FLAMES OF ADVENTURE EMBERS OF DARKNESS

C. C. MILTON

Edited by
MICHAEL SANFORD
Edited by
TAVLEEN KAUR

To my loving wife Myka. I thank you for the love and support you have given me. If it wasn't for you, I would have never been able to finish. You will always be in my heart.

Flames of Adventure

Embers of Darkness

C. C. Milton

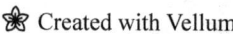 Created with Vellum

ABOUT THE BOOK

The Book:

Raised in an orphanage, Aluxes is the only survivor of the massacre of her entire village. Her life is not easy for she is only half-human and her other half is unknown. She tries to find out about her past and where she is from. Where will her adventure take her in this dark and unforgiving world?

The Author:

I hope you enjoy reading my first novel. I spent many years developing it. I am from a land far north that many barely know anything about except for silly lies. I am a father of three and I work full-time.

FLAMES OF ADVENTURE

Embers of Darkness

by

C. C. Milton

Papyrus Author, Inc. - Virginia Beach

1. Edition, 2019

Papyrus Author, Inc. - Virginia Beach

THE SURVIVOR AND THE DOLLY

The Survivor and the Dolly

The thunder roared and rumbled. The floorboards of the mansion shifted from side to side with each defining explosion. Little children sat nervously by the window. The youngest of them, who was five, clutched tightly onto her dolly for comfort.

"Be careful, Sue. That doll has been in the family for a very long time. You do not want to wear it out and ruin it with your tight hugs." Her mother calmly said as she sat there and continued to knit.

"But Mommy, I can hear voices in the thunder and I want them to go away," Sue cried out in a quiet whimper as she smothered her face with the doll.

Sam, the eldest, shouted, "Oh, you're just being stupid."

He always dressed like his father when he was away on his caravan trade and sat near the door. He wanted to be the first person to welcome him home. His head slowly shook as he grunted under his breath, but the slight twitch in his body gave away his fear.

"Oh, stop it, Sam. You have to remember that you are fifteen, almost a man, and she is only five, still a little child. It's all right, my dear." Their mother said as she took a deep breath and gently placed her knitted objects.

"The voices are just trying to tell you Father will be home very soon. Try not to let such things scare you. It is just the way nature is sometimes." She smiled at Sue, "Never lose that imagination of yours, my dear. For once it is gone, life gets boring."

Emmy, the eldest daughter of thirteen, held tightly onto Florence, her twin sister, as they trembled under a blanket. "But Mom, we hear the voices too," they said as they cried.

Their mother crossed her arms and stared at them. "Now girls, just calm down. It is only a really bad storm. Once it passes, the voices will go away." She stopped for a moment to look around. "Has anyone seen Jake?"

"No, Mother," the children replied.

"Sam, can you go look for him?"

"Yes, Mother." Sam rolled his eyes and moaned.

More thunder roared and sounded like it was right outside the house. The windows shook violently. "Mother!" cried the twins.

"It's all right, girls. It just means the lightning is getting closer, and then it will get further," she replied. Her face became sour as she looked at them, a shallow grunt escaped her throat as they whimpered.

"But Mother!" the twins shouted, "There is no lightning." Everyone ran towards the window to look outside. The clouds were dark, and heavy rain poured from them, but there were no strikes. Only the violent sounds, as if they were the footsteps of a giant or a dragon as he roared right before he ate his meal.

A blood curdling cry echoed throughout the house as the thunder stopped, "Mommy!"

They all ran towards the kitchen where the cry came from. There was not a single sound in the room, just a deathly silence. All they could hear was their own heavy breathing. Something was dripping from the kitchen table to the floor. Jake lay there with his father ripped to pieces as if by a beast. Large fingers wrapped around Sam's neck as a tall man stood there. He had bright crimson hair that glowed in the dark, crimson eyes that could send fear into their soul. He glared at them and then grinned. The girls stood there in shock, unable to move from terror.

"Master, I have finally found you. It is time now. The signs are there," the man said with a voice that shook their bones with its depth.

A female voice echoed in the back of their minds, "Finally after thousands of years, the time has come at last to get my revenge"

"What should I do with these lower creatures, Master?"

The voice echoed in their minds again as the family screamed in pain with blood pouring from their eyes, noses, and ears. "Dispose of them, and we shall be on our way."

"Yes, Master." The man opened his mouth, exposing large dragon-like teeth and devoured Sam.

The girls screamed and tried to run when a bright light came from the sky. A loud explosion echoed for miles away.

The villagers opened their doors and windows to see what had happened. All they heard was the sound of thunder that ripped the sky apart. No one dared leave their homes out of fear it may have been a hungry dragon. Some of them thought they could see something, but the cloud cover was too thick and blocked their sight.

The following day

"Hey, I found a survivor!" yelled a villager.

Sue, who tightly held her doll, lay there, still knocked out from the blast.

"That must be one lucky girl or that doll is a luck doll," another villager said with a smile as he rubbed the sweat off his brow.

They immediately picked up the girl and carried her off to the town healer. Hours later Sue woke up and screamed, "Mommy! Mommy!"

She kicked and punched at everyone like she was possessed, not knowing that the people there were the villagers who saved her. After a song from the local bard calmed her down, Sue finally stopped fighting.

The girl cried hysterically, "A monster ate them!" To them, stories of monsters were a common event for people that lived outside the village. Being near troll territory it was all too often. They were amazed at how this little girl survived such a terror.

She fell asleep, and they began to look for bodies and hopefully another survivor. After several hours had passed, all they could find were blood and body parts. But to their surprise, there were no signs of trolls, gnolls, dire wolfs, or bears.

The doctor ran out and shouted, "She is gone!"

Without a sound the little girl had left, leaving only the imprint that she had once lain there, and small black tar-like spots on the sheets. They looked for her but she was never seen again.

Chapter One

SWEET SIXTEEN

irds chirped around her ears, the smell of flowers filled the air, and the warmth of the sun gently kissed her skin. A soft voice rang through her mind, whispering, "Aluxes, wake up."

It was a heavenly sound that could charm the darkest of beasts. "Aluxes, you need to wake up. Your life is in danger."

The girl awakened. With a yawn, she stretched. She felt around blindly and could feel grass between her fingers. She softly rubbed the roots of a tree with her other hand. As her hand slowly moved up the tree onto a low-hanging branch, she realized she had been sleeping under the tree. The young girl opened her golden-colored eyes. She gazed at the beautiful scene and gently brushed her purple hair, which radiated a blue tone when touched by the light. Her skin was soft peach with a slight tan.

She slowly stood up and sighed with a slight hint of bitterness. "Great, I must be dreaming. Only I can have a nightmare like this," she said. A narrow dirt path shaped like an arrow aimed towards her. She looked around and viewed her surroundings.

"I must admit that this dream seems real. I can even smell the sweet aroma of sweet shrub around me." In an oddly calm manner, she took a step forward.

As a bright light appeared and forced her to squint slightly, a winged person flew a few inches from her nose. It was hard to make out much; the light was too bright and caused her vision to become blurred.

She closed her eyes, exhaled hard, and said, "Yeah, it must be a bad dream. There is no way an angel or a fairy would appear before me."

The winged person moved around and talked frantically. "Aluxes, you are in grave danger. The great evil is looking for you."

Aluxes turned her head. In the distance, she could hear crying. It began to grow darker as the sunlight faded, and her eyes adjusted slowly. She was able to see a little girl with a tattered dress who tightly held a tiny doll in a red dress, button eyes, and blond hair. The girl covered her face with the doll as Aluxes moved a little closer.

"Well, this is odd to have in a dream." She adjusted her breath, and as she walked towards her, asked in a calm manner , "What is the point of me having this in my dreams?"

She kneeled next to the little girl and grunted slightly. "What do I have to do to end this? Hey are you all right?"

As she leaned over with her arm extended towards her, the winged creature shouted, "No! Do not get close to that!"

For a moment, she looked away and something soft grabbed her hand. She turned her head and noticed that the doll had a hold on her. The field burst into hellish flames. The heat was intense, and Aluxes raised her other arm to cover her face. The little girl sank into a puddle of tar. The animals exploded, and their blood and other bits landed on her. The doll looked at her with a grin that sent shivers down her spine. "I found you!" it said in a dark, raspy voice.

Aluxes pulled away as a light blinded her. A loud thud echoed as pain shot through her body. She was tossed around side to side as she struggled to unwrap herself from her blanket. A ball of messy hair popped out of a tiny gap, followed by a deep breath. Everything was still slightly blurry, but as the dark gray color of the cobble stone bricks started to come into focus, she realized that she had fallen out of her bed and onto the cold floor.

She was barely able to make out the muffled voice behind the door.

"Aluxes, are you all right?" The constant knocking made it hard to hear.

The door burst open and a nun walked in with a sour look. "Aluxes, hurry up. You are going to be late." The nun ignored her as she lay there on the floor, grabbed her normal attire, and placed it on a chair near a vanity table.

"Today is your big day. You better get ready." She calmly looked around as she stood there.

Aluxes placed her hand on her head as she slowly rose. "Argh, my head. I guess it was all really just a dream." She blinked rapidly as she rubbed her eyes.

She looked right at the nun and said, "Hey! Thanks for the help, you crabby old nun. Just get out and leave me alone. Am I not even allowed to sleep in on my birthday?"

The nun took a deep breath as her skin became flushed. "Why must you always sound so bitter towards everyone? Some of us are actually trying to help you, you little wretch! Not all of us believed in the rumors."

Aluxes chuckled loudly. "Yeah, a rumor you started. You are about as holy as my ass."

The nun's face became more wrinkled as she deepened her scowl. "You better behave yourself young miss. You are a lady today. And at the looks of it, every bit of what I said was true."

She slowly walked towards a window, with one hand on top of the other. "Today is also your graduation. There are only three things a young lady like yourself can do at sixteen." She paused briefly as she composed herself. "Become a nun, become a holy knight, or get married."

Aluxes slowly walked around a little, resembling a caged animal ready to attack. "Yeah, like I can become an old nun like you, spreading rumors faster than a whore spreading her legs. As for getting married, there is no man alive that could meet my standards."

She smirked a little with a light laugh. "Just because I am an orphan does not mean you can waltz in here and judge me on how much of a disappointment I am every day. Now shut yer trap and get the hell out." She spat on the ground near the nun's feet as she walked off and mumbled under her breath.

Aluxes sat in her chair and unfolded the mirror from the vanity table. "I guess I should try to use some of this stuff to look nice." She fumbled around as if it was foreign to her.

She scoffed as she dug through the makeup kit and asked, "What is all this crap for anyway? I should have known better than to listen to Evalyn when she handed me this stuff." She tried to brush her hair, but it was too knotted. A soft hum came from her lips as she began and her muscles relaxed more. The song was the only memory of her mother that she had.

After a few moments, another voice synced with her hum. She looked in the mirror and saw a tall elderly woman dressed in a non-typical nun fashion. A bright blue uniform, headpiece higher than her hair, and some type of chain armor threaded into the sleeves. She came up behind Aluxes, slowly took the brush, and gently pulled it through Aluxes's hair.

She exhaled deeply and said, "Deary, you always hum this when you're upset. What seems to be on your mind?" Another deep breath with a sigh.

"The Balled of the Unknown Goddess. But you are never able to learn the correct words. Even as I sat there saying it with you word for word, you could never say it right." The head nun exhaled deeply, lost in her own thoughts.

A little smirk came across her face as she gazed out the window. "You need to stop hassling the other nuns. Many of them would admit that they do not like you, but they are willing to try and aid you if you only ask."

Aluxes looked down at her feet with a smirk and scoffed. "Like I care what they think. I can never forget the things they said to me. Like the one that was in here earlier. She thinks I forgot. During my first week, I heard her tell the others I was a whore's bastard, saying that I am part Mara." She tensed her muscles.

With a sly smile, she turned her head slightly and said, "You are the only one whom I can stand, Mildred."

The smile faded as she looked at the mirror with her normal bitter face. "They always tell me what choices I have in life. What I am allowed to read, who I am allowed to talk to, what my goals are allowed to be. They always guided the others by asking them about their thoughts. You're the only one who told me I may become more." She gritted her teeth slightly. "And the ones who never talked are just as guilty. I could see it in their faces. Not a single one of them liked me even on my good days. Everyone treated me differently because of the color of my eyes and hair. Not knowing what my other half is scares them. Other kids would call me a monster because of it."

"Well, my dear. Your voice is extremely aggressive, and you always seem angry when you are around others. Some would say it comes off as a bit threatening. Maybe if you didn't always look angry, even when you are happy, others might warm up to you, my dear."

With a gentle hug from behind, Aluxes's muscles relaxed. "If you are not careful, you will get wrinkles around your eyes from always having that irritable look."

Mildred smiled a little as she continued to brush Aluxes's hair. "I remember when the headmaster and I found you. We took you in. My, how have you grown. You were but a helpless child only three years of age."

She stepped back a little and held Aluxes's hair with her fingers. "At that time, your hair was a solid blue color. The head nun at the time said I should leave you; it would only bring misfortune if I took you in. Regardless you were my blessing." She tugged her a little. "And also, my curse."

She gently handed Aluxes her armor and said, "There are stories that say people born with unnatural hair or eye color have remarkable gifts. Like people who are half-elf have pink eyes, pink hair; or half-dwarfs with their gray eyes. I like to think which ever god blessed you had something important for you."

Mildred pulled out a red strip of linen from her pocket. "This was given to me by my mother when I graduated, but because I picked a life of devotion, I was never allowed to have any children so it will be best for you to have it." She tied it to the back of Aluxes's hair and slowly walked away.

Aluxes gently put on her armor. It was in the light class but had heavy elements. She had two chest plates that were divided in the middle with some padded leather and the mid-section was covered in padded leather. The upper legs had small plates with leather that covered the spots that the plates did not; the lower legs were the same. The arms had some thin metal plates with leather in between the exposed parts, and it was all mostly pure white. The odd thing about her armor was the lack of shoulder cover and they were exposed.

She opened her closet and grabbed her sword. It was larger than a normal arming sword, and it was heavy, six times the usual weight. To counter the sag, her armor had a loop that her belt clipped to for extra support. She took the red linen from her hair and tied it near the base of the pommel.

She took one last quick look in the mirror and rubbed the gold circlet around her neck, saying, "You are my only true friend. I hope this adventure leads us to our answers." The circlet had been around her neck when she was found, and it had never left. No one had been able to remove it, and except for the gold coloring, no one knew what it was made of. The oddest thing about it was that as she grew, it grew as well. With the right side of her lip curved up to make her normal smile, she took a deep breath and ran out the door.

The city was decorated for it was not only the graduation of the cadets to become adults, but it was also the anniversary of the Holy City of Cathair.

Booths sold rare, seasoned foods that were cooked for the occasion. The smell of rare herbs flooded Aluxes's nose. There were banners, flowers, and entertainers all over. People cheered as the actors preformed famous legends. A slight but cool spring breeze was in the air. Kids were playing games and everyone was in delightful spirits except for one. If it was not for her graduation, she would have never left her room.

She ran past a dark alley where she had a few memories of being a little girl that stood in the corner as other kids teased and tossed pebbles at her for being different. She ran by without a hint to slow down. Occasionally, she would bump into a person but her pace never changed.

The Grand Theater was an outdoor theater that could hold thousands. For graduation days, people sat in the stadium seats while the graduates sat in the open field.

The class this year was one of the largest in their history. Twenty thousand. As Aluxes tried to sneak through, her ears twitched as people whispered about the high graduation count as sign of a dark times ahead.

With a quick look around and a long exhale of air, she waited for a few moments before she decided to take another breath. When she looked ahead to see the headmaster talking, their eyes locked and goosebumps formed across her body.

The headmaster was a dignified man with scars on his face from past wars. He was rather short, even by normal human standards. He was more like a tall dwarf, stocky and broad. The crystals on the stage lit up. Magic amplified his voice as he began to talk about the history of the town and its importance to the world of mortals.

He stood there and cleared his throat. The faces in the crowd became long, knowing what was about to come next. "It was over thousands of years ago that gods and demons had their great war. The war so great that their realms could no longer contain it and it bled into the mortal realm."

He tried to clear his throat again. "Being mostly helpless, the humans suffered the most. Having no magical properties at birth, we were being wiped out. This would have been the end if it was not for one of the goddesses who took pity on us and made a stronghold to teach us holy magic, so we could defend ourselves from the demons who used us as food. But this was not seen as favorable to most gods, so she was slain by her own kind."

As he rambled on more about the history of how the city was founded, Aluxes's eyes began to feel heavy. She was able to see some heads slowly rock back and forth. She even pinched herself every so often to keep from falling victim to his speech.

There was a slight pause and everyone lifted their heads, ready to go on to the next stage of the ceremony, but the headmaster stood there and gazed into the sky. The last time he did this he talked about his younger days. A large grin overtook his face, a light twitch in his wrist.

With some stumbling with his notes and more throat clearing, he looked at his papers. "The citizens who decide to attend the Academy are free to live the life they want, but this Academy is mainly to raise orphans and orphans have only three choices. Men may choose to be in the work force. They are allowed to marry and have a family of their own."

Another deep breath. "Ladies are allowed to become betrothed and tend to the daily tasks of taking care of the home to help raise the future offspring. Both may also become dedicated to the Holy Teachings, and help spread the word as clerics but they are not allowed to ever marry or have children of their own for they are dedicated to the teachings of the gods. Lastly the Holy Soldier— you may never marry but are allowed to have children. However, you are not to raise them for you must be dedicated to be on call for battle at any time, and you are not allowed to have burdens."

He raised his hands and smiled. "May you pick wisely, and the heavens watch over you."

The cheer from the people and sound of the fireworks filled the air. The now young adults clapped and hugged each other. Most of the students were clearly dressed according to their decision. A few who were still undecided had on gowns. The booths where they were to sign up for their future filled up fast.

As Aluxes made her way to enlist as a soldier, she heard a familiar voice that sent shivers through her body. From about thirty feet away stood Evalyn. Her bright red hair, blue eyes, and freckles annoyed her to no end.

With her normal stuck-up voice, she said, "You thought you could sneak in without anyone noticing you were late, silly girl. You stick out like an elephant surrounded by zebras."

Her checks swelled up as laughter slipped out. "My rival daring to be late makes me think that I am the better person."

Most apprentice fighters typically trained with a sword, spear, or bow but Evalyn had became a master of the whip. A skill passed down through her family, her bladed whip was always on her side.

"Yeah, well, Evalyn. You can bite my ass. No one likes you and I sure as hell never wanted you to pick me to be your rival," she shouted with a sour face.

Evalyn pulled her shoulder back and said, "You are just jealous. My shapely body is a gift from the heavens. Meanwhile, your flat body just makes me more beautiful. So, I win."

Aluxes scoffed. "Why do you always try to compete with me on everything? Like I care about your tits. Let men grope them till they pop for all I care. As far as I am concerned, you have never defeated me in combat. That is all that matters as a warrior."

Evalyn chuckled. "I can see you did not even bother to try the makeup I gave you as a birthday gift. You do not even try to make it a challenge. Being a warrior is fine, but looking good while you fight is what makes legends. Your ugly face will disappear into history while there will be paintings of my exploits. So, in the end I will be the better warrior."

Aluxes scoffed, "Who would want to remember a total bitch?"

"That is enough, you two." The girls looked over and saw the headmaster. Evalyn quickly scampered away while he was focusing on Aluxes. "Such language is not fitting for a holy warrior. If you do not keep a clean mind and body, you will lose your ability to use holy magic."

With a little shrug, Aluxes looked at him and smirked. "I keep clean enough to still be able to use my skills whenever needed. Why am I always the object of ridicule?"

"Aluxes, my dear. You were obviously born with great abilities that would make anyone jealous. A noble of her type who views you as a rival is a great thing. Just be careful, my dear. You walk on a thin line with all that anger in your heart. I think you misunderstand her intentions." He took a deep breath and handed her an envelope. "I already signed you up for the army. It was obvious from the day I brought you into this school. I always knew where you would go."

Inside the envelope was a note of her acceptance into the elite squad which a small handpicked few were ever allowed into. It was one of those rare times that Aluxes gave a genuine smile.

She leaped at him with a hug.

"You are the closest thing to a daughter that I have," he said. "May the soul of the Unnamed Goddess protect you."

She turned the letter over. On the back was a list of supplies and a small banknote worth a very limited amount. With a quick trip to the bank, she withdrew some of her personal savings. The Academy gave orphans a tiny bit of allowance every week to be spent. It was so that they could have the enjoyments that normal kids have. But because she was different, even from other half-breeds, she was always harassed. The headmaster taught her how to save money in a bank so she could use it when she needed it later in life.

With no goal in mind, she walked around the town and looked at all the supply shop signs in an attempt to figure out where to go. *Shit, I wish I shopped more often. Where do I find these things?*

She wandered off into a random street. *Where in the hell am I? Great, I must ask someone for help.* Off in the distance there were other students. She tried to wave them down, but all they did was look at her and snicker as they walked away.

After an hour went by, she started to grind her teeth. *I am starting to get angry. Why do I have to put up with this? I am sure I do not need this stuff.* Then right when she turned around, she saw a little shop with a dwarf at the door with his arms crossed. Though the streets were full of people going into all shops, they were avoiding his.

"May I help ya, missy?" He looked up and down her body and spat off to the side. The sound of his voice had a weight to it, and with every motion he made, he never broke eye contact with her.

With an empty feeling in her gut she gazed at her list. Aluxes stuttered as she tried to talk to him. Her shoulders dropped a little, her breathing became unsure, her body shook, and she was covered in sweat. As she took another quick look at him, goosebumps enveloped her body.

He moved closer to her and slowly swayed his head from one side of her body to the next. " Aye, lass. Ya be a new graduate. They be many other shops more suited for a lovely lass like yer self."

Without warning, he took her sword. "This be trash. Not any good for a miss like yer self. I have decided my shop is the only shop for a mighty warrior." Her shoulders lifted up as did her head. Being called a warrior by a dwarf was considered great praise.

He snatched the paper from her hand. He had an air about him, and as she looked through his window, she saw that his shop was empty. He was an impatient man despite being the only one with no customers.

"Me shop be considered on the higher wee end of the prices. But me quality be a hundred times better than that human-made filth." He grunted as he waved at her to follow him.

They slowly walked into the shop. Aluxes's hands twitched as if they had a mind of their own. She touched objects carefully. Her eyes widened over the gold and silver trinkets, each masterfully crafted. A flask caught her eye. It had an image of a highly detailed castle. Before she could ask how much it costs, he ordered her to put it down. It caused her to jump a little and almost drop it.

He slowly walked up to her as he held a dwarven battle ax with both hands. "Aye, lass. Here, hold this." He said as he tossed it at her.

With quick reflexes, she caught it with a single hand. "What the hell is your problem?" He waved his hand around, and she imitated with the ax.

A grin overtook his face. "Aye, even a normal human or a half-breed dwarf would have a problem lifting that with two hands." He pointed a finger up and waved it around, saying, "All this stuff in shop be trash. Ya be something special. Aye, I got just the thing for you."

He moved quickly, and she was unable to follow as he snatched her coin pouch. "This wee bit will do. Everything be custom made. One of a kind, and only be for ya."

He waved at her. "Off ya go. They be delivered by me personally when done," he said as he shoved her out the door.

She looked around dumbfounded as the door slammed shut. "Well, shit! I can see the castle from here." She took a deep breath, and said,

"I guess I should go see my new home." Each step was faster the closer she got, but she was unable to smile. Her mind flashed back to when the other kids would pick on her every time she started a new class.

She approached the main office to check in and was greeted by a man in a fancy uniform. "We know who you are. The headmaster described you to us. There is no need for you to come inside the office. Your measurements have already been sent to us. I shall take you to your new quarters." She shrugged a little at the very sound of his high-pitched voice.

He walked in such a way that she struggled to keep up. They arrived at a dark gray building that hardly stuck out from the rest.

He placed one hand on the door and the other on her back, and said, "These are the quarters for the elites in training." He quickly opened the door and sent her in with a hard push. She was caught off guard and was barely able to prevent herself from falling over.

Aluxes stood there as her heart stopped for a moment. Everyone in the room looking at her without blinking. Unable to let any words escape from her mouth, her face became beet red. The others were like statues and stared at her with blank expressions.

A boy with bright blond hair slowly walked up to her along with some others. "Well, isn't she a tall one," he said. "I think she is the tallest person in this building." She began to shiver a little as she gazed at his hazel eyes.

Another boy that she could not see grabbed her shoulder and said, "I remember seeing her at the academy, I always thought she was sweet on the eyes. I could see myself getting with her even though she is a mutt."

A girl with dark skin, long brown hair, and black eyes walked up and took Aluxes's sword. "This be too heavy sword. It be useless. Girl like you do not belong in building." Her accent was slightly off.

Aluxes quickly tensed her body and gritted her teeth. Without looking at them, she raised her arms around her head.

As if time had stopped, everyone in the room rushed her. They pulled at her arms, punched her ribs, and kicked her mid-section. Some even screamed "half-breed!" as they tried to knock her over. Hit after hit, she stood like a wall.

A girl pulled her hair and said, "You know this group is for pure humans only, you mutt." As she yanked her harder, Aluxes's guard finally broke down. A few well-placed hits to her stomach knocked her to the ground.

One of the boys noticed the red linen that the head nun had given her. "Well, what do we have here. Looks important and valuable. I guess I'll keep it." He slowly put it in his pocket as he snickered at her.

Aluxes tightly gnashed her teeth, and her body started to shake. An eerie sound followed as the room shook. She used the distraction to stand back up with her fists clenched so hard that her nails broke the skin and blood poured from her hands.

One of the boys saw her and tried to take a swing at her, but she quickly tucked under his blow and shoved him with her shoulder. The others tried to attack, but she easily dodged and pushed them out of the way. The entire time, she did not take her eyes off her target. Her gaze locked on him like a lion's on its prey.

He looked up, and their eyes met. "Well, tall bitch, won't'cha be careful with my infighting." Sharp pain filled her face as he pummeled her in the cheek with his sword.

She took a step to the side to prevent herself from getting staggered. Blood tickled her skin as it flowed from her lips. He went in for another strike but she caught it. His arm twitched as she pushed. His veins bulged and sweat trickled down his head. His breathing was sparse and tense, and he tried to overpower her but it was to no avail. With her other hand, she reached for the red linen.

His breath became more erratic as his muscles strained. "Hey, it's mine you half-breed bit—." With an open-palmed strike to his chest, she sent him into the wall. A loud pop echoed and everyone stopped.

One girl shouted, "Get her!" but they were blocked by a magical barrier.

"When did she have time to cast?" a boy asked as they all slowly came to a halt.

The door burst open and slammed into the wall. "What in the hell is going on!" A man screamed as he held a runestone in his hand. It had a blue glow to it as he threw it at Aluxes's forehead. A sharp pain shot through her body as she dropped to the floor. Each time she tried to move, she received an electric shock.

As he walked closer, his footsteps echoed. He stood above her and looked right into her eyes. "I am your commander. You did real good, but going berserk on your fellow team will not do."

He gazed around the room as he turned his head side to side, saying, "The first rule to engagement is to know your enemy. As an unknown half-breed, you have no idea what her quirks are. If she were half-giant, you would have broken your hands on her thick skin."

He slowly walked toward the boy Aluxes had hit. Barely able to contain the smirk on his face, he said, "Boy, I say you flew over twenty-five feet. I bet you feel real dumb, son."

The boy coughed up a little blood as he tried to speak. "Sir, sorry sir. But she—."

With an intimidating shout that made everyone jump, the commander said, "It was passed by our king. Half-breeds will be allowed in the elite groups." He patted the boy's chest. "You broke a few ribs but you'll be fine. Maybe there was a sign it would backfire."

The spell began to wear off and Aluxes stood back up. Now without the pain, she was able to see and hear him clearer. His voice had a demanding presence but a subtle hint of sorrow. He had a scar on his left cheek. Jagged like it was caused by a dark elf dagger. Every time he closed his mouth, it pulled his eyelid down a little. His skin was extremely pale and rugged.

He looked at her and slowly walked toward her, one hand in front of him and the other near a pouch on his belt. "Missy, I am Commander Verus, and you do not understand the situation. See, the elites used to be for pure blooded-humans only."

He raised his voice. "It was not until a few years ago that allied races demanded that we put half-breeds in our ranks as well." He kneeled a little closer to her ear and spoke softly, "You have none of the traits that any of the allied half-breeds have. So you must earn that respect. It may have been better if you had joined the regular army. But your recommendation came from the top."

He walked around a little and picked up the stuff they'd stolen off her, carefully going over it. He took notice of her sword, "It is a little on the heavy side, and it appears to be damaged." Part of the sword had a deep crack, almost splitting it in half. With a quick twist, the blade snapped.

With a smile on his face and direct eye contact, he said, "It appears that all your personal belongings have been damaged. Consider it payment for his medical bill."

He turned and waved his hand back to front as he quickly walked. Aluxes tripped over her first step with a little twitch as she followed. He glanced behind him so everyone knew he was still able to watch them.

They moved out of the back door where there was an old run-down barrack. "This was the elite building before they built us the new one twenty years ago. We now use it to house our half-breeds because of the lack of numbers that actually try to join. Make sure you learn the ropes with them. One of them is a little colorful." He chuckled as he walked off.

The door creaked as Aluxes opened it. A foul odor overtook her. She tried to hold in her gag but it only made it worse.

There was a very deep grunt, but then a cheerful male voice filled the room. "Aye, that be the half-giant greeting. You better get used to it, lass." She looked up and saw see five people. A girl with pink hair, purple eyes, and slightly off-pink skin, obviously a half-elf. Three half-dwarfs, one was a very broad girl, the other two were men. One was taller than the other and was more human than dwarf. The smaller one looked like a typical dwarf but taller, and like all half-breeds, they had faded gray eyes and an offset tan. The last one was a rather tall man. He stood around ten feet tall with faded green skin and a foul odor, likely a half-forest giant.

The shorter half-dwarf male looked at her and in his deep grunting voice said, "Oi, you must be the new lass. I see they gave ya the intro-duction. If ya joined five years ago, it be much worse."

He moved his hand around as he talked. "I be Onyx. This be me twin brother, Ugthar. That lovely lady there be Lugathar. The ugly skinny lass there be Rosabud, and that there dim-witted looking guy be Udook, I think."

The half-elf rolled her eyes and sighed with her face still tucked away in her robe, and with a quiet voice that would give a mouse a run for its money, said, "I'm Rosaletta but dwarfs always get it wrong. You can just call me Rose."

Onyx dusted off an empty bed. "Aye lass, ya best rest. It'll help." Bruised and battered Aluxes made her way to the vacant bed and collapsed. Although it had been a harsh day, she felt somewhat relaxed and excited. As she slowly drifted away to sleep, her only thought was to become stronger so she could survive in her new hell.

The door busted open and the dwarf at the shop barged in. "Aye little lass here ye go," he said, handing her a receipt.

"What's this?" Her tone was a bit off as she turned her head to look at it.

"Why tis be ya bill. The wee amount ya had was not enough. Ya commander said percentage of ya pay will go towards ya bill," he said as a big smile came across his face.

"Uncle Ulbrek, I see you still have too much pride in your work to allow a discount to a customer you probably kidnapped," Ugthar said in his soft-spoken voice with a chuckle as his hand made a cutting motion.

Ulbrek walked toward him, grabbed him by the hair, and yanked hard. "Aye, I be ah true and proper dwarf. We be take pride in our craftsmanship and combat abilities. I be doing the best hand-crafted items in this wee city. If ya two were not such lousy soldiers, I be havin people flock to me shop." He looked over at Aluxes. His silver-colored eyes seemed to have penetrated part of her soul. "Aye, young lass. I be noticed ya trashy human made sword be broken. It be a good thing ya came to me shop." He let go of Ugthar's hair.

"You still after that human girl, Uncle Ulbrek?" Onyx started to chuckle.

"Yeah, I be short but she can't get enough of me thick stump." All four dwarfs began to laugh.

Aluxes noticed that Ulbrek was rather tall for a dwarf. She had not seen many but most stood in the four-foot range. If it wasn't for his extremely thick beard, she would have thought he was a half-dwarf.

Ulbrek took her sword. "Ya sword is a wee bit heavy. I might as well just sharpen me hammer and hand it ta ya."

He walked off while singing a Dwarven tune, "*Abec ueve ozeek obek ectatoa ucov evek Acovozucov.*"

As she watched him leave, she noticed that he'd left a bag near her bed. On it was a note on which it was written "*To the lovely tall girl.*" She was unable to hold in her smile as she blushed a little and looked inside. There was a small amount of equipment with amazing engravings, all images of dwarfs in mines or in battle. At the bottom, there was his seal engraved on every piece, a U and a B. She took hold of her water canteen and drifted off to sleep.

Chapter Two

THE HARD LESSON

A horn echoed throughout the quarters as a loud voice rang in Aluxes's mind. Her body was being shaken. "It be time for ya to learn, lass!" The bed pitched and she rolled onto the floor. She quickly staggered to her feet.

She looked around. "Where can I wash up?"

"There be no time for that, lass!" Onyx pointed out the door. Shadows of other new recruits could be seen rushing by the barracks.

She darted out the door in a panic. "Crap, I'm late. What a way to make a good impression." She rubbed her arms and said, "I should have removed my armor before I went to bed. Even my breasts hurt."

The area opened to a large courtyard. It was a little hard for Aluxes to see where to go as her eyes had not yet adjusted to the lack of sunlight. Onyx bumped into her and pointed to a formation.

There were three formations. One group was full of fresh young recruits that she remembered from the graduation. The second group was full of people that looked more defined in muscle and discipline. The third was full of older people; their gazes and battle scars made it clear that they were the veterans.

Shit. Well, might as well hide in the back. Maybe I won't stick out as much. She ran to the back. *Oh crap. I am the tallest person here.*

As the commander walked out, she noticed more things about him. He was a tall and slender man; he also had a slight limp as he walked. What stuck out the most to her was his voice that did not match his body type. His arms were covered with jagged scars.

"Today, we have the duty of training our new recruits so they will not embarrass us on the field of battle. Because we are the elite, and we must not only be the strongest but also the smartest." He eyeballed the new recruits and continued, "Thanks to yesterday's problem, one of our vets has several broken ribs, so I shall be doing the task personally!" He looked right at her and smiled, making her feel as if a piece of ice was sliding down her back.

"We shall be testing the new recruits on their combat skills today. They shall go one on one with our vets so that we'll know where they lack and we can properly train them." He walked off and a horn blew. Everyone dispersed to one of the three combat pits.

It was a decent-sized pit that could hold fifty fighters or more. Aluxes began to notice how the other half-breeds looked as they stood there watching the arena. Onyx was a little taller than she had originally thought. He had thick black hair and a beard. His brother Ugthar was the tallest. He was skinnier and had no beard. You could easily mistake him for a short human. Lugathar was between the height of the two with braided red hair, thick shoulders, dark skin, and a typical human face. Rose was almost six feet tall, not as thin as an elf, but she always hid her face behind her extremely long pink hair.

Two people entered the arena. It was easy to tell who the vet was. He mostly wore light plating and cloth armor. To him, the rookies were no threat.

She scoffed a little and said, "This is more like a mockery than an exercise." She threw her arms on the fence that surrounded the pit and buried her head in them.

"What type of person is she?" Aluxes heard the other recruits ask.

"All her bruises healed up overnight, and how was she able to cast a protection spell? I didn't hear her do any incantation or throw any runes."

At least they are whispering, I could pretend I cannot hear them,

Aluxes said to herself. Her hand twitched slightly as she rubbed the circlet around her neck.

"She was always like that in the academy. Any spells that required physical contact— she can do with just thinking about them. But because her mind tends to wander off from pure thoughts, they do not last very long," a boy said.

One of the female soldiers snickered. "You mean she has a dirty mind."

A few others whispered, "I heard her mother gave herself to a monster." They chuckled.

Aluxes scoffed as she tried to cover her ears as she buried herself deeper into her arms. Her mind filled with the head nun's instructions, "Remember, my dear. It is not the truth. So treat it like the water that runs off your hair." She tried to cover her ears in hopes the sound would block out their chatter.

"Aluxes! Front and center!" the commander shouted. "Remember, no magic. We need to test combat ability."

Rose walked over and helped her put on the required gear in a small room off to the side. It was a heavy plate with chain-mail to cover the exposed parts. She tried to shrug her arms a little and move them around.

"Aug, I cannot move in this crap. It is too heavy, and my arms are restricted," Aluxes cried.

"Commander said you must use this sword and shield," Rose whispered to her.

Aluxes picked them up. "How am I supposed to use this?" She walked out like a clumsy drunkard, juggling the sword and shield, not knowing which hand they went in.

As the match commenced, she moved her arms around. Her sword constantly collided with her shield when she tried to use her normal stance. Her helmet blocked her peripheral view, which caused her to shift her head from side to side. Sweat slowly ran into her eyes, and her breathing was getting erratic.

A man stood in front of her, ready to battle. She could barely make him out except for his dark olive skin. "Friend tossed you did. Me will seek vengeance Iayati SieGee."

"What in the hell is he saying?" Aluxes raised her helmet a little so she could see him better.

"Aye, lass, he be from the southern continent. They barely know common!" Onyx chuckled a bit. "She be fine, I guess."

The man moved in for the first strike. His attacks were not that strong, but they were consistent. No energy wasted on pointless swings. He was relentless and consistently aimed at the center of her mass. She was barely able to block him with her shield.

"Is all you got, Geetimwa?" In an instant, he rammed her with his shield. His cross guard hooked to her shield and with a quick jerk, ripped it from her grip. "No can block." He smiled and snickered as he said it.

Her ears burned as the people around them laughed at her. "Shit, I can't breathe in this thing." She hastily pulled off her helmet and said, "I wish these people would just shut the hell up." From the corner of her eye, she noticed Ulbrek. He stood there quietly with his arms folded. His eyes did not break their gaze. He motioned with his chin, telling her to focus on the fight.

"I finish now!" Her opponent charged and slammed his shield into her face. She staggered but managed to not fall over.

Her mouth slowly filled with blood as most of the others pointed and laughed. She screamed like a wild animal.

"To hell with this shit!" As if she were an angry bull, Aluxes charged at him. The man raised his shield as she kicked at him. There was a loud ringing sound as her foot slammed into it and he flew back like a ragged doll. The second his body hit the ground, he tried to use the momentum to roll up to his feet, but she was already on top of him. All he managed to do was raise his shield and sword to protect his body. There was a loud echo and everyone, even the ones in the other pits, stopped to see what had happened.

His sword had been cut in half and hers was embedded in his shield. Before he had time to react, Aluxes grabbed it, ripped it from his grip, and tossed it off to the side. Her blade snapped as she pulled it from the shield and aimed straight for her opponent's throat.

"Halt!" The commander stood there with a blank expression and said, "Well, young miss. It seems that your brutish strength is all natural. No magical enhancements, just like your academy instructor told me." He had on his full plate armor, his sword and shield at the ready. "It is also true about your weakness; you are over confident in your raw power. It is because of this that you lack the proper ability to defend yourself. Anyone who has fought a stronger opponent would know how to deal with someone like you."

A student tossed a two-handed sword into the arena. The commander stood at the ready. "You best pick that up, and I want you to make yourself comfortable. You need to be at your best to stand a chance." She looked at her sword and noticed that the blade was broken.

She unbuckled some of the straps that held on the parts of the armor, leaving only the cuirass and greaves. As she picked up the sword, everyone whispered since the weight difference had no effect on her motion. With one hand, she held it as easily as the short sword with no signs of muscle strain.

"I will tell you what, Missy. If you are able to land a single blow on me, I shall force everyone in this unit to treat you with respect," the commander said with a smile.

Aluxes walked around a little to look for a weak point in his stance. "Yeah, I do not care for forced respect. It is meaningless. I would much rather earn it." She readied as she gripped the sword tightly and rushed forward.

In one fluent instant, the commander glanced her blow with his shield and stabbed her in the shoulder. It was a pain she had never experienced before, but she tried to hide it as she mashed her teeth together.

"You went through your entire academy training overwhelming your opponents with your great power. You were only able to defeat your last opponent because you caught him off guard; he assumed you used enhancement magic the other day. Humans are weak, but we win battles because we are smart." He kicked her as he spoke.

She staggered but was still able to stand her ground as blood trickled down her arm. Her breath became heavy, and her vision had blurred as she tried to recover. She instinctively went into a guarded stance. Her hands shook and her legs were a little numb, but her eyes never broke. She slowly lost her grip on her sword, forcing herself to grab it with her other.

The commander readied himself again. The corner of his lip raised slightly. "I see you still got fight left in ya, but your lack of experience is your undoing in this match. Comparing you to an orc would be a disgrace to that race." He took a short step that made a small gap in his defense. She charged in with a strike but in an instant, the commander feinted, and she glanced off to his side. The forward momentum from her miss kept her moving uncontrollably. As she passed, he dropped his shield and grabbed her by the back of her head.

"It is over," he said as he slammed her to the ground. Before she could react, he kneed her in the back and punched her, knocking her out.

Blurred images slowly came into focus. Onyx had a small smile as he said, "Lass, should feel honored." Then, with a short breath, he added, "The commander taught ya the most important lesson someone like ya can learn. It means he respects ya."

Rose walked over with her voice a little shaken. "I will work on a healing spell at once."

"Thanks, but it is not needed," Aluxes said as she pushed her hand off to the side.

"I could not help but notice you have no scars on your body. Have you never been hurt as a child?" As Rose talked, the small bruises on her were mostly healed.

"Rosabud, ya better focus on ya healin on someone else or ya might heal her butt-hole shut by mistake," Lugathar bellowed out. These minor interactions made Aluxes understand that dwarfs were vulgar.

Aluxes looked around. Ulbrek nodded at her and walked off. "Why was your uncle here?"

"Aye, when he says he will forge ya a sword, he meant to say he will build ya a sword to fit ye fighting style. Which be the reason why we had this wee combat exercise right off the bat. Ulbrek made it a request to the commander."

Aluxes tried to get up, but a sharp pain ran through her body. "Ah four hells, my arms." She collapsed back onto the ground.

The commander walked up and examined her. "You fractured your wrist and dislocated your other arm. You have no idea how to properly control yourself." His tone was soft-spoken, and he carefully helped her up.

"This is your major flaw. Lack of defense is mostly due to your lack of experience. But this lack of control of yours is a problem. If something happened and you lost your mind in combat, I cannot have you become useless after one or two swings. Sadly, this is nothing a human can teach you. Controlling that power is the only way you can be useful as an elite."

She tried not to look him in the eyes, but something in her forced her to gaze at him. He popped her arm back into place. "If you want to earn respect, you must not allow that anger to control you. We all have had bad lives."

There was a loud noise, like an earthquake. Udook ran out of the barracks, shouting, "*Umma, Ick umander. Oood!*" He stopped in front of them.

The commander looked over at the mess hall and saw that troops were lining up. "Oh my, I am deeply sorry, brother. Chow time!"

They walked off with the commander's hand on Udooks back as they spoke.

"Yeah, they be in the army for thirty years, always be in the same unit. Whenever the commander got transferred, he made sure that giant be with him." Onyx looked at Rose. "It be what Rosabud told me."

She gazed towards the hall. "It happened almost ten years ago. He was much smarter and was able to hold a conversation. But that scar on his head was caused by a goblin blast stick."

Onyx folded his arms with his eyes closed. "That's right. Ya be in the regulars with them. I never met them before the accident but I heard it be aimed at the commander."

Ugthar looked at Aluxes as he ate an apple. "A goblin blast stick is a stick with an iron tube on it that uses blasting magic to propel an iron ball at high speeds. Goblins may be weak fighters but they are master engineers. Maybe if the spell was not such a drain it would be a common weapon."

"A giant's skin is mostly indestructible and half-giants are no exception. Unless you have a magical weapon or powerful magic, you will not be able to defeat a giant. However, the goblins lacking both magical ability and strength found a way to defeat the giants," Rose said as she sat next to Ugthar.

After breakfast was over all the new recruits were sent to their classes to learn the basics of their enemies. Aluxes had never been good at focusing in this type of environment, and it did not help that the teacher had a monotone voice. The first lesson was about orcs and she drifted off for most of it. She only stayed awake for the orc part because the commander compared her to one and she knew nothing about them.

"Orcs are ruthless, standing at eight to ten feet tall when adulthood is reached. They can become ten times stronger than a normal human. Savage in battle, they oddly lack in smithing technique, which makes their weapons slightly jagged. This makes it more harmful when one is wounded by them. Even though it seems that their main strategy is to overwhelm their opponent with their brute strength, they are very cunning and also expert fighters."

Two days later, Aluxes was lying in her bed. She heard a knock on the door to the barracks. It was Ulbrek, and he had a sword in his hand. "Lass, this be ya sword. Its name be Ulfberht."

He handed her the sword. It was a little heavier than her older one but slightly shorter to make it more balanced on her hip. The metal of the blade was almost mirror-like. As she touched it, a warmth radiated from it. The cross guard was the color of bronze and the handle was gold and had grooves for better grip. The pommel was dark red. She had never seen such a lovely sword in her life. On the blade was engraved "Ulfberht."

"Ya be my little walking advertisement, lass. So ye better do good in battle. The metal be only used for dwarfish lords so best be keep it hidden if in their lands.

"Sir Verus has arranged for me to be ya mentor. So, get ye stuff, ya coming with me, or my ax will hit ye ass." He chuckled as she slowly readied her belongings.

"I see ya take orders better. Be good for ya to listen better." He grabbed her hands, and said, "Only ya sword, lass. So, what brought about ya change?"

She cleared her throat a little. "The commander defeated me easily. He even allowed me a few rematches the next day. The calmer I got, the more he talked to me as if I were a person."

She slowly moved out the door with a softness in her breath. "The commander is the third person I respect. If he arranged for you to train me, then I must respect it."

She walked off with Ulbrek to a secluded area in the forest where they began to train. They used wooden wasters and padded armor, but his heavy-handed strikes still hurt Aluxes a lot. Every time, he attacked the same spot, which was difficult for her to defend.

"Stop hitting me in the ass." Aluxes tried to punch Ulbrek, but he swiftly dodged.

"Aye, we been at this for almost a week. Ya no getting better." He pulled out a small pipe and put some tobacco in it.

Aluxes sounded like an angry dog as she barked at him, "Maybe if you aimed for more than just my ass!"

He took a puff and said, "Me head be as high as ye cunt. If I went high, I only be able to hit ye tits. Ya ass be more padded."

He opened one eye and looked at the bushes. "Aye, we have a wee visitor." A child tumbled out onto the ground. The child was slightly shorter than Ulbrek and had a boyish figure. With hair a bright yellow and eyes of black.

The child stood up, "Sorry, master dwarf. I heard some shouting so I had to see."

Ulbrek waved. "Come a bit closer, lad. Me hearin be going." As the child approached, Ulbrek said, "Ah, ye be a dragonblood."

Aluxes looked at the child. "What is a dragonblood?"

Ulbrek choked on his pipe. "Ya be useless with info. They be dragons that breed with humans. After a while, they lost the ability to turn back into dragons but still be born from eggs."

The dragonblood smiled. "I am Rebecca. Father told me much about you, master dwarf."

Ulbrek looked up and down the dragonblood's body. "Aye, be female. Dragonbloods be always born female unless both parents are dragonblood. Then they all look male. Once they reach matin' season, they look adult." He grabbed a hold of her ear. "They be like a tree; each ring be their age. Aye she be an adult at twenty. Should have been breeded by now."

Rebecca giggled a little. "If we do not breed, we return to this until next season."

Aluxes chuckled. "I know the feeling. The date thing is overrated."

Rebecca looked at her with a blank stare. "How odd. You are the second person I've met that is immune to my aura."

Ulbrek laughed. "Aye, she not be into that, lass."

Aluxes smile faded. "What is so funny?"

Ulbrek slowly regained his breath and said, "They release a wee aura of pheromones to attract a mate. They can also direct it to a single person." He began to chuckle again, adding, "She be into lasses."

Aluxes eyes widened and her throat became dry. "I umm..."

Rebecca smiled and said, "It is all right. You are a very lovely lady." She turned her head to Ulbrek. "Father said I need to train. Maybe you can teach me."

He gently placed his pipe on a stump. "There be nothing I can teach ya. Dragonbloods be brawlers, but I may have a wee idea." He looked at Aluxes with a smile that made goosebumps appear on her body. "Be here in the mornin'." Rebecca giggled as she ran off.

"You think it will be all right to teach her?" she asked, staring at Ulbrek. "Can you just find someone taller I can spar with?"

He chuckled. "Don't be daft. Only thing your size be a young orc. The little lass be perfect for ya. They lost the ability to do breath attacks, but they still have that wee element. They able to enhance their physical ability for a bit of time."

Ulbrek picked up his wooden ax. "Aye, battle be full of monsters similar to her in size and ability. Unless ya fightin giants or orcs, all be shorter than ya. Most monsters try to out number ya. So startin' tomorrow, ya be fightin us both."

Chapter Three

PRELUDE OF FIRST BATTLE

"*A*ye, lass. You done well. Both ya make me proud." Ulbrek stood with a tear in his eye. "It been four months of hell, but ya grown on me."

Rebecca smiled and hugged him. "My father will be happy. I shall go back home now. Father wants me to learn the family trade."

She tried to hug Aluxes but was shoved to the side. "Hell no, I will not fall for that again. I told ya I am not interested."

Rebecca smiled and waved at her as she ran off towards the town. "I hope we meet again."

Aluxes looked at Ulbrek. "I thank you for everything. I promise I will not let you down."

He glanced up and saw a messenger bird fly towards the castle. "Aye, you may be tested soon, lass. We shall see."

Aluxes, with her shoulders held up, walked back to the old barracks that she had not seen for a while. A slight smile ran across her face as she placed her hand on the door, and a tiny breath escaped her lips as she opened it.

"What in the four hells is that smell?" She gagged as she closed her eyes.

Onyx looked at her. "Oh, good, ya here. It be time to wash Udook.

Normally, we knock him out with a sleep spell but he got wind halfway through the incantation. Now we be strugglin'.''

The half-dwarfs struggled to hold him down, barely holding his arms and legs pinned. Rose tried to use water magic to wash him but kept missing. Aluxes pummeled the back of his head and knocked him out.

Lugathar shouted, "Well, it be a good thing yer beast-like muscles showed up when they did, young lass."

"Does he always fight this hard?" Aluxes looked at them with a raised eyebrow.

Rose softly spoke, "We used to use the stuff from his hometown, but it had a really nasty smell to it."

"Made him smell like an orc's nut sack," Onyx boasted.

"Nah, more like being upside of an ogre's arse pipe," Ugthar added.

Troops quickly ran into the courtyard Commander Verus stood as he shouted for everyone to form up to be briefed.

"Hurry up, lass. It must be an important announcement." Onyx pulled Aluxes out the door.

As they were about to stand in formation, some people whispered, "I heard we are going into battle."

Commander Verus stepped onto a small box so everyone could see him with a letter in his hand. "*My dear elites. I only call on you when the time is dire. It is true these are just gnolls, and such are normally not worthy of your time, nor the money it would cost to send you out. Your talents were made for much bigger threats, but something has happened. They somehow became smart enough to split their army. One group went to fight in the battle, but the other group started to head towards the city nearby. I perhaps underestimated their numbers and should have sent more than just the royal guards. I ask that you show the unholy beasts your might. Signed, Your Holy Emperor Fredrick the Red.*"

They separated into their groups to prepare for war. Aluxes held her head as her feet staggered. Her breath became a little erratic, and she sat down on the ground. "What is this dark feeling I have? Am I scared to fight in a battle so soon?" She checked her sword a hundred times to make sure there were no cracks or blemishes.

"No worries, ye lass. We been in well over thirty battles, the lot of us. We will take care of ya." Lugathar chuckled as she patted Aluxes on the head.

Onyx kissed his double-headed hammer and prayed to random gods. Both Lugathar and Ugthar had war axes. Rose had a long-bow as a main, with a cross-bow and a short-bow as backup, and Udook just had his bare hands.

They all ran back after they had put their equipment onto a wagon and rushed into formation. The only one that stood near the commander was Udook. Like a personal guard, he shadowed his every move.

He took a deep breath and with slight excitement in his tone, said, "Some of you vets might remember that His Holy Highness use to be an elite, so this is a personal letter to us as his friends. We move out tonight, so say goodbye to your loved ones and meet up at the main gate." He grabbed Udook's hand, and they walked towards a cemetery nearby which was for the members of the royal family.

"Aye," Onyx said in a daze, "I got a lot of wee bastards gotta say bye to." He headed off to the dwarf district of the town.

Ugthar looked at Aluxes. "He has many kids. We may look like men in our thirties, but even us half-dwarfs live longer than humans. My brother and I are a hundred and fifty years old. A full-blooded dwarf can live to be six hundred if they take care of themselves. The previous dwarf king died at eight hundred and sixty." He smiled at her and walked towards Rose.

"Aye," Lugathar said with a cough, "I may look like I'm in me wee twenties, but I be hundred meself with six bastards."

Aluxes stared over at Rose and in a soft whisper said, "Two hundred and thirty."

She had felt at odds. Even among other half-breeds, she was different from them. She aged like normal people as far as she knew.

Her mind was buried in deep thoughts. As she rotated her hands, she looked at both sides. As she slowly moved one up, she nervously rubbed her circlet. *what am I?* constantly repeated in her mind. She didn't even notice that she was alone in the courtyard.

Bells echoed off in the distance and Aluxes moved towards the church. She thought, " I don't have any friends or family that I know of, and there are only two people I want to see before I go."

As she approached the church, a man standing there waved to greet her. "Oh, it is you headmaster. I guess with me out of the academy, you have plenty of free time."

"My dear, I remember that day well. When you were first found in that village, the only survivor of a dreadful massacre." He stood there, lost in thought.

He looked up at the tower as the bells rang again. "My dear, I hope you find the answers you need in this journey, and may whatever god made you always protect you." He glared at her with a tear in his eye. He turned around and walked towards the door of the church.

"My dear, how I always knew this was the path you were going to take. It still makes me worry so." The head nun, Mildred, walked into view from behind a shadow of the bell tower. She had a smile on her face, but her eyes were red and moist.

"I know you never liked other people, and you hate touching others even more. But can you forgive me for requesting a hug? They are so rare of you to give. I would love to have a final hug while you are still innocent."

As they hugged, Aluxes closed her eyes tightly as tears slowly trickled down her face. "The headmaster and you have always been kind to me. Even when I was unpleasant to you both."

They sat on a bench near the city fountain in front of the church. Mildred took a deep breath and scoffed, "Unpleasant is being kind about it, my dear. I remember when we visited that town where that boy tried to peek at you in the dressing room. You retaliated by covering the statue of the god that his town worshipped in cow manure. The towns folk wanted you hanged. They would have been allowed to if it weren't for that wild boar that tore through the market, which you killed with a single punch." She chuckled lightly, "When they saw an eight-year-old do that, they feared they would anger you."

Aluxes watched her shadow move around her feet as the sun disappeared into the horizon. "Yeah, well. They deserved my wrath." She looked up at the sky. "I am not afraid of the coming battle but I do fear something, and it bothers me very much."

Mildred smiled. "Dear, you could have married. You did get letters from boys that confessed their feelings of affection towards you."

Aluxes made a fist and gently punched the bench. "Yeah, they wanted to make me a trophy as if I was a wild animal to tame. I told them my requirement and none of them took it."

Mildred chuckled, "Deary, you might as well have asked that the sun turn into the moon or that cows produce cheese. They had to beat you in combat. When you said that, I knew the army was your destiny, but I know it would not be your end result. Just promise me that you will keep me in your thoughts wherever this journey takes you."

Aluxes looked over and noticed that Mildred had walked away. She placed her hand on her chest. "I hope my feelings are wrong. You better still be alive when I get back." The more she stared at the spot where Mildred sat, the more painful her heart became.

She headed toward the main gate and regrouped with her unit. The dwarfs were drinking and boasting of past killings. Rose was alone deep in thought, and the giant was with the commander. As she watched the commander helping Udook with his helmet, a little smile took over her normal demeanor.

"Aye!" Onyx shouted as the elites walked down the town road in a barely organized manner. "Aluxes, maybe ya can answer me this question?" He had a puzzled look on his face as he asked. "We be wondern if ya be able ta marry one of me bastards? Cause ya be so tall we think maybe it would make giant dwarf babies."

The three laughed as she punched at him, barely grazing his hair. "What the hell is wrong with you? You guys are just—," She stopped mid-sentence and rubbed her circlet. The more she looked at them, it was as if a dark cloud filled her heart.

A feeling overtook her as they walked out the main gate. "So, what made you guys join the elite?"

Lugathar replied, "I be a mighty shield maiden in the mighty dwarf army, but when me husband died, I decided to change my roots. Onyx here convinced me to come with him."

"Aye, your husband be a miner. Such a sad fate," Onyx replied. "The goblins had mined on the other side of the mountain and it be known to happen on rare occasions that the mines meet in the middle."

Ugthar cleared his throat. "My brother and I were asked by the king to represent our kind to the humans. When pressure from the allied races demanded that the elites at least add in half-breeds, Uncle Ulbrek persuaded the great dwarf king that we be picked." He smiled with pride. He kept looking at Rose, who was a tad bit slow and long in the face as she walked.

Aluxes noticed how different the brothers were in their speech. "Ugthar, you seem to speak more like a—,"

He put up his hand to stop her. "Ah yes, I can be speak like one. But I decided I should be better appealing than my brother." He had a grin on his face.

Onyx scoffed a little. "He be raised by our father. Mother be a temple maiden, so it be an unholy sin to allow him in dwarf lands. Uncle raised me, which be why I have a strong dwarf name. And what his name means, well, that be a story for a later time."

Onyx winked at Lugathar."I did it to prove myself to this lovely lady here." He looked at her and blew a kiss.

"Who says I'll have ya?" She threw a pebble at him.

"Ya probably did not know, Aluxes but elites be allowed to marry after they get enough points 'cause we be held to higher standards. I have two more years left." Onyx smiled a little, "I had a dwarf wife. She died in battle. I been with a human, I been with a hobbit, I think. I also been with an orc, I can't really remember. I was drunk, could have been a goblin. But anyways, I never been with a half-dwarf. Just think of it, they be double the human and dwarf."

"Brother, it don't work that way. Listen to me, I am the smart one." Ugthar covered his mouth as his shoulders lifted up and down to match his muffled laugh.

Onyx kept rambling, "Think of it. Fifty percent add another fifty percent makes a hundred percent. So they be two hundred percent!"

Lugathar chuckled uncontrollably. "And they be dumb as a stick." She calmed down and said, "But the thought be sweet. He once confessed to me by boasting." She tried her best impression of Onyx. "I be single handed defeat ah cave ogre and make a ring out of its testicles." She chuckled a little and added, "The gesture be a sweet thought though."

Rose turned her head towards them. "The commander is my brother-in-law." They stopped and looked at her. "That's how I was able to get into the elite. My husband and children were killed by dark elves twenty years ago. I had six children."

Onyx's jaw dropped so fast and hard that he almost fell over. "Well, that be depressing. Sorta ruined the mood. Me brother almost married a goat once."

Ugthar chuckled. "Her name was Gretta. She was a fine dwarf."

Lugathar laughed and added, "With a mighty fine beard she had."

Ugthar walked closer to Rose as he rubbed her back in an attempt to help her put her mind at ease. They talked quietly so no one could hear.

Onyx glanced a peek above the tree line and noticed a bright orange glow. He looked over at Aluxes. She was rubbing her circlet.

"So Aluxes, ya have any questions?" He asked softly.

"Yeah, what the hell is a gnoll?" she asked with the most puzzled tone in her voice.

"Didn't ya train under me uncle?" Onyx lifted one eyebrow higher than the other.

"Besides combat, all he did was boast about how thick his trunk for his tree was. Which is why human girls never leave him alone," she said as she blushed. With an angry tone in her voice, she added, "All he told me was I do not need to worry about them."

"Hahaha! Yeah, that be like him. He probably be right. Just imagine a dog breed with a bat, then mixed with a rat, and instead of wings, walks upright. They be ugly as hell. Not strong, mostly it be their large numbers that tend to be nasty."

He let out a deep breath. "Too bad they be shorter than me. Means can't end the fight real fast."

The people that could hear him chuckled. "Ya see, Aluxes. It be very rare dwarfs go to war, mainly with the taller races like orcs. We just be perfect height to take this war hammer right into their nuts. When entire front-lines take a hammer to the balls, the rest tend to follow suit." He chuckled. "Think of it. There be only one war between humans and dwarfs and it be a short one. Humans allied with them right after. The balls be the best way to end a war."

Aluxes blushed a little as Onyx talked more. They headed towards the city. The amber glow of fire above the tree line would have scared any new recruit.

Chapter Four

THE RIVAL

"Okay, class. Why is it that when it comes to magic we do not use it on a normal basis?" A nun asked, standing at the front in a class full of little kids.

A red-headed girl with a fancy silk dress raised her hand. "Because magic uses up life energy. Each spell drains the user. If they use too many spells, or a really big spell, they die."

The teacher clapped. "That is right, Evalyn."

Another girl, with a dirty gray dress, blue hair, and golden eyes cleared her throat. "Not always true. With humans, it only drains their stamina. Also, dwarfs created runestones to counter the life drain. However, it taxes twice as much stamina to get the same effect."

The nun snapped at Aluxes with her eyebrows furrowed, "Do you always have to interrupt? And why can you not stop looking angry? Just turn your seat around. The sight of your eyes bothers me."

Evalyn looked over at Aluxes and was captivated by the color of her eyes. During lunch break, she walked towards her with a large smile across her face. Her grin somehow gained in size, looking as if it could split her checks.

She extended her hand. "I am Evalyn, a new transfer. My father said this was a great academy. The others told me you are eight. Well, I turn eight tomorrow." She stood with her arm hanging, her smile never breaking.

Aluxes looked up at her. "You have an annoying voice. You must be rich. Are you not afraid that my dirty orphan clothing would stain that pretty dress?" She quickly turned her head and stared at a corner.

Evalyn's heart felt a little pinch. "You seem pretty smart. Why do you sit in the back? I saw you playing by yourself in the sand pit before class started."

Another kid came up to her. "Watch out. She is half-monster. One of the nuns told me that her mother was a whore to a mara."

The other kids pulled Evalyn away as they shouted "Sit with us." She looked back and noticed the tears that rolled down the girl's face.

During play time, the kids were around the sand pit. Every day, they played combat games. Evalyn made it obvious that she was experienced with weapons and she would always win. "Like my father, I will be a famous hunter. It is why I am the best."

She looked over, noticed Aluxes, and waved at her to join in. "Come on, you've been watching us for days. There is no point if you are curious."

Aluxes rubbed her circlet as she slowly walked towards them. Her head moving left to right as she watched the kids whisper. "It is all right. I will take it easy on you. My father has taught me how to fight. There is no need to be scared." The smile on her face showed her perfect teeth. Evalyn handed her a wooden sword and giggled.

Aluxes looked at it closely. The other kids snickered at her because she gripped it wrong. "We are not allowed to learn weapons until we are ten. You're just trying to get me into trouble."

Even though Evalyn had her whip by her side, she held a sword in her hand and tightened her grip. "All right. This is your first time, so I will take it easy on you. If I win, you will join my friends and I for lunch." With lightning reflexes, she attacked.

Everyone stood there in shock as Aluxes grabbed her blade with one hand. "You're too slow," she said with a bored expression.

Evalyn's face became red. "How dare you speak like that to me? I will show you your place." She released the grip on her sword and jumped back to gain some distance. "If I am too slow for you, then stop this!" With a quick snap of the wrist, she whipped Aluxes in the face before she could react.

She looked at her as blood poured slowly down her cheek from a deep cut that was half an inch long. All the kids ran off as they called for the nuns.

Evalyn put her hand in front of her face. "Oh my god, I am so sorry. Let me use a healing spell real quick so it won't leave a scar."

Aluxes growled and instantly attacked. Evalyn tried to hit her again with her whip, but she blocked it with her arm and let it wrap around it. With a hard yank, Evalyn flew toward her. A swift knee to her gut ended the fight.

Evalyn looked up at her and noticed that the wound was mostly healed. "What are you really?"

Aluxes gazed down at her. "You are too weak. The friends you have are asses. You will hate me like all of them do. Just don't bother me ever again," she said and walked off.

The next day, Evalyn declared that Aluxes was to be her rival in front of the entire class.

A handful of years passed and graduation was about to take place. Evalyn had always been one of the more beautiful girls in the academy. Her father being a famous war hero meant that she did not need to attend, but she did so to prove to herself that she deserved her family name.

As a normal human, she was not too tall and not too short, standing at five-feet-two, with red hair that ran all the way down to the backs of her legs, and eyes such a bright blue color that made the sky jealous. Like most of the students, she wore her armor to show that she was going for the army. It was a lightweight tan-colored leather with thick parts over the vital spots. Her shoulders were exposed but her arms were lightly covered, and she had her bladed whip at her side.

After her encounter with Aluxes at the stalls, she stood in line to join the Holy Army. *I will show her. She will be just a foot-note to my fame.*

She looked over at Aluxes as she was handed her letter from the headmaster. The large red seal on the envelope was easy for her to see. *Oh, that bitch! How dare she get accepted without registering. Of course, the head master pulled some strings, he always treated her like a daughter.* She scoffed as the heat from the sun beat down on her.

She clenched her fists so tightly that her hands shook. *To hell with this heat, and to hell with her not standing in line like the rest of us.* She controlled her breathing to calm herself as she waited.

As she approached the counter to enlist, she loosened the top strap of her armor a little and tried to flirt with the man who sat there. "Oh sir, can you please help me?" She smiled with a wink and leaned over the table to show some cleavage. "My friend and I promised we would be joining together but I cannot seem to be able to find her name on any of these sheets."

He tried to remain professional as he cleared his throat, but his eyes shifted their gaze down her loosened armor. "Well let's see. What was her name?"

"Aluxes!" She covered her mouth. "Oh my, I am most dreadfully sorry. I am just so upset that I could not control myself." She giggled a little and started to fan herself.

"Ahh, yes. She is in the elite. Sorry, not much I can do to help you."

She slammed her fists on the table. "I demand that you get me in that unit," she said with a soft growl.

"Sorry, ma'am. But only the king himself can say who is allowed to join. Sorry, you have to pick another unit." His voice was shaking and his nerves caused him to break into a light sweat.

"Ah, front-line soldier would guide me to fame faster." She let go of the man and signed her name on the paper.

The treatment was something she was unable to become accustomed to. Everything was standard issue. She was forced to put away her whip for the sword and shield. Her personal armor for light chain and plated armor. She even had to cut her hair above her ears as it caused a problem with the helmet.

After a few weeks had passed, she had proven herself to be one of the more able soldiers. *Oh my, look at this. I have been promoted again. At this rate, I should make the rank sergeant by the end of the year. I bet my rival has not even made it past the basic rank. I should probably check on her.*

She wandered around for a little bit before she ended up in the elite area. "Excuse me, good sir. Do you know where I may find Aluxes?" she asked a man.

He walked closer towards her. "Why would a lovely girl like you want to see an ugly half-breed bitch like that?"

She placed her hand over her mouth and giggled. "Oh my, sir. You must have her confused with some simple peasant." She quickly punched his throat. "A person of noble birth such as myself would only allow a lovely and talented person such as Aluxes to be my rival and friend."

The man coughed. "You are nobility. I can tell by the way you speak. Sorry for my rudeness. The half-breeds are over there in that run-down building." He slowly walked off and coughed out, "Whore!" but Evalyn ignored him and kept heading towards the barracks.

She knocked and Rose opened the door. "Ah, yes. I am sorry for disturbing you, but I am looking for Aluxes."

The half-elf looked up and down her body, and with a quiet voice that could be barely heard, asked, "And who might you be?"

She cleared her throat a little. "I am her friend."

"I thought she had no friends." They both stared at each other.

Evalyn moved her head to look around. "Her only friend and arch-rival."

Rose chuckled a little. "She been out training with a master for a few weeks and will be out—" Before she could finish, Evalyn let out a grunt and rolled her eyes back as she turned around.

She stormed off as she yelled to herself, "Of course she would get better treatment than me. I am only her better. I bet she did not even have to cut her hair. My lovely long hair."

She ran into the message office and wrote a letter to her father. *He will fix this,* raced through her mind over and over again.

A week passed by and a huge entourage came with a splendid white carriage. All who were there were stunned when they saw the extremely well-built man with faded red hair, a large scar across his check, and with signs of makeup to highlight it.

A personal announcer stepped out and cleared his throat, "Sir Edward L. Hossberg has arrived."

"Daddy!" Evalyn ran up to him and jumped into his arms.

His eyes twinkled as he looked at her. "Oh, my little angel. As always, I came the second I received your letter." His voice was extremely deep and carried.

"Oh, Daddy, did you cancel another meeting with regional lords to be with me?" Her eyes twinkled.

He gently pushed her forward as they entered the carriage and headed off to her father's favorite place, the Art Museum of History. As they approached, his personal announcer stepped out, and bellowed, "Sir Edward L. Hossberg and Lady Evalyn G. Hossberg have arrived."

"Daddy, must you have that every time we go anywhere? It gets embarrassing." She looked down at the ground as people whispered around her. Her face burned red.

"My dear, after all the things I have done for the world of the living, it is what I deserve. Even if I stop at a local shop to use the toilet, I want every man, woman, and child to know that I have arrived," he bellowed out.

As they approached the entrance, there was a statue of him at the main door, emblazoned with the words, *"Our hero and founder of this building."*

Inside there were paintings of every war to memory. They stopped at a mural of him fighting vampires when he was younger. The oddest highlight about the painting was that part of his thick mustache glowed.

"Ahh, I remember that day. They belonged to the vampire king so they were stronger than normal vampires." He looked at Evalyn. "So what is this problem you have, my dear?"

She stared at him with puffed eyes. "Oh, Daddy. I need to get into the elite. My rival is there and I cannot allow her to outdo me."

"You mean that half-breed mutt you've been complaining about all these years? You shouldn't bother yourself with such—"

"She always beat me in combat training. I have to prove that I am better," she snapped.

"Well, I remember that the prince and I where rivals." He rubbed his face where his whiskers used to be. His eyes widened as he noticed they were gone. *Damn it, I miss my mustash*, raced through his mind as he slowly removed his hand.

"Well, not even I can get you into that group. But I do know that when their numbers go down, they tend to pick people from other units. The royal guard is your best bet." He handed her a packet of papers.

"These are your orders to check in to the royal guard barracks. I do admire a good rival, but do not stain your hands with this mutt. We have a long line of fighting the armies of the undead. It's our legacy, and I am sure it is above her to be able to handle these monsters." They hugged as she ran off.

The next day, Evalyn arrived at the new barracks, and was greeted by a man on a snow-white horse. "I am Prince Loux. The third eldest brother of the king." He stood at five-six, with blue eyes and long blond hair.

"Lady Evalyn, your father requested that you be only allowed to use your personal equipment which he made for you," he said in a snooty tone. His pompous demeanor showed that everyone was beneath him. Even the way he turned and trotted off angered her to no end.

The maids came out and gave her the old leather armor and the whip she originally wore. They slowly guided her towards the dorm. It sat across the castle in the main garden. Right next to the door was a marble sign that read, *"Females' dorm—one thousand humans—five hundred elves. NO DWARFS ALLOWED!"*

"Dwarfs are too loud and foul-mouthed to be in the royal guard. The numbers are the total occupants allowed," said one of the female elves that sat near the entrance. Her long, flowing pink hair, green eyes, and long ears were things that Evalyn had always loved about valley elves.

Most of the time, they were being trained proper etiquette. How to be blend in with the rich as they had their parties and gatherings that the guard must attend. In total, there were four thousand troops in the guard but it always seemed much smaller. Rarely would they train for combat but when they did, Evalyn excelled at it.

At the end of the month, all the royal guard were in formation. Prince Loux was on his white horse and Evalyn's Father stood next to him, heavily muscled with an aura as if he were a god in human skin. The prince looked like a child, even on the horse, compared to him.

Loux held up a letter from the king and read, "My beloved guard. It is with great importance that I ask this of you. The army is doing very well on the battlefield, but they are stretched too thin and are unable able to stop the large formation of gnolls that are heading to the city of Angarth. This city is vital for our survival. Without it, they will have a chokehold on the supply line. It is my belief that the royal guard should also defend the people in this dire situation. You shall be reinforced by the elite the following day. May your gods watch and protect you. Your Lord and King Erwin."

The Prince trotted back and forth. "Do not disgrace me. We set out in an hour. Everyone get ready."

Evalyn was walking off when she was stopped by her father. He looked at her. His newly grown whiskers a tad wet from the tears he was unable to hold in. "My dear, I know you shall make it back safely. But even so, I hope you still come back as my angel."

He handed her a whip. "This has a new metal. A combination of elf and dwarf forge. It never needs to be sharpened or cleaned."

She looked at the runes on the whip and noticed that they were a little different from what was usually on her whips. "The normal holy soldiers have basic holy spells engraved on their swords so they do not waste time in enchanting; these are for something more than what a typical trooper would deal with." He smiled at her and hugged her before she walked away.

They set off in a standard formation, leaving five hundred behind to keep the castle guarded. It was a fast trip; barely two hours passed by as they approached the city. People cheered as they paraded through the town, greeting them as heroes. Banners were strung high and flower petals flew out from windows and balconies. Evalyn looked towards her sergeant with worry in her eyes that she was unable to hide. He waved at her. She did not understand the motion but it calmed her.

They set up outside the city and dug out a trench. They had barely started when a loud horn echoed, and out of the tree line in the distance, a formation of twenty thousand gnolls appeared.

"Sergeant, I read in the text book that they are incapable of military formations," Evalyn said as she tried to hide the fear from her voice.

"That is true. But sometimes, it is very rare, though they do scavenge enough wealth to hire an orc or a dark elf to be their officer." He pointed towards the tree line, and five orcs slowly walked out and stood behind the gnolls.

"If they paid them to also fight, we could have a problem. They seem very old which means they've seen more combat than our entire division put together," he said as he looked around to acquire a proper layout of the field.

The big orc who must have been over ten feet tall and was thickly-muscled, stood in front of the gnolls, waved his arms. They hopped around with excitement. *"Votaca kejauk tikka jeivu di kajaukvi ceivadeo di chuca koduo tekjauk di jeivata da kuvitik."*

They barked and howled; some made a cackling noise to imitate laughter. It was such an upsetting sound that even the seasoned troops were rattled a little. A handful of able villagers volunteered to help defend the city—around two thousand—but they were still outnumbered.

Evalyn's unit was placed on the flank. "This is the most important area," her sergeant said. "The gnolls will try to use their numbers to try and surround us. If we fail, we will all die." He handed her a luck charm.

As the beasts charged, it was as if a thunderstorm rolled through the valley. The very ground quaked as they rushed. The elf archers that were set up at the high points of the town started to fire, followed by the human archers but it still wasn't enough to slow them down. The gnolls smashed into the shield wall. The first line of beasts was crushed in between their line and the soldiers. Blood and bodies flew all over. The gnolls bit, clawed, and jabbed their swords at any exposed flesh.

The line flowed against the shield wall like water. The formation rippled and spread towards the sides. They quickly made it around to the flank in an attempt to encircle them.

Evalyn was able to take out a gnoll or two with each flick of her whip. *Holy shit, this is too much! No matter how many I kill, more just replace them. Their numbers seem endless.* The fight continued for what felt like hours. Everyone grew weary, but they held fast as the gnolls numbers were no longer an advantage.

"Evalyn, go rotate with one of the reserves. You have been fighting for a few hours," her sergeant said as he grabbed her shoulder.

"No, I can keep going. I—" He put his hand over her mouth.

He sighed a little. "Look, their numbers are no longer an issue, and we are winning. What I cannot have is worn out soldiers in case there is a second wave. The orcs have not entered the battle so we need to take rest whenever we can. More troops die from getting worn out in the field than from sword wounds." He placed his hand on her back and walked her towards the rear.

As soon as they sat down to rest, the ground rumbled a little and caved in. Goblins rushed out like ants and swarmed the area. Blast sticks took out archers with deadly accuracy. The loud thunderous sound that they made scared a handful of the troops, causing them to run off into a panic to their deaths.

As weariness began to take its toll, despair swept over them as well and a man shouted, "Oh, praise the gods. The prince and his calvary have arrived. We are saved." The calvary wedged straight into the flank. As night fell, hope filled the ranks and they cheered loudly. A war horn from the forest blasted its deafening sound.

The prince looked with his spy glass and could see thirty trolls that had come from the woods. They marched towards the battle alongside the orcs. He quickly rode off as he left his men to fight.

Evalyn's body shook as she saw one walk straight for her. Someone nudged her shoulder, and her sergeant's voice said, "They are not that strong as trolls go. They are only forest trolls, but they do have an amazing healing ability which could make them a problem." He patted her back.

As the orcs joined the battle, they quickly turned the tides. To them, the soldiers were no more than a mere nuisance. They swatted them away as if they were flies. People screamed and shouted as they tried to run but they were taken out just the same.

In a deep, low raspy voice, an orc yelled at Evalyn, "Girl challenge you I. Strike first you will!" He was muscular and large. He filled the entire view with his gigantic body.

She whipped him in the face multiple times, but she was too worn out from fighting and was unable to put in a full swing.

"Worth not my blade," he said as he looked around for another worthy soldier.

"He can have her." He walked off and the troll that she had seen earlier stood there in front of her with a large grin.

"Humm it'abe a long time'en from last time'en I had human meat." He had an extremely low and deep voice. He also drooled a little.

She managed to hit him a few times but his wounds healed up almost as soon as she hit him. "Ahh, poor girl be'a trying but she'd be'a get eatten by me." He swung his ax at her and missed.

"I'd be'a teasing you, girl. I'd like to eat'ed you still alive." He grabbed her arm and opened his mouth, ready to bite her when a glowing sword exited his chest through his back.

"Holy burn!" the sergeant shouted. He stood behind it with his hand still holding onto the handle. The troll screamed as he rolled on the ground and burst into flames.

"You can only hurt them with holy magic. Use your runes," he shouted as he stood ready for the next foe.

The orc turned around. "Trolls useless. Must do myself." The orc yanked a light post out of the ground and threw it like a javelin into the sergeant with blinding speed, killing him instantly.

The orc pulled out his sword and swung it at Evalyn. She closed her eyes tightly as she tried to block it with her whip.

Clank. She opened her eyes and saw a half-dwarf blocking the orc's blow.

"Aye, you be a berserker." Onyx stood there with a smile.

"A dwarf!" The orc backed up into a ready stance; his body shook a little, which made his sword waver off-target.

Onyx held up his hammer. The two faced each other with some excitement. With a quick leap to close the gap, Onyx changed his grip slightly to hasten an upper cut and cracked the Orc in his groin.

The orc let out a sound that could be heard for miles before he collapsed onto the ground.

Onyx swiftly bashed the orc's head in with a smile. "See, Aluxes. The quickest way is to the balls."

Evalyn looked behind her and saw Aluxes, covered in goblin blood. She was unable to hold back her smile. "Aluxes, I am so happy to see you." She jumped at her and hugged her tightly as tears rushed down her face. All the fear that she had been trying to hide came out in her crying.

Aluxes patted her back with her free arm. "You know, this means I am still better than you."

"The reinforcements arrived early," a troop shouted. Hope and joy filled the ranks. The battle raged on and was long from over, but their morale to win was greatly reinvigorated.

Chapter Five

LEGENDS AND FAILURES

*A*luxes put her arm around Evalyn and helped her walk. Every step made her moan. "Shit, I feel like I've been stabbed by a bunch of needles." Her body was covered in bruises.

"You got here late. Trying to make a heroic entry?" she asked with a little smirk.

Aluxes grunted. "We would have been here sooner, but we got ambushed by goblins. Just focus on breathing. It will dull the pain."

"I wish I could heal like you. I bet the pain would be gone by now." Evalyn coughed a little.

"Just because I heal fast does not mean I do not feel the pain. It hurts more when it is healing. For some wounds, I can feel the pain for days—" Aluxes grunted as they stumbled.

She shoved her onto an area full of injured soldiers. With her usual annoyed look, she said, "Sit there and do not move." A troll stood there with a smirk.

The beast was about eight feet tall with tusks for canines, and green skin. "I'd see you'd be diff from others. Maybe you 'd be a good eat'en."

Aluxes stepped away from the wounded and worn out soldiers with her sword ready. She slightly lowered the tip as to invite the troll to make the first move. Her body was calm as she slowly took deep breaths.

The monster ran towards her fast. As he swung for her head, she tucked and rolled her back against his chest. Before he could noticed her, she hit him in the teeth with the pommel of her sword and broke most of them.

He screamed in pain as he held his face. "Little girl, you'd be regrettin that!"

As he removed his hands, she grabbed him by the neck and rolled him over her shoulder. A blue glow covered her body, and then the troll was engulfed in a blue flame. He instantly burned to ash. Before she could look up, another troll came up and grabbed her face and squeezed.

"You'd be too dangerous to try'ed eat'en," he snarled at her.

She kicked him in the ribs. Each time she struck, the sound of bones breaking echoed. After a few moments, the pain forced him to let her go and he hunched over.

"What'en kind a monster are be?" he asked before she chopped off his head with her sword. Again, she burned the troll the same way to make sure he stayed dead.

Even though she had seen it in the academy, Evalyn was still shocked as she watched. "If I was more brute than brain like you, I could have made short work of them as well."

Aluxes looked at her. "Yeah, well. If you were so smart, then why didn't ya remember to use your runes on that fancy whip?" She turned and walked into the battlefield.

She was stopped by Onyx. "Aye, lass. We have here a rare moment." He pointed over at an orc.

The orc looked at her; he was around ten feet tall with faded green skin, almost a gray color, long white hair, and a beard. He was not as muscular as the other orc, only the size of a well-built man.

"Aye, that there be a real orc. The other a berserker. They be focus on raw power. An orc like that would not fall for me golf trick. To look like that, he be around five hundred." Onyx was barely able to hide his excitement to see an orc of that caliber.

The orc walked closer. "Human girl pup. It is a rare honor for me to challenge a warrior to a duel. No tricks, no magic, just a simple battle. Will you accept?" He had an extremely deep but sincere voice. He stripped off his armor which was covered in runes, and put down his enchanted sword and drew a normal one from another sheath.

Onyx looked at her. "If ya accept and beat him, this battle be over. Ya chances be based on luck but who knows? He may be wee sick. In ya case I hope so."

Aluxes nodded and stood in a ready stance. She took a deep breath to stop her body from shaking. They locked eyes, trying to spot an opening.

The orc chuckled. "Pup, I see you have trained well. However, you lack experience."

The orc smiled a little and lunged forward with a fast and powerful swing. Aluxes was barely able to block in time and managed to break his sword, but not without complications. The shear might of the strike knocked the blade from her hands. An anticipated move that the orc immediately followed with a punch to her gut.

She coughed up some blood but did not lose the chance to grab his wrist. She used it to help her as she kicked his legs and brought him to the ground. She managed to twist his arm behind his back and dislocated it.

With some joy, he said, "Human girl pup, you are a mighty warrior indeed!" His other arm, which was under his chest, reached up and grabbed her hair. With a hard pull, she was on the ground. He stood up and reset his injured arm without a single flinch. "I have heard rumors about your kind and they were not exaggerated." He chuckled.

Aluxes dropped her guard as her mind raced. Her eyes wandered off her target a little. All she was able to do was to think about what he'd said. *I might finally have an answer to what I am.*

Suddenly, a thunderous sound echoed, and a goblin snickered as he raised a blast stick. The impact on her shoulder knocked her to the ground immediately, and she passed out.

The orc grabbed the goblin by the head. *"Koca ceica kaka. Jeivo deoko jeivu touvadi vokidi."* He squeezed it like a tomato. Green blood oozed from his lifeless corpse. He tossed him to the side as if it was trash.

He walked over to her and picked her up. "Dwarf, what is pup's name?" He gently lowered her by Onyx.

"Aye, her name be Aluxes." He never took his eyes off the orc.

"Our duel was tarnished. By orc law, I cannot allow any harm to this girl. To make sure no harm happens to me, I shall pull my troops back so we may duel again," he said in a calm manner.

He put on his armor and grabbed his enchanted sword. He took a medal off his uniform and tossed it to Onyx. "Dwarf, make sure she gets it when awaken. Tell her show it any orc if she wishes to duel me again." He walked off.

"Aye, noble orc. What be ya name?" Onyx asked.

He turned his head with a smirk. "Krull," he said and continued to walk off. The other orcs, trolls, and goblins slowly leave through the hole they'd dug, but the gnolls stayed to fight, only to be slaughtered.

A horn could be heard, and off in the distance where the sun met the cliff, there was a man with a small band of horsemen.

Prince Loux shouted, "The battle is won." People ran out to celebrate. A handfull recognized who, in reality, had saved the day.

Aluxes awakened in a soft bed in a makeshift hospital for the wounded. By her side, Onyx and Rosaletta sat talking among themselves. The room was filled with the smell of flowers and fragrance. She tried to get up but she was buried in gifts from the people she had saved from the trolls and the orc general. As she struggled, some of the items fell off her and alerted the two that she was awake.

"Aye, little lass, ya should slow down a wee bit. Ya were shot and had a lot of broken bones." Onyx softly smiled at her. "Glad to see ya be awake."

Rose looked at her and said, "You should be fine tomorrow." She hummed a little as she gave her water like a mother does with a child who is sick in bed.

"Ah shit, my body feels like it is on fire." Aluxes coughed as flashes of the battle raced through her mind. "Who was that orc?"

Onyx answered with excitement. "That be no other than the mighty Krull. Just seeing him was an amazing sight, let alone surviving him."

He handed her the medal. "Krull be a legend of sorts. If he deemed it more honorable, he would side with his enemy and fight his own kind. He helped the dwarfs with the last war in fighting the orcs."

She looked at the medal. It had orc runes engraved all over it and was made of a rare metal that she had never seen. It had a rainbow coloring to it when light hit it. There was an image of an orc holding an ax leaping at a dragon. The odd thing about it was that the dragon's head followed her as she moved it.

Onyx stood up and slowly walked out. "Aye, gotta drain me snake. Enjoy ya fan mail." He laughed as he left.

She looked over at a stand near Rose and saw that there was a pile of letters on it. She grunted a little and pulled the blanket over her face.

Rose moved them closer. "There are over a thousand letters here that consider you a hero. They should cheer you up," she said with a cheerful yet empty tone.

Aluxes's hand came out and touched the stand, and the letters burst into a blue flame. She then grabbed some of the flowers and threw them. "How can I be a hero? I lost my battle. Heroes save the day by winning. I know how they truly feel about me. How could I forgive and forget how these people treated me? Most of them grew up with me in the academy."

She looked out the window. Outside and right under her window, children played near a fountain. "These people only praise the ones they want to topple over. They will build me up like a statue to pull down so they can feel stronger later. They are all useless."

Rose looked at her and tried her best to hold back the tears in her eyes. "I was told your holy powers are unstable because you are immoral, but I can see it is because of the deep hatred you have for others. All that rage and anger will consume and change you."

She acted a little motherly by cleaning up the room. "It is easy to hate but harder to move on. Even after all I've been through, I still have time to find love in my heart."

She started to hum, which soothed Aluxes. Her chest became

lighter as if a weight were removed. She lay back down in her bed. She was unable to help but wonder about Rose's story. Whenever she thought about how Rose looked and acted, it was hard not to be a little sad. It was as if you could read it in her body about the sadness she must had been through.

"Knock knock," someone whispered as the door opened and Ugthar entered. Aluxes noticed that Rose blushed every time they talked and that they stood close. He handed her a letter and a flower before he walked away.

Rose held the letter close to her heart. "Aluxes, these people think of you as a hero because the times seem terrible, and they want someone strong to have faith in. You always seem to be very strong yet you act very weakly. I know that someday, you will be the hero that we see you as. You just need to fall a little to learn how to stand up." She walked off and gently closed the door.

An odd hum slowly became louder next to her bed. There was a strange orb where Rose had been sitting that was emitting a blue energy. Her eyes were heavy and she drifted into a coma-like rest. Her dream was filled with a young half-elf. It was Rosaletta.

$\mathcal{A}$n elf girl ran down the halls, passing by the maids and the other occupants with a large grin on her face. Her ears were not as long as an elf and her eye color was a faded pink— all the typical signs of a half-blood. She ran up to a man at the end of the hall who stood with dignity like people in paintings do. He had the air of someone who was kingly, and the pride he had in himself was easy to see. "Father, gather," she said, "Are they here?"

The man turned around, displaying the crown of the high elf king. "Yes, my dear. The human delegates are here, so you should behave accordingly, Rosaletta. Make sure you wear something elegant."

As a full-blooded male elf, his hair was magenta and his eyes were a dark green color. He had an elegant green silk robe with long sleeves. When he walked, it was as if he was gliding on the air. Despite his age, he looked like a man in his thirties.

Rose rushed into her room. "Oh my goddess, I can barely move from blushing so much." She placed her hands over her face and looked in the mirror. "Oh, I hope today is the day. I wonder where I placed it." She rapidly searched her room.

She pulled out a white rose dress. "Ah, Mother's dress. I hope this impresses him." Next to her was a little lock-box. She sat down and opened it. Inside, it was full of love letters. The blood rushed back to her checks. She dug around and sifted through the box and pulled out a necklace with a glowing white stone in the middle. Her head swayed from side to side as she hummed a little while putting it on.

She walked towards the dining area and peeked around the corner. Her father, brother, and three humans sat chatting. One of the men wore fancy armor, and as she gazed at him, her cheeks turned bright red. In time, their eyes met and everyone stopped talking.

Her father looked towards her. "Ahh, there she is. Our person of honor." They all stood up and waited for her to be seated.

He waved her to come over and cleared his throat. "So, under these delegations, it is normal for a truce to end with a marriage. Yet you still saw it fit to honor our traditions of proposal to her."

Everyone looked at the glowing white light in the gem. "The light of a star root is very hard for a human to obtain. If my son did not witness such a feat, I would have thought you stole it." He unsuccessfully hid the enjoyment in his voice.

He rubbed the mole on his face, and with his other hand, fidgeted with a locket he wore around his neck. "You do know this is for a full-blooded elf right? You could have asked for one of her sisters. Why choose the half-blood?"

The man in the fancy armor stood up. "My king, might I explain why I picked your lovely daughter here. After your kind saved me, she looked after me while I healed. I have known her for three years and would rather be with a woman I know than one I hardly know."

Her father stood up with a cup held high. It was full of *olaitay*— an elvish wine. "Sir Walton, fine words. You have my blessing to marry my favorite daughter."

They all stood up, and her brother said with authority, "*Iayati.*" The others joined in with the humans. "For honor"

Everything faded into a cloud. Random sounds echoed through her mind as a new image formed. Some years had come to pass and Rose was now a mother. She lived in a huge mansion in the holy city of Cathair. The kids lined up oldest to youngest: Adalolf, a boy of sixteen;

Arculf, a boy of fourteen; Geva, a girl of ten; Ria, a girl of nine; Ronnie, a boy of seven; and Samantha, a two-year-old girl.

No matter how the story unfolded around Aluxes, she was unable to take her eyes off Samantha. Even when she tried to force herself to turn away, there was a glow that radiated from the little girl that made her want to keep looking.

Rosaletta stood in front of them with a huge smile, wearing a fancy summer dress. "All right, kids. Uncle Verus and his wife are on their way. We must be ready for the picnic."

Three men walked in: Rose's husband the elite commander; his brother Verus, the current commander; and another man.

"Dear, you're home a little early. Is everything all right at the castle?" She looked over at the bald man who stood behind him. "Who is this?"

He smiled and kissed her. "This is the new commander of the elite, Commander Largo."

Largo looked right into her eyes and smiled as he bowed polity and kissed her hand. His voice sounded a little off, like he had an injury in his throat. "It is an honor to meet you. I have heard tales of your beauty."

"Uncle Verus!" The kids shouted as they ran to him.

Adalof was the only one who did not hug him. "Uncle, congratulations on your promotion to lieutenant."

Verus shook his hand. "Congrats on being accepted into the royal guard." Both of them smiled.

A large carriage pulled up and an attractive blond-haired woman who was pregnant slowly walked out. Verus ran up to help her up to the door. She nodded at him. "My husband may not be the smartest of the bunch but he is the sweetest. I cannot believe you forgot me in the carriage."

Rose hugged her tightly and kissed her checks. "You look like you're going to pop, Tanya."

Tanya looked around. "I got the ride for our trip. Let's go and have some fun. It may be the last time I can enjoy myself this year."

Everyone piled into the carriage except for Largo, who helped the servants put the baskets of food in the storage area and walked off. For just a moment, he had a little smirk on his face that Rose noticed.

Rose stood there in a daze. Her kids were trying to push her to hurry, but she was unable to shake off how the smirk bothered her. They dragged her halfway to the carriage.

As they moved, Verus and Walton talked. "So, brother. How is that giant of yours?" Walton asked.

Verus chuckled a little. "He is off visiting his mother. It is a big day in his village. She is to match him. That poor simpleton is worried he will miss his chance to mate."

Rose sighed as she fanned herself. "I would have loved to have him here. He is very good with poems."

Verus nodded. "Yeah, he has a heart of gold that one. He may have a future once he retires from the army."

After a few miles into a field with tall grass, the kids complained that they had to use the bathroom. They pulled over and everyone rushed out. Samantha waddled off toward a pond and picked flowers. The adults were busy with conversation, talking about how Rosaletta would make a fine delegate to negotiate half-breeds into the elites.

Samantha let out a little scream. Sir Walton ran over to see what had happened.

"Samantha!" her father cried out as he ran towards the pond, but she had disappeared.

Rose became ghostly pale as she tried to find her voice. "The pond!"

As her husband turned to look at her, an arrow pierced the back of his head. Before they could react, dark elves with gray skin and hair leaped out of the tall grass. The few bodyguards they had were overwhelmed by the numbers. After it was all done, the only survivors were Rose and Verus.

Rosaletta sat in her bed surrounded with the belongings of her family. She was so lost in her thoughts she did not notice her father had walk in.

"Dear, the maid has said you've been sitting here for a week. You do remember that the funeral is tomorrow. I know you begged us to find Samantha before we have it but we were unable to find her." He stood there calmly, but he was clinching his fist in frustration.

Rose looked at him and tears ran down her eyes ,"She is alive! We must find her now!"

He grabbed onto her shoulders tightly. "Rosaletta, the dark ones never leave any alive. If she was taken, it must have been for a sacrifice for their goddess, Melaina."

She cried as she held onto one of Samantha's dolls. "I know she is alive. I can feel it in my soul and heart." She tried to cry, but her eyes had no more tears. "She is alive. Even if I have to spend my entire fortune, I will have her found. She is all I have left."

A huge tombstone was erected that had their names engraved with red sapphire in the lettering: "*Sir Walton, Sir Adalolf, Sir Arculf, Lady Geva, Lady Ria, Sir Ronnie, and Lady Samantha.*" Next to it was a smaller gravestone that read "*Lady Tanya, and Sir Lucas.*" Lucas was the name of the unborn child.

A week passed by and her brother showed up to pay his respects. He noticed that Rose still had on her clothing from the funeral though it had become faded. As he approached her, she said, "Yavandir, please just go away." Her face had been deformed by her tears.

He gently put his hands on her shoulders. "*Ulaaol ya elail ulyue aaol,* Rosaletta."

Her face regained some color as she looked at him with a tiny smile. "You promise you will bring her back to me?"

He nodded and walked off accompanied by his eldest son and two of his wives. They had on light leather armor which was normally for scouting and hunting. She quickly dried up her tears and headed to the home of Verus.

"Oh my goddess. What is that awful odor?" She followed the smell and found Verus and Udook. They stood near the bar. Udook noticed her and waved her down.

She grabbed Verus by the collar, "I demand you teach me how to fight!"

Verus had left the royal guard and joined the regular army with Rose and Udook.

Her brother's search for Samantha had put a strain on an already sketchy treaty between the dark elves' kingdom and the high elves, inevitably triggering a war that lasted fifteen years. As allies to the high elf king, the Holy City had to enter the war alongside the dwarf army.

Every hold and keep that they raided, Verus and Rose searched. They checked ever temple and sacrifice pit for signs of her missing daughter. She showed no mercy to even the helpless.

"Verus, is this the keep?" She walked back and forth, ready to rush in.

"Yes, the dark elf we captured on the battlefield said they had a little quarter-elf girl here. But something feels a bit off." Verus spat on the ground. "I think we should wait for Udook and his men to arrive."

She scoffed and said, "There is no time. Mommy is coming, my angel." She rushed off towards the keep. None of the troops were able to stop her.

She ran through the opened door and was ambushed by a group of dark elves. "Grab her! The elf prince will surrender now that we have his sister." They tied her up and tossed her into a pit.

"Where is my baby!" She screamed at the top of her lungs.

They started to laugh. "You dumb bitch, it was a trap. She was already gone before your family was killed." One of them shot an arrow into her leg.

Screams bounced off the walls as the sound of metal clashing followed. Rose tried to climb out to see what was going on but the pain in her leg caused her to fall back to the bottom.

A short figure stood above the pit. "Princess, are you okay?" The man lit a torch to see inside. It was Ugthar, and he still looked the same as he does presently.

He helped her out and showed her a rose that he had picked. "I found this on the battlefield. It is only fitting to hand a rose to a princess after you rescue her."

She looked at it, "It's half dead."

He chuckled a little and said, "It had been three days when I found it. It was hard to give it to you in the middle of a battle. This just happened to be the right moment."

She smiled and blushed. "Thank you, my brave dwarf knight."

As the war came close to an end, she sat at her father's table. He was unable to hide his anger, "I've heard rumors that you've been smitten with a dwarf. Must I remind you that even though we are allies, we are not allowed to be with them. They are foul and disgusting."

She looked down at her plate and played with her food a little. "He is only half-dwarf Father."

He stood up and raised his voice. "I do not care if he is half-god. Our gods decreed the same with their gods. We are too different and must never break this taboo."

He walked towards his throne. "Your brother's antics in the dark elf territories caused a war. He did it for you. Many of the other elf tribes agreed with the war, and even I agreed. It was my grandchildren that were killed. But some of the other tribes are not happy with the cost. Arrangements have been made; you will marry the prince of TielZi. If not, they will break away from the Tribal Alliance. I will hear no more of this dwarf fling."

She returned to the Holy City and headed straight for the Temple of the Thirteen. It was made to represent the twelve named gods and goddesses that took pity on mortal beings and the unnamed goddess. "Moerae, you are my favorite of the gods. Please hear me out. Show me what I must do to keep him in my destiny."

She kneeled in front of the statue, "I was born in the month Mora. My mother was one of your maidens, so please hear me."

In the middle of her prayer, a flash of light struck her and she was visited by a sight. She stood there in a daze and spoke in an unknown language. Tears of blood slowly flowed from her eyes before she returned to normal.

"I must write a letter to Father. I knew it. Thank you, Moerae. I shall follow your instructions." She smiled and ran off.

A man came and visited Rose shortly after. He had green eyes and hair, and no imperfections in his face. His voice also seemed to be perfect. He was rather tall at six-feet-five. There was a little sadness in his eyes and though he looked young, his voice had such wisdom that it made him seem much older.

She bowed with great respect. "Lord Azaroth, you must have for more than a friendly visit. What do you think I should do?"

He was blunt and straight forward. "The only way to avoid this is to follow your father's wishes and leave this town. You already have the graves of your late husband and children moved. Also, to marry your fiancé."

She looked at him and couldn't help but to feel some attraction towards him. "Same as always, you never beat around the bush. You are lucky that you are handsome. I cannot do that. My husband's wishes are starting to come forth. Half-breeds are allowed in the elites, and I plan on being the first."

He nodded, "If you still decide on this action of yours I will respect it. But also know that if you stay on this track, I will see you one more time before the event. I hope I am able to give you good news at that time. Whoever took her is extremely good at covering his tracks."

His warning hit her like an arrow to her heart. "Is this a message from the gods?"

He smiled a little. "I have known you for your entire life. I say this as a friend. Mora visions are not always perfect and can be avoided. Do not let anyone know that secret."

He left with the remains of her family to deliver them to the elf sanctuary to be put in the Tomb of Nobles.

A few days passed and an elfish man burst into her house. His face was red red his eyes were like daggers. Even the people on the street could hear him shout. "Is it true that you decided to stay? Your vision will come to pass if you stay! Why fulfill the wishes of a dead human?" The way he said 'human' made her blood boil with rage.

She looked at him with a smile. "I am to be accepted into the elite next year, a royal decree from my king. I cannot disobey."

He slapped her across the face. "We pure-blooded elves can only reproduce every ten years; you will be dead by then in some battle. The gods said that one of your children will become very important. All of them are dead which means it must be one that we make. I already have you father's blessing; we are to be married."

She spat in his face. "I will never marry you! Even when we were little, you were always a snob. Demanded everyone to do as you say. Your clan has always been no better than orcs."

He looked at her with determination in his face. "I am ripe today, and you being half-human means you should be ready as well. We do not need to be married as long as I can put my seedling into your belly. My child will be destined by the gods to be great."

He forced himself on her and tore at her clothing. She fought back and was able to overpower him. She kicked him a few times as he lay on the ground.

"I fought in a war while you sat fucking your whores. You are weak, worthless, and a fool." Her body became stiffened.

He had slapped her leg with a rune. "*Elailau!*" he shouted and snared her to the ground. He then used magic to silence her voice and raped her.

The next day she ran to Ugthar in their secret place of meeting. "Sleep with me now! You must." Her face became red as she had cried all night.

"My lady! We—I dare not treat you like a whore. We shall wait till we can marry. What is wrong, my love?" He held her close.

"The monster that my father wanted me to get married to. I cannot bear his child. You are strong. I know your seed will kill off his." She tried to kiss him but he pushed her back.

He looked over her body and noticed the bruises. "That little shit of an elf is no better than a thug. Did he force himself on you?" He grabbed his ax and tried to walk out the door, but was stopped by Rose as she leaped on his back.

"No, you cannot. It will cause a war between the elves and the dwarfs. I cannot bear it if we have to fight. Just lay with me and help me erase his seed." He nodded, and they slept together.

Rose became pregnant, but because of the long term, she knew that the baby belonged to the prince. She hated the prince but not the baby. After the two-year term, she gave birth to the child, but before she could see the new-born, she was put under a sleep spell and the baby was taken away. She never learned of the gender.

Aluxes woke up next to Onyx. He cleared his throat a little. "Aye, that be an elf memory stone. It keeps record of their life, a journal of sorts. They can relive it while they sleep. Rose must've wanted ya to see it."

He slammed his fist on a table. "I remember when me own brother used one on me. It's how he told me he been having an affair with that elf wench."

He walked off still talking, "Tomorrow ye be summoned to meet the prince and Lord Azaroth. So try not to look too angry, and clean up. Ya smell like a horse's nut sack."

Aluxes looked over at the stone and held it gently. Tears fell from her eyes; she never knew that the innocent and shy half-elf had such a tragic story. It made her understand how much simpler her life seemed. She gazed at her sword and armor and decided that she had enough sleep and should train for the next time she would face Krull.

Chapter Seven

THE GIRL AND HER DOLL

A dull poke forced Aluxes to awaken. The first thing she saw was Ugthar. He gently nudged her with a long stick. "Where in the hell am I?" she asked.

"You fell asleep on a park bench," he said, still poking her.

"What in the hell are you doing?" She tried swat at it like a fly but missed.

"I heard from your friend that you get really violent when you are forced to wake up. I was worried you might snap me in two if you attacked me. In war, the weapon with extra each provides more safety, so I figured it be the same for waking you." He tried not to laugh.

She slowly opened her eyes more and could see some kids staring at her. One of them walked a little closer and asked, "What are you? I have seen half-elves, half-dwarfs, half-giants, and even a half-orc bard but none of them look like you."

Another kid whispered to his friend, "One of the soldiers said she is half-mara."

The kids ran off as she tried to sit up. "Run! She must be a monster."

She sat there with a blank expression on her face. The emotionless stare was something Ugthar understood. "It is nothing I haven't heard my entire life. I always tried to just shake it off but I always questioned myself too. Am I really a half-monster?"

"Aye, Aluxes!" He tried his best to sound like his brother. She turned to look at him; he was in formal attire. "You need to get ready. You have a formal meeting with Prince Loux and Lord Azaroth." He tossed the stick and walked away towards the town hall.

She ran to her room. "I never packed a bag, oh crap. Shit, I guess I will just mend my armor." She tried some mending magic but all it could do was some minor repairing. With no time to spare, she rushes toward the town hall which had a huge garden clearing in front of it. All the soldiers were there in formation, dressed in formal attire—bright white with gold trim.

She stood next to Onyx. "Aye lass, we knew ya would forget to pack ya stuff so we packed it for ya. Rose went to ya room with the stuff but a wee bit late, ya be gone." Her eyes widened and she found herself at a loss for words.

He smiled a little. "Aye, but ya better dressed than Udook there." She glanced over and saw that he was struggling to keep his pants on.

A horn blew and everyone stood at attention. Prince Loux and a man with green hair and eyes walked out. She was unable to take her gaze off the man; he looked the same as he did in Rose's memory stone. She had been out of place her entire life. The average human being five-four, she had always been taller than everyone else but this man made her seem normal. He was the only person she had met that was taller, other than half-giants.

The prince cleared his throat and said, "My loyal troops and fellow elites, it would not have been a glorious day if it was not for your gallant efforts to depose of the vile forces of evil. We hereby give thanks to the messenger of the gods, Lord Azaroth. If he did not show up when he did, we would have lost many more troops. It was as if the orcs saw him and ran out of fear."

He looked over at Azaroth. "But it came to my ears from Lord Azaroth as he talked to the troops that they were already starting to leave before he arrived. The word was, an injured, brave, and strong elite recruit had a duel of honor with their leader and managed to drive him back."

He reached over for a tiny box that was being carried by his aid and pulled out a medal from it. "For true gallantry and duty, I present this honor to Lady Aluxes. If it were not for you, many innocents would have perished at the hands of that vile orc."

She stood there paralyzed. Not being properly dressed had already made her feel embarrassed but everyone was staring at her. All she had on was patched-up armor spattered with plenty of blood, and dirt from the fight. Onyx chuckled like a little kid and pushed her out.

Loux looked at her and the rage on his face was obvious to all. "And what foul monster must you be? You dare come here dressed like filth? Is the honor of being in my presence not understood by a half-breed mutt? You look no better than the vile beast I trampled with my horse. I should have you arrested for such a manner, forcing royalty to be greeted with something beneath a peasant."

He started to put the medal away when Azaroth grabbed his hand. "Surely the prince has a good eye to notice a true soldier that is so dedicated that she is always ready in case the enemy attacks again while we are out in the open. It is common for orcs to raid troops that think the battle is over."

He smiled a little. "I would hate to think that the prince would dare not think it was possible. This place was indeed a battlefield just two days ago. I think a soldier's honor should be given to a real soldier who thought of this. You are not a foolish person now, are you Prince?"

Loux scoffed a little and held the medal out. Azaroth waved at her to come forward. She slowly walked towards them, her limbs stiff like boards of wood. Her knees and elbows were unable to bend and her eyes were as wide as boulders. She locked her joints as she stood in front of them. Her body swayed back and forth as everything started to fade out.

The prince looked at her and spat near her feet. "You are a half-breed mutt and you smell worse than the peasant that wipes my arse. Now hurry up and get out of my sight!"

Azaroth took the medal, leaned forward, and put it around her neck. He softly whispered into her ear, "Unlock your knees or you will pass out. It may be harder to defend you from the prince a second time." She pulled her head back and their eyes locked. Her heart skipped a beat and her face turned as red as an apple.

Azaroth gazed at Loux. He was unable to look at him directly. "Ah yes, my Lord Azaroth. I agree with you. I hope I did not offend you with my outburst. I did not mean that about half-breeds, I only meant that about half-humans." His body shook and beads of sweat trickled down his face as he spoke.

The prince walked towards the steps of the town hall and made some announcements as he tried to glorify himself. Aluxes, in a daze, slowly shifted her way back next to Onyx in line.

There was a slight chuckle as he said, "Aye, if I be a woman that close to him, I be a wee wet too. As a man, he gets me excited."

She reached for her sword but stopped herself. Onyx pointed to a group of female soldiers. The redness in their faces as they watched Azaroth was enough to make the men a little jealous. He looked to be in his mid-twenties but his voice had the sound of a man beyond his years.

After the ceremony, everyone bunched up in groups and talked. Aluxes gazed around the area to see what Azaroth was doing. She saw him hand Rosaletta a note, and they said a few words to eachother. Rose quickly teared up and smiled as she hugged him, and then ran off towards Ugthar. They hugged each other in excitement after they looked at the note.

Onyx grunted a little when he saw them. "Disgraceful."

Aluxes smiled as she saw them. "I think they make a cute couple. It is nice that she has found someone to love after everything."

Onyx scoffed before she could finish her sentence. "I not be drunk enough to hear about a dwarf fucking an elf."

The bell by the mess hall rang and everyone was just beginning to grab food when it suddenly became silent.

A chill that ran down Aluxes's spine along with a slight burn on her neck from her circlet. She turned around and there, walking towards the prince, was a young girl in ragged clothing with a cute little doll in her hands. Everyone stood in shock as they looked at the poor child.

She slowly stumbled as she walked. Her clothing was tattered as if it had been snagged by bushes. Her color was pasty as if she had not had any sleep. Her skin was so tight that one could see the details of her bones. Her feet were worn raw and she left bloody footprints with each step. Even Azaroth was stunned by the girl's ghoulish looks.

She stood in front of the prince and held up the doll. "This has been in my family for hundreds of years. Please take this as a token for saving our city." The girl's voice was hard to understand; it was so raspy from dehydration.

Loux kneeled next to her and hugged her. "My poor little girl, I will gladly accept this gift." He took the doll and walked off.

After a few moments, she let out a loud hellish scream of pain. A dark tar-like substance oozed out of her eyes and ears. The scream that seemed as if it would last forever abruptly came to an end, and she collapsed.

Azaroth ran over to check on her. "She is dead!" He held her close and cried. Everyone looked around to see if anyone would claim the little girl, but no one showed up.

Aluxes looked at one of the bloody footprints and noticed that there was a black tar-like substance in the blood. "What the hell is this stuff? That poor little girl. Something about this makes my circlet burn more than normal." She looked around. "Oh god, I cannot think on an empty stomach." She walked to the mess hall and stumbled into a table.

Shortly after she had sat down, Ugthar and Lugathar joined her. "It be a crime, I say." Lugathar's words seemed lifeless as they came from her mouth.

Tears rolled down her cheek as she cried. "I think she be hit by a blasted dark spell during the battle. I have never seen a curse like this before."

Ugthar rubbed his head. "The event sent Rose into shock and she is resting." He tapped the table lightly and said, "I've never seen the prince hug someone before."

One of the soldiers from the royal guard shouted at Aluxes. "You really are a monster, being able to eat after seeing an event like that."

He slapped her plate off the table and placed his face at nose-touching distance. "I bet your mommy was fucked by a demon and loved it. I bet you're just as much of a whore as she was."

Aluxes sat there quietly and slowly closed her eyes. She tipped her head down a little so that the shadow of her brow covered her eye.

"I bet if I showed you mine, you would jump me in a second. I bet that was how you got that orc to go." The man laughed as loud as he could.

Lugathar grabbed the man by his balls. "Sir, ya be a wee little shit, ain't ya?" She pointed to her plate. "As ya see, little lad. I also be eating." As she began to squeeze, he whimpered as his feet lost their balance. "Now be a good boy and be on ye way."

She let him go, and he tried to stumble away before Aluxes tightly grabbed his arm. "Where the hell do you think you are going?"

He looked at her and smiled, and with a slight tremble in his voice, said, "So, bitch. You want me that bad? I never fucked—."

With a smirk, she squeezed his arm. The sound of his bones cracking echoed and he howled in pain. She stood up slowly and placed her hand on his back. His head slammed into the table. With his arm being held behind his back, she slowly pushed his head into the table. Ugthar and Lugathar tried to pull her off but she was too strong.

"Filth like you do not deserve to speak ever again." She grinned as she pushed harder. People panicked and rushed off. Between the chaos, a crossbow dart flew through the air and hit her in the shoulder. Rose stood near the entryway with another bolt loaded.

A tear slowly rolled from Aluxes's eye. "You think I can be a hero to these filthy people?" She let go of the man as he fell to the ground. He screamed as he held his now disfigured arm.

"All they ever do is see me as a monster, call me filth, and say that I am a whore." She sat back down as more tears rolled off her face. "A little girl just died, and all they can think of is to still bring me down. I curse my parents. I should have never been born."

She took a deep breath and calmed herself. "Humans are the

monsters that do not deserve to be saved. Like unwanted bugs, they should be squashed."

The man stood up. "You're going to wish you accepted my offer to my bed. I am going to report this incident to the prince, you dumb bitch."

Rose shot off the bolt, barely missing the man's head. "I am the widow of Lord Walton who was the cousin of the king. If I report this incident, who do you think they will believe?"

The man grunted as he left.

Rose rushed over to tend to the crossbow bolt, but it was removed already and the wound was mostly healed.

She sat down at the table. "Care to join me?"

Aluxes looked at her. "Why did you show me that dream? Why would I care about your history? What did you think I would do?" She was out of breath; each question was forced from her throat.

With a smile, Rose looked at her and said, "Because you are the one who will find her. And I want you to tell her about me."

Aluxes stood there unable to talk. All she could do was rub her circlet.

Rose noticed that it had been tarnished a little. "Aluxes, dear. How do you feel?"

Aluxes breathed heavily. "Something about that event bothers me. Not just the kid dying but the black stuff. When I looked at it, my circlet started to get hot." She rubbed it a little more, then stood up and walked off.

"And where ya be goin lass?" Lugathar asked.

Aluxes slowly headed towards the exit and said without a glance, "I need to find out what happened to that girl."

Lugathar looked at Rose. "What be that look on yer face?"

Rose watched Aluxes walk out the entryway and then said, "Her golden circlet is tarnishing."

"Aye, gold never gets tarnished. Ya eyes must be goin bad." She stared into her eyes. "Aye, I see ya be tellin the truth. I wonder it be? I noticed she have a wee blister as well."

Aluxes walked towards the hospital. People stood around in

groups. All she could hear was how frightful the girl looked. She stood there in front of the entrance and asked where the child's body was being kept; the nurse pointed her in the direction.

She opened the door and the smell and taste of chemicals nearly overwhelmed her. There was a lady there that looked at her without blinking. She was an elf, young looking with pink hair and eyes. She had the little girl's body cut open to study the insides.

With an extremely monotone voice, she said, "how may help young miss?" she had a weird accent, like she had barely grasped the hang of human language.

It always boggled her mind how young they seemed and sounded. She looked at the little girl's body. The insides were full of the black substance. A sharp burning pain shot through her neck and the golden circlet turned dark again. "Ah shit!"

"What wrong? Who you? Neck has blister," the woman said. She tried to examine Aluxes but she brushed her hand aside.

"You must be a doctor. I am from the elite division. I would like to find out what happened to this girl." She looked right into her eyes.

The elf rubbed her chin a little. "Yes, doctor. You just interesting as little girl." She covered up the body. "If not have permission to be here, then you must go."

She placed her hand on Aluxes's chest and tried to push her out when Commander Verus walked in. "It's all right. She can be here."

He stood in front of the body and removed the cover. The girl's insides were full of blood and black goo. The sight was ghastly, and it caused all three some issues to look at it.

Verus rubbed his brows. "It is odd that there's no odor. Normally someone that looks like that has a smell to them. There's not even the smell of internal rot."

The doctor mumbled, "No idea what black stuff is. Tried remove with tools but it consumed it." She pointed to a scalpel that was slowly being dissolved into the goo.

The commander looked at her. "The stuff that was on the street was safe to touch. It was oddly cold." He placed his hands over the body.

"The body is slowly cooling off; the same type of cold air is being emitted. I think whatever was inside her is slowly dying."

The doctor poked around again at the cold spots with some instruments. "Ahh, not consume. Inside blood not normal. She bleed inside."

She walked over to her desk with some papers. "We find girl's parents. She not from here." She rubbed her chin again, and asked, "Maybe Azaroth knows?"

Aluxes leaned towards the body to have a better look. "Oh, be careful. Warm spots active, I think it living organism. Lost connection to host, it slowly dies."

"Verus, I have a weird feeling about this stuff," Aluxes said as she gazed over and saw that her commander's face was red and he was gritting his teeth.

"Someone set this up. It may be a trap." He looked out the window and could see the horse of the prince. "Someone has started to make a move."

The doctor stood in between them and said, "*Yultay hogeauit.*"

Aluxes stood with a blank look on her face as Verus explained, "She said there is no life flame. It is what they call the soul in common reference." He never took his gaze off the horse.

The doctor looked at her and tried to find the words. "Elves created by magic like dwarfs. Dwarfs see dark while we see energy of beings. When someone dies flame, slowly burns out. Humans have bigger flame than most. When human dies, takes days or weeks to disperse, but girl has none, she been dead weeks."

Aluxes walked out. Right away, she tried to ask some of the villagers if they recognized the little girl, but then she remembered that the doctor said she was not from that city. She pondered more as she rubbed her circlet intensely. She leaped up and thought, "Azaroth! He must know something." She asked some people if they had seen him, eventually finding one that suggested she try Loux's quarters.

On her way there, she saw him with his hand on his horse, ready to saddle up and leave. Her cheeks became red and her words came out in a forceful manner. "Hey, you need to explain yourself!"

He turned to her and smiled. "I was hoping I would have a chance to meet you before I left." Though his smile seemed nice, it had an empty look to it.

She closed her eyes and focused her thoughts. "Do not try your charm on me. Who was that little girl? Do you even know what is going on?"

He stopped smiling and adopted a concerned look on his face. "I had never met that girl. I held her so that her last moment would be loving. She had been suffering for a long time. It is sad when you see a curse like that befall a little child."

She looked down and rubbed her circlet, and then snapped her head up. "A curse?"

He was already on his horse and was on his way to leave. "I have only seen this once, a few thousand years ago when one of the Fallen tried to invade the mortal realm. It was called *the abyssal disease*. I must do more investigation to know more." He snapped the reins and rode off. All he did was leave her with more questions.

Aluxes was unable to take her eyes off him as he left, watching until he was out of sight. As if she had no control, she placed her hand on her breast. Her heart was going to burst out of her chest. *Why am I feeling this way? When I look at his eyes, something forces me to keep looking as if I am looking into a mirror.* She stood there in a daze. *His gloves, he no longer had them on. He touched the girl's face with them.*

She was interrupted by a loud voice off in the distance. It brought her to the building where the prince was staying. She placed all her loose stuff on the ground and tried to peek in through an open window. Verus and Udook came around the corner.

She stood there holding a box. "Commander, I need—"

He waved his hand around. "We were also able to hear it. Udook here said that a strange voice came from the prince's room." With ease, Udook lifted them both close enough to the window.

"Yes, I know the plan, but it was not my fault. Orcs are not the same as you remember. They've now started to embrace peace, grow farms, and establish a civilization." The prince walked around and pondered nervously. "Look, the second I got a message, Lord Azaroth was showing up I had to change the plans. See, even with the orcs leaving, it still could have worked but not with him there." They tried to peek in to see who he was talking to, but there was no one there, not even a voice.

He became angry and shouted at the fireplace. "Look, if you did that to me, it would have drawn too much attention and ruined your plans. He was born after your fall; he is a threat. It was your fault for not looking up the current history of things once you reawakened."

Loux calmed down a little and slowly walked backwards towards the window. In an instant, the prince thrust his sword through the glass, shattering it. There was a knock on the door and he ran to answer it.

Aluxes and the commander stood there. Verus talked in a low tone, saying "Sir, we are ready to move back to the capital when you are ready."

Loux chuckled a little. "Yes, yes. Give me a few hours."

Verus looked around. "Sir, heard yelling. Are you all right?"

Loux smiled and pulled out a communication stone. "I was talking to the king. We had a disagreement on some matters. Just brotherly stuff." He closed the door.

Verus and Aluxes walked out. "He is lying, girl. A communication stone has a two-way sound. We would have been able to hear who he was talking to." He put his hand on her shoulder. "We must get ready to leave ahead of them so we can alert the king. I have a bad feeling."

Aluxes was heading off when she noticed Evalyn sitting near a fountain. She was ranting to herself. Aluxes sighed a little and slowly walked towards her. There was an odd voice in the back of her head that nagged at her as she sat next to Evalyn and stared at her. Though she tried to look like she cared, her facial expression was still angry.

Evalyn gazed up at her. "Aluxes, I cannot take it. It's just too much."

Aluxes looked around and took a deep breath. "Yeah, I know. First battle, seeing that happen to a poor little girl— it's a little too much to handle."

Evalyn scoffed at her and the tears stopped. "No, you moron. My dad took me on some of his missions. He fought vampires, zombies, and other nightmares. Seeing dead children is sad, but it is normal for me. It is the fact that you get a medal and had the chance to get close to Lord Azaroth, and he did not even notice me." She teared up again.

Evalyn laid her head on Aluxes's shoulder, still sobbing. Aluxes at first made a fist, but then she opened it and patted her. "Evalyn, you are the only person who never called me a monster growing up, so I will allow you this one time to use me as a rag to cry on."

"You are not a monster," Evalyn said with her head still on Aluxes's shoulder.

Aluxes scoffed a little. "How do you know?"

Evalyn looked right into her eyes. "When the other kids called you a half-mara, I knew it was a lie. A half-mara has normal human eyes and skin that looks like it is about to rot off. I only played with them because in order to survive, one must learn to hide among real monsters." She chuckled a little. "They were also just jabbering peasants, and I am a lord. I never pay mind to the words of the lesser."

She held back her tears. "You are no peasant. You are my equal and rival."

A loud horn echoed throughout the city. All the troops gathered. Instead, of marching they staggered out in an unorganized fashion. Aluxes tried to find her way towards her comrades. As she was about to give up, she heard a song.

"*I bust their balls on me hammer, and they may howl the words most foul. The others cower like a wilted flower when they see me mighty hammer.*" Onyx smiled. "Ya like me song, boys?" The solders chuckled as they walked.

"Hey, Onyx." Aluxes said in a hurry as she caught up to him.

"Aye, lass be looking for me? Sorry but you're not me type," He laughed but then saw her face and became less joyful.

"Well, lass. What be on ya mind?" he asked gently.

She looked at him. "Who is this Lord Azaroth? I know I've heard the name somewhere, but I cannot remember where."

He choked a little out of shock. "I knew book studies be not ya thing, but this be beyond insane," he said with a chuckle. "He be not only in ya history books. There be paintings of him all over, and a huge statue of him in the Hall of Heroe's."

She looked up in shock. "That cannot be the same guy. That would make him three thousand years old."

He rubbed his beard and sighed. He smiled since he was now in his talkative groove which he enjoyed. "Aye, there be legends about him in every kingdom in the world. He has had huge impact on nations. But what do ya expect from a half-demon and half-god? No one knows how old he be but he be the only one out of that union to survive to adulthood."

Aluxes noticed she was surrounded by Rose, Lugathar, Ugthar, and Udook. A soft groan escaped her lips as she looked up at the sky, and everyone chipped in with what they knew about him.

Chapter Eight

LORD AZAROTH, THE LEGEND

"Aye, he be a legend among the dwarfs. There be one I know to be true. A wee confrontation he had with the great dwarf king almost a thousand years ago. The thing to remember is he be some sort of messenger boy between the realms of mortals, gods, and demons," Onyx said as he rubbed his beard.

"Azaroth rode his horse towards the Great Dwarven Gate—a huge double door, large enough for a dragon. Three times the thickness of a normal heavy gate. It was said to have once withstood a fireball from a demon during the ancient war. He stopped in front of it and announced his arrival.

"The guard looked down at him from atop and shouted, 'By the order of the king, no one is allowed in!'

"Azaroth stared at him dead in the eyes. 'I have a very important message for the king. It is from the God Orehelm.'

"The great dwarf king walked out onto a balcony above the gate. 'Ahh, the messenger of the gods has arrived. I chose to not allow you in here. Ye half-demon spawn caused bad luck. Now be off or be killed on the spot.'

"The king walked off and archers lined at the top of the wall. Azaroth snapped his fingers and they all burst into blue flames. A survivor said that for a wee moment his eyes and hair turned crimson red. After that, he placed his right hand on the door and just forced it open with his own amazing strength. This claim not be disputed because his hand print still be on the door today.' Onyx took a sip from his flask and continued.

"He slowly walked through the main hall that led straight to the throne room. Soldiers tried to attack him but were disposed of with his bare hands. Every now and then, an archer would come out to take a shot but would burst into blue flames.

"He stood there in front of the king and said, 'Sir, I insist you stop this attack on me or your entire race will be exterminated.' His eyes and hair became a crimson red as he gazed at the dwarf.

"The king held his chest as if his soul was on fire. 'All right, ye win, we stop.' Azaroth's eyes and hair turned back to green.

"The king glared at the messenger, tried his best to look refined, but the smell of piss stank up the area. 'Ya had a message for me from one of our gods?' He asked as he attempted to clear his throat.

"Azaroth smirked. 'Yes, he was worried about how you run the mighty empire. He said you must step down and let your grandson take the throne. I shall be the one to train him for a month.'

"The king's face turned red; his veins started to show as he reached around for a sword. 'Ya dare say this to me? Was it not you three hundred years ago that appointed me this title? Now ya take it from me?'

"Azaroth's smile vanished. 'You were once a great hero, a wonderful visionary, and a loving friend. But you allowed power to rush to your head. It is time you step down; your grandson has shown to be a great leader.'

"The king ordered for the boy to come out. A lad of barely sixteen stood in front of them, 'Son, this be Lord Azaroth. A half-demon and half-god, messenger of the realms. He claims that the gods have chosen you to succeed me.'

"The boy looked at Azaroth. 'Sir, my grandfather be a strong and mighty king. Our people have not known these types of riches before. I ask of you—please let him reign a little longer to redeem what he lost in the eyes of the gods.' He was a well-spoken boy who oddly did not have the normal dwarf accent.

"Azaroth looked directly into his eyes, and the boy held his head as he searched his mind. 'Tell me, young lord. Are you aware that he taxed his people to the point of starvation? Have you noticed how the lords of the clans are in the middle of revolting? Maybe you also noticed how he destroyed the temples of your gods? He also killed off family members who dared questioned his choices. I am here because your aunt survived and asked the gods for help.'

"Sweat poured down the boy's face as his body shook. 'Sir, he is still a strong ruler who has never been defeated.'

"His grandfather interrupted him. 'He be right me, boy. I am overall a bad ruler. I have tried to find a way to kill a god and give myself more freedom. Ya would be a great choice, but I not done with me throne.'

"A blade burst from the boy's chest and blood poured down his body. His grandfather then slit his throat to ensure that his death would come. He snickered at Azaroth, simply saying. 'Oops.'

The boy slowly fell with a look of shock still imprinted on his face. From his shirt pocket a carving of a dragon made of gold hit the floor and rolled over.

"When the king stared down and saw the figure, he smiled and his eyes began to light up. He fell to his knees in tears as he lifted the boy in his arms. 'I made this for his birthday last week.'

"He looked at Azaroth. 'What have I done out of anger and greed? He be the only blood left in me line. Is there a slim chance he and I can exchange places?'

"Azaroth patted his shoulders. 'This is the last act you shall do as a king.'

"A blinding light came forth and the king lay dead, and the boy lived."

Onyx walked with a large grin on his face. "That be an epic tale no one can beat."

His brother looked at him. "Some of that was made up by you."

Rose quietly said, "I have met him a few times in my lifetime, but my father has a story about him that became a legend among our people; it was when he became the high elf king before the orcs started to have times of peace. A great war which raged for a hundred years started to take its toll on the elf kingdom."

"The sky darkened, filled with smoke that covered the sun. Tress burned and orcs screamed to be in joy all over. The high elf king looked out of a window and stared at the large army that stood outside his lands.

"Orcs were made for war, perfect warriors with no equal when it came to brute strength and natural intuition on the battlefield. The elven army was battered and mostly destroyed. The empire as a whole was on the brink of collapse.

"A soldier walked up to him. 'High king, the orcs are about to breach the gate and swarm the city. We must get you and your wives out of here.'

"He looked at the guard, unable to hide his disappointment. 'How can I abandon my people? Ready my armor; I shall ready for combat.'

"He walked off towards his personal armory and heard the orcs shouting. He quickly looked out and could see a modest gap that would allow a single man to ride through on his horse. It was Lord Azaroth; they even had legends about him and dared not interfere with him when he was on his missions.

"When he arrived at the main gate, he quickly got off his horse and looked up at its height. With a little squat, he readied himself for a jump and leaped onto the high wall. He ran along the walkway towards the castle. The king ran out to meet him, and they embraced as if they were old friends.

"The king, out of breath looked at Azaroth. '*Taygee humlao,*' he said, and they shook hands.

"Azaroth turned towards the field. His gaze was hard to read. 'The gods have decided to end this peacefully. Even the orc god, Grimshaw.'

"He called out for the orc lord. It was said he was the last remaining true orc that was hand-created by the gods before they added reproductive organs. A relic of a long-forgotten war.

"The largest and tallest orc anyone had ever seen walked up. Covered in scars with skin that sagged and was barely held together, he stepped forward. He sneered at the man and spat at him.

"The orc growled, '*Deoko tikjauk vijou caveku,*' he drew his sword and stood in a battle stance.

"Azaroth grinned a little, 'I shall honor your request.' He drew his own sword and leaped off the wall to meet him.

"As per the honor fights of orcs, no magic was allowed. It was only raw skill. The old orc showed his battle expertise, and his knowledge of combat had no equal. If it were not for Azaroth's youth and strength, he would have met his match. The battle lasted for days but soon the orc tired out, and Azaroth was able to get a decisive blow in to end the duel.

"The orc raised his hand, and Azaroth held it out of respect for their tradition. '*Tikjauk kocaveku.*' He smiled as tears ran down his eyes.

"Everyone said an orc prayer to honor a hero who was tired of immortality, and the elf king joined in.

"The orcs stowed their weapons and walked off. Azaroth built an honor grave out of respect for the last survivor of an old forgotten war. The end of a beast that could only end his life the way he was made. To this day, the elves have a celebration in which they honor him by decorating his statue every year."

Everyone stared at Rose. "That be more crap than me story, lass," Onyx had the look of disappointment.

Over the edge of the horizon, the Holy City could be seen. Aluxes started to think they embellished their stories to make the trip seem shorter. "None of you really told me anything about him. All you did was tell me folktales."

Lugathar looked at her. "The only real truth that we know of is that after the war between the gods and the demons, they formed a wee peace pact. They have no written language so the pact was made with a wee offspring of mixed blood. They not god nor demon and be abandoned in the Mortal Realm. This happens every hundred years, and they get hunted for wee sport by anyone who wants to brag. Azaroth be the only one to survive to adulthood."

She rubbed her circlet. "I wonder if we will ever meet again."

Rose gently placed her hand on her shoulder. "I noticed that thing around your neck has tarnished a little, and you also rub it a lot. What is it?"

Aluxes smiled a little. "I do not know. No one knows. It is all I have from my real mother and father." She glanced over at her. "It is hard to explain but when it feels upset, I rub it to calm it down. When it gets bothered, it heats up. At times it burns my neck. And when it gets mad, it tarnishes."

Evalyn popped up behind her. "She used to talk to it as a kid. At times, she would play games with it like it was alive. But I have noticed it reacts to her mood. The madder she gets, the darker it becomes."

Aluxes scoffed. "Where in the hell did you come from? Always popping up when you are not needed. I thought you royal guards were going to leave tomorrow."

Evalyn pointed at the tree line. The prince was riding with his calvary ahead of the group. "He said he must get there before you guys. Something about the king's orders and favors."

She smiled and winked at her. "So, I heard you asking about Azaroth. You in love?" she asked as she giggled.

"Shut the hell up, just because he was good-looking does not mean I'm in love!" She blushed a little.

"Aye, so ya think he be good lookin. High standards ya got." Lugathar chuckled as Aluxes scoffed.

"I just wonder if he knew my parents and why they had to die." Onyx patted her back as they kept marching.

Chapter Nine

FALL OF AN EMPIRE

*A*s they approached the city, they quickly formed into proper formation. They slowly marched pass the grand gate. As it opened, they could hear people scream. They tossed flowers and other objects that were scented with perfumes as they cheered them on as if they were heroes.

The royal guard, minus Evalyn, was overjoyed and acted the part. The elites gave blank looks. The crowd was silent towards them; the regular army was still out there in a war. All they did was defend a city, yet they were treated as if they had won the war.

Prince Loux was at the front. He waved his hand and smiled. Every now and then, he blew a kiss to a maiden. Oddly, he also held the doll in his lap.

Often, Aluxes would notice small black dots on the road. She immediately remembered the little girl. She broke formation and disappeared into the crowd. Evalyn saw her and slipped out to follow.

She quickly caught up to her, "Psst. hey listen."

Aluxes stared at her. "Huh, what? Why are you whispering?" She looked around. "Why are you following me?"

Evalyn smirked. "It looked as if you were going to do something fun." She took a deep breath. "Something did not feel right the entire trip. When I was near the prince, I had this weird feeling that the doll was looking at me." Her body shook the more she remembered. "At one point, I swear I saw its head had moved and it was staring at me."

They ran to an alley for a better view of the prince. Aluxes carefully watched, "I do not see any symptoms like the little girl."

Evalyn pointed "See that? The doll just moved. I swear."

Aluxes stared at it but she saw nothing, not even an inch of movement. "You sure the orc didn't hit your head?" She snickered a little.

The girls were bickering when they were interrupted. "Ya ladies wanted ta fight over me, it be all right I have enough energy for both ya." Onyx chuckled as they became flustered and stopped.

The parade ended when they reached the inner gate where the castle was, and the groups dispersed for their quarters. They hurried to rush in before they closed. In the distance they could see Ugthar and Rose as they wandered off. They held hands and smiled. Onyx grunted a little and tagged along after them.

Evalyn grinned, "I am also going to see what they are up to. It looks more interesting."

Aluxes tried to see if she could follow the prince, but he was surrounded by people. "Shit! Looks like I'll have to wait till nightfall."

She had an odd feeling. A voice in the back of her head was guiding her towards a park full of trees.

She ended up in an area that was fenced off by shrubs and thick bushes. Nearby, there was a small plaque that read "*Made by Ugthar and Rosaletta.*" It was a private garden that they had built for themselves. She looked off to the end and could see Rose, Ugthar, and her father. She'd never met him but remembered him from the dream.

She started to walk towards them but was halted by Onyx's voice. "This be a private affair. Not even I was invited. But they wished for us to see." Next to him was Evalyn, and her bright eyes looked as cheerful as a child surrounded by candy.

Aluxes peered over to watch what was going on. "So, what am I witnessing?"

He took a deep breath. "You be a witness to a breaking of a taboo. The first dwarf and elf marriage," he grumbled. "As a dwarf, I am angered by this. But as a brother, I be very proud he found someone to share his life with. I never told him when I found out about them two. All I could do was yell at the wee bastards." A tear fell from his eye. "Please tell no one." He said and walked off.

Aluxes smile a little, something warm in her heart pulsating as she watched. But she was confused as to why her father would allow it. In the dream, he outrightly forbade it. She was unable to help but think it had to do with the vision that Rose saw and the letter that Azaroth gave her.

"I wonder why they're keeping it a secret; this is something we should celebrate." Evalyn could not look away. Her mind was in a different world.

Aluxes wandered off to her barrack and was interrupted by a messenger. He told her that she was to attend to the castle immediately. He handed her a letter— an invitation to tend the king's speech. As she headed towards the door of the Grand Hall, she came across the commander.

He looked at her. "Aluxes, you skipped out of the parade. Normally, you would have been sent to prison for that but the prince and the king insisted that you must attend this for your reward." Thou he said it kindly, there was an angry tone mixed in.

A little shocked, she said, "Sorry, commander. I will not do it again."

They both headed into the hall. It had amazing red drapes with a gold trim that hung from all the windows, and a large velvet carpet that extended from the castle door towards the throne room. Inside were officers, nobles, and the royal family members.

The prince glared at Aluxes with disgust. "Still wearing that disgraceful armor. A filthy mutt like yourself probably has no idea what a formal attire is."

Her face turned bright red as she looked down. The heavy regret she had in her gut would have taken over if it were not for a loud boastful voice that came forth. "Ahh, brother. Do not judge a soldier. It is the only way I would imagine she would show up. It reminds me of the days I was in the elite fighting ghouls and vampires." She looked up and saw that the king stood a few feet from her.

He was a rather tall man for a human at five-eight with blond hair, blue eyes, and an impressive beard that could rival a dwarf's. He was extremely cheerful and had a deep voice that echoed.

He walked up to the commander. "Verus, my cousin. How are things looking? It has been ages. I never see you these days." His smile became even wider, which seemed impossible.

He stared at Aluxes. "You are rather tall. I am among the tallest of the humans. It is impressive to see a woman taller than me."

He was a straightforward man and was unable to hide what was on his mind. In books, kings never mingled with people, but he walked towards everyone, shook their hands, and boasted of his past glory.

Verus mumbled to himself, "He never truly acted like a king, but he will force his views if he knows he is right." He began to look for the table with food and wandered off.

Aluxes eyed Loux and noticed that the doll was not with him. She headed towards one of the back doors but was immediately stopped by Evalyn and her father.

She smiled. "Daddy, this is Aluxes. The girl I've been telling you about."

He looked her up and down. "You did tell me she was tall, but it is amazing to see it in person and up close. She's even taller than me." He smiled at her and said, "I think you are a fine rival for my little girl here."

Aluxes stuttered as she searched for words. She was caught off guard by what he had said. All she could do was nod.

He patted her on the back. "Aye, yes. I will leave you two to chat. Being around a hero like me has left you breathless."

She tried to regain her composure. "How the hell did you get here? I thought you were too busy with the wedding?"

Evalyn smiled a little. "Oh, you! It ended after you left. So afterwards, I went to meet my dad. He was kind enough to bring me this pretty outfit. It's not a fancy dress but he said if combat broke out, I would still look fancy."

Aluxes glanced towards a corner and looked at Verus. He nodded his head, and she walked over to him. He looked around the hall and talked softly. "You have a small window. The doll is in Loux's room. It's at the top of the third tower." He used his chin to point to the door.

"I have not forgotten what happened in the city. I watched you when you left the formation and I have my suspicions. But I am too well known. If I walked off, everyone would take notice. You do not blend in very well but you're still a nobody. People pay no mind to nobodies wandering about."

She grunted a little as she slowly moved towards the door. She watched the guest as she stood by it. It was as he had said, no one really cared about what she was doing. She slipped out quickly; the sound of music was muffled but it could still be heard. Goosebumps formed on her skin as she inched herself away from the door. The air was colder than normal, cold enough that she had to use her breath to warm up her hands. A small piece of paper was stuck to her wrist, a note from Verus. It told her which door to enter and whom he had bribed.

As she slowly walked up the stairs, the air around her became colder and colder. She approached a door halfway up and peeked through it into the hallway. There were two guards that stood near the middle. She noticed that they were not bothered by the cold. They actually had no reaction to it. It was only something that she felt.

Both guards looked the same, but he had only bribed one of them. All she could do now was to take a deep breath and walk.

As she approached them, one of the guards whispered into the other's ear. The grin on their faces made her a little bit uneasy. One guard looked her up and down and chuckled as he slowly walked off. The other opened a door that led into his quarters. It must have been a supply room at one time. It barely fit the two beds.

"I told him that you are my date for tonight," he said with his voice broken. "Verus says to puts on this lipstick and kiss to my cheeks to make look like we had a good times." He paused a little and out of pure reaction said, "Please miss, do not kills me."

She looked at him with her face as blank as the wall. "Why did you say that?"

He barely glanced at her. "Verus says you might get violent. After hearing whats you did to an orcs, I fears what you may do to me."

She looked at him and grunted like a beast. He jumped a little and ran into the wall. She giggled as she helped him up.

The guard dusted himself off. "Ahh, umm yes. That doors there leads to a small halls. Beyond that is, um, yeah, anothers door that leads to his room." His voice was less broken but more flustered.

As she slowly opened the door the guard pointed to her neck and said, "Miss, that circlets around your necks is now red."

She acted like she did not hear him but her gut turned on itself as he said it. The closer she got to the room the colder it became. Eventually, a burning sensation caused her to curse.

Not being able to contain the suspense, she darted down the hall and bashed through the door. Inside was fancy...*everything*. It overwhelmed her at first; never had she laid eyes on furniture made from rare wood, linen, and stone. As she stood there, she imagined what it would be like if it were hers.

The only odd item was an old wooden desk. It was of poor quality and needed to be repaired. As she walked closer to it, she could hear footsteps. The sound was that of someone extremely light; it had a padded quality to it. Her head moved around but she saw no one. She could feel vomit rising in the back of her throat.

She regained her composure and shouted, "Who is there?" Again, she saw nothing but she could hear footsteps.

From the corner of her eye, she saw that the doll was over by the fireplace. She slowly walked towards it. "I do not remember you being there. Why do little girls enjoy playing with these ugly things?"

In the back of her mind, there was a voice. It was soft and gentle, whispering, "You are not Etharia. Where is Etharia?" The closer she got to the doll, the louder the voice became. It asked her over and over "Where is Etharia?" It got to the point where it blocked out all other sounds.

Aluxes picked up the doll. "I never had a doll. Never saw the need for one. The faces always bothered me, so ugly." She swallowed the saliva that had built up in her throat. "You are just a simple raggedy doll."

She tried to move her head away but was unable to. The doll's eyes moved like there was a liquid trapped inside them.

She tried to get a better look, and the doll grabbed her head from both sides and shouted in a hellish voice, "Where is Etharia? I demand you tell me now!"

Aluxes tried to pull the doll away but it had unimaginable strength. As she tugged harder and harder, the monster chuckled. She was able to force her tiny arms from her head, and tossed it into the fireplace. The doll walked out with not even a single hair singed.

It stared at her. "Your smell and your looks remind me of her. You are not her, yet somehow I cannot devour you yet. I am still too weak."

The doll floated in the air and a storm-like breeze blew through the room. Aluxes, with all her might, tried to walk towards the beast. The wind bruised her skin, and in some places, it caused her to bleed. She pulled out her sword and thrust at the doll but right before she was able to pierce it, a huge shock-wave exploded from the doll. It threw her out the window and into the moat, barely missing the stone and wood that fell with her. She looked up and noticed that the entire tower was now large chunks flying towards the earth.

High up in the sky, she could see the doll, hovering in the air. It raised an arm and black bolts of lightning struck the ground. The area shook and cracks formed all over the city, flames as dark as night spurting forth from them. Numerous people were caught off guard and burned. More in the unlit parts, where the fire was mostly invisible. A loud sound ripped across the sky as portals opened in the sky.

In the center was a white light and little black dots that could be seen as they fell towards the ground. It was not long before people started to scream. Aluxes quickly turned around and saw a tiny black creature with huge glowing white eyes. It was about a foot tall, but when it grinned, the teeth seemed larger than its head; they too glowed an eerie white in the dark. She could see some eating people like

Paraná, devouring them in an instant and leaving nothing but blood behind.

One talked in a low growl. "What manner of creature is this? Her aura is not human. Is she tasty? May we eat it?" Before Aluxes could start to swim to the other side, one leaped at her. Though she was about thirty feet away, it covered the distance in a single jump. She quickly grabbed the creature and it burst into a blinding blue flame. Some scattered away as others watched her as she swam off and climbed out the opposite side.

Chaos and panic filled the air as people started dying all over. Those who could use magic managed to fend them off for a while, but their sheer numbers overwhelmed most.

Aluxes tried to run into the castle but was blocked by more of these creatures. They looked at her with huge grins. It was mind-blowing how large their mouths and teeth were considering their tiny bodies.

Some of them stared at her. "Smell no good." They seemed to leave her alone but refused to allow her to pass by. She drew her sword and tried to swing it at them.

Each time she would manage to hit one, it would burst into blue flames. "Her weapon burns," one shrieked, and they quickly scattered.

When she entered the door, she could hear Loux yelling, "It was not time yet!" The doll hovered at eye level with him.

He talked more respectfully. "I know you have your goal, but we agreed to do it after I found it."

The doll's mouth moved and it said, "I encourage you to find it now, or else I shall replace you with someone that has less ambition." Her dull tiny voice now sounded more horrific and sharper.

The king ran up to Loux. "Brother, what is the meaning of this?" he asked, confused. His face panned around as people fended for their lives.

Loux chuckled. "You have always been an improper king. Being friendly with those that are lesser than you. Ignoring my advice to be proper for them to respect you. You know you're a joke in the minds of the elf king and dwarf king." He pulled out his sword.

"I must be the king to put them in their place." He tried to lunge in for a killing blow, but being a vet of war, the king outmaneuvered him easily and knocked his sword out of his hand.

The king had a disappointed look when he said, "I took care of you after Father died. I raised you. To think you were driven this mad for power." As he went in with a thrust, a black tar-like vine wrapped around his wrist.

The doll chuckled. "Must I do your task as well? I shall enjoy this." And in the blink of an eye the king's hand turned to dust.

He cried out in pain as he fell to his knees. Blood poured as if from a pitcher of wine. The doll was about to strike again when a whip, glowing in a blinding holy light, wrapped around her. Evalyn's father with his teeth bared had his eyes closed.

He griped the handle with all his might. "*Ho, nal hokken, das huse.*" Each word made it glow brighter. There was an explosion of white light at the end of the whip, and the doll screamed as if it was in pain, a type of sound that could pierce your soul. Such a horrific noise forced all who heard it to fall to their knees and cry in terror.

After the light died down, the doll was still there, smiling. "You silly mortal thought that would harm me. I hope it made you feel like you had hope with that amazing scream of mine."

Her little doll hands touched the whip and a black flame rushed down from it. Sir Hossberg tried to release it, but one hand was still in contact. He screamed in pain as it exploded. Blood and bone flew through the air as he fell to the ground.

Aluxes stood there and watched the chaos unfold. The lump in her throat prevented her from breathing. The screaming blocked out the ability hear most noises, which made it hard for her to focus. Fear froze her in place. Unable to move, everything around her unraveled in slow motion. She quickly noticed. that Evalyn was trying to repeat what her father had done and knocked her out with her hand.

Sir Hossberg looked at her and smiled with a little nod. She knew he wanted her to get his daughter out. She picked up Evalyn and tossed her over her shoulder. As she tried to run out the door, she was stopped by a larger shadowy creature. This one stood about six feet tall, had a mouth for a face, a mouth where his stomach should be, and teeth for fingers. Carrying Evalyn with her, Aluxes was unable to fight.

A glowing sword cut through the creature, and it split it in half from head to legs. "Commander Verus," she shouted. There was a warmth in her chest, as if everything was now going to be safe.

He waved his hand. "Hurry, we must get to the gate."

Aluxes looked back as she ran off and could see the doll. Her shadow turned into a tar beast and devoured the king. There was nothing left, not even a puddle of blood. They ran up to Onyx, Rosa, Ugthar, and Udook who were running towards the gate.

Onyx looked over. "Any ya seen Lugathar?" They shook their heads. He darted off, saying "I must find me love."

They stood at the gate where thousands of people were trying to open it with great desperation to escape. They frantically clawed at it until one of them shouted, "Stop!"

From the other side, a loud thud rattled the gate. Something pounded it and shook it violently. Cracks formed in the walls. The people backed away right before it exploded. It sent debris in every direction. Dust rose and blocked the view. As it slowly faded, Aluxes saw a tall man with huge muscles, dark tanned skin, glowing crimson eyes, and glowing crimson hair. Aluxes tried to do something, but part of the gate hit her and knocked her out.

Chapter Ten

FAREWELL MY LOVE

*O*h my god, my head, What happened? Shadows faded in and out as her consciousness drifted back and forth. *That horrid smell, Udook. His face is close. Is he carrying me?* Her eyes wandered before their weight forced her to shut them again. *He has Evalyn. That is good. I need some rest. Everyone will be fine if I drift off for a bit.* She smiled with one thought as she fell back asleep. *I hope they all got out to safety.*

Halfway across the city was the tavern Slouchy Dwarf Keep. In the front, Lugathar tried to save the citizens that were inside but to little avail. Every time one of the creatures got around her, they would eat a person or two.

As her swings got slower and weaker, she used runestones. Each time she tossed one, her breathing became heavier. She would stop to try to enchant a spell but a monster would attack, preventing her from completing one. It was not long before she realized that she was surrounded and everyone else had been eaten.

Out of breath, she stood there and talked to one of them, "What manner of monsters are ya?"

They all chuckled and a small one replied, "We are the nox. The larger ones are the nal. We were created by the Fallen to help our master destroy all living things in this land. We come from the Abyss." Its voice was raspy. There was a gargle in it as if there was liquid stuck in its throat. It must have been blood from the people it ate.

One of the nal leaped at her and she hit him as she casted the *holy strike*. They kept doing it one at a time as if they were toying with her, with no regard for their own life. After a few dozen attacks, her stamina ran out and she fell to her knees. A nox tried to bite her and she whacked it.

Her arm shook as blood poured from her hand. "Four hells, I be out of me mind, I musta hit a brick wall." The nox stood there, immune to her attacks. It grinned at her with its freakishly large teeth.

"Lugathar," Onyx shouted her name from the distance. She looked over to see him as the nox bit off her arm.

With his war hammer, he leaped into the group and smashed the ground. A bright light encircled the area, and the nal and the nox burned in a white flame. He bandaged her limb and helped her walk. He held her up on his shoulder.

Despite the pain she was in, she was able to talk calmly. "Onyx, ya dumb bastard, ya took ya sweet time to save a lady ya swore to love."

He cleared his throat. "Aye, sorry about that. Part of the gate landed in front of me. A bit of delay."

There was a bell tower nearby full of elven archers who were skillfully plucking off the monsters. One of them waved at Onyx and said, "Enter here. We will keep you safe, friend." Right as he was about to head towards the door, a loud thunderous roar ripped through the air, and a large ball of fire hit the tower, causing it to explode.

The dust cleared, and they were able to see what had happened; a tall dark tanned man with crimson red hair and eyes. He opened his mouth and a large fireball blasted out, destroying another tower.

Lugathar breathed frantically. "What in the bloody hell is that?"

Onyx tried to run with her over his shoulder. "I use to hear stories when I was a wee lad. That be the cursed dragon in human form. Me only think that because of that blasted dragon fire that came from his mouth." They had managed to run a few blocks when he slowed down a little.

His legs started to give way, and his run became a fast walk. A sharp pain shot through his body. A nox had bitten off his foot by the ankle. They both fell over as he screamed.

Lugathar pulled out a dagger, "*Holy strike!*" It had a faint glow but it was enough to kill the beast.

Onyx sat up. "I guess that be as far as we can go. Am sorry I failed ya, lass."

She looked at him and smiled. "Even though ya be flawed and dumb as a rock, I would have said yes." His eyes widened and shone brightly.

She cleared her throat. "I saw ya working on the ring. I knew it be for me."

He pulled out a ring made of solid diamond from his pocket. "It be no oger testicle, but it be the purest diamond I had ever seen."

He looked up at her as she stood there. In that moment, time slowed down. He was unable to tell whether or not it was from the blood loss, but he could see a halo shine above her head. He reached out to slide the ring on her finger as she smiled.

Before he could snugly put it on her, a nal with its large hands and teeth for nails that were as strong as steel, grasped Lugathar's head. Fingers dug into her neck and ripped it off. The monster laughed as it dropped her head in front of him.

Onyx slowly picked up her head and cradled it; he tried to cry but no tears would flow. He looked and saw men, women, and children being eaten all around him. The death and carnage, mixed with screams became dull in his mind. He stared at the nal as it laughed at him with both of its mouths.

His body started to shake in rage as he chanted, "*Abud tiarak evebuk ukthtiartievoz utito utaukul aozeek tuuculev obo. Tyarab ecud-ab,yaec ecgeo yeyek utito. Akoz yeguk ulek!*"

As he spoke, his body emitted a white glow. The light that emanated from him became brighter with every word he said. The nal in front of him disappeared, engulfed in light. His hammer glowed with the purest of light.

The entire block was brighter than the sun as dirt was lifted into the air. He raised his hammer above his head. Tears finally rolled down his face. "Aye, ye wee bastards. Ya now show up. I will see ya soon, me love." He slammed the ground with all his might shouting, *"Grand smite!"* Two city blocks exploded, killing every nal, nox, and person.

Aluxes slowly opened her eyes. In front of her was the head nun who had just finished tending to her wound and was starting to walk towards Evalyn. Everything was blurred; she tried to rub the pain away as she struggled to keep her eyes from closing.

"Here, my dear. Have some water." Mildred turned around and handed her a cup. "You are lucky to be as hard-headed as you are. A big chunk of the gate hit you on the head. Any normal person would have been dead right away." She smiled and hummed the song that she had always hummed to Aluxes.

She drank the water and looked at her. "Why are the monsters not attacking us in here?"

Mildred stared at the wall and sighed. "I would tell you how there is more to the history of the Unnamed Goddess but we do not have the time. Let's just say this is the part that she built herself—this closet-sized room. I think it was a room in which she could hide from the mobs of people that loved her." She smiled a little and put a wet warm rag on her head. "She also wrote that song you love so much in this very room."

The walls cracked, followed by a loud thud as someone pounded on them. They stared out the window and saw the crimson-haired person. In a deep voice that shook their bones, he cried out, "Old woman, I know you have it. Give it to me!"

She looked at Aluxes. "The spell holding this place will not hold out for long. Take Evalyn and get out of here."

As soon as she finished talking, he smashed through the wall. He smiled at them and growled with each breath. His glowing eyes burned into their souls.

He looked at his hands which were covered in blisters and opened wounds. "If this spell was renewed, I would have not been able to break it." He stared at them again. "I am Aeron. I am here to reclaim what is mine so I can return to my proper self."

The nun gazed at him, unmoved. "I read abut you in one of the forbidden books. The Fallen dragon god—so it was true. Your punishment was to be stuck in the human form forever."

He looked at her with an angry frown on his face. "It is more complicated than that, old woman. Your ancestors were entrusted with a part of me and I want it back."

Aluxes pulled out her sword and swung at him. He blocked it with his arm and the sword barely cut into him. He looked at her from the corner of his eye. "That actually hurt me, little girl." He flexed his muscle and moved his arm with such force that she flew back and smashed into the wall.

He looked at Mildred and grabbed her by the neck. He pulled out a hair from his head. It slowly morphed into a dragon spine and with it, he stabbed her hand, nailing her to the wall. He did the same to her other hand and smiled in joy she screamed in pain.

He put his face against hers, nose to nose. "I know it is here. I can feel it. Where is it?"

She spit in his eye. "I am a nun. I have no items of value."

He sniffed the air and stared at Aluxes. Tied to her sword was the red linen that had been given to her. She looked up at him, and with a sinister grin, he slowly put his hand inside the nun's stomach.

Aluxes screamed, "No, stop it!" as the nun cried in pain.

Mildred smiled at her. "You were like the daughter I was never allowed to have. I am proud of you. I never told you this but you remind me of your father. He was a wonderful man." Right at that moment, Aeron gripped her hip bone and pulled it down, ripping her in half.

He licked the blood off his fingers and grinned at Aluxes. "Girl, give me back my scale. I will allow you to live if you give me that which is tied to your sword. You have no need for it, child."

Aluxes sat there and watched the puddle of blood grow bigger. She had a flash back of how the nun always helped her feel better and played with her because none of the other kids would. As more blood spilled out, she felt a sharp pain in her heart. She looked at Aeron with hate in her eyes.

She rushed forward and hit him in the ribs with the pommel of her sword. He cried out in pain as his bones cracked. She quickly stabbed his foot with a dagger, pinning him to the ground. He tried to headbutt her but she dodged and spun around behind him with her sword, and pierced him through the back. The blade stuck out of his chest. Blood dripped all over the floor, and he laughed.

With joy in his voice, he said, "Girl, you are no weakling. If I were a normal dragon, that would have killed me." His hand morphed into a claw and he hit the tip of the blade, forcing the pommel to strike Aluxes in the stomach.

Aluxes vomited a little and collapsed onto the ground. He looked at her with a smile. "I can only manipulate parts of my body for a short time. I shall take back my scale." As he glanced at the weapon from the corner of his eyes, he became bothered by one of the runes. "That is not a normal sword. How did a mortal like you get—."

He was unable to finish, being interrupted by a heavy hammer as it smashed him in the face. Ulbrek followed with another hit to his balls and then to his chin. Each blow caused major damage.

Aeron quickly healed as he laughed. "I see, so you survived. She got that from you."

Ulbrek looked into his eyes, his teeth bared. "Aye, I be ah waiting for ya. Four hundred years ta see ya again, ya bastard." He shouted. "Go, lass! I hold him off while ya go. Ya in no condition ta fight him."

Aluxes looked over at Evalyn and saw Udook picking her up and trying to run. She followed suit, glancing back to see Ulbrek attack Aeron with a fury of blows, not a single one being missed.

They met up with Verus who was fighting off some creatures that looked like ghouls— ugly dog-sized monsters covered in a slimy substance.

Aluxes came up from behind and cut some of them down. A few tried to take a bite at Udook but their teeth shattered on his unbreakable giant skin, which remained undamaged by the biting.

Verus smiled. "If I had your hide, I would not have been missing this." He held up his hand— a finger had been bitten off by a ghoul.

Verus slowly walked over as he wrapped his stub. His lips opened, ready to speak, but a dragon spine pierced his armor, straight into his heart and killed him instantly. Aeron stood there laughing. They turned around and saw that in his hand, he held Ulbrek's hammer. He tossed it at them like it was a ball. He had a small wound on his cheek which was not healing.

He rubbed it. "That was a fine mortal; I shall cherish this scar," His grin faded and his eyes focused on them like spears.

Udook gently laid Evalyn down and charged at him. Tears flew as he yelled. All he was able to do was babble and stare at his dead friend. He pulled out a streetlamp and with all his might, uppercut Aeron, sending him flying as the streetlamp exploded into a million pieces. Udook followed.

A recognizable laugh came from behind. Aluxes turned around and saw the doll floating at head level and clapping. "You have done well to survive this long but it ends now." A lighting bolt flew out of her hand and hit her on the shoulder. It caused her body to twist. There was a burn mark but it healed faster than the other wounds.

The doll looked at her with a smile. "I see. So that's who you are. Magic has less effect on a being like you. Well, time to end this." A black tar-like vine popped out of her back and stabbed Aluxes in the shoulder, pinning her to the ground. It wiggled around as she screamed a little. She mashed her teeth and struggled to get up.

The doll moved in closer with another vine that came out and aimed at her neck. But before it reached her, a bolt with a blue tip struck her and exploded, encasing her in ice. In the distance, on top of the city wall, Rose was setting another bolt. Ugthar was fighting off the nox that tried to get at her. Evalyn grabbed Aluxes,and they rolled into the river that went through the center of the city.

The ice casing glowed red and then exploded. Before she could look at where the bolt came from another, one impaled her with a red tip and the doll burst into flames. The fire extinguished faster than Rose had anticipated, so she grabbed her short bow and shot an arrow. With a smile on her face, a black vine caught it out of the air and another vine came out and formed a bow. The arrow was nocked and released. It moved with blinding speed; Rose was unable to dodge it and was impaled in the chest.

She let out a scream that was quickly silenced by the blood that she was vomiting. Ugthar turned around and caught her before she fell off the wall. He moved her to a nearby tower and gently set her down. He tried to wipe the blood off her face so she could breathe. He reached to pull the arrow out but it was covered in the black tar and wouldn't come out. His hands trembled as his eyes swelled with tears. His cries became louder as he tried a healing spell but her wounds would not close. She whimpered as she screamed out a sharp, "Stop!" as more blood came out of her mouth.

She pulled out a pocket-sized piece of paper. "Azaroth handed this to me the other day. They found her—my baby. She is alive, my Samantha." Tears flowed out of her like a waterfall. "I knew this day would come. I just wish I could have seen her."

She handed him the paper. "Please make sure Aluxes tells her about me. Promise me she will find her like in my vision. Promise me —" her tears turned red and the blood from her mouth thickened. "My baby, Mommy is sorry. Please be safe. I know you're there." The blood had become black and resembled tar.

She cried out more and twitched violently. "Mommy will find you, I promise. I will never give up. You are alive. I know it." He was now holding her lifeless body. Her eyes were still open and black tar oozed from her eyes, mouth, and ears.

Ugthar held her tightly in his arms and cried till his tears ran dry. His cry became louder, turning into a raging scream. The black tar moved to his gloves, so he took them off. He inspected himself to make sure that was all of it.

Outside, the nox giggled at his pain. They even mocked her last words. "My baby, I am sorry." He picked up Rose's body and carried her down some stairs. He saw a large chest full of wood. After he emptied it, he gently placed her in it.

He closed it as his body trembled. "Stay safe here, my love. You shall have a proper burial after this is over. But I am sorry, I might not be able to keep that promise."

He gently opened the door at ground level and looked outside. He noticed his uncle's hammer a few feet away. Body parts littered the streets. Without a nox in sight to worry about, a few ghouls were busy as they picked at the fresh meat for their feast. He grabbed the hammer and ran off deeper into the city. His face trembled more as he ground his teeth. Like a wild animal, he growled, "Bitch, I will end you!"

Chapter Eleven

THE END OF PEACE

*A*luxes and Evalyn quickly climbed out of the water. They ended up near the elite barracks. No one was around. There were only ghouls looking for scraps to eat. They decided to rest and laid down on the grass. The beasts grunted and snarled at them but left them alone.

Evalyn stared at the pools of blood. "Is it all over?" She breathed faster and cried a little.

Aluxes looked at her and punched the ground. "Calm down! We need to survive this. If you lose it now, it might make the ghouls think we are easy targets and they may attack us."

Evalyn took in a few deep breaths. "That's not what I mean. Do you understand what would happen after this city falls? It was the bridge between the races. It was what made them unite. An age of unending war will come."

Aluxes sighed a little. "It is all right. I know what you are doing. This is not the time to think about it yet. You can mourn him after we escape. We will honor your friends and everyone else." She held her head. The vision of the closest person to a mother she had being ripped in half played over and over in her mind. Her eyes grew wider the more it repeated. A tear slowly fell and hit the ground between her legs. She looked around and noticed a water grate at the end of the stream. All that would prevent them from escaping was the heavy iron cover.

Before she could tell Evalyn, a cry for help softly echoed. They ran towards the sound; it was Sir Hossberg. His eyes had been removed and he staggered around blindly with no shirt. It was a miracle that he had been able to survive so long.

"Oh, Daddy!" Evalyn shouted as she ran to him. They hugged, and then he pushed her hands away.

He cried out a little. "My dear, it hurts too much." The skin on his back had mostly been removed.

"It has only been through sheer will that I made it this far," he said as he tried to hide the pain in his voice. He stumbled to the ground. "The evil bitch left me to live. I have fought vampire kings, ghoul lords, and a demon. But I have never met a beast so evil in my life and so powerful."

Ghouls moved in closer. The smell of fresh blood that poured from his wounds attracted them. Just as they were about to pounce, they lifted their heads and sniffed the air. They sat there for a few moments and then scattered.

"I guess you now owe me for saving your lives from the ghouls," a voice pierced their minds like a needle. They all held their heads and screamed in pain. They turned around and there was the doll, hovering above the ground.

She slowly moved closer to them. Evalyn tried to help her father step backwards. Though Aluxes was filled with fear, she stood fast. She quickly drew her sword and slashed at the monster. The doll split in half. Her stuffing was nothing but black tar. Before any of them could take advantage of the situation, she reformed and giggled.

The doll looked at her for a moment. "You seem to be immune to my hunger. The essences of the Abyss that I use to consume. I remember stabbing you with it, yet you seem undevoured."

Another vine came out of her and pierced forward. Before anyone could react, a hammer hit the doll in the head, smashing her into the ground. Ugthar screamed as he kept pounding her. He screamed till his voice was hoarse.

Before the doll could move he recited the same spell that his brother had, *"Abud tiarak evebuk ukthtiartievoz utito utaukul aozeek tuuculev obo. Tyarab ecudab,yaec ecgeo*

yeyek utito. Akoz yeguk ulek!"

Just when he was about to strike down on the doll, she grabbed the hammer with two black vines. She opened her mouth and breathed in deeply. Each time she did so, it caused the light he emanated to slowly fade. After a few moments, the glowing vanished and Ugthar fell over; she had consumed his spell.

She looked at him and gave a smile that could freeze one's soul. "Was that elf important to you? Well, I hope you know that I safely consumed her. There is nothing to worry about, like her getting lost in whatever afterlife they believe in. She is forever inside me, giving me energy."

With a wide grin on her face and tar that resembled teeth, she mimicked Rose's voice. "Save me, my love. I need you to join me. With you inside her, we can be at peace forever." She coughed a little. "Kill us. It hurts so much. Please, my love. Release me from this hell."

With his rage, he tried to take another swing. With all his might, the hammer almost touched her tiny head. She snapped her fingers and his arm folded in half, forcing him to drop the weapon. She snapped again and his body rose.

She floated up and put her face in front of his. "Silly mortal, part of me was already inside you. However, I do not like the taste of dwarf so be happy that you will be alone in the next world. Alone." She moved her head slightly and a spear that was laying on the ground pierced his stomach.

She snapped her fingers again and Ugthar fell, barely able to breathe. The doll glared at the girls. "How shall I deal with you?" Aluxes waved her arm and blue flames engulfed the doll.

She chuckled as the fires went out. "You are also able to use magic by will. I feel that if I try to deal with you properly, I would use too much of what little power I have at this time," she said, looking around, "And there might be more survivors, so I need to kill all birds at once. You will probably survive but by the time you find me, I shall be in my real body."

The sun barely peaked over the castle wall. She raised her arms, and the ground around the entire city began to glow. White and black auras engulfed everything.

Evalyn's father pushed her into the stream. "Father, no!"

His mind flashed back to when she was a little girl, and he said, "Live well, my girl. Be strong and do not forget how much you mean to me. Your mother told me she was proud of her blood in your veins."

Evalyn smashed into the grate. It was old and worn, and it buckled and broke when she hit it. She was flushed out into a lake. A bright light covered the sky and a large cloud of dust rose. Though she was underwater, the sound still deafened her. The waves violently pushed her to the shore. She slowly crawled out. Surrounded by falling stone and brick, she lay down and passed out.

Off in the distance, outside the city wall, Udook and Aeron were still fighting. As the explosion happened, both of them stopped to look. Aeron was unable to hide the amazement on his face. "My master is truly more powerful than the mightiest of the gods."

Across the continent, the explosion could be seen and heard; almost the entire world could feel the quakes from it. The city that was the bright hope for mortals was now gone.

Aeron moved side to side as if to dance. "I guess I should end this now, you poor halfwit. If I were a normal dragon in human form, you would have killed me." His wounds started to heal except for the scar that Ulbrek had put on his check.

Udook charged at him. There was a loud thud followed by a cracking noise. He stood there and looked down to see that Aeron's hand was inside his chest. Aeron pulled his now dragon-shaped claw out and held his heart. He ate it in front of Udook as he slowly died.

After the dust cleared, all that was left was a barren wasteland. Somewhere, Aluxes was lying on the ground, barely conscious. A man with green hair ran up to her before she passed out.

She woke inside a house. The bed felt like it was made of straw and rocks. She slowly looked around and saw a middle-aged woman sitting next to her.

The woman glanced over and noticed her. "Oh good, you're finally awake." She had a high-pitched stuck-up voice, and the way she looked at Aluxes was as if she was beneath her.

The lady left a plate of food that was half-eaten. "You've been out for weeks. You may thank us by working off your debt." She quickly walked off.

Aluxes tried to get up but her arms and legs were weak. Her gut started to moan as she hunched over with tears. She felt as if she had not eaten anything in days. She looked at the plate and saw that all that was left were some breadcrumbs, minor scraps of meat, and a carrot.

Aluxes scoffed. "It seems the old hag ate all the good stuff and left what she did not like on the plate." There was a cup of water that had an odd odor to it. She took a little sip and spit it back out. "It tastes like diluted piss."

She got up and noticed a uniform laying around with a letter on top of it. It red "*You owe us for medical and food. You shall work it off as a house servant. Wear this outfit or you will be punished.*"

Aluxes made a fist and grunted. The image of the doll appeared in front of her and she punched the wall as hard as she could. A sharp pain shot through her arm. Her skin broke and her knuckles bled. It was soft wood but there was no dent nor a single mark.

She looked down and saw that was wearing a nightgown that went to her toes. Under it, she was wrapped in bandages. She took a peek and saw that her body was still bruised. After a little while, she started to sway from side to side as her head became light and she fell over. Unable to pick herself back up, she grunted as pain shot through her entire body.

She managed to climb to her knees. *Why am I not healing? How come I feel so weak? Is this how normal people feel?* She wondered.

She got up and held the dress. "Who the hell do these people think they are? I am no slave." She stared at it and slowly put it on. "I need information first; if I play along, they will be more willing to talk. I also have no idea how long I will be in this weakened state. It's best if I stay here till I heal, I guess. Shit."

Slowly, she walked down the stairs. Her hands gripped the rails tightly as each step was a struggle. At the bottom was a huge room. At a table there was a man, his wife, a young boy, and a girl.

The man sat there reading a paper and glanced over it. "Ahh, you're awake. Well, get to it and make us food." He talked as if he owned her. The tone of his voice was making her vomit inside her mouth. "You owe us a lot of money, so start working now or there will be no food for you tonight."

Aluxes slowly walked into the kitchen. *What the hell am I doing? How dare he talk like that to me. Filthy, fat, rich human. I have to find everyone. Why am I standing in front of this stove?*

She grunted under her breath as she stood there. "What in the hell is this stuff?" The room started to grow bigger and her mind spun around. She scoffed a little. "Well, I hope they like broth."

The wife walked up to her. "My goodness. What type of peasant girl are you? I think you have never cooked a meal in your life. Broth is something only beggars get. Not even you are a beggar." Her voice was higher pitched than the last time. She pushed Aluxes aside. "Well, I guess I have to teach you. This will add on to your debt."

After the food was served, she noticed that the front page of the paper read "King Loux Cuts Relations With Dwarf High King."

Aluxes face turned red and her body began to shake, "Loux survived?"

The husband looked up. "A peasant. A woman peasant that knows how to read. It is a wonder why you cannot cook."

He scoffed at her a little. "I am Sir Belmot, and that is all you need to know of our names."

Before he ate, he placed the paper down. "You are no longer what you were in the capitol. You must get that out of your mind. A peasant servant is who you are." He nodded his head and took a spoon full of stew.

After a long day of house chores, Aluxes was about to make herself dinner when she was stopped by Lady Belmont. "Dear, you already had a meal today this morning. You are to only get one meal a day. That is all. Now get some rest."

Aluxes growled as she threw her pillow. "This is hell, I am not going to stand for this shit. I do not care about information; I can force it out of them."

The door opened and Sir Belmont stood there. "Young lady, I do not think you fully understand your situation. A lot happened during the week you were out. All the survivors of the fallen capitol are wanted. I am the only person who knows what you are, and it shall stay that way or my family will be executed if anyone finds out. Get it in your head that you are a servant, an infertile dragonblood. They sell their young to slavery if they are unable to produce a litter. This is the last we will speak of this or I will turn you over." He closed the door softly.

She sat on her bed. *What is going on? Wanted? I guess I will serve for one more day till I understand my situation better. Maybe I should just kill them all.*

The next day, she peeked at the paper before anyone woke up. It read*"The high elf king refuses to negotiate with King Loux. Without our support to form an alliance, the kingdom of the dark elves is to wage war on the elves."*

Sir Belmont suddenly grabbed everyone. Aluxes worried that she had been caught reading the paper and tried to hide it. He took her arm tightly and pulled her outside to stand next to the family. There was a group of knights that was talking to each household in the village.

One of them walked up to Sir Belmont. "I see that you look good in your retirement." They both chuckled a little. "We are looking for survivors from the Holy City. The king has had attempts on his life by a few."

Sir Belmont nodded. "I have not seen any survivors here."

The captain stood in the middle of the town and announced, "If any of you find a survivor of the Holy City, they are to be executed on sight. By order of the king as many of them have made attempts on his life." He put up a decree on the post board. In bold letters, it read *"Fifty gold reward."*

Sir Belmont guided everyone back into the house. "These are dark days indeed."

Aluxes stared at the knights from the window. "The knight said he was retired, but he looks to be only in his thirties, and he did not have the same build of a typical troop. Who is Belmont?"

There was a sharp snap as Sir Belmont slapped her. "Peasant woman, you are to work. Not to be a statue."

She tried to lash out but stopped herself. She was still very weak, and the army was looking. The sir's warning filled her head as she stood there. She needed to stay silent until she fully recovered.

She grabbed a broom. "I hate them all. Every last one of them. I will kill Loux."

Chapter Twelve

HAPPY SEVENTEEN

*I*t had been a full year. Aluxes woke up and felt a little different. Maybe it was because her body was older, or maybe she'd become accustomed to the work.

She started the day like always, slowly putting on her uniform, but there was a small problem, she was now six-five and the dress no longer fit her. She walked down the stairs and began making breakfast before everyone woke up. She had become somewhat of a successful cook. People would come by and pay her under the table to make them extra food as they headed off to work.

She set up the table and waited. The kids came bursting out first like rabid dogs and tackled the food. Then the parents slowly walked out.

Aluxes handed the paper over to Sir Belmont. "You did not read it, did you wench?" He checked to look at the seal to make sure it had not been tampered with.

She cleared her throat. "Sir, it is my birthday. I was wondering if I may have some time off."

He looked at her over his paper. "You, a day off? Might as well. Just use your own money. I know you been earning some." His tone had changed. It was harder for her to tell if he was talking down to her, or if he was being complimentary. It still had that stuck-up tone to it.

She put on her shoes and headed out. They were a little tight and caused her to stumble. Each time she tripped, she would have memories of the doll. As her mind came back to the moment, she was standing in the blacksmith shop with her hand on a sword hilt. A voice nagged at her. *Get a sword.*

She stared at the heavy blades. The price tags on them were a little high. *This will cost me my entire earnings. I need new shoes and an outfit but damn it. I need a sword.*

The smith looked at her. "Oy, a lady like you might get hurt. Best step away." He showed her a short sword. "A lady like yourself might want to use a blade like this for protection. But ladies tend to go for the small daggers to hide up their nickers."

Aluxes looked at it but then pushed it away. "I would like to try that blade, sir." She pointed at the largest blade there.

He laughed. "That is a funny joke, lady. That is heavy even for a man. Now scamper off before you cause an incident."

He was about to chase her off when she grabbed it out of the display with one hand. Her arm quivered a little which caused her to also grip it with the second hand. The people nearby stared at her with widened eyes.

She smiled at the smith. "What in the hell is this for anyways?"

He looked at her and tried to find his voice. "It is ahh, umm, for taking out a horse and the rider at the same time."

She put it away and wandered off. "I guess my strength is returning. If I need a sword, I am sure I can mug someone for one."

She headed back towards the Belmont's residence and entered through the door. She handed him all her money. "Sir, here. I hope this is enough. After adding in the work I have done, I hope I have made enough to pay what I owe you."

He looked at her and laughed. "You dumb girl, your stay was already paid for by the guy that saved you. Now, we talked about this. I am keeping you safe and alive."

She mashed her teeth. "Why in the hell did you tell me I owed you a large debt?"

He stared at her as if she were a child. "A mind-altering spell would have been better but you were immune to it. You owed me for making sure that the soldiers did not find you. I put my family at risk by keeping you here." He looked up and down her body like she was his property. "Stay with us and you can live out a life of simple means. I can even order my wife to do more if you let me bed you. You are a rather attractive woman and I am a noble."

He put his hand around a mace that he had hidden behind his chair. "I risked everything when I agreed to care for you. It is not as if you blend in easily. Being a mistress can be exciting."

She stood there in a fighting stance. "I am going to avenge my fallen friends. I will not allow anyone to stop me. I will kill you if I must."

He placed his mace on the table and chuckled. "I will not stop you, but just watch what you say and do. If it comes back to me, I will put you down."

He handed her some of her money back. "Half of this will be to pay for the supplies you used to earn this money. I saw you fight Verus on my last day."

She stood there dazed. "I do not understand I—."

He chuckled more. "I was told to keep you here till you recovered and you made your choice. I owed the lad my life. Please forgive me for what I am about to say and do next, but it is the only way you can leave without suspicion. Just never return."

"You have been doing what? You filthy whore! Fine, this is enough to buy back your freedom! Now get the hell out and raise that bastard on your own!" He pushed her out the door and slammed it shut.

She stood there as people stared at her. Unable to move or speak, she blushed as everyone gawked at her. Before they walked off to continue their day, someone shouted. "Which lucky lad is the father?"

What the holy fuck? why? I can never show my face here again after that. What the four hells just happened? She moved towards the road and looked both ways.

She picked up a stick that she saw laying on the ground and dropped it. *Well, I hope fate guides me on the right way.*

As she passed a few houses, an old woman stopped her. "I hear you got pregnant and were kicked out. You do not have to tell me but I bet it was that bastard Belmont, and he is trying to save face by throwing you out." She handed her a basket. "There is some food and a blanket to keep you warm. May the Unnamed Goddess watch over you."

As she walked along the road, she heard a soft female voice in the back of her mind. It was annoying and had a pitch to it, but she followed the direction it told her to go.

After a day of travel, a group of bandits jumped out. "Well, what do we have here," one of them said, drooling as he looked at her.

Aluxes barely glanced at them and counted that there were four. She could smell another one behind the bushes. She reached for where her sword should have been but quickly realized that she was unarmed. She stood there with her hands halfway up and palms opened.

One of the bandits walked closer and sniffed her. "I bet she be a virgin that one is. She will sell for a nice price."

Another gave her a dirty look. "What! I never been with a half-breed, and she is half something. I hear half-breeds have the best tasting cunts. Maybe we fuck her mindless first."

One of them walked around and stood behind her. "Maybe we can all have a piece. It's been ages for me. She be tight and in need to be used. She probably able to handle all of us at once being so tall." He pulled out a dagger and lifted up part of her dress. "I wonder if she wearin' any nickers."

In an instant, his head was smashed in. She punched him in the center of his face. His skull caved in and bits of blood flew off in every direction. One of them was quick to react and reached for his sword but Aluxes lunged at him before he could draw it out. She grabbed him by the back of the head and slammed his face into her knee, killing him instantly.

An arrow flew through the bushes, hitting her in the shoulder.

The bandit chuckled. "Bitch wounded." The others swung at her with their blades. She easily dodged and grabbed the neck of one of the men and snapped it.

She picked up a sword and threw it into the bushes, hitting the bandit archer that was hiding behind it. The last one tried to make a run for it but Aluxes was able to catch up to him. She grabbed him by the head and pulled him down to the ground.

She opened her hand and a fistful of hair fell. "You got my nice dress all dirty."

She looked at the man as he cried. "Please, ma'am. I meant no harm. Times be tough, just tryin' to get by. Please, I have a son."

She kneeled down and punched the ground next to his head. "Take me to your camp. Give me all your supplies and I will let you live."

He took her to a clearing not too far away. "What the hell is this? I made better camps than this at the orphanage. That firepit can barely hold a single log. Of course this shit will be my luck."

She scoffed a little. "Pathetic, you probably need the money more than I do." She took a sword, a dagger, a bow, and a few arrows. "This is all I need for now. I am not desperate enough to take that slop you call food."

As she walked off, the bandit tried to stab her in the back with a dagger, but she swayed to the side and kicked his leg. Like a twig, it snapped.

She took one last look at him. "Maybe you need to learn a proper skill." She said with a scoff. "Learn to fight or beg. Just remember I never forget a face. If I see you again, I will kill you, yeah?"

She pulled the arrow out of her shoulder and walked off. The man lay there on the ground crying, the stench of his own piss surrounding him.

He coughed when he tried to find some words. "I'll get you, little bitch. I swear it. I will have me cock in ya cunt after I kill ya."

Aluxes calmly turned around and threw the arrow into the man's chest, and then ran up to him and made a tight fist that broke her skin. "I will never be called that again," she said as she pounded the ground over and over. Each time she slammed down, she saw flashes of class-mates that had teased and bullied her. The words mara, bastard of a monster whore, and slut ran through her mind. She screamed at the top of her lungs when she saw the doll in front of her and in the same instant, it all stopped. Her face became blue, and she collapsed to the ground. The man curled up with his arms covering his body, laying between busted roots.

Standing over Aluxes was Mildred. "Why can't I just murder a worthless scum? Is it a sin to destroy the ones that deserve it, nun?"

She cried as she curled up. "Should I forgive him?" Mildred began to hum. "Mother? Can I call you Mother? You are all I can think of when I try to remember my real—."

The nun softly whispered, "I will always watch over you. I love you my dear." She sat in her rocking chair, holding a young blue-haired child who was covered in bruises and was crying.

Chapter Thirteen

HOLY CAPITOL OF GRAVES

Shit, how much more do I have to walk? I've been walking for weeks. That annoying voice better not be a sign that my mind has been damaged from the city exploding. Aluxes looked at her coin pouch, *Useless. I am almost out of money from the last job I did.*

She plugged her nose and tried to impersonate someone. "Good pay to build my fence, throw in a bonus if you finish in a day." She scoffed. "All that rich snob offered me was to marry his son." She grabbed her nose again. "I am the richest man in this town, it would be an upgrade for you."

Aluxes put her hand on her belly and talked to it. "I know you want food. But I need to replace my boots as well. Maybe if you could work jobs, we would get paid more."

As night fell, she set up camp and cleaned the random wild berries she would find. *Aluxes keep going down that road. I beg you. You are running out of time.*

Her eyes opened. "Fuck, voice. I swear by the name of the Unnamed Goddess I will stick this dagger in my ear." She sat up. "It keeps getting louder and louder. You know, if I do not get any sleep, I won't be able to keep walking."

The following day she approached a mansion. When she stood in front of it, the voice simply said *"thank you"* and then it was silent.

Well, I finally have peace, and I do not wish to enter this run-down dump. She tried to walk away but was unable to take her mind off it. *Alright already, fine. Here I am talking to myself. I swear to the gods— if there is a werewolf in there, I will kill that inner voice.* She huffed as she walked towards the door.

As she approached it she realized there was an odd smell around it. The pungent odor of dust and newly formed mold irritated her nose. She tried to knock to see if anyone would answer, but the door fell off its hinges. The walls inside were covered in a layer of dirt and deep cuts across the paper. Every few moments, she could hear crying that echoed throughout the house.

She trembled a little. "I swear if it is a ghost, I will burn this shit-hole down. I know wards to help you cross over." She tried to swallow the lump in her throat but it was too big. She hummed as she rubbed her circlet.

She followed the sound of crying towards a hall. "Little girl, I do not mean you any harm. If you need help to cross over, I promise I will find a priest. Do not haunt or take over my body." Her sword rattled as her hand shook uncontrollably.

She managed to find the room where the crying was originating from. The door slowly opened as she pushed it. There was a fireplace that was lit and a large fancy chair covered in rare furs. She took a few steps, each creaking on the floor.

A swoosh whistled in the air and she barely had enough time to block it. A girl jumped out from the chair. "Who dare tries to rob from me? I am skilled and armed." She held a bladed whip and was ready to strike at Aluxes again. Aluxes was able to dodge it but still received a slight cut on her arm.

Without hesitation, she lunged forward and punched the girl in the stomach with the pommel and knocked her on the ground. "Evalyn, calm down. It is me. You are lucky I am smarter than you." Though she was covered in dirt, smelt of smoke, and her hair was blackened with ash from the fireplace, her voice was still the one attribute that Aluxes hated the most.

Evalyn looked up at her and immediately cried and hugged her, "It has been such a nightmare. Almost an entire year. I thought you were dead."

Aluxes looked around. "What happened here?" All over the walls were deep cuts. Some blood spots stained the carpet, and Evalyn had scars on her arms.

She took a few steps back and sat on her chair, looking into the fire as if she could see the events. "Some of the monsters followed me home. They ate most of the guards and servants. It took a while, maybe a few months, to clear out the entire house. After that, there were only maybe a handful of house workers and five guards." She looked at Aluxes and smiled. "Mother and Father would have been proud of me. I was strong."

She stared back at the fire. "Then it got worse. When that little shit King Loux put a bounty on the heads of the survivors, one of the maids contacted him about me. The knights came in and slaughtered everyone. I have been fighting them off this entire time. They come. I kill most of them. Then, they retreat and come back. It is as if they have made a game out of it. But the worst are the bandits that from time to time show up to take what little I have left. The things I had to do in order to survive. I know that I had no other choice, right?"

Evalyn cried some more. "I have nothing left. No one left."

Aluxes grunted. "Come on, now. This is not the brave girl I knew from back at the academy. I think it is high time you grow up and put yourself back together. I would even allow you to join me if you wish. It is the only way a rival can find out if she is better." A foul smell flared her nostrils. "After you take a bath."

Before Evalyn could smile, horses stumbled through the hall. A man's voice echoed. "Did the little whore kill herself yet? Or did she enjoy our last visit that much and is wanting more?"

Aluxes turned around and saw that there were three knights on horseback lined up in the hall. They climbed off their horses and drew swords.

"I see that the bitch has a new friend," one said in a joyful tone. "I was worried the three of us had to fuck one girl again but looks like I can have one to myself. She is tall, just how I like'em."

"They raped you?" Aluxes whispered to her.

"No, I managed to overpower them, but one time he snuck in when I was sleeping and touched my perfect skin. After that, he claimed I allowed him into my bed." Evalyn tried to pull out her whip but was too tired to fight.

Aluxes looked at her. "I got this. Just rest. You have been through enough."

One knight laughed. "What can a girl in a green dress do?" Then, changing his tone a little, he said, "Better just lift it up and ride me. Less pain that way, princess."

Aluxes pulled her dress away, revealing her full chain armor suit underneath with a sheathed long sword. She stood in a ready stance. "Come at me, you bastards. None of you filthy humans shall live."

They laughed a little. The one in the front tried to swing. Aluxes grabbed his wrist and punched his elbow, breaking it. The other two pulled back. "He is wearing heavy armor and she crushed it like it was nothing." The plate was smashed in and bits of the metal splintered into his arm.

Before they could think of a plan, she grabbed the injured one by the leg and threw him at them, knocking them over. She leaped up and smashed one of their faces in with her foot. She then pulled out her sword and stabbed the injured one. The third knight managed to get up and tried to swing at her, but she blocked him and counter swung, cutting his weapon in half and embedding her blade in his chest plate.

Cold sweat ran down his face. "Please, I don't want to die. I was just following orders. It is nothing personal."

Aluxes looked at him. "You are no knight. Holy Knights uphold justice even if it means disobeying their king because you are loyal only to the thirteen, yet you decided to rape a girl and kill her when she has done nothing. Can you not see that she has lost everything?"

Snot rushed out of his nose. "I am sorry, miss. I swear I shall leave and you will never see me again. I never bedded her, I only touched her knickers, but she woke up and beat the shit out of me. I seen your wanted poster. You know the oath, you are an elite."

She looked over at Evalyn. "I cannot kill someone who is unarmed and begging to live. I am not a monster." Before he could make a move, Aluxes smashed both sides of his helmet and crushed his head. "But I am sick of you humans talking down to me."

She walked over to her discarded dress and wiped the blood off her hands and sword. "I no longer need this. I only wore it to draw out bandits."

Evalyn stood there, face pale like a ghost. "You did not have to kill them all. The guy was begging. They taught us to be better than that."

Aluxes put her face close to hers. "If he'd gone back and described me to the king, it would cause him to send out a larger force. It would have been more of a problem."

Evalyn nodded but was unable to take her eyes off the man's smashed head. "How can you do that and not feel a thing?" She glanced over and noticed that the circlet was black for a moment.

Aluxes found a bucket and filled it with water from the pump in the kitchen. She put it near the fire to warm it a little. "Here, have a quick wash for now."

Evalyn stood there unable to take a step closer seeing how cold Aluxes was. "I spared a bandit once who begged. He came back with his friends to attack me. He came at night while I was asleep. He tied me up and tried to—well, if I was not me, it would have been my end or worse. So I learned pretty quickly that when you stick out like me, it is best to remove the problem."

Aluxes searched the horses' saddles and found some food. "This will make stew for us for the week. I will prepare it while you wash up."

Evalyn noticed how skilled she looked as it was being cut up. "How the hell you learn to cook? I remember the one time you had to make soup. It almost killed everyone. Your year must have been a dreadful one for you to learn how to cook."

"It was not so bad. I was a house servant for the year. I had to learn how to do many things that are now helpful skills." She smiled a little as she talked.

Evalyn glanced over and noticed that the circlet was a bright gold again. "The mighty Aluxes a servant? Why did you not just kill them or just bust down the door and walk off?" She moved the basin away from the fire and stripped.

"I tried. I even snuck into the master's room to slit his throat but mother, stopped me." Aluxes stared at the knife, remembering the night.

"Mother?" Evalyn slowly lowered herself into the water.

"Head Nun Mildred." She continued to cut the food.

"Ah yes, the daughter she was not allowed to have and the mother you were robbed of. Father told me she was pregnant once but the baby was born dead. It was a daughter." She splashed some water.

"Every time the kids would bully me, every time I would get angry, every time I cried, she always calmed me down." She put the food bits into a pouch.

"Why did you not just use your muscles and force your way out?" She glanced at her to see if there was a reaction.

Aluxes pulled her armor up a little to show a scar across her belly. "Something happened during the explosion. I lost all my strength for almost a year. Even my ability to heal. I was human." She tossed her some soap.

"Ahh yes, and now you understand how we all feel. So were there any men you were weakened towards?" She lathered up and chuckled.

"I am not like you, giving it up to a boy just to make me angry. There is only one man." She placed her hands over her lips.

"One man." She slowly turned her head with a snake-like glare. "Oh, I know. Is it the green-haired man who is the messenger of the gods?"

Aluxes blushed. "He did save me from the prince and found me after the explosion. His face was—" She placed her hands over her lips again.

Evalyn squeezed her breasts together. "Oh, mister messenger. I have an important delivery you must take a look at. It is right here on my nipples." She giggled as Aluxes grunted.

"I am sorry. That boy was not right for you. He would say such sweet things to you. Behind your back, he said some of the worst lies about—" She stopped herself.

"I know. He said that up close, my breath smelled like cow shit. I also know he lied about sleeping with you. One of his friends tried to pick a fight with me and he told me everything. But you had to act as if it really happened. Why?" They looked at each other.

Evalyn smiled as she rinsed off the soap. "I wanted to spark something inside you. Maybe if you got laid, you wouldn't be so uptight and angry. Sex was so relaxing for me." She stood up. "Look at me, my skin is all cut up from that day. But my privileged skin is still silky soft. It is what any lover would want to feel regardless of how it looks."

Aluxes scoffed. "How can you think about that at a time like this? For me it has more value. Time to get dressed, princess."

"Dear, the man you decide to give it up to would have to be the luckiest man who ever lived." She winked and smiled.

After they were prepared, Evalyn was about to climb on one of the horses when she was stopped by Aluxes. "Only a fool would take a marked horse."

She closed her eyes and stuck up her nose. "But this would make moving around a lot easier. I cannot walk forever."

Aluxes scoffed a little and grabbed her by the collar. "If we stop in a town with a horse marked with the king's seal and not wearing his knights' armor, the locals would get the authorities. Also, horses have to be taken care of. Seems like a waste of money that we do not have. We cannot even sell them because they are marked!"

Aluxes shoved her out the door and they walked on the main road. Evalyn gazed at her as if she were trying to burn a hole into her head. "Why are we heading this way? Why have you allowed me to join you? Do you want to be my friend now? If so, what—"

"Oh my god, you are so annoying." Aluxes rolled her eyes. "There is something guiding me, like a heavenly voice telling me where to go.

It says *go this way* so I go. If I ignore it, I feel pain. If I feel pain, I will make sure you feel pain too. So shut your mouth so that I can hear it."

Evalyn said sarcastically. "Being led by a loon that probably has a brain tumor is not a good plan if you ask me." She pointed at her and chuckled. "Must have hit your head."

Aluxes stopped and stared at her with her typical look. "The voice told me to save your sorry ass and told me you must come with me. But I will tell you this, annoy the piss out of me and I will kill you with my bare hands faster than you can blink." Evalyn felt a little chill down her spine. "I plan on killing that doll. I hope this voice is leading me to it."

After a few days of walking, they noticed a broken road post. On it was written "*Holy City of Cathair.*"

Jittery and annoyed, Aluxes looked at the ground. "I been heading home this entire time. Was it you guiding me this entire time? Were you still watching over me like you have been doing my entire life? Have I disappointed you?" She fell to her knees. "I am sorry, Mother."

They kept walking till the trees no longer blocked the view. It was a sight to behold. The greatest human city was now the largest cemetery in the world.

What used to be thousands of buildings were now millions of gravestones that scattered across the entire area of where the city once stood. Human stones were straight up and down marble slabs with rounded corners, elf graves had the star of the Everlasting, and dwarfs' were carved up gems in the shape of axes and hammers. In the distance, what looked like the center was a hill with green grass and a tiny building on top.

"Well, I guess we should head there. Probably a caretaker I must save or something." Aluxes let out a loud exhalation. "It better be a secret and powerful weapon."

"No more walking. My feet cannot take anymore. I am a noble and not a slave. Carry me, my dear." Evalyn laid down on the ground like a dead animal.

"Move it or I will drag your ass. Better yet, stay here. I am sure there are a few ghosts in this place. with grave this large I doubt they have decent ghoul removal." She walked off.

"Ghouls? I was only kidding. Hey, wait up." Evalyn tripped as she tried to rush up.

It was a Doric-style build with huge pillars that had detailed carvings on every inch of people that lived there. The steps were made of marble and they looked like they were cleaned on a regular basis. The climb was long and seemed to last forever until they reached the top, where they were greeted by a marble casket with a carving of a woman and a man on the top.

When Aluxes and Evalyn looked at the engraving *"Here lie Rosaletta and Her Beloved,"* tears fell from their eyes, and on the other side, they could hear a man crying. He had gray hair, one arm, and one leg. They could tell he was a dwarf by his majestic beard.

Evalyn slowly walked up behind him. "Excuse me, dear sir. Are you in charge here?"

He moved away a little and they could see that the gravestone where he sat read *"My Beloved Lugathar."* Aluxes looked at him closer. "Onyx?"

He smiled and tried to speak but his voice was a shadow of what it once was. "Aye, it be good to see ya survived, young lass." He pulled himself over to a makeshift wheelchair that was off to the side. "I was starting to think it be all in vain."

Aluxes hugged him and he chuckled. "It tickles me balls to know ya came to see me." She jumped away.

He rolled his chair towards a small wooden box with a few of his belongings. "I live here now by the order of the high elf king to watch over this wee mound. King Loux made a wee few attempts to get me, but I be protected." He looked at his brother's grave. "It be sad his name not be on it but I understood the elf kings position on it."

He pulled out a tiny piece of paper. It was a little burnt and torn. "Me brother did not die right away. He suffered for three days after we found him while that black evil ate him from the insides. No elf magic or Azaroth himself be able to cure it. I only survived 'cause the bloody building that fell on me managed to miss most of my body and shielded me from the explosion."

He looked at the girls, his eyes worn and aged beyond his years. His face was drawn and his head no longer held up with pride. He was tired of life. He tried to smile but it was forced. His jokes no longer carried the joy he once had.

Aluxes stumbled for words. "What happened to you? You look like you aged a hundred years."

He chuckled. "It be the only spell I actually know and this be the after effect. It drained most of me life force. The *grand smite* would have killed a normal dwarf but being half-human, it only drained me mostly. I no longer can cast any spells."

He handed Aluxes the paper. "Aye little lass, please. Me brother's dying wish was ya to find this missing child. Once he understood his fate, he told me to give it to ya." He looked down with an empty expression. "I thought ya had died but he somehow knew ya lived." He stared at her as his eyes swelled. "It be Rose's youngest daughter, Samantha. She be somehow survived the attack. This is where Rose's brother heard she be living."

As he let go of her hand, the effort caused his entire body to shake a little, "Please bring her here when ya find her. Problems between humans and elves have sorta forced the elf prince ta return home. I beg ya, their souls need proper rest."

Aluxes gently smiled. "I promise I will find her. You rest now, old goat. I will bring you a present when I come back."

Aluxes stared at the paper. It was all in Elvish. She looked at Onyx. "Aye lass, nor I cannot read Elvish. And apparently the elves that come here to take care of me cannot read the blasted thing neither. The prince be an odd way of talking. He speaks straight to the point and leaves out words he thinks are unnecessary. Only people that under-stand be his family."

Evalyn took a gander at it. "I heard a rumor there was an elf outpost not too far from here. An elf in the guard told me it is the home of her princess."

She pulled out a little map that she had in a pouch. "My father once told me that when he saw Rosaletta—he remembered one time they dined with the high elf kings family after he saved them from a vampire, and that she was the king's daughter. He mentioned that her sister has a small outpost nearby." Evalyn rolled her eyes a little. "Hard to tell if his story was true or not. He loved to embellish a lot."

Aluxes looked around his place and noticed that there were no signs of dwarf goods. "Why are your people not helping to take care of you?"

He smiled a little. "Once they found out me brother married an elf, they worried I might tell. So, I be banished from the dwarf kingdom." He looked at his grave again. "Might as well. After we left, I sorta started to feel more distance from it, ya know. Not let the elves know, I enjoy giving them a wee run around."

Aluxes headed off. "I will see ya around, old man. I promise I will bring that girl here. Rose told me I was going to find her anyways." She stopped for a moment. "Where is Mildred buried?"

He rubbed his beard. "Ah, aye. Yes, head nun. What little be left of her remains was taken by a young lass. She be not much older than ya. Said family, though she reminded me of you if I being honest. It be the brows and bit of the stern face."

She continued to walk. "She never told me she had any family. I need to find out so I can place flowers on her stone."

Evalyn quickly followed, observing the graves. Something about them shook her to her bones. "I wonder if I should visit Father? I hope I get to take a look when we get back."

Chapter Fourteen

SHE WAS LOVED

They headed southwest for a few days to a territory called Lugshire. It was mainly a farming community with a small hub at the forest border. The town where the bazaar normally happened was now mostly deserted. Fallen relations between the humans and the elves had made trade almost disappear. Empty buildings scattered about and the only people that remained were the ones too poor to leave.

Villagers whispered as Aluxes walked by, "Look at her, a half-breed. I wonder what her other half is? Watch your things. She will steal from us. I bet she is a rare type of half-elf and will kill us in our sleep."

Aluxes tried to ignore them but some of their harsh statements did make her scoff a little. "Like they are any better." For a moment, she balled her hands into tight fists.

"It amazes me that relations have fallen so fast in a short time. It just shows how fast good propaganda can work in the minds of the simple." Evalyn stood in front of a poster that read *"Elves cannot be trusted. They allowed the fall."*

They approached the edge where the forest began and were stopped by guards. "I would not venture there if I were you. Elves have a small outpost in that there woods. They tend to shoot on sight any who they catch walking in there."

They looked around and could see the start of a wall being constructed. Aluxes took a breath. "I will take my chances, but if you try to stop me, I will break your arm."

He stepped off to the side a little. "I would not stop a half-breed bitch. I be trying to save the human girl beside you."

Another guard snuck up behind and hit Aluxes in the back with a club. "Half-breed bitch needs to watch her tongue while talking to a human."

The hit barely moved her as she expected it and she braced herself. The pain was dull and flat; she was used to it. She turned around and kicked his chest plate, causing part of it to cave in a little. The people that checked on him shouted that he was dead. Aluxes grabbed Evalyn's hand and ran into the forest, knowing that the guards would not follow.

"Aluxes, why did you kill him? It was not needed." She was barely able to shout since she was out of breath.

She looked at her without slowing down. "I did not kill him. It was only a light kick. They only said that to fuel their hate. After what he said to me, even if he was dead, he was just another filth that needed to be wiped."

Arrows from behind hit the ground around them. The guards tried to use long bows between the gaps in the trees. But as they ran deeper into the woods, the gaps became narrower the thicker the forest became. The air had a different weight to it, making it harder to breath. The girls stopped to rest in a clearing.

Evalyn looked over. "Oh my god! Hun, your body. It is glowing."

Aluxes quickly moved her body around. There was a slight white light that emanated from her like a flame. She tried to put it out in reaction but there was no heat. Before any of them could say a word, two stones hit them. Vines popped out of the ground and Evalyn was pulled down and became entangled in them.

Aluxes was able to break free and stood ready to fight. "It is an elven snare spell."

A young female voice echoed. "Intruders of human realm. You trespassed, be executed." She looked up and saw five elf rangers in the trees. Like her, there was a light coming from them but it was green and much smaller.

Aluxes tightened her muscles. "Like hell you will." With a quick and powerful kick, the thin tree that one of the elves was perched on snapped and fell. The elf jumped to the next one.

She looked up at them. "We are not here to fight. Do not escalate this any further."

Some sat there, a little shocked by what they saw. The young female voice shouted again, "You magical properties which why you glowing. Mean half-human. We not hesitate to kill." Before she could finish speaking, an arrow hit Aluxes in the shoulder.

She dodged them the best she could and managed to block a few with her sword. Each time one of them hit her or grazed her, it made it harder to continually be successful.

"Aluxes, I know you can do better. Why do you not just attack them?" Evalyn struggled with the spell.

"If I moved off to the side to attack, the arrows would hit you. If you have not noticed they are aiming for that perfect skin you love so much." Another arrow hit her arm.

The elves stopped shooting and the sound was replaced by some minor chanting for a spell. "*Hogeauit geatay.*" For a brief moment, she could see a little pink-haired elf girl and a fireball forming.

Aluxes quickly cut the vines. "Shit, no time. Be useful and cover your head." She jumped on top of her. A small explosion with a loud noise echoed and flames swirled around the area where the girls were. The elves gathered near the fire and waited for it to burn out.

The little elf girl patted them on the back, "*Taygee.*" One bobbed his head around and pointed. He moved in closer for a better look. A sword popped out of the fire and stabbed him in the heart.

The flames died out, and Aluxes stood there in a fighting stance.

She was surrounded by a barrier that faded away. The elf girl gasped. "How have time cast protection spell?"

Without hesitation, she plunged her sword into another ranger. Before he could fall off her blade, she grabbed the other one that was trying to run off by the neck and a blue flamed burned him to ash.

The elf girl nocked an arrow. "She magic at will." When she drew back her bow, Aluxes charged at her. The elf let loose without aiming. The shot flew and bounced off the circlet around her neck. She swung her sword, cutting the bow in half.

"I am sorry, but you left me no choice." Aluxes grabbed her arm and twisted it behind her back and used her as a shield.

She pulled out the paper and placed it in front of her eyes. "I know you are the princess. You look just like Rose. Is this your brother's writing? Her dying wish was that I would find her daughter."

The elf stared at the note and shouted, "Auti!" They put down their weapons.

She turned her head and tried to look at Aluxes. "Old man Onyx had this. How you get hold of this?" Her hood fell off and exposed her face. She was a shorter version of Rose but full-blooded Elf. Her skin had a pinkish glow to it and her ears were twice as long.

"I was in the same unit as them before the fall. Old man Onyx handed this off to me." She pulled the arm tighter and said, "Your older sister said that I was the one who would find Samantha."

Aluxes let her go, and she turned to look at her. "Younger. I older sister." Her accent made it hard, but it was understood.

"Pure elves age differently. You rather tall for human. You no half-giant. What manner being are you?" When the elf looked at the aura closely, she could see gold and black specks in the base of the glow. She held her arm. "Broken, like twig to you."

Evalyn jumped into the conversation. "My daddy said you were younger." She stood there with a dumb grin on her face.

The elf stared at her with a blank expression. "You look like father. He dined with us. Only talked to my father. He based everything on looks. He a very brash oaf." The elves guided the girls towards an outpost made of thick red iron wood.

"So, what do we call you?" Aluxes asked.

She looked at her with a blank stare. "I refuse let you know real name. You use human name I picked, Myka," She gave a creepy smile. "You lower tongue probably not even pronounce name properly."

As they entered, there was a large hall with a small throne. Myka walked up to it and sat down. She wrapped her arm in a green bandage. "Because you here for sister, I grant you night rest and point you to go. Because kill my men that all I allow you."

Aluxes balled her hands into tight fists and ground her teeth. They had attacked first. But she kept her mouth in check and swallowed her anger.

She looked at her and was about to ask but was interrupted. "The auras. It common question first time one steps in elf territory. Original all creatures created by gods. Left marker on beings. These forests from the time so allows us to see marker. Each race has own marker, except humans. Humans magical essence internal. They have power to create and jealousy gods tried copy but still not fully copy mother creation."

Aluxes stood there and rubbed her circlet. "So, you are saying that the gods could not copy the mother earth who created humans. Their creations are flawed and the glow is their essence."

She took a deep breath and displayed that creepy smile again. She started to think it was a new concept for the elf. "When magic used, it drains. You see effects on half-dwarf. Powerful spell constant use for beings like us drain force, ages us quicker. Forest replenish some, not all making effect lessen cost. It why dwarfs created runes. They drain physically, not spiritually so you recover. Draw back a weaker spell."

She stood up and walked towards Aluxes, closely looking at her aura. "Half-breeds have same effect but never seen before. When you cast two spell, did not drain or effected slightest. It remind of Lord Azaroth. Aura is similar. Eternal." Her cheeks turned bright red.

As soon as his name was mentioned, both of their hearts skipped a beat. She stood there, rubbing her circlet. Her mind filled with the moment she first saw him.

Myka looked deep into Aluxes's eyes and tried to speak in proper human. "Err, umm… how err, did mmy sister die? Father err, never let see the body. Onyx refused umm, to tell me anything." Unlike before, she spoke slower and tried to pronounce every word without skipping the ones they had no concept of. Her tone was also softer and easier to understand.

Aluxes told her everything about the little girl and the cursed doll. When she reached the fall of the city, she was able to speak from her point of view because she never saw how Rose died but she speculated it was from the doll. It took an hour to explain it but time did not matter; Myka hung on every word. Evalyn, in the middle of the story, ran off into the guest room and cried.

Then she looked down and removed the bandage. "When elf die, soul go ring eternal. There short moment when powerful spell bring one back before absorbed into the stream to feed earth. Price is caster's life. Father willing make but soul not there. Was devoured. Same happen to dwarf. His soul devoured by black stuff."

Myka looked at her and patted her now healed arm. "She never met dwarf she never died. I hate her." She ran off.

Aluxes was guided to the guest room by a servant. It was a large room with silk curtains. More impressive was the bed that was as soft as a cloud. She had never been in such luxury. To not be spoiled with the new comfort, she claimed the sofa instead of the bed. Also, there was one bed and the thought of sharing with Evalyn made her gag.

"Oh my, goodness! Look at this. And I thought *I* was rich." Evalyn sat down on the bed and curled her hair with her finger. "I've been meaning to ask. I have noticed you've been angrier. Things you used to brush aside now make you attack without thinking. You also call people filthy humans from time to time. You are half-human."

Aluxes let out a slight scoff. "And what would a spoiled girl like you know of it? Being bullied and teased more than normal, Mildred would sing to me every night to calm me down. All that humans see when they look at me is my non-human half, and other races only see my human half." She sat there, not bothering to look at anything.

"I guess we owe that nun more praises. If it was not for her, we would have all been dead a long time ago. But you do know I never viewed you as anything else but Aluxes. And I am human. Same with your commander, the nun, and—" She stopped and laid down on the bed.

"Are you unable to finish anything you say?" She glanced over and noticed that Evalyn had fallen asleep. "I know you treated me like a friend but I am a monster, and monsters are not allowed to have friends."

Aluxes woke up covered in a cold sweat and screamed. "This place. Who was that?" She tried to close her eyes but had to open them again. Every time, she glimpsed a woman with pure black hair. It was so dark that not even the light was able to reflect off it.

She closed her eyes and tried to force them to stay shut. *All right bitch, let me see if I can get a good look at you.* Still, all she could see was the back of the girl's head. *To hell with this, might as well just stay awake.* Right before she opened her eyes, the girl turned around. A chill ran through her body and she was paralyzed. The skin was void of any real color, and the eyes were gold but the whites were black.

Aluxes sprang up and screamed. She looked from side to side but the fear still lingered. She got up and ran towards the mirror.

As she stared into the reflection, her eyes became as wide as door-knobs. Her hands covered her mouth to muffle her voice. *What the fuck? What the fuck? Is this a dream? Or a sick joke?* The person that was looking back at her was the girl in her vision. No, it was really her. Even the aura was black. Lightning flashed and the body jumped out and grabbed her. When the thunder followed, she was gone and everything went back to normal.

Aluxes's body trembled and her arms twitched. She was unable to make any sound. She smiled. *Was just a dream, might have been a mara.* She tried to laugh, but realized that on her neck was a wound in the shape of a hand.

After a while she did what she could to brush it off. *Dose this aura stuff ever stop? Maybe this is why I cannot sleep.*

She tried to close her eyes again, but someone was playing a lyre.

She walked out and looked over. On the balcony next to hers was Myka gazing at the moon. The song was the human version of the folk song to the Unnamed Goddess.

Aluxes stood there, trying to remember the words. "She came from the realm of divine, came down to save all mankind.

"Ended war that raged across the land, saved everyone with her mighty hand. Lived in the realm which broke the god king's ancient law. She paid the price, which ended her own life."

Myka stopped playing and looked at her. "Words not right, you switch some. But thank, was in tune." She gazed back at the moon. "Unknown Goddess never came to realm. We all perished. My father said so. I worship instead of elvish gods."

She held up a note. "Messenger bird came. You wait here. Lord Azaroth arrives." Her face turned red again as his named slipped from her mouth.

Aluxes looked at her and noticed that her aura had stopped. "Excuse me, how long will I keep glowing ? It is keeping me up."

Myka stared at her and giggled. "Only go until replenished spiritual energy. Maybe healing burns without you control it." She looked at her some more. "You uncomfortable in armor. No take it off sleep?"

Aluxes smirked a little. "For a while now, I've lived on the road. Most of the nights I would get attacked by a beast or the rare bandit during the night. I made it a habit to sleep battle-ready. I would admit, my old armor would have made it easier to sleep."

Myka gave her a blank stare. "You unknown breed, not human. You cannot sleep your bad blood. Maybe like dwarf, no deserve to born?"

"Why sister with dirty dwarf? It disgraceful." She tried to throw her lyre but stopped. "They filthy, greedy, foul mouthed. I not know why father try for peace with them." She looked down from the balcony and stood there silently.

Aluxes walked back inside. "I will try to nod off again. It seems you have more problems than I do."

The following morning, a horn blew to signal the arrival of Azaroth. Every elf soldier there stood in formation, ready to greet him.

The numbers were small. The gaps between the troops and impressions on the ground indicated that there use to be a lot more. It could be seen in their faces. These losses were recent.

The gate opened and Azaroth rode in. Behind him was a hooded figure wearing a white robe with a red trim. Evalyn and Aluxes stood next to a little throne that Myka was sitting on. The guest trotted straight through the courtyard till they reached the carpet.

When Azaroth dismounted and walked up to the lower part of the throne steps, Myka's little hands unsuccessfully hid her smile. The makeup she wore was unable to hide her flushed checks.

He kneeled in front of her. "Lady, I hope all is well for you. But I do bring news from your father." He stared at her in a way that made her smile fade. "Your father is angry with the tactics you have been using. This was once a flourishing trade post with the humans. He planned on it returning to the way it was." As Aluxes watched him, she noticed that his aura was white and gold, and like her, it also had no signs of stopping.

Myka crossed her arms and pouted. "*Auaaoumwa tihatul ousoo. Hummao, ellauit zihaga ooyeo tayzaga.*"

She looked around and took a deep breath. "Dwarfs greedy, foul, evil. They stop when enough will eventually *siegee.*"

He stood up and stared into her eyes. "Act your age, young princess. You may look young, but you're eight hundred. You know this will end badly."

She stared into his eyes. Her checks became red and she calmed herself down with short breaths. "*Meotah yale titul?*"

The other person removed her hood. It was a female elf that looked like an older Myka. Her mouth gaped open and her eyes widened. "*Moatay!*"

Her mother stared at her and scoffed. "I never cared for Rosaletta's mother. Her human stench ruined the palace, but I loved Rosaletta. This was originally her post, and you bring dishonor to it. Your latest antics got three of your rangers killed." She took a deep breath and looked around. "Today, I will be in charge of this post, and you shall accompany Lady Aluxes on her journey to find our kin, Samantha."

Myka stared at Azaroth but was unable to meet his eyes. *"Hagee elul sieual?"*

He smirked at her a little. "I think it would be a learning experience for you. You have never left the world of the elves, thinking other races are a burden."

Myka's mother clapped her hands and all the troops dispersed. She pulled off a box from her horse. She nudged her head at the girls. "Onyx forgot to give this back to you. It is a little heavy for me to carry." Aluxes ran up to her and opened it. Inside was her sword. "This was made very special, so do not lose it again."

She tried to swing it around but her armor restricted her movements more than she was used to. "I think I need to see an armorer."

As they began to get ready, Myka came out in a dark gray robe and a hood. "Trying to blend in? It does not help that you're a little short for a human. People might mistake you for a tall gnome." Aluxes chuckled.

Myka looked at them. "Better find her. Watched sister go mad over years thinking still alive. My heart broke."

They walked off but Azaroth stopped them. "I am not ready to go yet. I heard a rumor that Samantha is no longer in that town. She is in Valburg and I have heard some interesting rumors about that town."

Myka blushed. *"Tiailul yale ooleol mwagee aulatay?"* She placed her hand on her chin. *"El oula."*

He looked at her right in the eyes and coughed on his sleeve. "I have been telling you this for almost five hundread years. I will never marry you." He said under his breath and shook his head. His tone was unpleasant.

Aluxes noticed from the corner of her eye a painting of Rose from when she was younger. Under it were fresh flowers and some of the troops were adding more. A handful were dressed in the same attire as her and kissed the portrait.

She sighed a little. "I hope to someday find someone who can love me the way everyone loves Rose."

There was a tap on her shoulder and Azaroth cleared his throat.

"There is something I have here for you." He had an elf drop off a chest by her feet.

She kneeled and slowly opened it. Her original armor was inside, slightly modified for her new height. She looked at him but was unable to form any words. He winked at her and walked off. She stood there as if she was in a daydream. Her face became bright pink.

Chapter Fifteen

THE CURSED

They slowly trotted through an unmarked trail to avoid any towns that may border the forest. Everyone but Aluxes were riding on their own horses. Myka, having the biggest one, had to share, with her.

She growled. "There horse for you, why you take?" Aluxes just sat there with her usual frown.

Evalyn chuckled. "When we first started our trip, I asked about horses. She claimed we did not have the money nor the food to care for them. After looting some bandits along the way, I noticed that we had more than enough. I figured she does not know how to ride horses."

Aluxes snapped back. "The horses were marked."

She smiled. "That one bandit had five non-marked horses."

They exited the forest and stopped for a bit. Myka put on some makeup and her glasses. Her elvish features disappeared. Evalyn stared at her with a funny glare. "Blue eyes just look odd on you."

Myka snapped back. "Red hair ugly on *hummao*." Unbothered the comment, Evalyn just chuckled.

Aluxes looked at her arms. "Finally, the aura thing stopped." She sighed.

Evalyn rubbed her head as she stared at Aluxes. She gazed at Azaroth. "Have you ever seen anyone else like Aluxes?"

He smiled as they moved. "She is the only one of her kind that I have ever seen. Her father was a mighty knight."

Aluxes looked back at him. "You knew my father?" Her body was a little shaken when she asked.

He stared up and watched the clouds. "He was a good friend. A mighty warrior. He died very young. He never saw you after you were born. His death still bothers me today."

Evalyn tried to pry more. "What about her mother?"

His face became stern. His eyes narrowed and the tone of his voice was was no longer cheerful. "I never knew her personally. Only met her three times." He refused to say anymore.

Evalyn kept trying but he changed the topic, treating the questions the same way he acted with Myka when she flirted with him.

Aluxes rubbed her circlet. *He knows more. I need to know everything about my parents, but how do I get him to speak? Damn, he is too old and smart to fall for any tricks.*

She coughed a little. "So, Samantha. How old is—."

Before she could finish, Myka interrupted, "Twenty-two. Was two when taken. It twenty years."

They picked up the pace and rode the horses as fast as they could. They did not talk during the rest of the day. Night was coming when they saw a village not too far in the distance. The sign on it read *"Welcome to Huldenberg."*

They dismounted and tied their horses to a post. Evalyn looked at her map. "Valburg is the next town over. I hope it's a nice town."

Huldenberg was mostly a village that had more farms than buildings. Dust and mud covered everything. There was an odd smell in the air but there was a tavern.

They entered. People were cheering and singing. A drunkard slapped the wench on the ass as she served food and drinks. Azaroth walked up to the counter to request a room.

Aluxes stared at a table full of people singing. "Something seems off. My neck burns like mad. Four hells, I wish I could remove the blasted thing at times." She sniffed the air. "What is that foul smell?"

She looked at Azaroth and for a second, one of his eyes was gold-colored like hers.

Myka gazed around. "Place is off."

Evalyn grabbed her by the shoulder. "Just act normally, and let's go to our room." Her grip became a little tighter. She did not take her eyes off the dining area.

Azaroth talked quietly, "I will stay with the horses. Evalyn, you know what is going on." She nodded and guided them up some stairs. Aluxes was still staring at his green eyes.

When they entered their room, Evalyn pushed them in and locked the door. "Do not fall asleep."

Aluxes looked at her. "What is it now? It seems a bit off but there's nothing out of the ordinary." Myka nodded as to agree with her.

Evalyn snapped back, "You always think I am dumb. There are times you are right about things. But this time, please listen. It is a trap." She grabbed her whip. "Vampires. Every single one of them."

Without time to process what she had said, a vampire jumped through the window. Evalyn quickly hit him with her whip. The metal burned him, and he turned into ashes instantly.

Myka stood there stunned. "How you know?"

She looked at them both like they were stupid. "My father took me on some of his hunts. Remember, he was famous for killing the vampire king."

Aluxes drew her sword and stabbed it threw the door, impaling another vampire. "I thought your dad killed them all?" she said in a stern tone.

Evalyn looked out the window. "He always assumed he missed a few, or that there was another vampire lord in hiding." She could see a few dozen running off. "We must help Azaroth. Most of them are heading towards him."

As she turned around, a vampire jumped through the window, knocking her over. He tried to bite her but Myka was able to put a bolt into his heart. He burned to ashes before he hit the ground.

Evalyn stood up. "Thanks, but what happened to your bow?"

Myka grunted a little. "Not hide under robe. Crossbow better for. Reloading getting on nerves." She tried to load another but failed because of the panic.

Aluxes walked up to the door and placed her ear against it. There was the sound of a dozen vampires on the other side scratching at it, slowly wearing out the wood. She looked back at Evalyn. "I am going to put a barrier on the wall." She grabbed Myka and jumped to the other side of the bed.

"What's problem. Just barrier spell." She grunted as she talked.

Evalyn covered their heads with the blanket. "Aluxes's spells are very powerful but not stable, so they Explode at times." Before Myka could respond, Aluxes placed her hand on the door and grunted a little, causing the wall to burst. Killing some vampires and making the rest scatter.

Myka peeked out. "Why no cast holy ward or protection spell?"

Without looking at her, Aluxes calmly replied. "I am limited to what I can touch. Also it is very short-lived. There is also a small chance I could kill you with the spell. I have very little control on my energy flow."

Evalyn chuckled. "When we were learning the healing spell on mice, Aluxes managed to make the mouse explode." Myka stood there staring at her.

They rushed down the stairs, killing vampires along the way. They were able to make it to the horses. Azaroth, with great skill, was picking them off with ease. It made them look defenseless at how easily they fell to his blade. One of the horses let out a horrific noise as a group of vampires ate it.

Azaroth looked around. "Well, it was bound to happen." They were surrounded and outnumbered thirty to one. He backed up a little towards the girls. "I can take out a lot, but this many means they are trying to wear us out."

Than the vampires burst into ashes. Small bolts flew through the air, each shot hitting their vitals. They turned around and saw an old person with a repeating crossbow. The stranger, with a woman's voice, shouted "Duck!" and tossed a flask. There was an explosion of light and all the vampires that looked into it died. The group took care of the ones that covered their eyes.

Evalyn smiled. "Thank you, old sir."

The old person scoffed at her. "I am not a man. I am a girl." She had a youthful but drained voice.

"Thank you, old ma'am?" She stood there with her finger on her chin.

"I am not old, I am twenty-two." She took off her helmet which covered most of her face. Her skin wrinkled and had the shape of an old person who was burned out on life, and her hair was faded brown, almost gray. She looked to be in her fifties and her ears were slightly pointed like an elf, but she was as tall as a normal human girl at five-two.

Aluxes walked up to her. "I thank you. We were headed towards the city Valburg—"

The girl stopped her. "Dead, well dead-ish. Some of these people came from there. They are all vampires." She reloaded her crossbow, checking each bolt to make sure nothing was wrong with them.

Aluxes, not realizing she was speaking out loud, said, "Fuck's sake. I hope Samantha was not in there."

The girl walked around trying to see if there were more bolts. "Well, maybe I can help you out. I am really good at finding people. My name is also Samantha. What does she look like?"

Everyone, even Azaroth who had seen it all, stood there not knowing what to say or do. While they were trying to find their words, there was clapping behind them. From the shadows stepped out a man. He was seven feet tall with skin that looked decayed. His hair was a solid white—not an old person white but the kind that is dignified. When he opened his eyes, they were a golden color like Aluxes's but bolder.

When he spoke, his voice had a divine yet a little out of tune sound. "Well done, you have finally found me my Samantha. I see that you also saved some rabbits." He talked with such confidence yet he bantered like his mind was gone. "My love, Etharia. This is what I get for loving you. I am punished." He held his head as he ranted.

Evalyn looked at him. "My father never mentioned a vampire like you before."

Samantha quickly answered. "He is the first, the original. He has been hiding. but now he has decided to rebuild his kingdom."

The vampire looked at them. "I'm rebuilding nothing, I need to feed and this is the result," he rambled. "I consume to create and create to consume. I am cursed by my gift."

Azaroth tried to make a surprise attack as he bantered, but the vampire caught him and threw him to the ground. "Rabbits should know their place."

Samantha took a few shots, but the bolts bounced off him like they were paper. Evalyn hit him with her whip but he did not even notice. Aluxes moved in for an attack and he looked right at her.

She stopped in her tracks. His eyes glared as he smiled with his fangs bearing their full glory. "Etharia you have come back to me, my love. You smell of her and look of her, but you also smell of him. You dare try to trick me. I must think of what you are." He walked back into the shadows and disappeared. Aluxes stood there with her head slightly tilted.

Samantha ran to the area where he'd vanished. "Shit! He got away." She checked her bolts that bounced off. They were now all useless.

She fell to her knees and cried, "Shit, I thought I had him. All this time, I thought these would work."

"*El aulatay hasie zati!*" Myka ran towards Azaroth who still was on the ground after he had been thrown away like a rag doll.

Aluxes walked over to him and scoffed. "You will heal. Now tell me, what do you know about him? You've been alive for a while now. You must know something."

He looked at her and chuckled. "I never got around to asking who he was. I have an idea but he does not seem to be what I've been told. My father once told me of a dark lord who was consumed with devouring. He did not say much. When I was a small boy, I only saw him when one of the Fallen tried to escape from the Abyss. I never knew his name, but I do remember that face."

Samantha shouted, "He is a monster and nothing more!" She dropped her crossbow and cried, "He kidnapped me for fifteen years. He was feeding off my life energy and making me look this way. He kept promising that I would be allowed to see my family."

Myka placed a hand on her shoulder. "Escaped five years ago. Why no see family?"

Samantha tightly shut her eyes and made a fist. "Looking like this? I need to kill him to get what he took from me."

She looked at Azaroth. "What are you? I can see past your illusions." She tried to calm herself. "You do not look like him but there is something about you two."

He chuckled. "I am assuming it is part of the gifted curse from him." He stood back up with his arm fully healed. "I will answer your question after we get him."

Samantha looked at Aluxes a little closely. "What are you?" Aluxes took a few steps back. "That is what I am trying to find out. That vampire seems to have a clue."

Samantha paused. "His name is Turiacus. I am not sure he can be of any help. His mind seems to be gone. At most he bellows out something but then rambles about someone named Etharia."

Azaroth grabbed her arm. "You sure his name is Turiacus?"

She looked at him. "Yeah, why?"

"You know where his castle is?"

She quickly moved her arm out of his hand. "Yeah, but he abandoned it. That's how I was able to escape."

He grabbed her shoulders. "Take me there now!"

They tried to ready their horses when Samantha stopped them. "Those are large beasts with blood. They will attract more vampires. It is not far from here. Maybe three days at most." Aluxes smiled as she stretched her legs.

As they were walking, Evalyn ran up to Aluxes. "Why did we not tell her?" She looked at the back of Samantha's head. "We know it's her, right?"

Myka interrupted. "We tell her now, will make things worse. She would storm off, get killed because not thinking clear."

Aluxes stayed silent. Her mind kept on flashing back to Turiacus. Over and over, she tried to tear apart every word to see if there was a single hint as to what she was.

She looked at Samantha and thought about what she had said to Azaroth. "That she can see what none of us can?" she whispered to herself.

Evelyn nudged her shoulder. "If your father and him were good friends, he would have known more about his wife."

Aluxes walked a little slower. She rubbed her circlet differently than before. She wondered how it got damaged. Under her finger, there was a tiny dent.

Myka overheard Evelyn. "He has rules. He messenger for immortals. Maybe not allowed tell you."

Azaroth turned his head. "They are not immortal and yes, I can hear you."

Evelyn walked closer to him. "So, want to tell us about Turiacus?"

He looked forward and rubbed the back of his head. "History books have it wrong. There was no war between gods and demons. It was a civil war between gods. Eventually, they divided between gods and devils. Demons are just like angels—creations made to do their bidding. The war ended when a new group started to form among the gods and the devils called them the Fallen. They were defeated and banished into the Abyss. When I was still very young, the king of the Fallen tried to escape. I only got to fight the lower monsters, but a rumor was that a man named Turiacus defeated them along with the Unnamed Goddess." He looked right at Aluxes. "I think he knows who the doll is and how to beat it. I believe the doll is a Fallen that went into hiding." His mind flashed back to the girl in the city. "That is why I cried when I saw the little girl. She was touched by a Fallen, just like my sister. It must have been a very slow and painful death and she must have suffered the entire time."

Chapter Sixteen

THE CURSED GOD

After a few days of travel, they could see a castle in the distance. It was not large but it was decent-sized. It had moss growing all around it and some parts were in shambles as if it were abandoned.

Samantha stretched her arms out to stop everyone. "He is here. I can feel him." She looked back at them. "He tends to not have vampires near him. He is disgusted by them. But he does sometimes have them as guards along the tree line." They slowly moved closer to the castle, and piano notes echoed from inside.

Evalyn smirked. "My dad said it is normal for higher vamps to play music. I am glad he was right about this."

They walked into the main reception area without running into any problems. There, in the background, they could see Turiacus stroking the notes with his eyes closed.

Samantha whispered. "He only plays when he is worried about something." Next to the piano was a nal who was bound by a magical rope.

Turiacus stopped playing. "Etharia, you have returned to me. My love, I can smell thee." He turned around. "Oh, my little Samantha. You have come home. Are you ready to thank me yet?"

She grabbed a glass flask and threw it at him. "You can burn in hell." As it hit him, a bright light came out. It was like looking into the sun. Everyone moaned in pain. The nal screamed as it burned some of his skin. The light dissipated and Turiacus stood there unaffected.

He sighed in a loving manner. "My Samantha, you have grown strong. You have learned a lot." He rambled again, "They have returned. This is bad. Can you not see that they are back? What are the gods doing?" He walked up to the nal and kicked it.

Myka stared at it. "What is beast? Never seen it."

Aluxes, without blinking, said, "It is a beast from the Abyss. They devour everything."

Turiacus gazed at her. "Etharia, this is a bad omen." He looked at her some more. "You are not her. You smell of that man. He took her heart from me."

Azaroth walked a little closer. "Turiacus, I've heard your name before, when the Fallen tried to escape. Is this a sign that they are trying again?"

He looked at him and clinched his fist. "Boy! Do you not know a thing? You're a useless god. An unimportant devil. Do I have to explain it to you? The Fallen cannot control these. That boy was just a puppet, not even worthy of being considered a king. Only I can build an army to fight it. The other gods do nothing." In the blink of an eye. He was in front of Azaroth, and he uppercut him. He flew twenty feet in the air.

Evalyn tried to hit him again with her whip but he grabbed it with his hand. "Little girl, this was made for vampires, and other undead, but not for me."

She replied, "It killed the vampire king, so it can kill you."

Turiacus pulled her toward him and grabbed her by the neck. "He was my son. You smell of your father. I am not a vampire. I am a god!" He tossed her off to the side and sent her flying into the wall. She slammed against it, coughing up some blood and then fell the floor.

Samantha tried to sneak behind him and put a stake through his heart, but all she managed to do was put a hole in his shirt. "Did you go see your mother?" He smiled at her. "My dear Samantha, I allowed you to escape to find her. I hope it was a joyful reunion."

She cried out, "How can I face her looking like this?"

His smile faded. "Oh, I am sorry, my dear. I did not know. But your mother died. She started a war trying to find you. Well, I guess it is as it should be."

Samantha fell to her knees crying, "You're lying!"

He sniffed at Myka. "She smells of your mother. Probably her sister. I assume she was here to find you. Poor little Samantha, your entire family is dead. Now give up this dream and return to me."

He raised his hand and caught Aluxes's blade before she could sneak attack. "You smell and look of her. But you're that mutt that she bore. You are his seed, Reinhard." He grabbed her by the neck with his other hand. "I killed your father so she would love me."

He let go of her neck but still held her blade. She clinched her teeth and put all her might into pushing the sword, cutting his hand.

He quickly let go. "This is the gods' metal. It must be you, Etharia. See this." He stood next to the nal. "These beasts you remember these, Etharia? She is back. We must attack before she finds herself." He kicked the nals head and it popped like a tomato.

"Did you also kill my mother?" she yelled at the top of her lungs.

He looked at her and gasped. "Etharia dead? Oh, no, no, my love. Without her, Agrona will devour all. I never would have imagined my love could die. I killed your father because she was my love first. I became cursed for her. I was not always like this. I created flowers, whales, and healing magic. I was one of the few gods who were able to create more than one thing."

Azaroth stabbed him in the chest and blood poured to the ground. As it dripped the moss caught on fire as it touched it.

Turiacus looked at him. "Silly boy, only Agrona can kill me." He grabbed him and slammed him to the floor. He then pulled the sword out and stabbed Azaroth through the stomach and pinned him down. Turiacus rapidly healed his wound.

Myka sneaked over to Samantha. "Come with, you in no condition to fight."

She looked at her with tears in her eyes. "Is it true?" Myka grabbed her and pulled her away from the fight. "Yes, I your aunt. Now got think how to—." Right in front of her, Turiacus stood there, blocking the exit with his body.

He smiled, "Samantha is mine, little bunny. Now begone." He slapped Myka across the face and knocked her out.

Aluxes leaped towards him and tried to swing but was stopped in the air. His hand was glowing, and she was unable to move.

He took a closer look of her neck. "That circlet has me wondering about you. It appears to also be damaged." He reached over and rubbed it. "An arrow must have hit it and made a small crack."

He slowly moved his hand down her body to the red linen tied to her sword. "You do know that there is a dragon scale on your sword?" He reached up and grabbed the circlet with both of his hands and tried to pull it apart.

He grunted and moaned as he struggled. "This has me intrigued as to why this item is on such a little girl."

Azaroth tried shouting at him to stop, but each time he shouted; it made him pull harder, till a loud cracking sound echoed with a bright blinding light.

Turiacus screamed in pain. Aluxes had cut off his arm. The spell he'd casted gave out and she landed on the ground. Her fall was a slow glide as if she were a feather. Black and white auras formed around her. She slowly swayed from side to side. Her eyes were blank and her drunken smile sent shivers through everyone. The energy around her made a strange afterimage of her as she moved.

Turiacus looked at her and held his hand up in praise. "You are Etharia, in body and soul. My love, I do not need Samantha anymore. You have returned to me."

She walked towards him and lifted her foot up and kicked him in the chest. Though her motions were slow, it caused him to fly through a wall and roll like a tumbleweed on the other side. The crack slowly grew bigger and the aura that came out of her grew. Her smile filled her face. Drunk with her own power, she started to giggle.

As Evalyn looked at her, she had a flashback of the black aura that had come from the doll. Except for the size, it was almost the same.

Turiacus gazed up. "I see. So that's why it was placed on you. You cannot control her power." He stood up and wings came out of his back. They were not made of flesh or feather but of the raw energy of golden light.

He flew away and waved. "I will see you again, my love. My Samantha."

The girls surrounded Aluxes. Myka tried to talk to her. "Hey, we won. Let stop now." Samantha tackled Myka as Aluxes's sword flew over where she was standing. Her sword embedded itself into a wall.

Azaroth pulled the sword out of his gut and rushed to grab Evalyn. He yanked her down as Aluxes's fist appeared right where her head had been.

He shouted, "She has no control. We have to subdue her!" Evalyn was breathing frantically. "What's wrong with her? Where did all this power come from?"

He grabbed her arm to calm her. "The circlet was forged by Sirenisteen. It was a dampener created to hide her power as she traveled the mortal world. I was gifted it at the request of Reinhard for his daughter. Aluxes's human half is unable to contain her mother's half."

Samantha tossed another flask of sunlight. When it set off, Myka used Samantha's repeating crossbow to hit Aluxes's arms and legs. Evalyn took a chance at whipping Aluxes's legs, and pulled her to the ground. Azaroth ran over and placed his hands on her. Vines and roots come out and wrapped around her. He signaled everyone to hold her down.

He moved his hands over the crack and chanted a language they'd never heard. As it started repairing, Aluxes grew weaker, eventually passing out when it was fully repaired.

Samantha, not breaking eye contact, asked, "What in the hell was that?" He tried to avoid answering her but everyone crowded him.

There was a small crack in his eye. He took out a thin film that covered his eye. It was a bright crimson red. He stood there and looked at them, trying to find his words as they kept pelting him with more questions.

He cleared his throat. "She has been cursed by Grimshaw. It was passed from her mother."

He sat down and took a deep breath. "Her mother was a homunculus created by the gods as a weapon. She started to turn on her creators and faked her own death to hide. Aluxes is a half-human half-magical creation," He looked at her as she slept. "When she was born, they found out that Etharia was still alive and destroyed the entire village just to kill her. Aluxes survived because one of the gods had a vision about her importance in the outcome of their survival. Sirenisteen gave me that circlet so her powers would not become uncontrollable. The village was full of those unwanted by the gods who were tired and wanted to live a simple life."

He looked off to the side and rubbed his nose. "Her father and I were originally sent there to kill her. But they fell in love and I kept it a secret." Everyone was sitting there dumbfounded, not knowing how to react.

"Do not tell her this, because her life may become at risk if she knows." He got on his knees and begged.

They gathered their stuff and headed out. Azaroth was tasked with carrying Aluxes. They did not say a word on the trip. They walked for four days till they reached the town where they'd left the horses. They were drained by vampires.

Evalyn broke the silence. "How come you and Rose are sisters from different mothers? I also noticed that your brother has a few wives as well."

Myka looked at her, a little annoyed. "You know nothing about elves? Female outnumber men fifteen to one. We not know why more girls born. They just are." She found something to sit on. "Depending on status, lowest have two wives, and highest have seven. This because female only fertile two to three times a year, with low chance fertilization."

She looked at Samantha. "That why lot of female elves take liking to human men. Human men tend take single wife. Because Rose half-elf, she reproduce like human."

Samantha, barely able to speak, cleared her throat. "How did they die?"

Myka looked at her. "Your father, sisters, brothers, and aunt died day you taken. Group of dark elves attacked. Thought you also died. Rosaletta refused, convinced uncle find you."

A tear fell from Samantha's eye. "She did not look for me herself?"

Myka took a deep breath. "She sorrowed months before would even leave house. She had Uncle Verus train her to fight. She looked for you when war broke out."

Samantha stared at her hands. "I caused a war? Did she die in this—"

Evalyn stopped her. "No, she died in a much worse way." She told her about the day the Holy City fell. "She remarried. Your stepfathers brother would very much love to see you. He guards her grave."

Samantha looked at her. "She remarried?"

Evalyn sighed. "The day she died."

She hugged her, crying. "I need to see her."

Azaroth came back with a handcart that he had found to move Aluxes, who was still unconscious.

Samantha wiped away her tears and checked her vitals. "How long do you think she will be out?"

He pondered a little. "She expended a lot of power, so I will say maybe a month."

Samantha, still puffed in the face from crying, moved her lips near Azaroth's ear. "I know you were lying."

He scoffed a little. "Of course you would know. What gave it away?"

She took a step back. "I read two of the books of—"

He quickly placed his hand over her mouth and looked up into the sky. He slowly lowered his head. "The gods do not watch us, but they do listen for key words. That name is one of them. I wish I could tell you the truth but it is not safe here. The Watcher and the Seer have their sight on us right now."

Samantha was a little confused. "How do you know?"

He looked back up into the sky. "Mother and Father always watch me."

Deep in Aluxes's mind, she was dreaming. She was standing in a dead world with ashes that fell from the sky. Volcanos were erupting in the background. In front of her was that same girl that looked like her. They stood there, staring into each other's eyes, barely ten feet away.

Chapter Seventeen

AN EMBER OF DARKNESS

The eyes deadlocked on each other, not blinking or budging. Both had the same angry expression on their faces. It was as if she was looking in a mirror of a different version of herself.

Before she could ask, it replied as if she knew her question, "I am you." Her voice had an echo about it and it lacked emotion. They stood there staring. The figure spoke again, "I am you; I am what you are."

Aluxes looked around at the barren wasteland. "What is this place?"

The dark one responded without hesitation. "This is the mortal realm. It is what we make it." She smiled. "It is what it will be." When she grinned, it could be seen that her teeth were black, and her mouth was full of a dark liquid.

Aluxes looked right into her eyes. "I do not understand." Dark replied, "Your birth was already written in the fabric of time. I am what you could have been if your mother made a different choice." She walked closer like a mindless zombie with each step. "I am what you still can become. I am deep in your heart. I am what you should become."

She stopped when their noses touched. "Deep inside you know I am there. The darkness to consume. The being in the shadow in your heart. I am what you need to be to make your wish happen." Aluxes tried to take a step back but tripped and fell on her butt.

Dark kept talking and hunched over to get her face closer. "The gods will die and you will help. All will be consumed in the Abyss,. Even the Fallen will fall to nothing. When Agrona makes you the deal, take it."

Dark stood straight up and turned around. She looked back at Aluxes who was still sitting there, but now her body trembled uncontrollablly. "I must go. She needs me. She beckons for me. It can only be done by me, or I must kill her. Those are the only two choices you have. This world or the world as it is." She walked towards the base of a cliff.

On the top, staring over the edge was a tall woman standing. She was taller than Aluxes. She looked almost the same as Dark but her skin was darker and more lifeless. Her clothing was pitch black. It was like it was eating the light around. She had huge black wings that flapped out. There was a black Aura irradiating off her body. It covered much of the view and was solid enough to make it unable to be seen through. She stared at Aluxes with a look of hatred on her face.

She started to sway from side to side. Each motion left a little bit of an afterimage. As Aluxes looked at her, she saw that there was a pit in her soul, as if something were telling her that was the end of everything. Dark stood at the base of the cliff and this woman jumped down. The dust that lifted up as she landed was consumed by the body of this creature. She grabbed Dark Aluxes and they flew off.

Before they left, Aluxes swore she heard Dark say, "This is Agrona." It was hard to understand over the sound of the wings as they flapped.

After they were out of sight, the sun turned red, and the sky was the color of blood. The sun rotated around and became an eye that was looking at her. She tried to run from it but the ground became liquid.

She began to sink. She tried to push down with her hands to stop herself but there was nothing solid, only liquid. She lifted her hands to see what it was—blood. The ground had turned into an ocean of blood.

She looked up at the sun as she slowly sank more. There was loud breathing that echoed in the sky. The red sun grew brighter while it slowly started to shrink. Eventually, it disappeared.

The sky became pitch black. She could not see a thing as she slowly sank further into the ocean of blood. In a panic, she started to frantically move but it made her sink faster. Not being able to tell how deep it was or if there was something to grab onto, she stretched her arms out in every direction but she still sank.

She screamed and cried as more panic overtook her. She begged for help as the blood reached her chin. It was thick and heavy. She could no longer raiser her arms.

She softly said, "Mommy, please save me, Mommy. I promise I will be a good girl, Mommy." She was silenced by the blood that filled her mouth, and she became fully submerged.

Images ran threw her mind. Memories that were locked deep inside her. She saw her mother rocking the crib gently. Her voice was soft. "My baby, the only creation I am able to make." Her smile made the emptiness in Aluxes disappear. Her blue hair was bright as the light shined behind her head. Her eyes a bold gold.

Agrona's face appeared next to her mother's. The two stood side by side, identical except for the obvious. The length of their hair, height, shape of the face, and even the nose were the same.

Her mother hummed as the other face slowly vanished. She then sang as she tucked Aluxes in, "My legend will be spread across the land. I ended war with my own hand. When the Darkness tried to consume the world, I ended it with my mighty sword." She kissed her forehead. "My precious creation, whatever may happen, I am glad that I was able to have you in my life. Your father and I have truly been blessed."

There was a bright light in front of her and all her fears vanished. The light was warm and yellow. Dark Aluxes's face appeared in front of her and shouted, "Get up!"

She opened her eyes to see an old dwarf in front of her, too close for comfort. She screamed a little and pushed him. He hit the side of the boat and almost fell over.

She sat up and looked around. Samantha, Myka, Evalyn, and Onyx stood there watching her. For the most part they seemed fine. Azaroth was beside her with a bloodied bandage wrapped around his chest.

She placed her hand on him, "What happened?"

Samantha, a little annoyed, looked at her. "Well, my princess. You were out for almost two weeks. We almost died trying to save you."

Onyx stumbled back up. He had replaced his missing leg with a fake leg. He chuckled a little. "For good guys, we be good at getting our arses kicked." He slowly staggered to a seat. "This elven metal leg be hard on boats."

Aluxes looked at Azaroth. "What happened to him?"

Onyx scooted his seat closer to her. "Well, remember that man that kept using dragon magic? Well, he be try to kill ya. And this lad here, well, he took the hit."

Myka teared up and cried. "He got bitten for you. How dare you make him do that." Aluxes, still a little confused, sat there unable to talk.

Evalyn walked up and sat next to her. "I should tell you what happened."

Chapter Eighteen

DRAGON'S SCALE

*T*hey slowly walked the main road. Every few hours, they would rotate as to who would pull the cart that had Aluxes in it. As they approached the large grave city, the very sight of the sheer numbers of graves still shocked them to their very core. They made it to the steps in the center and painfully walked up the hill.

When they reached the top, Onyx was prepared for them. He had some small cups with tea already made for them. He smiled as they collapsed and offered his bed for any of them to rest on. Samantha stood there staring at the memorial for Rosaletta and her husband.

"Aye, ya look just like her. A wee bit older." He tried to say more but had to clear his throat. "I have seen this curse before. Orc shaman drained the life force of his enemies. It caused them to age rapidly while it renewed the shaman." He lunged out of his wheelchair and hugged her. "I am glad ya be found, lass. It was me brother's wish."

Samantha looked at Myka. "Yes, filthy creature your uncle."

Onyx sat back down and sniffed himself. "I bathed I think?"

Samantha looked around. "So, you buried all these people?"

He chuckled. "Nah, most of graves be empty. Other territories had records of relatives who lived here. All races gathered for the last time to make this place what it be." He wheeled himself to Rose's grave. "Ya grandfather, the high king, buried your mother and stepfather here to be a memory. Their bodies be here but sadly, probably not much left."

He looked over at Lugathar's grave. "All I could find of her was a wee head." He wheeled to the gravestone and brushed off some dust.

Azaroth rushed to the steps and looked over to the edge of the grave site. In the distance, a tall man could be seen. His body started to shake. "Aeron."

Evalyn and Onyx panicked a little as he walked towards them. Myka and Samantha had never seen him before, but his intent to kill gave off an odd aura that terrified them down to their core.

He was still some distance away, but when he said, "Here, chick, chick, chick." like he was calling out to chickens, they could feel his deep voice shake their bones.

He stopped halfway. "Give me what is mine and I shall be on my way." Samantha looked at the linen tied to Aluxes's sword and remembered Turiacus saying it was a dragon's scale.

Myka rushed for it when Samantha grabbed her. "Let go, I your aunt. I trying save us." She was frantically reaching for it.

Azaroth shouted at her without turning his gaze from Aeron, "He will kill all life if we give him that scale." She stopped.

Samantha calmly tried to talk to her. "When monsters like that want something, it means it is a bad idea to let them have it."

Myka grabbed her crossbow. "Should never left fort." She fired off a bolt, hitting him in the mouth.

Aeron pulled it out with a smile. "I will give you the respect and fight you away from this place. But if you take too long, I will blow up this entire grave before you can even blink, children."

Azaroth slowly walked towards him, followed by Samantha. Myka tried to stop them. "It suicide, he a real monster. He more a threat than Turiacus."

Samantha looked at her with some disappointment. "If we run, we will die. If we fight, we might die. I lived my entire life with a monster. Running only makes them stronger in here." She pointed to Myka's heart and walked off.

Evalyn stood there, tears rolling from her eyes. "I am utterly useless. Nothing I do can even hurt him. Aluxes, what do I do?"

Azaroth grabbed Samantha's shoulder. "We do have a small chance with him. Unlike Turiacus, who is a being that lost his mind, making him unpredictable. Aeron is a devil, which means a dark god. He was trapped in a human body by his own kind out of fear. The human part has limitations. If he gets his scale back, he will regain his true form." Samantha checked her repeating crossbow and made sure it was loaded.

They approached Aeron. He smiled with excitement in his eyes. "Pup, I am glad to see a whelp like you is willing to fight me. That mutt of girl is also brave. That smell on her, I know it." He sniffed in so much air that she could feel the difference in the pressure around her. "Turiacus, I have not seen him in thousands of years."

Samantha unloaded her magazine into him, each piercing a vital spot. They slowly ejected from his skin as he healed. "If I was a normal mortal, that would have killed." Before he could finish talking, Azaroth cut off his arm with his sword.

Aeron grabbed him by the head and slammed him into the ground. He walked over and picked up his severed arm and reattached it. Samantha tossed a flask—a blinding light burned his eyes as he screamed. Azaroth stabbed him in the stomach and pulled it upwards, cutting him open, and spilling his guts out.

Aeron smiled. His hand turned into a small dragon claw, and he punched Azaroth, forcing his body to fly a good distance. He put his insides back and healed.

"Silly, mortals. I am a true god. You cannot kill me so easily." Samantha lunged in, stabbing him in the throat with a dagger. She pushed a small button in the handle and oil covered the blade. She took her finger off the button and a spark ignited the oil, catching his face on fire.

He laughed demonically. "Silly pup, this attack was made to fight strong vampires. I am a dragon, I am living fire." He inhaled, consuming the flames. He tried to claw off her face but she was quicker at dodging. He closed the distance but became covered in roots that came from the ground.

Myka tried to chant a spell. "*Satay hogeauit geemwa.*" The clouds darkened above and a lightning bolt crashed into him.

After the dust cleared, he stood there with a large grin, healing from his wounds. "That actually hurt. Allow me to return the favor." He pulled out another quill from his hair and threw it, impaling Myka's leg. He grabbed Samantha who was trying to stab him in the back and tossed her aside like trash.

He chuckled when Azaroth stabbed him in the back. "Boy, I am growing weary of this game." Large wings protruded from his shoulder blades, knocking Azaroth to the ground. He flew off towards Aluxes. Azaroth ran as fast as he could to catch up.

Aeron landed on the top step. "Woman! Fetch me my scale." He looked at Evalyn who was gripping her whip as tightly as she could. She let out a scream as she entangled his legs.

The metal glowed and burned him. "You bitch, where did you get that steel?" He fell over, holding his leg.

Azaroth caught up and tried to cut off Aeron's head. Aeron bore the pain, grabbed the whip, and pulled Evalyn into Azaroth. He quickly untangled his legs and made his way towards Aluxes. Onyx tried to stop him by ramming into him, but all Aeron did was push him down the steps. He pulled out another quill and was about stab Aluxes when he stopped.

He looked at her unconscious body. "I do not find honor in killing you like this. But it is my master's wish." He raised the quill for the kill, but Azaroth jumped in the way and got stabbed in the arm. Azaroth's eyes glowed red as he grabbed Aeron by the neck.

Aeron smiled. "This is what a half-breed mutt is able to do. I will finish you off first then." Azaroth broke his neck and tossed him aside like a ragged doll. Before he hit the ground, a small fireball smashed into him and exploded. The explosion destroyed some of the gravestones and made a decent-sized hole in the ground.

His neck cracked and it slowly healed. The girls quickly grabbed Aluxes and Onyx and tried to run. Azaroth collapsed from blood loss,

Evalyn stopped and removed his armor. His chest was covered in wounds, and they were not healing fast enough.

She looked at them. "Will he be able to die from this? I thought gods were immortal."

Samantha poured some medicine over his body to help stop the bleeding. "If that was true, why are the books full of gods dying?" With no time to bandage him, they propped him up so Evalyn could move him while Samantha carried Aluxes.

Aeron jumped into the air. Large twelve-foot wings popped from his back and propelled him higher into the air. He opened his mouth. Air around him grew thin as he inhaled, and a ball of fire formed.

Samantha looked back. "He is about to breathe fire."

The girls tried to move as fast as they could, but there was no cover. There was nothing they could do but hope he would miss. *Woosh.* The sound could be heard as hundreds of arrows flew through the sky, hitting him. Most of them found their target but were still not enough to make him fall from the sky. He gently lowered to the ground as his wings retracted. An elven army stood at the edge of the graveyard.

Myka excitedly shouted, *"Moatay!"* as she ran towards the army while Aeron was still pulling out arrows.

Myka's mother was wearing full-plated armor and helmet. "This is a real monster you have found."

She looked at Samantha. "You look just like your mother." The soldiers quickly tossed them onto a wagon.

Myka cried to her, *"Moatay, yale elul titul."* More arrows let loose, keeping Aeron busy.

Her mother looked at her. *"Yeosieol, taygee ya aulatay. Iayati hogeauit geetul."*

Myka's eyes watered up as the driver of the wagon whipped the horses to speed up faster. In the back, a huge dragons head could be seen. Arrows bounced off his scales. His gills on the side lit up as air flowed through them. He opened his mouth and it glowed bright red. The girls in the wagon covered their heads when a loud explosion echoed.

A giant mushroom-shaped cloud could be seen. Body parts rained down. More arrows flew off as Aeron returned to his normal human form. They were at a distance where all they could see were shadows of people being killed. Myka cried as in front of her was her mother's arm with her royal ring on the finger.

She looked at the linen on Aluxes's sword. Everyone stopped her from grabbing it. "No worth it keeping safe. Just give him, he stop."

Azaroth held her hand while Samantha bandaged him up. "If we give him that scale, he will return to his godly form. He was a devil that is now a Fallen. Legends say he is as big as a mountain. My dear Yeosieol, if he gets that, all life is doomed."

The top of a tree crashed down on the path. The driver barely dodged it, swerving so fast that they flew out of the wagon. Aeron's head was in dragon form, about to bite Aluxes. Azaroth tried to body slam him but was slightly off. He managed to knock him out of the way, but Aeron whipped his head to bite Azaroth's chest. He held on but barely. His body was slightly disfigured. More arrows rained down on him and he was forced to drop Azaroth. He quickly ran off into the woods.

They arrived at a port owned by the elves. The driver helped them board the ship. "You be taken to port in Northern Amazonia. Your father still has friends in the dwarven kingdom. You be safe there. *Iyati*."

The ship was a small vessel but was made for speed. It was a little narrow for cargo, but fifteen people could fit in it. They were given some supplies and then they set sail.

Samantha gave Azaroth some medicine to help with the pain. He quickly fell asleep. A few days went by and Aluxes woke up. When she was told what had happened, she was at a loss for words.

They had been unable to win a single victory. It bothered her to her core. "Hell, if we keep losing like this, we will all die eventually." Her mind filled with her dream. "I better keep what I dreamed of to myself."

She kept blushing every time she saw Azaroth. His tall body, his perfect face, and even the way he smiled in his sleep sent tingles down her spine. *Every time I look at him I feel weak. Why does this have to happen during a time like this? Be better if I was dead inside.*

Evalyn noticed how she blushed a little when she looked at him and chuckled. "Oh my sweet angel, Aluxes. You are starting to grow up."

Aluxes saw Samantha near the supplies. She was taking note of what they had. She slowly approached her and without turning said, "Yeah, can I help you?"

Aluxes stood there. "Your mother—she was a very good person. She tried her best to help me when I was in a bad spot. In a forceful manner." She smiled a little. "She aimed a crossbow at my head."

Samantha turned slightly. "And what did she tell you?"

Aluxes's smile faded. "She told me I would find you."

Samantha counted more boxes with her finger. "I wish you never found me. I am a cursed monster."

Aluxes walked a little closer. "Your mother told me her story, sort of. It was to help her heal." She took a deep breath. "So...what is your story?"

Chapter Nineteen

SAMANTHA

Rose yelled out, "Samantha dear, do not waddle off out of sight." The young girl explored the world around her and found some tiny stones. She grabbed as many as her little hands could carry and walked towards a pond. She tossed them in one at a time and clapped in excitement as each one splashed and rippled out.

She eventually tossed them all in at once. "*Splosh*. Hahahaha Mommy, *splosh*," A dragonfly buzzed by her face and landed on a flower. "I will get you, bug." She ran up towards it but it flew off. She stood there and watched with her eyes wide open.

"Psst." Her older sister Ria tried to get her attention. "If you pick a bunch of them lovely flowers, Mommy would be happy." Samantha looked down and saw a red flower.

She picked one up and said, "Red one." She then found a blue one and picked it up with a smile. "Blue one."

Near the pond was a yellow and green flower. The multi-colored flower intrigued her. "Oh, pretty. Mommy will love it." She wandered close to it.

Ria watched her carefully. "Samantha, do not get too close. If you fall in, you might drown."

Samantha gently put the other flowers down and patted them. "You wait right here." She reached for the flower and managed to touch it. The tall grass behind it suddenly grew eyes which looked at her. She gasped and jumped back.

The voice was very soothing to her ears. "It is all right, my dear. I did not mean to scare you. I am Turiacus. My, are you a lovely young lady." Samantha giggled and talked back. Ria tried to see who she was talking to, but her head was blocking the view.

Turiacus looked to both sides. "Little lady, you must come with me. Something bad is going to happen." He quickly grabbed her by the arm and pulled her into the tall grass.

"Ahh! Mommy, help!" But she was drowned by more screams. No one came to her rescue.

He took her to his castle, which at the time looked kept up. "Mommy, Daddy, help me! Save me brother, sister, uncle! Mommy, Mommy!" She cried but was ignored.

Turiacus put her in a well-made room. There was a queen-sized bed, fancy table, and a large dresser with an elegant mirror that had a gold trim.

Every day, he brought her new toys but she would cry for weeks. Soon, she did what all kids do. She made the best of the situation and played with the toys. He would bring a tutor every day to teach Samantha. To educate her as she grew. The tutors would only last a week, maybe two, each day becoming weaker and frailer. They would age day by day as he drank their life force when they were not in the room.

She would ask, or demand at times, to see her family. Every day he would tell her that if she pleased him, she could see them. He always treated her to fancy foods and drinks, some that would make the rich jealous. He kept her room locked and never allowed her to go out.

"Turiacus, I demand that I see my mother. I promise I will not tell her about you. You've had me locked in here for eight years now. Just let me see her." She threw a tantrum and broke some of her gifts, only to have them replaced the next day.

Each time, he would smile at her. "My dear little sweet girl, do you even remember her name? I bet you do not even remember her face. If you left, how would you find her?" She sat there with a look of shock.

She was unable to remember any of them. No matter how hard she tried to think, their names and faces were not there.

One day, Turiacus brought out a stone. "Dwarfs call this lovely item an elf stone. During the times of their great war with the elves, the short elves would dress up as a dwarf to spy on them. People of elf blood that got near this the stone would glow a lovely blue." He held the pearl-white stone next to her face and it started to glow blue. Her eyes lit up; it was one of the prettiest things she had ever seen.

"It is a late birthday gift but you turned ten not too long ago. I made it into a necklace for you." He carefully put it around her neck. She looked in her mirror and smiled. Her reflection reminded her of her mother, but with her father's eyes and hair color.

He tried to smile back, but his hands started to twitch. "You are growing into a very lovely lady." He began to quietly mumble, as his hands twitched more violently.

She watched his reflection. "Are you all right? Do you need me to find you a doctor?"

He pulled out some books. "This is the latest in science. I will not educate myself. You my dear, must self-learn from now on. If you please me, I will allow you to leave this room."

Well, this place is really nice. I am so glad I did good in my studies. Turiacus seemed very pleased with my progress. She walked down a hall and heard a voice. *He has a guest?*

She peeked around the corner and saw that he was alone. "Etharia, my love, where have you gone? He is dead, so there was no need for you to think about it. That god king should pay for what he did to us. The prince, my friend—how your grace left you. I wish I knew she did that to you." Every week she would spy on him. Some of the times he would pass out from his fits.

"Oh my Turiacus, are you all right?" He was laying in the middle of the hall. "You hit your head, my poor Turiacus."

"Etharia, I am sorry for what I have done. She is now twelve. I kept her to keep her safe. That wicked man took you from me." She rested his head on her lap and gently brushed her fingers through his hair.

"My poor lord. You are your own hell. Being tormented by a past love." She looked down and kissed his forehead as he slept.

She continued to do this every time she saw him pass out. "My dear little Samantha, how old are you now? Time escapes me." She rubbed his checks and smiled at him.

"I am now fourteen. My birthday was last month." She twisted his hair around her finger.

"I forgot your birthday. I am sorry, my dear. It has become harder to control my mind. To make up for it, what is it you want?" Their eyes locked and her heart pounded like a hammer. She leaned over and kissed his lips.

"I cannot live without you. Allow me to be the one to help bring your mind to rest." She tried to kiss him again, but he pushed her back.

"My dear, do you understand what this implies? This request you ask will have dire outcomes." He regained some of his vigor.

She looked into his eyes and held her hand over her heart. "Yes, my heart feels for you. Allow me to help your suffering. Allow me to be your Etharia." They were words she later regretted in life. After she escaped, she learned about the condition that means falling for your kidnapper.

Without hesitation, he took her to her room and gently laid her onto the bed. Each time they kissed he removed some clothing. It all changed, however, when he had another rant and became aggressive between her legs. For her, it was a nightmare, The pain she felt and his ungentle manner made it an unforgettable moment. When she fell asleep after, he would take a small breath over her nose and mouth.

A few months passed. "Oh, my head, my entire body feels like it was hit by rocks." She fell as she tried to walk properly. "My head, what did he do to me last night? He seemed gentle this time around." Her voice became horse. Barely able to move, she managed to make her way to a mirror. What she saw sent cold shivers down her spine. Her reflection was that of an eighty-year-old man looking back at her.

"Oh...oh...what? No, no, no. I remember that I brushed my hair yesterday. I know I was still me than. He may know how to cure me.

He has to cure me. He loves me." She stumbled towards the door and into the hall.

As she reached the door, her mind flashed to every night that he bedded her. *He took a deep breath over my face every time. No, he could not have done this.* Each step fueled her anger to move more.

With whatever energy she had left, she hurried to Turiacus's throne room. "What the hell did you do to me?" She collapsed to the ground with each breath being a struggle.

He looked at her with a blank stare. "I simply could not help myself. My little Samantha, my Etharia, my love. I admit I went overboard last night and drained you too quickly. But my love, you are a lower life, not my Etharia." He stood up and walked towards her. He fought hard to control himself. "You fell for my spell perfectly. My dear, you were under an illusion this entire time." In the middle of the room was a family of four travelers.

He appeared in front of the man faster than one could blink. "You have trespassed into my kingdom and for that you shall serve me." He grabbed the man as he was screaming for forgiveness, and he bit his neck. He filled up a cup with the blood and tossed the man, allowing other vampires to drain him. His lifeless body was all that remained.

He picked up the wife and placed his face in front of her nose and breathed in heavily. A green gas flowed into his body, and it caused her to age rapidly. Her screams came to an end when she became a pile of dust.

"You see, my love. I am not a vampire. I do not need the blood to live. I, however, drain the very energy that gives life. If I am not careful, it can kill them. At first, I would only drain a month or two out of you, but last night was a little wild and I got carried away. The vampires were created when my first wife gave birth to our son. He was known as the vampire king." He looked in the cup as if he was bored.

The two kids sitting there cried. They met the worst fate. The father was raised as a vampire and was ordered to drain his own kids.

Samantha sat there scared and helpless. "Please, miss. Save me. I will tell you where my father hid our savings. Please save me." One of the kids reached out to her but she did not budge.

Turiacus appeared in front of her and slowly twitched again. "Oh my love, Etharia. I must admit I did enjoy you." He helped her up and gently walked her into a room. He opened the door and inside were jars full of fetuses. "Yes, my dear. You actually became pregnant a few times. I had to use my magic to pull the babies out without you knowing. You are not my Etharia, so an offspring with you would not be fitting."

Chewing noises echoed from around the corner. She slowly followed the noise and covered her mouth as tears fell from her eyes. The vampires that were too weak for the hunt were eating the fetuses.

"Not to worry, my love. Not all of them are yours. Sometimes a pregnant girl wanders into my domain." He gently placed his hand on her shoulders.

Samantha screamed at the top of her lungs and lashed out at Turiacus, but he did not budge. She was weak. He locked her in a cage in his throne room so she could see the horrors he caused from day to day.

"I do love you, my dear. So I shall keep you alive. Who knows? I may grow tired of this and let you go. If you drink this, I will restore one year of your life force back." He handed her the cup.

After a year, Turiacus had a violent attack and ranted more strongly than normal. Samantha pretended to be asleep in her cage. "Etharia, can you forgive me? I am sorry, I never thought I would hurt you. My love, the only one for me, what have I done? This girl—would she make it up to you? I had no idea how much you loved him." He walked closer to the cage. "I will fix it. I am sorry. I shall keep my promise. My poor little Samantha, I wanted to protect you. I never meant for this to happen. Poor innocent mortal. I shall forever hold you in my heart, my love."

A small bit of energy flew out of his hand and was absorbed into her body. He unlocked the cage and left.

Samantha woke up feeling more energetic. She was able to see things that had been unnotice before. Objects that were covered with magic before to hide their appearance now seemed like see-through drapes. The castle was more broken down. Areas that she did not know about appeared before her, and she felt younger. She rushed to her room which seemed as if it had been decaying for centuries. The only new objects in the room were her bed, her clothing, and the mirror.

"My, I am younger. Why did he not just kill me instead?" A man who looked to be in his fifties stared back at her in the reflection.

There was a small note on her bed. All it said was *"Kill me to restore your youth. Please, kill me. I need you to kill me, my love."*

She stormed out with vengeance on her mind. Not knowing where to go, she wandered aimlessly for days till she passed out along the road.

She woke up in the back of a covered wagon. There was an old lady spoon-feeding her broth. "There ya go. You are finally awake," The old lady sat down next to her.

Samantha was wrapped up in a blanket. The old lady smiled. "When we first saw ya, we thought you were a dead ol' man. If it was not for you being mostly naked, we would have never thought you were an old lady."

She handed Samantha the bowl. "Yep, life must not have been too kind on ya to make you look like that."

She stared at her reflection in the broth. Her cheekbones could be seen. Her face was lifeless, and her hair was faded.

She cleared her throat. "Thanks, ma'am." Her voice was still that of a young girl. It was an elegant sound, no doubt due to the education. Her speech was the same as that of nobles.

The man driving the wagon said cheerfully, "That is an amazing voice you got there. Maybe you were blessed with a singing voice."

The old lady looked at her. "Do not mind my husband. He is a bit strange in the head but he is full of honor."

They stopped off at the nearest town. They gave her some clothing and wished her luck. They continued on the trail south. Their wagon read *"Roaming Fun Wagon"* on the side. She waved at them till they were no longer in sight.

"Oy, you need to look out, you troll." She turned and saw two men.

"I think that old man dressed like a woman hurt my shoulder. I think he needs to pay up." They smiled a little as they walked closer.

She patted her sides to gesture that she was broke. One man pulled out a dagger. "Well, that stone around yer neck be worth a bit. You must be part elf for it to glow like that."

One of the men tossed up some powder that exploded. "That's me illusion dust. It distorts your vision and hearing." She was able to see him just fine. To her, he was moving from side to side, waving his hands.

Maybe he is a poor simpleton and was scammed or the spell just did not work, and he has no idea. She looked around and noticed that the people that were watching had their eyes covered.

She saw a sharp stick laying around and picked it up. One of the men giggled and said, "You dumb bitch. It will do ya no good if you cannot see." And then she stabbed him in the eye. He screamed as she grabbed his dagger and slit his throat.

The other man slapped her across the face. "That moron probably grinded up the powder too much and it didn't work. Now hand over that stone." He punched her in the stomach and she collapsed to the ground, gasping for air.

He was about to go in for the kill when a man in full chain armor came in from behind and knocked him out. He looked at Samantha. "That be a useful gift, my lady. I am the sheriff and I could use a set of eyes like yours."

She then became a sheriff and learned how to fight. Her ability to see through illusions made it easier for her to catch criminals. She would often think about finding her family, but every time she would look in the mirror, her mind would fill up with anger.

After a year on the job, she decided to leave with the money she had earned. She decided to head towards the city of Wiss because it had the largest book collection open to the public. She started to read up on everything about vampires. She mainly tried to look up Turiacus, but he was not in any of the books.

"Four hells. Of course he is not in the books. He told me he was not a vampire. Well this one seems to be new." It was the only book that was not torn or covered in dust.

"Sir Edward L. Hossberg who killed the vampire king and wiped out all the vampires.

She threw away the book. "That moron missed a few." After a while, she picked it back up and kept reading. "Well, he is not in any of the books so maybe he did not know about him."

When she opened the last page a piece of paper fell out. It read:

My family has spent many generations fighting the vampires, but I have achieved what they could never do. The only thing that bothers me is all the text and all the stories that say the vampire king was not the first. Even when I killed him, he cried out to his father. I fear that one is still in hiding and is rebuilding so slowly that time will have passed and forgotten about them. Then, they will attack when all have forgotten how to kill them. I hope whoever reads this will know that I am sorry if it is too late.

Sir Edward L. Hossberg.

"Afterwards, I decided to go into the vampire hunting trade. It was not an easy task because everyone thought they were all killed off. I did manage to find a small group of hunters that knew their numbers had started to grow." She leaned over to the side of the boat and looked at the water. "I spent all that I had earned to buy the needed supplies— holy metals, stakes, magical sunlight, and thick leather armor."

"Why that type of armor?" Aluxes stood next to her.

"It had to be light enough to move, but it had to be solid and tough enough to prevent me from being bitten or clawed." She gazed at the sun. "One of the good things about my curse was that I could see past the illusions. Vampires stayed hidden in plain sight by using this type of magic. My skills became a highly valued asset."

"After the Holy City was destroyed, the vampires no longer stayed hidden. They attacked small towns to grow their numbers faster. I was on the hunt when I ran into you guys." She sighed as she looked at Aluxes. "They raided five towns, but it seems that all that I learned was pointless. He was immune to all of it."

Samantha was carefully studying a dagger that she had pulled out of her pouch. "That is my story."

Aluxes sat there searching for her words. "So, erm. I noticed Myka is starting to talk better."

They looked over. She was trying to tease Onyx but he was brushing it off with lewd jokes. "Yeah, I have been teaching her. It will be important for others to understand her more."

Aluxes tried to look at her neck to see if she was still wearing the necklace. "So, do you—"

"No, I sold it. That monster gave it to me to make me fall for his tricks. I sold it to pay for my crossbow." She scoffed before she spat in the water.

She slowly walked towards the front of the boat. "I wish to be alone now. I need to think about what to do next. For now, it seems I am stuck with you." Aluxes nodded and sat there as she headed off.

"So Evalyn, what do you have there?" Aluxes walked over towards the rest of the group.

"Oh, yeah. You have a letter here, from a Rebecca? She said she survived. Oh, and your old commander Verus says hello. I thought he was impaled and died?" She handed over the letter.

Samantha stared at them as they read. She scoffed as she watched. *Of course, I never told her the real truth. The real story is much harder than the lie. For people like her, they would never understand.* She pulled out a blue leather pouch. Nearby, there was a barrel that was made into a table. She sat and dumped out the necklace and letters.

Her eyes teared up as she read them. *"Please kill me. My love, Samantha. I beg you to kill me. I need you to kill me, my love."* Each note begged for death.

She let out a soft sigh. "I am trying, but you do not make it easy." She looked at the clouds as she cried, "My love."

INTERLUDE

"My dear Aluxes, how have you been? After the fall of the city, I knew you had to be one of the survivors. I learned of this information when I visited a small elf outpost. The lovely lady there told me you had left just a day before we arrived. I hope all is going well with you My party has had its share of bad luck. Not all was bad. After we departed ways, I found the love of my life, Lilith. So, you do not have to worry about me trying to molest you in your sleep anymore." Evalyn chuckled as she read it out loud.

"You have no shame, Rebecca. Did you really try to have your way with a sleeping girl?" A girl with split-colored hair read over her shoulders. One side was brown and the other was red. Her eyes were also two different colors—one was gold, the other brown.

"Do not be jealous, Lilith. It was when you left to visit your mother. Like you, she was immune to my pheromones, so I thought I could get her in the mood. All I did was touch her breasts in a cuddle and she broke my arm like a twig." Rebecca chuckled. "Her eyes are like the one you got there, gold. But not as bold, more of a dull look."

Lilith stared at the letter. "You said her eyes were this color? I think."

Before she could finish, Rebecca interrupted, "You do not need to be jealous. I promise I will never."

Lilith returned the favor. "Why do you always assume my feelings wrong?"

We have been together for over a year now and you still have that emotionless voice. The only time you show any hint of emotion is when you talk to your father." Rebecca began to pout.

Lilith sat down on her lap with her legs on both sides facing her. She leaned over and kissed her deeply, their tongues mixed as they held each other closely.

I hope that erased any doubt of jealously in your mind, and if you want to hear how emotionless my voice can get, I guess you have to hurry up with that letter and meet me in the bed for a refresher. Just do not take too long or I will fall asleep." She kissed her again as she stood up and walked towards the bed, shedding her clothing.

"We found a friend of yours before we escaped the city, Verus. He sends his love and wants you to know that he is now at peace. Apparently, Lilith is his daughter. It is a long story. Best way to put it, she was created by magic. I hope we meet again soon.

Love Always,

Rebecca."

"He was impaled right through his heart. I know he was dead. How could he have survived?" Aluxes looked at Onyx.

Azaroth coughed a little. "There are only two things I can think of. I think he had a clay doll. I doubt he befriended a dream beast."

Chapter Twenty

THE RESTLESS

$\mathcal{A}$fter a week, they arrived at the port town Osburgda. They slowly walked off, trying to regain their balance for being on land. Onyx moved his wheelchair down off the docking ramp as if he were in a race. There was a dwarf with thick black hair and beard there to greet him. They hugged when they were close. He was the spitting image of Onyx.

The dwarf looked at him. "Father, I see ye wanted to be short enough to give ye fellows a proper hello." They laughed.

Azaroth walked a little slower. His wounds were mostly healed, but they still gave him some pain. They met up with the two. Onyx smiled in a way they had never seen before.

He pointed at the other dwarf. "This be one of me bastards, Tourmaline."

He bowed and shook their hands. He had rough skin that was also dry. He was a little shorter than his dad but not by a lot. He was bulkier, likely because his mother was a dwarf. His eyes were also much more of a bolder gray like his Uncle Ulbrek.

He had a deeper voice. "Ye all be with me dad. I'll treat ye as blood. My kin." It was a little hard to understand him. He walked them towards a small house near the docks. Aluxes was amazed to see so many dwarfs in one area.

Tourmaline opened the door. "Welcome ta me dwellings." It had a large dining table that took up most of the space. He grabbed some filled bags and handed them one each.

"Young elf, ya father sent me tis letter. Bags be filled with camping supplies." He tried to speak in a way they could understand, "Ya must head towards Amazon tribe. Ya be safe there."

When he handed Aluxes her bag, he almost fell over as he tried to look at her face. "Ya be a giant. Ever breed with a dwarf? They be giants, rule the world the will." Everyone laughed.

"Like father like son. He said the same to me." Her mind flashed back.

Onyx talked to his son quietly. "*Uudab evulyek yekon?*" Tourmaline moved his head a little.

He looked at them and smiled. "Here, take this letter into the forest. Ya will know who ta give it to. I shall see ya guys in a day or two. Now go, ye pups." He sounded odd and moved with an uncertainty in his eyes.

Aluxes took the letter and hugged Onyx. "You be careful, old man."

"I still have many of years left in me. I be not even middle aged." She put on her pack and looked at him. There was a feeling she was unable to shake.

They walked towards the edge of the harbor. Outside, there were no roads. Only a thick jungle. Some self-made foot paths could be seen but they could have been easily missed.

Tourmaline came up to them. "People of this kingdom not want roads, so try ta keep to the path. If ya stray off, ya can be lost forever. Just remember ta go north." He headed back to his father.

Everyone looked at Azaroth. "I have only been to the capitol once over two thousand years ago. Just aim north and do not get lost." Aluxes grunted a little and walked into the forest. The rest followed.

The brush was thick. Keeping on the path was close to impossible. The mixture of heat, moisture, and bugs made it the most undesirable trip. As night took place, they opened their packs. Inside there was a note that read *"Do not sleep on the ground. Set up these cots high above the ground."*

Samantha and Myka climbed up the trees and set up their cot tents. They were cozy-looking with a loose flap that could cover them up like a tent. Evalyn tried, but she was not good at climbing. It took her a little bit, but she managed to do it.

"If I was to sleep in a tree, I would have been a bird," Aluxes said in her usual annoyed tone.

Evalyn snickered at her. "Are you still afraid of heights?" She fluttered her eyes at her. "It is sad when my rival can barely challenge me. I guess you do have me beat in fear."

Aluxes used thick roots from a tree to set up a barrier. She did what she could to cover up and set her back against the tree. Azaroth joined her by sitting next to her.

He smiled. "I will keep you company. I heard the night creatures that roam on the grounds here can be dangerous."

She blushed a little, lost for words. "Thanks, I guess." She looked right at him. "Have you ever been to the Amazon capitol?"

He rummaged his hand inside his pack for a can of food. "Yeah, once. I almost died there. Back then, they would kill any outsider no matter what. I was still very young and new to the role as a messenger. I never bothered to come back."

She grabbed a can from her pack and was trying to open it when a tongue popped out and snagged it with finger-like ends. In an instant, it pulled the food into the thick bushes. A beast leaped. It was as tall as a man and as long as two horses. It walked on all fours with six-inch razor-sharp claws. The most noticeable aspects were its giant teeth and the thick shell that covered its entire body.

Like a frog, the tongue projected towards Aluxes. It stuck to her shoulder and pulled her to its mouth, but Azaroth quickly cut the tongue, saving her from the monster's jaws. The creature's missing part regrew rapidly. She acted quickly and stabbed it in the skull straight through the brain, killing it instantly.

In the background, they could hear more of them on the way. They hastily climbed a tree, leaving their gear below. The creatures tore the packs and scattered all the equipment.

Azaroth chuckled. "This is what happened the last time I was here."

Aluxes grunted a little. "I thought you said you did not remember much."

He looked at her. "It's slowly coming back to me." He pulled out some rope that he had wrapped around himself and tied it to the tree. "Time to rest, I guess. Maybe you should also get some rest?"

"Where did ya get that rope?" She crossed her arms.

He smiled and winked at her. "I grabbed it from my pack. It would have felt silly to be the only person in the group to make a mistake." He rested his back against the tree and closed his eyes. "If two people make a mistake, it is harder to feel as bad."

Aluxes stood there and understood his hidden message. Now she would not be singled out as a fool. She stared at him as he slept and her heart beat rapidly. Her cheeks became flushed and her eyes locked on him, unblinking.

Evalyn giggled as she watched. "Oh, my cute little Aluxes is in love!" She covered herself with a blanket. "Hey, get some sleep!"

Aluxes sat down and nodded. "I cannot sleep, I do not want to have that dream ever again." Every time she closed her eyes for more than a blink, she could see the figures. She stayed up all night watching the beasts rummage through their stuff. As the sun came up, the monsters ran off. She climbed down and tried to find anything that was still usable.

"My, my. Looks like you had a hard night there." Evalyn stood there with a grin on her face. "That nasty beast almost ate you. We could have helped you but we knew you were in good hands."

Aluxes looked at her a little and scoffed. "You sat up there and watched as my stuff got destroyed?"

Samantha picked up a destroyed can. "We thought it would be a way for you to learn. We also knew you could handle yourself." They managed to find a few supplies from the packs, mostly bandages.

After an hour, Aluxes struggled to keep up. Her eyes felt heavy and she slowed down a little. Every once in a while, when no one was looking, she would pinch herself to stay awake. Samantha took notice and kept an eye on her.

Azaroth chuckled. "It is all right, Sam. She is just worn out from not sleeping for a few days." He walked a little closer. "It started after she woke up on the boat. I do not know what it was that she saw in her dream, but it has been bothering her."

Samantha saw her rub her eyes. "I am more concerned with needing her power. Can we trust her? I am also concerned about her going berserk again."

He looked at Aluxes. "I was like that when I was young. She needs to learn how to face her demons, or they will face her." Aluxes turned her head and saw him smile at her. She blushed a little, and it caused her to trip over a root.

Evalyn helped her up. "My, my. You need to watch out. The love bug might take off your head."

Myka bumped into Aluxes. "Do not get funny ideas, you child. He mine to marry."

Aluxes pushed the girls to the ground as a spear flew over their heads. Azaroth and Samantha kneeled with their hands in the air. The bushes rumbled and thirty women came out into the opening. They were wearing hide armor that looked like it'd been crafted from a leopard. They each had a hide shield and a short spear.

One that was on horseback rode up. Her accent was the same as that of an elf, but she had no problem with human words. Her voice was muffled with a mask which had a baboon face on it. "Who dares enter the Amazonian lands without an invitation?"

Azaroth looked right at her and bowed his head. "I am Azaroth. I am sure you have heard of me. I come with a letter from the high king of the elves. I also have need of aid."

She took off her mask. Her skin was dark brown. She had blue eyes and long brown hair. Her armor was made from black leather with some metal protecting the vital spots and she had a spear with a large head. "We've heard of you but you cannot be him. The stories are thousands of years old." She looked at Aluxes who was slowly standing up. "She wears one of the missing treasures. Who are you people?"

They made some clicking noises and slow hand motions. A group of girls came out and cuffed them. "I Alisa, and you be brought to before our queen."

The cuffs were tied together by ropes made from vines. The metal was made from an unknown material. It was tight and it caused some pain when they moved. Aluxes dozed off a little. Her head bobbed up and down as she tried to keep herself awake. For a moment, she drifted off enough to see a glimpse of the woman in her dreams. Dark Aluxes hit her shoulder with a fist.

Aluxes woke up in a panic as one of the guards on a horse jabbed her with a pointed stick. She broke the cuffs, grabbed the stick, and immediately hit the guard, knocking her out. Another guard came in with a spear. She sidestepped out of the way and grabbed the shaft.

The guard struggled to pull it back. "What monster are you?" the guard gritted her teeth.

Aluxes let go with one arm and grabbed another spear shaft as a guard tried to flank her, but before they could let go, she yanked as hard as she could, causing them to hit the ground. Alisa managed to sneak up behind her and put a thick stick over her throat and tried to break her neck, but Aluxes was able to grab her hands and pull her arms away like she was a frail child.

Alisa tried to find her words. "You must be strong. Only can imagine how much power that circlet is holding back." She kneed Aluxes in the back and tried to regain control of her arms so she could pull the stick.

Aluxes managed to toss Alisa over her back onto the ground. Before she could smash her head with her foot. Azaroth rushed up and knocked her out with a sleep spell. More Amazons were rushing in, ready to kill her, when he ordered them to stop.

His loud voice echoed. They stood there a little scared. "She is under my protection. She is not well. Her mind is not at ease."

Alisa walked up, "Have strict rules how to deal with. Our laws say kill you all now. You both will die today." She and some of the others stood in battle stances.

Azaroth smiled. He gently raised his hand and snapped his fingers. The ground trembled a little. The Amazons panicked except Alisa— she stood on the ready, waiting for an opening. Roots started to rise from the ground and entangled the Amazons.

When the roots came to trap Alisa, she quickly sliced them with a small blade that she had hidden as she jumped out of the way. She then lunged at Azaroth, going for a killing blow. Right before her blade met his flesh, he grabbed it with his bare hand. Blood dripped to the ground but he did not flinch. He grunted and snapped the dagger in half.

She looked at him and gasped. There was also a hint of fear in her movements as she tried to take a step back. He grabbed her head and pushed her to the ground. A large beast lunged at her and barely missed her. The beast had a hide as tough as a turtle shell. Was as big as a bear with nine-inch razor-claws and walked on two legs. It leaped at Azaroth, bearing its large, sharp canines. Azaroth grabbed it by the mouth, with one hand holding the bottom jaw, and the other holding the top. He stood right in the middle so he could dodge the claws easily. He quickly ripped the jaw off and snapped its neck, killing it. The Amazons gawked in amazement at his raw power.

He walked up to Alisa and surrendered. "We will go with you if you will not harm us." He raised his wrists, ready for new cuffs. She took out another pair.

She looked at Aluxes. "I will accept, but she is a problem. Even you, she might attack." She stared at him. "Her mind not at ease and her soul in conflict." She noticed that Azaroth was unsettled with her words. He knew that she was asking him to end her.

She put her fingers under Aluxes's chin and rubbed a powder on her neck. "We keep her sleep with magic. She get rest that needed and we be safe?" Azaroth nodded in agreement.

They had been walking for an entire day when they came into a clearing. It was a huge city with tall, decorated pyramids that blocked the view. It was an amazing sight to behold.

Chapter Twenty-One

THE DAMAGED SOUL

*A*s they were being walked through the city, they noticed how the women wore armor and the men were dressed for domestically. The number of men were limited, but they looked like they could handle themselves in a fight. The children tossed clumps of dirt at the prisoners and everyone laughed.

They were brought to the largest of the pyramids. The inside was draped in red silk, gold and silver trim all over, and a huge ivory throne. Sitting on the throne was the most beautiful woman they had ever seen. Her red silk outfit left little to the imagination. Sitting in smaller seats were a man and some children. She looked right at Samantha; her crimson eyes penetrated her soul.

Her voice was soft but demanded respect. "My dear sweet child, you have been cursed by a great evil. I bet if it were not for the curse, you would look just like your mother."

Samantha stood there barely able to speak a word. "You know my mother?"

The queen looked at her softly. "She came by once with her father many years ago. It was right after she got married. She was a good friend." Her face became stern. Samantha was able to feel her in the back of her mind. "Only the one who cursed you can restore you. His power is greater than anything in this realm."

She glanced at Azaroth. "Lord Azaroth, you look the same as the last time I saw you." Her crimson eyes had a slight glow in them as she spoke in a more demanding tone, "Release them at once! If we anger him, he can burn this city down within the hour."

As they removed the cuffs off the prisoners, Azaroth smiled. "You have grown. I am surprised you remember me."

The queen smiled back. "It was true I was only a little girl. But I never forgot the face of the man that killed the dragon. You avenged my father that day."

Some of the troops gently carried Aluxes and laid her down. Alisa kneeled. "This girl, my queen, has powers that are terrible. She wears one of stolen treasures."

The queen stood up and removed her crown. Long crimson hair which almost touched the ground became exposed. They had an unnatural flow to it as she slowly walked up to Aluxes.

She had an expression of slight excitement. "In the long years that I have been around, I never thought I would see this day." She stood so close that her breath caused goosebumps on her skin. She hovered her hands over the body like she was able to read a vibe off it.

She looked at Evalyn. "With this on, how strong is she?"

With a blank stare, she pointed to herself. "Umm, me?"

"Well," she said clearing her throat, "she did fight a troll and made it look easy, but the orc overpowered her. She did put up a decent struggle. But lately, it has been bouncing around."

The queen looked at Azaroth. "Is it true?"

He smiled. "Yes, Riviana. She is almost like you."

Riviana did not take her gaze off Aluxes. "Alisa, do you know what this treasure was?"

She kneeled, "Was treasured gift from the Unnamed Goddess. Granted to ones worthy, it suppresses energy for longer life."

The queen laughed. "Rumors about artifacts have changed in the past thousand years. It is a power limiter. When the Unnamed Goddess lived in these lands, she had to limit her powers. Her very presence would destroy lesser beings. My mother made this for her."

She walked over to Alisa. "My dear knight, it took the Goddess many human lifetimes to learn how to control her power. That was how we got the circlet. If you wore it, or even someone of my ability, it would kill us."

Queen Riviana signaled for everyone to leave. She pointed to Azaroth, Alisa, and Samantha to stay. "If anyone shall harm the redheaded prisoner or elf, I will personally kill them. They are our honored guests. Show them to their room." They grabbed them and rushed them out.

The queen took a deep breath. "Alisa, remove the sleeping spell when I tell you to."

"But my queen, she may attack."

Riviana smiled and chuckled. "Her soul is in torment. Right now, she is having a nightmare. I hope she will attack. My aura gives off a dark aroma to her kind. She looks just like Etharia."

With a shout of "Now!" Alisa removed the sleeping spell by breaking the rune that it had been cast on.

Aluxes leaped to her feet and panicked. She frantically looked around for an enemy to fight. She shivered as fear overcame her. She tried to reach for her sword, but it was gone.

Riviana's voice could be felt in the souls of everyone nearby. "Child, look at me." Red wings made of energy shot out of the queen's back. They covered the entire field of view.

Samantha froze still like ice, Azaroth talked quietly, asking, "Remember what I told you? In the world of gods and mortals, there are no straight lines. There are actually two factions of gods. The dark gods are devils. The queen is half human and half devil."

Samantha quickly replied, "I heard something like that during my years of captivity. But he also mentioned there was a third faction, the Fallen." She looked at the queen, unable to blink. "But it still shocks me to see it in person."

Aluxes stared at Riviana, and with a voice filled with rage, asked, "How did you get into my head? Get out of my head, monster!" She leaped at her with amazing speed. She pushed off with so much force that the stone ground under her feet cracked.

Right before her fist could connect, Riviana grabbed her by the wrist. "My dear, you truly are strong. It takes all my power just to block you." Aluxes punched with her other hand but got the same result.

"Just so young, my dear. I'm afraid the influx of power is due to your shorter life span."

Samantha, confused, asked Azaroth, "Is she studying her?" He chuckled a little. "She is excited like her mother. The both love new things. Also like her mother, she tries to rescue the souls of the tormented. We are here in case it gets dangerous."

Alisa stood there watching, trying to fight her instincts. *My queen, I understand but our laws—I have been trained to uphold our laws from birth. She dares attack my queen, she must be killed before she harms her.* Her hands trembled as they held on to the spear, fighting the urge to stab her through the heart from the back. She fixed her sight on the spot. The tunnel vision took control. She slowly moved by instincts.

Aluxes tried to overpower the queen with brute force. "I will decide my own fate. It is mine to pick. Stay away from me." Still in a dream-like state, she was unable to tell the difference between the two.

Riviana tried her best not to be overpowered. "So, that is your curse. My mother told me a story once. But Aluxes, open your eyes. Your mother's curse is not yours." She could feel that she was starting to take notice of where she was, and began to lower her arms when Riviana saw her. "Alisa, no!"

Alisa looked at the queen as she thrust her spear into Aluxes's back, but she missed her mark. Full of rage, Aluxes kicked the queen, knocking her to the ground. Blood came up when she coughed. Before Azaroth and Samantha could leap in to stop her, Alisa was punched in the ribs.

The sound of the bones cracking echoed through out the halls. Alisa flew down the steps onto the carpet. Blood flowed out of her mouth and head. Her eyes slowly turned red as they filled with blood. Everything she saw turned red.

Riviana placed her hand on the back of Aluxes's head. The gravity around her quickly raised and forced her to the ground. She ran to Alisa. "My poor sweet child. I am so very, very sorry. I will fix you."

She used her fingernail to prick her finger. As the blood dripped, her eyes and blood glowed bright red. It dripped into Alisa's mouth. She then put her lips over her mouth and exhaled over them. The bones popped back into place and Alisa started breathing again.

Azaroth looked at Riviana. "You do know if they find out—"

Before he could finish, she yelled, "I know the rules! My mother told them to me for over a hundred years. She is the only pure-blooded mortal left from my father's side. All the rest are dead or have been tainted by my blood." She slowly stood up, still looking at Alisa. "I am not mad at you. Your rules are worse than mine, sir. Do not interfere with the actions of the mortals unless they affect your mission or it was requested by the gods."

She looked right at him and scoffed. "But after taking that girl in, your rules stopped having their meaning. You need to decide what has more value to you."

He moved over to Alisa and picked her up. "I will heal her tonight. It was my fault for allowing it to happen. A part of me is trying hard to keep my old habits." He slowly walked off towards his guest quarters. "If I remember, my room was this way."

Samantha checked to make sure Aluxes was all right but was unable to do so. "Why did you choose for me to stay?" Aluxes was stuck to the ground, screaming and unable to move.

Riviana stood next to her, looking at Aluxes. "Because you can keep a leveled head. Also, you two are not so different in your torment. You have the emotional. Ehe has the spiritual."

Riviana kneeled next to Aluxes and placed her hands on her head. They started to glow red and she closed her eyes. She calmly spoke so Samantha understood what was going on. "I am trying to look into her mind to see what is bothering her."

After a few moments, her wings dissipated and she moved her hands away with a gasp. With an expression of terror in her eyes, she breathed slowly, looking blankly into the wall. Tears started to roll down her face.

She tried to speak, but the words were hard to form. "Her soul is divided." She removed the spell from Aluxes. Too exhausted, Aluxes still lay there in tears.

Riviana held up her hand and water slowly poured out of there. "Here, drink some." Aluxes drank it without hesitating. "Unlike you who was blessed with amazing strength, I was granted a long life and amazing magical abilities." Riviana looked at her, she gently rubbed the circlet.

She gasped. "Ah, it has been damaged."

Samantha quickly shouted out, "He tried to break it but—"

"I understand, young one. I can already see what has happened. We are lucky it was not removed, or he would be the least of our problems." Riviana put her hand across Aluxes's eyes, casting another sleeping spell.

"Unlike her, I was blessed by my mother who was around for the first thousand years to train me. She is not ready to know who she is yet. She and I are alike, but I am ruled by my birth and she has to make a choice. I envy her a little. To have freedom must be a nice thing."

Riviana slowly walked towards her throne. "The small cracks in it are causing some power to leak. It is too much for her human side to control. Also, the dark secret of the gods has a hold on her. These secrets are why everything is now falling apart, child. Remember, hiding things will always come back to hurt you. Of course, you already know that."

"It is why I wrote it all down. To say the things that my lips will not. When I pass, everything will be known." Samantha tried to make a fake smile.

"Dear, I fear it will all come out before that happens. Some of which you are unaware of." The queen's eyes glowed for a moment.

She waved her hands and hidden doors opened from behind the throne. "Lady Samantha, you shall watch over her tonight." She helped carry Aluxes into a small room with beds. "Only a handful of people in the world know of this room. It has properties that allow me to recharge."

Riviana slowly walked out, and the doors closed as she left. Samantha looked around and noticed murals of angels and devils fighting a dark void. In the center of the void was a face, a man with dark blue skin, gold eyes, and a red diamond-shaped object in the center of his forehead. It was hard to tell what it was by the painting. The longer she looked at it, the more uneasy she felt.

"Every time I see one of these magical murals, they creep me out. Like the one of his beloved, Etharia." She slowly nodded off as she lay in one of the beds. Before she closed her eyes, the dark figure moved and looked into her eyes.

Chapter Twenty-Two

THE AMAZONS

The following morning, Samantha could hear a voice. It was soft and soothing, yet it scared her. It seemed to be random mumbles, but she could tell that it was a man. Vivid flashes of the face in the painting filled her mind: the man in the void.

She woke up screaming, her fists ready to fight. She could see Aluxes. She stood there staring at the murals, her fingers gently touching it. On the field, there was a girl who looked like her but was clad in heavy white-plate armor. Next to her was another one but she had crimson hair and wings.

"That is the missing history that the gods and devils erased from the minds of mortals," a voice softly said from behind them. They turned around, caught off guard. Riviana stood there smiling. "It is also part of the history of how I was born."

She walked up to the mural and pointed to the one with red hair. "That is my mother. She was the second one to live with the mortals. She was with Etharia, a mighty warrior."

Riviana looked at Samantha and smiled. "You have questions?"

She pondered with her finger tapping her cheek. "I thought the Unknown Goddess was the only one to live with mortals."

Riviana chuckled a little. "My dear child, you have met Turiacus.

You have been cursed by him. He was once a high-ranking god. His story is tragic. He too was cursed by his greatest success. It was also his greatest failure." She pointed to one of the white-winged characters ready to stab the face that filled the void in the center. "That was Turiacus. It was before his curse took full control and he lost his mind."

Aluxes looked at them both, confused. "Excuse me, but how did I end up here?"

Riviana spoke to Samantha telepathically, "I erased her memory of the past few days."

Aluxes rubbed her circlet. "I remember that we got on a boat, but I do not remember much after that."

Samantha looked at her. "Well, we got into a bad storm, and you got hit in the head pretty bad when the mast broke. The Amazons helped us bring you here."

The queen led them through some halls. Aluxes shaking her head, trying to remember what had happened. They ended up in a room, Evalyn and Myka were waiting for them.

Queen Riviana smiled. "Now, before you guys go, are there any questions you wish to ask?"

Myka had her finger on her chin, mulling over something that had been bothering her. "Well queen, everyone speaks in broken human with an elvish accent, yet you speak it perfectly."

Riviana slowly walked towards her. "The Amazon history started with a war. You know of the seven elf tribes but there used to be eight." She reached for a book on the shelf. Inside it were pictures that moved. It was the history of the people there.

Riviana tried to explain by pointing at each page. "You see, humans started to tire of being around other humans. A large tribe made many boats and traveled by sea. They soon landed on this land that was lush with forests. It began with high hopes as all new adventures do."

"It ended when they found out that there was a tribe of elves that was also sick of living with other elves. They were too filled with pride to seek peace and a war started. It lasted for over a hundred years. It ended when a bigger enemy showed up: dragons."

"Dragons had been hibernating here for centuries. After the civil war between the gods, they had no need to be awake, but the fighting between the two tribes woke up a few. The humans formed an alliance with the elf tribe, and they together pushed the dragons out of the forest. This, however, came at a price. The alliance was formed because two beings got involved; my mother and the Unknown Goddess. After the battle was over, my mother stayed to rule over them. Because she was a devil, it was a strict rule."

"She also planned for a future of her not being there, and so she made the two races intermix, bearing half-breed children. After a few generations, there was no longer a difference between the two." Riviana closed the book and slowly put it away. "That is the history of our people. My mother stayed longer than she intended. She fell in love with a heroic man."

Aluxes had a flashback of the man she fought in the training pit. "This is the southern continent?"

The queen giggled a little. "I see you met someone, yes. Men here are only allowed to be in the home guard. The ones that want to make a warrior name for themselves join human armies."

A well-built man rushed in with a scroll. It was the same person that had sat next to her the day before. She looked in his eyes and shook her head. "Take this scroll. You must find my mother and hand it to her." Evalyn grabbed it and put it in a handbag.

Riviana smiled at Aluxes. "My dear, seeing you has brought much joy to my heart. I wish we could chat a little, but we will never meet again."

She leaned and whispered in her ear, "Take a boat and follow the star of Caelus for three weeks. You will find a continent called Kitezh. Look for Lilith. She will have your answers." She held her hand gently. "You look just like your mother." Samantha grabbed Aluxes by the shoulder and pulled her out.

"Wait! My mother? Let me go! She knows my mother." She tried to struggle but was too weak.

"We must go. Can you not feel it in the air?" Samantha grunted as she pulled. "You are more of a pain in the ass. Why does half the group value you so much?"

They rushed out into the main hall where Azaroth was waiting for them. "We must go before the clouds get here. If you or Aluxes are seen by what that storm brings—well, we must not find out." He tried to smile but was unable to hide his sadness.

He turned to Riviana. "She will live. I made sure they do not find out that it was her. But they will be here, you know it."

She smiled. "Do not worry about me. They need me to bring her out of hiding." She looked past him at Aluxes. "She is very lovely like her mother, and strong. She will need your protection more than I. If we shall meet again, show me your true face. I want to know what you really look like." She kissed his lips. "I wanted to know the taste of the cursed born before I go. I will never return here, I fear, knowing him. Now go and catch up before they find out you are also here."

After a few hours had gone by, the storm hit the city. Lightning lit the ground and the main door to the throne room burst open and flew off the hinges. A large muscular man with blond hair and blue eyes walked in. He wore blue pants and a white robe.

Riviana sat on her throne with her husband and three kids. She smirked. "He still refuses to get me himself. Is he afraid to set foot in his own creation?"

The man stood there and opened a scroll. "You are under arrest by the god king. You showed your divine form to mortals and used a divine power to save a mortal without permission. This is treason."

She stared at him as if he were a prey to a snake. "He sends an angel to fetch me. It means he does not wish me dead. How is my grandfather anyways?"

Like the prey trapped in the eyes of a snake, he stood there unable to speak. He refused to even flex a muscle. It was apparent who was the stronger of the two. Each time he tried to utter a word, his voice would crack. He resorted to hand motions and bows.

He looked at her kids. "He has not said anything about your family. I promise you that they will be unharmed." He was a little nervous but had full confidence.

She hugged her family and slowly walked towards him, still giving off an overpowering presence. "He must be getting desperate to use me as bait to lure out his daughter. Normally, an execution squad would have been sent for these matters. He must be growing old. Now, you better hurry with me before you piss yourself on my floor. I would hate to make you lick it clean."

As they slowly walked outside, the angel looked at her. "He wishes to speak with her. He has been bothered that his eldest—"

She quickly snapped at him, "If he was that concerned, it would have been easier to talk to Uncle Apophis. I am sure they have loads to speak about." He raised his hand as if he wanted to hit her but stopped.

Without flinching, she stood there and smiled at him as he regained his composure. "You know that name is forbidden to speak of in the mortal realm and the holy realm."

She scoffed a little. "It has been a few thousand years and the Fallen are still a forbidden subject. That is why my mother left. Remember this—one whose name I care nothing about, forgotten history has a way of striking back."

She slowly followed him outside where a beam of light came down on them. In a flash they disappeared, along with the storm.

Alisa woke up and saw a man watching over her. "Queen, where she?"

The king stood up taller than he appeared, no longer slouching, and handed her two scrolls. With a deep dignifying voice that demanded respect as he talked, he said "Her grandfather has taken her. The one is for your eyes only." He held her hands as if to beg. "The other is for her mother. Do not fail, or we will lose her."

Amazed at how he sounded, Alisa sat there in shock. "You never spoke before."

He scoffed a little. "I am a dead hero from a far land." He continued to walk off towards the throne room. Alisa looked at the scroll meant for her. She thought about not opening it.

She headed off to her house which was attached to the castle. Her home was small, had little in it. Some extra warrior clothing, a few weapons, one dish, a set of utensils, and a bed. Anyone would think her life had nothing in it. Her body quivered as she opened the scroll.

"My dear Alisa, I do not blame you for what you did. You have devoted your life to the very laws I set forth. But we are entering a new era. The forest is getting smaller and smaller, and our trades with the outside world are more frequent. You are the last surviving pure-blooded human in our kingdom, and are in direct line to the throne. A new era is approaching, and I need you to be at the forefront to help usher our people into it. Your new mission is to be banished from the Amazonian kingdom until you understand the outside world. Their rules and laws are different from ours and must be understood so the right choices can be made. I need you to accompany Aluxes on her journey to find my mother. I hope that by then you will have learned something. DO NOT FAIL ME."

She was confused. Never had she ever broken a rule and she enforced all laws. Yet, she was being punished for it. She sat there as her body quivered. She hesitated as to whether or not to obey. She just sat there staring at the wall.

She clinched the other scroll. "Mission important. I never fail queen. It is law I obey all and every order." She gathered a few items for the trip.

When she was about to exit, the young prince stood at her door. "Her memory was erased from the event. Do not make her remember." He pointed north. "They are a day ahead of you. Hurry and catch the boat."

He was a well-spoken boy. People thought highly of him. He would make a wonderful king. His dark red eyes with his olive skin made him look even more handsome.

She set off and ran towards the forest, her mind fixed on Aluxes who had almost killed her with a single blow. This was a new emotion. One she didn't know. Being the leader of the knights, fear was some-thing she was not allowed to experience. When she would stop to take a break, she would remove her shirt. There was a large scar from where Aluxes had hit her. Though magic could have healed it perfectly, it was left there as a reminder.

Swiftly, she closed the distance, hoping that she would be able to catch them before they could exit the forest. She ran faster, not stopping to eat or sleep as she rushed towards them. She made it into a clearing and random voices filled her head. Unable to see properly as her eyes had not yet adjusted to the blinding light, she tried to speak in the hope that the person near her was someone she was looking for.

"My queen been taken. I go with you," she said, barely able to speak from being worn out. Once her eyes adjusted, she saw Samantha and Evalyn packing up camp.

Shocked, they stood there. Myka, who stumbled towards her, asked, "Taken? We go rescue her?"

Azaroth shouted, "We cannot save her. Where she is at, none of us are allowed to go." Alisa noticed that he did not seem at all bothered. It was as if he already knew.

He helped pick up camp. "Aluxes went on ahead to get the boat tickets. All we can do to save her is to complete our task."

Samantha looked at Alisa. "Who would take—"

Azaroth interrupted her, "Her grandfather. She will be safe for now, but we have a time limit."

They walked towards the harbor and met up with Aluxes halfway, who was returning to the camp. She had with her Onyx who had decided to join them.

He had on him magical relics attached to devices on his arm and leg, covered with dwarf runes. "Aye, me son had made a name for himself as a doctor." He moved the arm around to show it off. "The we bastard invented these. This be his latest model." They were all happy to see him well. "Almost as good as me real limbs."

As they headed towards the docks to board, Aluxes tried to hand Alisa her ticket. She jumped with her arms up, ready to block. Aluxes stood there holding the ticket.

Her eyes went back to their usual angered stare. "Look, I paid for your ticket. Azaroth said you would show up. For a kingdom full of mixed-breeds, you should have no problems with a half-human like me."

Alisa tried to smile as she slowly grabbed it. "*Taygee.*" She nodded her head.

Aluxes scoffed a little. "I wonder what type of beastly tales your country has about unknowns. I can tell that you are afraid of me and it's pissing me off." She stormed onto the boat.

The boat was rather large compared to how it had seemed, nearly barren of cargo. It was made for passengers. Boats like these were rare, and they all could not help but be excited. Even the cheap rooms they paid for were bigger than a tavern's guest quarters. As the ship set sail, Alisa stood on the deck, gazed at the open sea, and wondered what the new world would bring to her.

Chapter Twenty-Three

THE CURSED OCEANS

*A*lisa had never ventured outside her kingdom. She was homesick and seasick. The motions of the boat had her hunched over the edge every day. When the waters were still, she managed all right, but on good sail weather, her day was full of throwing up.

"Eww, Mom. She is vomiting again," said the kids that teased her during the day.

"Be careful or she may get a wee bit on ya. I bet with this bit of candy she vomits three more times." Onyx sometimes chipped in, making bets with the children for candy on how many times she would vomit by the end of the day.

Myka, not looking much older than the eldest kids, joined in on some of their games. It helped pass the time. She oddly had taken a liking to a young mother with a new baby. She would watch the child when the mother needed a rest.

"Aunt, why do you seem to like that human? The way you talked made me assume you hated all humans," Samantha asked.

Myka giggled a little. "Because of the baby. I plan on having one with Azaroth. I will assume it will look close to this. Also, when the baby smiles, it is so cute."

Samantha remembered reading about how when female elves get close to their sexual cycle, they tend to be extra joyful around babies.

Myka held him above her head. "It is amazing. Only a few months old. This little guy has more exploring experience than an old elf alive for a thousand years."

She handed the baby back to the mother. "He is the joy of my life. My husband is waiting for us at Rumland docks. They've never met."

Samantha stood next to Azaroth as he watched the sun. "Why does she? Is she not happy with how she looks?"

He barely glanced at her. "I forgot you can see past illusions. I always wondered how it works. Can you tell there is something there or does it all look normal?"

She hummed a little. "Well, it is like holding a clear cloth over what it is they are hiding. It is faded but everything they are hiding—I can see clearly. Like you. I can see your real face, and her, who is older than she appears."

"I can only sense illusions. For me there is a feeling of where it is at. For Myka case, she thinks if she looks young and cute, she will attract more attention. It is not really an illusion. She uses magic to make her look that way. Someday, she will learn like many others, a life with me can never happen." He chuckled in a depressing way.

In the distance, they could see dolphins leap out of the water. The baby giggled each time he saw one. The deck crew yelled to the people it was almost dark and they should head back to their beds. Alisa, still not feeling too good, stayed up top.

A crew member walked up to her. "Ma'am, for your safety, please go back to your room. These waters are different."

She glared at him. "I am fine on my own. I—" Before she could finish, she vomited all over him. He stormed off, cursing at her under his breath.

Samantha walked up behind her. "Here, drink this. It is not easy to brew on this ship. When I first went on a ship, I had problems as well."

Alisa drank it and instantly felt better. "What this potion?"

She hesitated a little. "It is best you do not know."

Samantha pulled out a pillow that she had in her other hand to catch Alisa as she passed out. "It prevents motion sickness for a while but the side effect is that you sleep."

A young woman off to the side who was trying to calm her baby down noticed the incident. "Is she all right?" She looked over and saw the young mother with her baby.

Samantha snapped at her. "What are you doing here?"

The mother stared at her baby with a big smile. "He was unable to sleep, so I was hoping we could see some dolphins to wear him out."

Before Samantha could say or do anything, three human-looking creatures appeared behind the young lady. They had green skin, long black hair, black eyes, and long fingers.

Two of them grabbed the mother as the third snatched the baby. "Yes, this will keep us fed for a while."

Samantha quickly bolted up but stopped when the creature held the infant over the edge. "Move and I will drop this baby." She stood there, not knowing what to do.

The monster pulled the child close to its chest. "This nice young baby. So full of youthful energy."

The mother screamed at the top of her lungs, "Do what you will with me, but please spare my baby!"

The monster smiled. "Why would I waste such energy from its youth." The beast opened its mouth and was about to eat the infant when an arrow hit the creature in the head. Myka nocked another.

Samantha ran up to grab the baby, but before she could do that, the beast snapped its head forward and bit him.

A loud scream of pain from the child woke up most of the crew. The monster jumped back into the ocean and the other two followed. Everyone stood there, not speaking a single word. The mother collapsed to her knees without a sound.

The captain ran out. "We warned ye to stay indoors!" He gently put his coat around the young lady.

"That be a qalupalix. They feed on the youthful energy of children. It heals them, and makes them younger. I am sorry, miss, but you're still young. Let this be a lesson if ya have another one."

Myka stood at the side of the boat, looking into the ocean and crying. Her mind filled with the baby as it smiled at her. She tried to say something but was only able to cry.

Samantha walked up behind her. "I have seen this so many times, so I tend to forget how hard it is for someone who has never witnessed such a horrific event."

Myka rubbed the tears off her face, "I am not crying for these hummao. They are beneath me." She was trying to sound like a high-born elf but the sadness in her voice could not hide how she felt.

The following morning, Aluxes walked out and noticed that the poor young mother was still sitting there, mumbling the baby's name—Nathan. She kept saying it over and over again. Her voice had gone hoarse.

Samantha sat nearby with Myka's head resting on her lap. "She passed out after crying. It was a hard night for us all."

The young mother stood up. "I can hear him. He is giggling. He is waiting for me; he is still alive." Before anyone could grab her, she ran towards the side of the boat and jumped into the water.

Aluxes was about to leap in after her but was stopped by Azaroth. "It's too late."

In the ocean, there was a massive creature. It looked like a fifty-foot-tall man with pale skin floating in the water. The monster poked its bald head above the surface, just enough for the eyes to peek out. The eyes were a dark red. The corner of its lips could be seen as it grinned.

It lifted its hand out of the water and the young mother was in his massive palm. The creature's mouth opened, and it slowly moved its arm closer to its face, angling it enough to cause her to slide in.

Myka ran over to the side of the boat. The woman's lips were moving, and she could hear every word. "Nathan, Mommy is coming. You will not be alone anymore." The young lady slid into his mouth. She held her arms out as if she was reaching out to hug her baby. Her body had made it halfway through when the monster bit down. Blood leaked out of its lips and it opened to swallow the rest. It quickly disappeared into the water.

Everyone stood there in horror. The captain walked up to Aluxes.

"That be a ningen. They be a very rare sight back in the day but within the year they have been on migration. They only be in dark waters of the cursed isle, but now the entire ocean is be cursed."

Azaroth took a deep breath. "They are what remains of the Fallen war. Monsters of the Black Islands of Thule."

Aluxes looked at him. "I have heard of this Fallen from you before. What are the Fallen?"

Samantha added, "I have spent years living in a library and I've never heard of this Fallen war."

He looked out across the ocean. "If we ever wind up in Thule, I will tell you. I myself was not in the war. I was then a young boy. But I did fight the monsters it created."

The following day, they could see land in a distance. One of the shipmates had a box in his hands. He stood near the gangway. The wait took forever, but they eventually landed.

A young man ran up to the gangway. The shipmate handed the box to the man, and he soon dropped to the ground and cried.

Myka watched closely. "That is the father of the poor baby." She kept her gaze on him as a tear rolled down her check. The man slowly stood to his feet and stumbled off.

The captain cleared his throat as he tried to speak to the remaining passengers still on board. "Our next stop be Kitezh. It be a long trip. You best be wise to do as we say. These waters be legendary. Only a number of boats be allowed in its docks, so you all be prepared for when we be docked." He walked off a little bit and turned around. "Ahh ye. Best not be fishing off the boat once the waters become a different color. Be more nasty monsters than that there what we saw not too long ago."

A sailor shouted, "Anyone be not wanting to continue on this journey, get off the ship now!" Seven people slowly walked down the gangway.

The boat sailed off with twenty passengers remaining on board. Kitezh was a land of legend. The things there could only be found on that continent. Brave adventurers or thrill-seekers are the ones that dared to take the trip. The ships charged outrageous prices to detour some people. Rarely had anyone returned which added to the mystery.

Aluxes's anxiety built up as she walked up to Azaroth. "Hey, what type of place is this? The sailors do not want to talk about it and the air seems to be off. And for the past few days, you have ignored me."

He smiled at her. "I have been there maybe a handful of times. It is a place I never wish to visit." He looked down at the water.

"When I look from the side, you look older. The decades of life, pain, and sadness become more apparent the closer we get." It was obvious he was unable to talk about it. *He is the most human person I have ever met.*

She held his arm. "Did something happen? Was it bad? You can trust me. I swear I will not tell anyone."

He patted her arm with his hand. "My best friend died there. Him and his wife. He was an amazing warrior." He looked out to the sea. "There used to be songs about him and statues all over the Holy City."

She tried to think who it might be but was interrupted by a scoff. "You will not know his name. They erased him from history."

Her voice skipped a little as she asked, "Wha—what happened?"

He looked her in the eyes, which made her blush. "He disobeyed the commands of the gods and I was sent to kill him. I was forced to watch him be killed when I refused. His wife understood and allowed herself to be killed to save their only daughter." He looked out into the ocean again. "The entire village was killed. The angels lied and killed everyone."

In a soft tone, unaware that he was talking out loud, he said, "To every living being a human is viewed as an annoying bug. Even the gods and their armies."

She released his arm. "How do you view us?"

He looked at her and took her hand. "I have always loved humans. They have treated me better than my parents."

A man in the distance shouted, "I caught a bite!" It was a world-class fisherman who was unable to help himself but to fish. The waters were no longer blue but a shade of red. Some of the sailors shouted at the man to release the rod.

They rushed over to him in hopes to stop him but it was too late. He pulled up a tiny fish. It was able to fit in the palm of his hand. "Well, look what we have here. You put up a huge fight for such a small guy."

The captain calmly shouted at the man. "Ye have but a few seconds to toss ya fish back to the waters now, boy."

The fisherman chuckled. "This little thing you are afraid of?" He lifted the fish with a large grin. At a closer inspection, it looked like a tiny dragon.

"What in da—" He was unable to finish his sentence as it grew rapidly and bit the man's head off. It kept growing.

Azaroth grabbed his sword. "This is a problem."

Aluxes jumped into action before he was able to lop off its head. The dead body twitched and was becoming bigger. It thrashed around, causing damage to the ship. They both pushed the beast overboard.

Aluxes caught her breath. "Wha—what in the hell was that?" He looked at her. "A coinarain. It is a water dragon that can hide itself as a small fish. But they can get as big as whales."

He stared out at the horizon and said in a monotone voice said, "It means we are getting closer." He sighed a little.

He slowly walked back to his room, she was still watching him as he vanished. "He seems troubled, I wonder if..."

I faint whisper from behind her said, "My dear, next time, kiss him deeply, embrace him in your arms, and confess your love. Then take him to your bed and make super babies. In all honesty, you two seem made to be together." She blushed and frantically turned around. Evalyn stood there giggling like a school child.

With a dumb grin on her face, she said, "My lovely Aluxes, I never thought this, and on a boat of all places. Sounds like something out of a romance story. Maybe you will no longer be a virgin by the end of this trip. I hope you are not a load moaner. The walls are very thin and I need my beauty sleep." She put her hands under her chin and sighed.

Aluxes, a little annoyed, asked, "Are you going to pester me every time I look at him? You said almost the same thing last time. And why does everything have to lead to sex with you?"

Evalyn grinned wider, which seemed impossible for her tiny lips. "My poor Aluxes, I remember when a guy wrote you a love letter once. You beat him so bad in combat class that day and made the poor thing cry. You also made your famous announcement of only dating a guy who could defeat you in combat." She looked over the horizon. "He is half-god and half-demon, maybe a few thousand years old. It is almost like you two were made to meet."

Aluxes rested her arm on the side of the ship and gazed out. "You think I have a chance at love? Most guys view me as a prize to dominate. I never really cared for it, but now I think I am starting to feel lonely." She looked at Evalyn. "You always had boyfriends. You were always going out and guys were giving you fancy gifts. I always hated you because you rubbed it in my face. I still hate you because you annoy the hell out of me."

Evalyn giggled a little. "That is the closest thing to a compliment anyone can get from you. I am honored to be your only friend." She sighed, and it slowly grew into an uncontrollable laughter.

"My dear Aluxes, the more you act like you hate the world, the closer your real friends will get. You will not notice it until something happens, and it shall be too late."

She touched Aluxes's shoulder. "Dear, we have other problems to deal with." They turned around and some of the ship's crew gave them angry looks.

One of the members had an odd tone to his voice that made it sound more like a threat. "We understand that you're not fully human, but it is the other half that has us concerned. If your other half snaps it could mean the end of the ship."

Evalyn's face turned red as she yelled, "Azaroth is on this ship and he is a mixed breed!"

Another member spoke, trying to keep his voice down. "Yes, but we all know what he is, and the legends about him. But her—we have never seen something like her. All we are asking is that she stay in her room."

Aluxes stared at them in her usual angry look. She closed her eyes and took a deep breath. "Do not bother. I've heard it all before. I will be in my room if you need me." She slowly walked by the crew mates. One of them was shaking a little as he tried to look composed.

She could hear him as he whispered, "She is so tall."

She quickly planted her face in front of his. "Boo!" He startled and fell over. She giggled with her eyes closed as she walked back to her room.

Later that day, they could see their destination. The trees had black leaves, making it look like a dead island from the distance. A small port barely stuck out with only a tiny storage shed for the sailors to drop off supplies. Black stone brick had been used to make the dock, which allowed it to blend in from afar.

When they attached the gangway everyone was rushed off. The crew acted as if they wished to not stay long. The dirt was red, almost like it was made of dried blood. The air was thick, making it hard to breath. Aluxes and Azaroth were the only ones that were fine but the others gasped as if needles pierced their throats.

The captain shouted at everyone as he walked back on the ship, "Ye best be get to town before too long. If ye stay here too long, the air be kill ya." He pointed towards some bushes and rotting dead bodies could be seen in random places.

"They not like folk to linger. Harder to watch unwanted folk if they be wandering." He turned around and jumped onto the ship.

Everyone followed the path of the black stone bricks. Each step was like walking on sharp glass. Some of the weaker people fell dead from the air. It caused a panic but Samantha tried to keep the group calm and told them to focus on the town, which could be seen.

Evalyn tapped Aluxes on the shoulder. "I am glad to see you are fine." Her body weaved as she collapsed. Her breaths became quick and short.

Azaroth picked her up and handed her to Aluxes. "She is full human. The effects are worse on her. Take her and run. I will help the others." Soon after, Alisa showed signs of weakening.

She ran as fast as she could, eyes fixed on the gates. "I need you to stay with me, I cannot lose you too."

As she approached, a guard shouted, "Halt!"

Chapter Twenty-Four

ERASED HISTORY

"Halt!" A guard stood atop the wall. He stared down at her and looked over to the other side. "Quickly, open the gate!"

"Why!" A hatch popped up from the wall. "Her eyes, her hair, hurry. Open the gate!"

When it was barely cracked, she rushed in. "Please, my friends are on the way. Leave the gate open."

When they looked at them, they immediately notice Azaroth. "It's him again. I was hoping we'd seen the last of him."

One guard was about to close the gate but the other punched his shoulder. "You know the laws. We have to let him in."

Another took a deep breath. "I do not want to feel his wrath."

As the group entered the city, the guards spat at his feet. "We only allow you to enter because of the law but if it was up to us, we would never allow you to even look at our gates."

Azaroth smiled at one of them. "I see you've been made guard captain. Last time, you'd just made sergeant." He glanced around and could see some people looking at him in disgust.

An elderly lady dressed in a white robe with a few young men beside her walked over and checked Evalyn. "If anyone is still having problems, please come with me for medical attention." The people that were more human than others followed her to the hospital building.

Aluxes tried to look around but the guard captain stood right in front of her. He cleared his throat a little. "Miss, we have not seen one of your kind since a long time. I would watch it with him if I were you. Last time he was here, many died."

The guards marched off but the captain stopped and without looking at him, said, "I know it was not your fault, but he was also my friend. I can never forgive you for what happened here." He walked back to his post.

Azaroth found a bench to sit on. He sighed and stared at his feet, unable to raise his head. It reminded Aluxes of how she used to act after a long day of being bullied.

She looked around at the buildings and noticed how oddly they were all shaped, like rain drops. The material was unknown to her. It must have been something from the island. She sat next to him and stared at his feet, imitating him.

He chuckled. "The buildings look new, but the youngest one is over a thousand years old. They were willed into existence. They never age."

She tried to use a caring tone but it came off as a little rude. "What happened here?" She attempted to cover her mouth but decided to continue. "Might as well at least tell me. I have a right to know."

"Remember my best friend that I said died here? Well, many were killed. It was because I refused to follow orders." He looked at a group of kids playing ball near a fountain, "I was told to execute someone. My friend and I were both sent to kill her. He fell in love with her, and I kept it a secret."

He smiled a little. "They had a daughter and that was how they found out. So, the gods sent in their army and forced me to watch. They slaughtered thousands, entire families, so they could keep their secrets. She was a powerful person, you see. If she wanted to–"

He looked around her and memories flashed in his mind. "She made a deal in exchange for her own life. They only kept half of the deal. They killed her husband right at that gate in a very brutal way."

He pointed at a spot as if he could still see it. "It was to serve as a warning to the residents. To not defy them." He looked in her eyes. "His name was Gaius Antonius."

As soon as he said that name, her body trembled inside. The more she sat there, the more uneasy she felt. Her hand shook a little. She tried to hide it but was unsuccessful. Her vision spun as images of flames filled her mind. The houses were on fire and dead bodies were all around.

She tried to cover her ears to drown out the screaming and quickly closed her eyes in the hope that it was a dream. She could feel someone tapping on her shoulder; it was a little old woman with glasses.

In a dried-up voice, she said, "Excuse me, dear. Are you Elpis?" She looked at Aluxes and smiled. "Ahh, it is you. My dear child."

She pulled out some baked bread. "Do you remember this? It was your favorite, Bierocks." Aluxes had no idea what to do and tried to push the old lady away.

A young woman ran over and shouted, "Grandma!" She grabbed her by the hand. "Sorry, miss. Her mind is going from age." She gently pulled her towards the shop. The bread roll fell onto her lap.

Azaroth touched her shoulder. "We must hurry and look for Melaina. Last I heard, she lived near the old town." He headed over to the others of the group and handed them some coins. He whispered in their ears and they walked off into a shop.

Onyx was the only one that refused to move. He was staring through a window. There was a stone glowing, his face lit up and his eyes twinkled as he gazed upon it.

Aluxes walked up behind him. "Do you know what that is?"

He looked at her with a faded smile. "Aye, that be a soul stone. The mightiest dwarf king, Halguard—he used it to slay a demon. It be a stone that could keep ya soul safe. The elves be use them to find lost souls for resurrection."

He looked at it and sighed. "But I be told her soul was gone into nothingness." Tears fell from his eyes, and he turned towards the shop with everyone else.

They came out with amulets to wear around their necks. The gems on them glowed a florescent pink. Aluxes looked at them, wondering if she should buy one.

Azaroth stopped her. "It will keep them safe outside the city for a few days. You and I do not need these." He waved at them to move closer. "It is a two-day trip north. Some of the things you will see will destroy what you know of history. Whatever you thought about the gods will be torn away."

As he walked off, he raised his head and relaxed his shoulders. Every few moments, someone would catch him staring at Aluxes and he would look away when he noticed they were watching

Evalyn, with her perverted grin across her face, said, "You know he has been watching you." She gazed back and smiled. "He also seems more relaxed. Maybe he will confess his love for you."

Aluxes choked on her own saliva. "What the hell is wrong with you? Yeah, I have noticed, but I think it has to do more with the fact his rules do not seem to apply here. He always acted like he was being watched."

The path was full of large stones with murals that moved. Words appeared, depicting what was happening. Samantha stood in front of one. Evalyn noticed that she was way behind and told everyone to stop.

They walked back to see what it was. "It is about Turiacus." She pointed to the text.

Azaroth focused on it. "These are the histories of the gods. The daughter of the god king made these." He took a deep breath. "These are the true histories of the world from the perspective of the gods."

Onyx looked at it. "I am impressed ya can read Dwarfish, lass."

Azaroth interrupted him. "It translates to 'the eyes of the seer.' She made it so all can read without misinterpretation."

Samantha teared up and was about to hit it but stopped herself. "This is not true!" She turned towards them and said, "It says he was a great hero, and he saved the world of the mortals twice."

Alisa took a closer look. "This story I know. Queen said great man mind was lost this day. Became monster he fought."

"I remember the parade in my village. There was a woman there in snow-white armor. He was also there. He spoke to himself and twitched a lot. The woman would whisper in his ear and he would calm down." Azaroth stood there looking at another stone.

They continued to move. "It was the first time I met her—the Goddess. She was very beautiful, and strong." Myka helped to calm down Samantha as they walked.

Aluxes tried to read all the stones quickly and ran into one that read *"You will not find what you're looking for here. What you are is a miracle that the gods were never able to foresee."*

Myka noticed the oddness of the pictures. "Events not in order. Mind seems to be gone for this one."

Azaroth chuckled and continued walking. "They are not in order because if you learn the true history, you would die. She made these to defile the god king's law. It was the only safe way to teach people."

They all stopped when they saw a familiar site; it was the same as the one that the Amazon queen had in her chamber. A dark face with red eyes in a hole. Goosebumps formed on their skins when they focused on it.

Onyx looked at it closely. "Our high king's throne room has this. Be about the end of times that almost came to be."

Azaroth touched it. "I was a young kid when this happened. I was not in the main battle, but I did have to fight the monsters that were made from it. His name is Apophis."

"So, Aluxes. You should walk closer to him. Maybe you two might even kiss by the end of the day?" Evalyn lightly jabbed her in the ribs.

"So I guess she is a virgin?" Samantha chuckled a little. "I mean my first time was not ideal, but I've been with others after. It does help with my anxiety."

"I been breed age and tried, not take. Queen says I find man right for me to mate with. It does feel good when done right." Alisa patted Aluxes on the back. "Just give it try. Be a woman."

Myka scoffed at them. "I save self for Azaroth. Also I princess, so I must wait."

Onyx pushed them to move faster. "Ya sister told me ya touch yaself thinking of him. Dwarf out walkin' ya long legs." Myka blushed and froze up.

"Well, I've only been with three people but I am still young and very desirable," Evalyn nudged her chin at Azaroth. "So, you've been around for thous—"

"None." He had an angered look. "The god king law. If I were to sleep with a woman, she is to be killed along with her family. It is to make sure my tainted blood will stay with me."

Aluxes walked next to him. "I personally see nothing wrong with that." Their hands kept bumping into each other with the occasional finger lock.

"You're welcome," Evalyn whispered to herself.

After what seemed like a two-day hike, they approached the largest image of them all and behind it was a destroyed village. Aluxes looked at the mural and fell to her knees. The person in her nightmares was there. The movements were more lifelike than the others and the detail more realistic. Goosebumps started to form on all of them. The shivering fear was impossible to hide. Even Azaroth himself was uneasy as he saw the image. The size of it filled their view, and her wings looked like they were moving towards them.

"Her name is Agrona. It is best not to stare at it too long," a powerful female voice echoed. The sheer energy emanating from her words put them to their knees, except for Azaroth.

Onyx, barely able to speak, said "Wha—what kind of power be this?"

"This is what happens when mortals hear the true voice of a god," Azaroth wiped his brow.

Aluxes managed to stand up and ran around to the other side of the mural with her sword drawn. "Stop now or you will kill us!"

There in the ruins was a destroyed city with skeletons scattered all over. And in the middle stood a tall woman. Her wings were a crimson red. Her eyes and hair were the same color. Like the Amazon queen but more intense and dignified.

She was much taller than Aluxes and Azaroth. It was hard not to feel a little bit of fear when looking upon her. She glared down at them as if they were mere bugs.

Aluxes stared into her eyes. "Why is she just standing there?" "She is trying to remember how to speak to mortals without killing them. Not all gods share the same power. Being the daughter of the god king, she is gifted with such power that her voice could kill lesser gods."

Onyx pointed out, "Why does she look like that dragon fella?"

"Because they are both devils." Azaroth kneeled in front of her. "She is their queen."

With a voice that had a commanding tone that demanded respect, she said, "Mortals, you should not have come here. You know better than to bring her here."

Azaroth smirked at her a little. "Being here for a while might have made you forget that the world outside still moves. You are unaware of what happened off this island. The monsters that your brother commanded are back, I feel he may be escaping."

The goddess looked with furrowed brows and spoke in an unpleasant voice. "Young man, I do from time to time check on his prison. He is not escaping. You are aware that he did not make them." She looked at Alisa. "I am aware that monsters are more active, and that there was a great disturbance, but my job is not yet done."

The goddess placed herself in front of Aluxes. It was obvious she was trying to block her view. Aluxes moved to look around her, but her aura was too thick to see through.

"You are from the Amazon. Tell me, how is my daughter?" The goddess noticed the parchment. In an instant, the paper appeared in her hands. Her eyes widened and she lost her concentration allowing Aluxes to see what was behind her. It was a destroyed house, and inside of her, something snapped.

The goddess was annoyed. "My father finally found a way to—" Before she could finish what she was saying she noticed that Aluxes had seen the house.

She had flashbacks of her mother watching her while someone else held her with a knife blade pointed at her little neck. There was a man with wings and hair as white as snow speaking in a language she did not understand. Her mother, holding a sword covered in blood that was not hers, stood there and begged the man.

Another person with gold-colored wings made of energy walked up to her and stabbed her. She was smiling at Aluxes as she was falling. They put the baby next to her and the woman died holding her. The winged people laughed and one pulled out a blade. He slowly moved up to Aluxes and was about to kill her when he was stopped.

A man with golden eyes walked out. He sounded like he was demanding something, though she did not understand the language; it seemed that he told them to stop. He gently lifted the baby. He placed her in a soft flower bed and casted a sleeping spell on her. When she awakened, she could see the high priest and head nun picking her up.

Everyone was crowded around Aluxes, trying to not to let her swallow her tongue. Onyx held her head and tears fell from his eyes.

In a quiet tone he said, "Ya scared me, lass. Ya all I have left. Ya had a wee seizure."

Azaroth checked on her to see if she was all right and looked at the goddess, "Melaina, your memory spell has lost its control. It may be time to tell her." He sounded a little angry, unable to hide it. Melania shrank herself so she was as tall as Aluxes.

She looked down at them. "Yes, you were born here. Your parents died here." She pointed to an area near the center. "That is where your mother died. She died for you, the only thing she cared for most in this world. She died because of you."

Chapter Twenty-Five

THE FLAMES

*A*s Melania moved, there was an afterimage. It waslike a shadow following her.

Azaroth tried his best to explain. "It is the energy she emits. Mortal minds cannot comprehend the energy of a god. So, it creates an image made of pure energy as she moves. Like a double."

She looked down at Aluxes. "Yes, my little one. You were born in this village. Your parents died here, and you were the only survivor." Melania's stare was like a snake ready to pounce at its prey.

Aluxes closed her eyes and cried out, "Why has no one told me this before? They all knew—the people in the church. Why did they have to die?"

The goddess gave her a smile that had no feeling of joy behind it. "It was because you were born." Her expression quickly vanished. "You were spared because after her death, your importance was discovered. Her fate became yours."

She walked over to a large stone erected in the center of the town. It was glowing blue like the memory stone that Rose had used on Aluxes, but it was as tall as a tree.

She rubbed her finger across it. "This is why I am here. I protect this. It is the true history of your world. Etharia was my greatest friend and rival. I was doing other duties when this happened."

Everyone slowly walked up to it. Before anyone could touch it, Melania stopped them. "It is not ready yet. I have not finished it." She moved towards Aluxes. "I never liked your father, and you smell of him. He was sent here to kill her. I told her to snap his neck. She refused to listen, and they fell in love in the middle of a duel. She was the greatest creation of the gods, and she fell for a simple human who was blessed."

Samantha cleared her throat. "May I ask—you remind me of Aeron. We have had a battle with him."

Melania laughed. "That is because we are both devils. The darker side of the gods' powers. The ones that interpreted the rules differently were cursed by my father to look like this." She then sighed as her face dropped. "And then there are those that made their own rules and fell down an unforgivable path."

She looked at Aluxes and made eye contact. "We do not have much time. If Aeron is attacking you, it means you must learn of the Fallen."

Azaroth also showed interest. Even he was not fully aware of what the Fallen were. She handed them each a tiny memory stone and told them to close their eyes. In their minds, they could hear chanting. They fell into a deep sleep; drifting in a stream with waves slowly moving them around.

A voice echoed from every direction, "These are the waves of time. The memories of events that cannot be changed. They are the true history that all chose to ignore."

The shadows of the waves became images of people. Soon, it turned into a scene of a war. Thousands of orcs, elves, dwarfs, gnolls, trolls, goblins, dragons, wyverns, and other beasts battled. There were no sides. Each on their own for survival.

The voice spoke again, "This was near the end of the war. The gods had become so confused that their alliances broke down. This was the war between the demons and gods, as you mortals call it, but it was really a civil war between the gods. It was a creation by these two individuals."

The entire view became covered by two beings with black wings of energy. The whites of their eyes were black and they had golden-colored eyes. They were whispering to each other.

They were interrupted by Melania. "All sides have collapsed. We are lost and confused. If both of you pick a side, it will tip the scales and end this war, and we shall truly know who was right."

The voice echoed again, "I was foolish. I knew what they were doing but like the others, I was enchanted by their power. They had the ability to kill gods. It was intoxicating to be near them. Both sides, gods and devils, enjoyed thinking we were taking advantage of them. But in reality, they made us fight each other. It was their game from the start."

Melania appeared in front of them and forced the streams to move. "Let us fast forward to the important part of the story. The second creation war."

It showed the two beings; one walked off while the other looked down at the mortal realm through a view mirror. A man came in. He had white hair and golden eyes.

Samantha ground her teeth. "Turiacus."

Melania smiled. "He was once a beloved person by all. He stayed out of the war, but he had a minor problem that set forth everything. He fell in love with one of them."

Turiacus walked up to her. "What is it you see? I often see you standing here, without your sister, gazing at the war."

She stared at him. Her voice sent fear into their hearts, and souls. Though it was a view of past events, it still had its effect. "What are these beings?" He looked at what she was pointing at. There were a family of humans trying to hide.

He chuckled a little. "Well, they are humans. They are nothing to pay any mind to. The only thing they seem to be good for is fodder for the others."

She looked at him without any emotion. "You say these things because they were not created by a divine nature. Yet they managed to survive this long."

He was a little upset at how she worded it. "Well, my dear. What do you think about them? To the gods and the devils, they are just a stain on our perfect world."

She looked back at the view mirror, still emotionless. "I can see what you are unable to. Their life energy is very strong. Almost as bright as a lower god. I feel that they are the future of ending the war."

Melania's image moved in between them as if they were statues. "While watching the humans, she started to develop a personality. At first, the two sisters were alike in every way but their roles affected them differently. She became admired by the humans. They had the ability to overcome the harsh world and survive. But they were starting to face the end of their race, and she decided to help them."

Melania fast-forwarded the time again. The one sister sneaked to the mortal surface. A family of three that she had been watching was about to be killed off by orcs. Her aura drained them of everything, even their physical bodies. The humans that she tried to save were devoured just the same. She held their ashes in her hands and cried as they were slowly consumed.

She was seen again sitting by the viewing mirror, with an emotional and depressed face. Black liquid oozed from her eyes like tears.

Turiacus rushed to her. "What has happened to you? What is this black stuff pouring from your eyes?" He was about to wipe it from her face but she grabbed his hand stopped him from touching it.

She looked and tried to regain her emotionless composure but failed. "Do not touch. It will consume you." Her facial expression started to resemble anger. "Do not tell my sister, but I will tell you everything."

The waves moved a little faster and ended in a moment; she was now alone with Turiacus in what appeared to be a lab.

He looked at her and tried to hold onto her shoulders. "Are you sure you want to do this? It may even kill you. It is a new spell that has never been tested."

She gazed at him and smiled in a strange way, as if it was something new to her. "I have trust in you, and the humans need someone. Fate will show that they are needed in this world."

Azaroth, lost for words, slowly found them. "She did everything for humans, so they would have a future in this world."

Melania stopped the images. "She did it all for the mortal realm. No higher being has ever cared for mortals as much as her. I followed her to the mortal realm and ended the war. She was the greatest person I had ever met."

An image of the man that they had seen in the murals showed up. "That is my brother; he was influenced by the other one. After her sister left her, she became unstable. She changed her plans and made an army. The vile filth that was inside her body could also influence others. They created the dark monsters for her. This was the war you were born into, Azaroth. Her name was forgotten by all as her reward, and death was what she earned."

She placed her finger on her chin and her other arm folded across her chest. "If he is breaking free, then it can be."

Azaroth interrupted her. "It was not him. The leader was a little doll, and she created the black substance from her body."

A look of shock overtook her. "Sirenisteen, it cannot be. She has been awakened?" She quickly ended the dream and everyone woke up.

Melania walked over to an orb and touched it. It slowly turned black and oozed out the dark liquid. "This is not good. I should have paid more attention to the human side of the world. Where is Lilith? How long has she been gone? I sent her on a simple mission to gather information." She looked over at a locket. "She is with her. I told her to end it. I must make what I need quickly to fix this."

She looked at Samantha. "Cursed girl, how was Turiacus's acting when you last saw him?"

She made a tight fist. "He was ranting and raving. His mind was gone like always."

Melania walked over to Aluxes. "He was desperate to remove your circlet. I can see the damage he made to the seal." A blinding light glowed around her neck. "It is repaired, my poor girl. You are not yet ready. If you remove it now, you will be consumed by the evil that has affected your heart. I blame your wretched father for that weakness."

She pushed Aluxes away gently. "That cloth that the nun gave you

—make sure that the dragon Aeron never gets a hold of it. If he does, he will return to his true state. I must go and deal with my father."

Melania glared over the group. "Dwarf, you have any questions?"

Onyx stared into her eyes and she nodded. "I can see that you have lost a loved one. I am sorry that she has been consumed by nothingness. Not even their soul survives." She looked over at Samantha. "I am sorry, poor child.His powers are stronger than mine. Only he can remove this curse." She never allowed them to speak. They could feel her in their minds. She rushed around and gathered a few random memory stones and placed them into a bag.

She looked over at them again. "You are still here? Of course, you are. You are needed someplace else."

She waved at them and suddenly, they were someplace new. Evalyn vomited. Myka was turning green. They all had a hard time walking and fell over. Azaroth was more stable but held his head and rubbed his temple to ease the migraine.

Myka looked around. "Are we near mountain elf lands?"

Azaroth coughed up some vomit. "Yeah, she teleported us." He sat on the ground before he fell over. "She moved us at her maximum range, halfway around the world. We are about a year's trip if we wanted to go back."

They were in the middle of a field, highlands to the south and a swamp to the north. In a distance they could see some elves watching them. They had the typical elf-colored hair but their skin was a little on the green side.

Onyx waved at them. "Ay, swamp elves."

He looked at Aluxes. "Better cover ya nose, lass. They have a wee odor to them."

One of them slowly walked over towards Myka. "*Humloa iayati, geetimwa.*" He kneeled in front of her.

Azaroth smirked. "Well, some luck is better than none. They are one of the loyalist tribes."

Onyx sat back down. "We always had bit of hard times with the swampies. Some be loyal to the dark elves, some be high elves, and some just grow moss out their arses all day."

They waved their arms as if they wanted them and the group reluctantly followed. They staggered at first but slowly regained the ability to walk at a normal pace. They were brought into a mid-sized town with a small castle. It looked like a trade hub between the different races.

There were dwarf crafts, gnome seeds, elf weapons, giant produce, and a handful of others. The swamp elves held out their hands as if asking for money. Myka gave them a gold coin each.

Onyx boasted out a laugh. "Give them a high reward for taking us to a town we would have found on our own."

She looked at him. "Their kind just get on economically. As princess, I do what I can to help. Though they are foul."

Evalyn wandered around. "I feel like I know this place. I think."

Before she could finish, she was interrupted by a loud voice that shouted, "My dear!" There stood a finely dressed man that almost looked like her father but smaller.

Her face broke into a smile, but her eyes feigned the happiness. "Uncle, how have you been?" The sound of her voice made it obvious she did not wish to see him.

She introduced him to the group. "This is my uncle. He is the lord of this town, Idielbuerg. He is Regent Lord Ludwig."

Aluxes whispered to her, "I am surprised you did not know you were in his lands."

She grunted. "How was I supposed to know she transported us thousands of miles? We are almost ten thousand miles from the Holy Capitol."

Azaroth walked up and shook his hand. "It has been a while, sir. Last time I saw you was at your wedding." They smiled as they greeted each other.

Ludwig clapped his hands together. "Well now, you guys showed up during our festival. Our lands have had peace for almost five thousand years."

Aluxes and Onyx looked over where they heard some loud laughing, and they saw a stall with orcs behind it selling food.

Onyx talked with a slow and calm voice. "I heard that during their non-war seasons, the bastards do trade with others. I never seen it, and I must admit, startles me bones a little."

Azaroth smiled. "It's hard for a dwarf to know about the doings of the orc lands. But in the last few decades, more tribes have started to give up war and focus on economics."

Ludwig, wanting to sound important, added in the last word, "Many tribes were almost wiped out. They understood that for the race to survive, they must find new ways. We are one of the three cities that allows them to trade."

Aluxes sat there, just watching them. Even though her eyes looked angry as usual, she was actually impressed.

Ludwig pulled Azaroth aside. "Sir, it would be an honor if you attended the ball tonight. You normally say no, but today is different."

He nodded in agreement to show up. Ludwig's smile was so large that the points of his lips almost touched his ears.

Samantha nudged Evalyn. "Your uncle is kind of creepy." She nodded with disappointment on her face.

Azaroth took them to a large house. There was a magic lock that kept the door shut. but it broke apart in a bright light as he touched the handle.

Evalyn stuttered a little, "This is bigger than the place I grew up in, and my father was a noble. Who lives here?" Azaroth tossed up a powder that imitated a flame and lit up the entire building.

He looked over his shoulder. "It is my home. I was raised here. I was found by the family that lived here and they adopted me. They had no children of their own, at first."

Myka's eyes and face lit up in excitement. "This where my love grew up? A building over ten thousand years old?"

He chuckled a little. "No, it has been remolded a few times. It is actually half the size. They died during the war with the Fallen gods. This city was how I got involved. The first attack was here."

He slowly walked towards the main stairs. "The changing rooms are down the hall. You need to dress up nicely. You're invited to my birthday party."

Chapter Twenty-Six

YOUNG LOVE

*A*zaroth led them to a room. The door was labeled as the dressing room. Alisa opened it and the girls crowded in. The inside was as large as a house and was filled from wall to wall with women's clothing.

Samantha found a chair and sat there staring at the dresses. "With a face like mine, it does not matter what I wear." She tried to hide it, but she kept glancing at a light-blue dress enchanted with gnome dust that made it glow. Every time she looked at it, she turned her head to stare in the mirror. All she could see was her curse.

Aluxes sat next to her. "It's all right. I never see any point in parties like these. I went to one once. All that happened was Evalyn trying to brag about how much better she was than me." She looked over and Samantha was still depressed.

She scoffed slightly. "I know you probably had a hard time growing up. To others, you are a freak, but to me, you're a very pretty girl. I wish a guy would look at me without thinking I needed aid to cross the street." She walked up to a red velvet dress with gold trim. "I think this will look perfect on you."

Alisa stared, not knowing what to pick. "We have nothing like this in the Amazon. I once saw the queen wear a fancy dress."

Myka was still looking at the dresses. "I want to ask—how come you not bring armor? I thought in pack but was full of stones."

Alisa stopped what she was doing. "I banished. I forbidden to wear armor of queen."

Evalyn picked up a dress. "This will look great with your dark skin. Maybe we will find you armor later." Aluxes tried to see the dress but was unable to.

Aluxes looked at the one that Samantha held up next to her and said, "I have no intention of attending this party. I need to do mo—"

Before she could finish, she was cut off by Samantha, "Out of all of us, you should be the one to go. You are the only one he gets close to. The little princess is always trying to get at him and he ignores her. Evalyn tried to use her body to get him to peek and he ignored. You, however, he takes the effort to speak truthfully to. He always seems to care about what you think, and when you make a mistake, he makes it with you so you're not alone." Her eyes swelled up as she tried to hold back her tears.

"I know why people do not like you. It was something that I noticed after we met that goddess and the Amazon queen. The uneasy, unnatural shape, the perfection." She looked at her closer. "No marks, no misshape. Everything is perfect. It is why people treated you badly. It is uneasy on the mind to see a face with no imperfections."

She rubbed Aluxes's arm. "When I touch your skin, I feel nothing hindering it. Not even marks from an old pimple. You give off a feeling when people look at you. The same intimidation they give off when I look at them. People hate it and they hate you for it. They can never be you."

Aluxes tried not to stare at her. "What does this have to do with me attending the party?"

Samantha glanced at her reflection. "The way he looks at you when you are not looking is... I have seen how you look at him. I feel it is something that has to happen." She slowly rubbed the mirror. She was able to see herself without the curse.

She sighed. "I wish someone would look at me the way he looks at you. I wish I were a beautiful freak instead of a cursed monster."

Evalyn screamed and rushed out into the hall. She barely had time to cover herself when Onyx ran to see what had happened. "Ya be giving this old dwarf his final dream with ya tits as perfect as yours." She quickly backed up to the wall and lifted the dress she had in her hand to cover more.

There was a girl that walked out. She looked like a bird. Stood about three and a half feet tall with bird feet, a small beak, and fingers instead of feathers at the end of her small wings; but she had a human figure.

Onyx laughed. "It be a kikimora. Made me think there be a monster."

The kikimora picked up the dresses that Evalyn had dropped and hung them back up. She then walked off, dusting around the halls.

Samantha watched it carefully. "It is a house spirit. If they like the dwelling they are in and you treat them with respect, they help with the house. They come from the dream realm. There is a space between the mortal realm and the divine realm."

Onyx rubbed his chin and pondered. "Aye, mine was a wee bit destructive. Must have been a time I was drunk. She ended up smashing all me belongings."

Myka, still angered that a dwarf saw her partially naked, said, "You probably tried sleep with, you dirty dwarf." Then as if lightning hit her, added, "Onyx, how you get here fast?"

He walked off whistling, not answering. He slowly disappeared down the hall. He was wearing what looked like a pirate's outfit. The girls stood there, a little confused. They realized that they were mostly naked, standing in a hallway. They all blushed a little and rushed back in.

Aluxes picked up the dress that Samantha had showed her and stood in front of a mirror and held it up to her neck. "I wonder if he would notice me in this? Will he like it if I wore something like this?"

Evalyn took a glance. "Oh, that is a good color for you. I wonder who Morsha is?"

On the hanger of the dress was a small tag that read *"Morsha."* Half of them had that name. Evalyn helped her put it on. It was a thickly layered dress and it weighed almost half as much as Aluxes. Inside it, there was a small pocket that held full-length formal gloves. They were pearl white with gold and silver trim.

Myka and Samantha made her hair match the formal dress. It was something any girl but Aluxes could dream of. Her sour face threw off the image but she smiled. They tried to make it look better by putting on a flowered hairband. It worked a little, but she was unable to change her furrowed eyebrows.

Evalyn smirked with a face of defeat. "Your scouring look is your gift, I guess." They walked off to finish getting dressed.

After two hours had gone by, Azaroth returned with a carriage to take them to the castle. Samantha, still in her usual armor, sat with the driver. Evalyn had on a pearl white dress which almost looked like a wedding dress. Myka was wearing a pink silk dress, something that was found in the Far East Empire. Onyx was wearing something that a pirate captain would wear during a formal party.

The girls chuckled. "Aye, I once saw a brave seafolk wear something like this when I was a wee lad and I thunk it looked amazing." Azaroth chuckled a little, and they rode off to the castle.

When they walked inside, they were greeted by nobles and rich people who were scattered throughout the halls. In the center of the courtyard were the rest of the townspeople were gathered, celebrating their hero. Paper lanterns hung all over along with white flags that had a red eye in the center.

Aluxes looked at the flag and asked quietly, "Why the red eye?"

Azaroth grunted a little and was about to change the subject but he decided to answer, "When I show my true self my eyes turn red, and my hair turns white. It is the cursed power of my birth, but it was the only way I was able to save the town."

Samantha and Onyx joined the party in the courtyard. Even though Samantha looked happy, her fake smile conveyed every bit of her anger. Generally, people would have mistaken her for one of the male guards. Onyx was dancing around drunk and getting along with the seafolk that happened to be in the town when the party started.

A fancy style of music with a slow tune played. People separated into pairs and danced. Evalyn was having problems. A bunch of attractive men surrounded her asking for a moment on the floor. Myka found a young elf boy and decided to dance with him. He had never seen the elf kingdom. They were lost in conversation as she explained it to him in detail. Aluxes stood there alone in a corner.

She could hear the men whisper, but they were too afraid to ask her. "I wish my ears would fall off. I do not care for the rituals of these kinds of things, but it would still be nice to be asked." Most of them were intimidated by her height. The only man taller than her was Azaroth.

Some more songs played and then the music stopped. Everyone stepped aside. "Let's all praise our hero and honor him during his birthday. Cheers to his heroic deeds!" one of the guests said out loud as the people clapped. Azaroth was wearing the formal attire of a noble lord. It was dark green, with a red sash around the waist, and white pants. Aluxes's entire face was as pink as a peach when he approached her.

He held out his hand. "It would be rude of me if I did not ask the loveliest lady in the room to dance a single dance. Will you honor me with your beauty?" He smiled with a bow.

All she could do was stare at his hand. She looked over at Evalyn who was giving her a thumbs up. The people outside crowded the windows to watch. Samantha and Onyx were in the front with large smiles as she took his hand.

The conductor tapped a few times to hint which song to perform. They played *Greensleeves*. Aluxes looked down at her feet, trying not to step on his toes.

"Relax and follow my lead." They danced as if it was meant to be.

As they waltzed, the burning feeling of everyone watching faded from Aluxes's mind. She slowly become enchanted by looking into his eyes and everything in the room disappeared except for the sound of the music. Time for her stopped and they danced endlessly. It was as if she was flying in the sky. She was unusually gifted, like it was second nature. For a moment, her eyebrows, which were always furrowed, showed signs of happiness.

The song ended and a new one played so they kept moving. The other guests danced as well. "I can say I had a hand in this. If it were not for me, she would have ignored her feelings." Evalyn smirked.

"Aye, that boat trip be a wee bit annoying with them glancing at each other. I must say, lass. Ya be doin' well for ya self despite the tragicness," Onyx said.

"I was around monsters my entire life. I knew Father would die eventually. When she found me alone, crying for my father, I decided to do what I could to give her a good life. She is all I have left." She smiled and closed her eyes when she looked at them.

"Aye, she all I have left as well. If anything happen to her, I think me old heart would stop." He turned around to rejoin the party.

Aluxes broke the silence between them. "Who is Morsha?"

He looked over her shoulder and sighed. "My sister. The family that adopted me had a daughter a few years afterwards. Almost all the clothing in there used to be hers." A tear fell from his eye. "She died on her wedding day, when the Fallen unleashed their hellish monsters onto the world."

"How could the clothing be kept looking new for so long?"

He smiled at her. "If you take a closer look, there is some pixie dust woven into the fabric. It prevents the clothing from aging."

After the second song ended, he spun her and bowed down, kissing her hand. Their eyes never broke contact as time returned to normal and the room slowly filled with people. Everyone clapped as they walked off the floor with their arms locked together. They moved towards the balcony.

Azaroth took a deep breath. "I needed to get some fresh air."

Her face still red, she said, "It's all right. I needed some air also. I've never danced before. I am a bit nervous. I guess it is normal for you."

He rested his arms on the railing. "I have not attended any parties in over five hundred years." He looked at her. "I only came today because we just happen to be here. It is not even my birthday. I am rarely home, so if I happen to be here when they are having their biweekly festival, they say it is my birthday. I also thought it would be fun to dance with you."

It seemed impossible, but her face was able to turn redder as she looked down at her feet. "So, what is it like being immortal?"

He chuckled a little. "I am not immortal, and I am younger than the legends say I am." He lifted up his sleeve. Under his skin, his veins were turning black. "I have a longer lifespan than normal mortals but I am not immortal. I was born to die, like others before and after me."

He stood up straight and looked at the stars. "To keep the peace the gods and devils made an alliance not from paper but from blood. Once every hundred years, they renew it by making a half-breed like me. Since no one wants them, they are stripped of their divine aura and sent to the earth. We are stronger than mortals even as infants, but there are hunters whose sole purpose is to kill us before we can grow up." He looked into her eyes. "I survived because a kind family found me and adopted me. Some of the legends about me are actually that of others. The one thing that is true about me is that I was there during the war with the fallen gods, I defended this village and the kingdom of this land. Also, the one with the dwarfs."

Aluxes stood there unable to speak but understood the pain he was in. Not being able to open up to anyone, people only viewed him as something he was not. It was a constant struggle that she was aware of. She nudged herself towards him. The closer she moved, the more she could feel the warmth radiating from his body, and it drew her in.

As he talked, she rubbed her elbow on his arm. "I have maybe a few decades left, but I am glad I got to meet you."

She grabbed him and looked into his eyes, holding his shirt around the shoulders. Her breath became heavy, and she was sweating. Her mind was telling her to kiss him. Their lips moved closer but before they could follow through with it, there was a loud explosion.

Random people that were not at the party ran towards the castle screaming, and in the distance, glowing crimson hair could be seen. It was Aeron.

Chapter Twenty-Seven

THE DOLL AND A PRINCE

*A*month after the disaster in the Holy City of Cathair, Prince Loux's coronation took place at the Holy Alter of Kings near Fuirborlg. The first rule he made was to move the capitol to Angrath. Though he had rebuilt the city, and boosted the economy, the survivors of the event were disappearing.

To make it easier, King Loux had the castle built around his vacation home. This already gave him a study and a bedroom. He also had no need to move his belongings.

Rumors circulated among the workers. They swore they could hear screams from time to time, and few said that they saw the new king talking to himself. The ones that decided to peep in on his conversations were never seen again.

One of the maids who had been there for a week became curious and put her ear to the door, trying to listen in.

There was fear in his voice as he yelled, "Look, I know you want it found now, but we cannot afford to be discovered right now. You are still in a weakened state, we need to bide our time. Dig slowly."

A female voice that sent shivers through the maid's soul replied, "I have been waiting for ten thousand years. I need it now to return to my original form. If I did not need your resources, I would have devoured you the day we met."

Before the maid could move, a black tar spear flew through the door and penetrated her head. The door opened and her body was pulled back towards the doll. The black substance attached itself to the doll, and the maid's body slowly drained into nothingness.

King Loux tried to sound angry to hide his fear. "You have to control your eating habits a little more. People are starting to spread rumors."

Though she had black eyes made of stone that made her look like every other doll, when she turned her head to stare at him, he could feel her anger and trembled uncontrollably.

She pointed a finger at him. "Remember whom you are speaking to. Our deal was that you will find my body and I shall grant you rule of the world. Even in this weakened state I am still able to devour anything you mortals can summon."

With a shaken voice, he regained some composer. "You've never heard of Lord Azaroth? He was the one that defeated your armies when your disciple tried to bring you back. There is also another wild card that roams these plains that can hinder you."

Her little doll hands rubbed her chin. "Aeron has told me of this boy. He said he could be a major problem." Some of the flames of the candles turned black.

"Turiacus is to blame for all of my problems. He was the very center of all of this. But I've been told that he has become a new monster." She slammed her stuffed hands on the arms of the chair. It made almost no noise. "I will allow you to advise me this one time. What you say is the reason why I should slow myself down. Just remember, King. You read the book and awakened me, knowing what I was."

He felt uneasy about her, but his overconfidence in the summoning spell relaxed him. "We know where your relic is at. It has been a slight problem, though, the dwarf that survived lives there, and he is closely watched by all of the races. So, our work can only be done when no one is watching."

The doll used some magic to make a round crystal. "Aeron, I need you to do something for me."

His deep voice echoed through the halls of the castle. "My master, it may take me a while. I am still recovering. This body that I am trapped in has weaknesses." There was a short break. "It shall be done soon, my master!"

After a month, the rumors died out. Workers stopped disappearing and returned home at night. With the king's son Prince Tourmaline arriving, everyone started setting up for a party.

He was a tall young man with full plate armor. It had a fresh polish to it for the occasion. It was not decorated like most high-borns but was simple and elegant. He had a tattoo on his neck in the shape of a diamond with a three-headed dragon in the center. He was barely eighteen but still looked like he had seen his fair share. He slowly walked over the red carpet with a flock of people that kneeled as they watched him pass by.

His father stood there and embraced him. "It has been three long years. I missed you." He tried not to cry with joy but a tear made its way through.

With great joy, he shouted, "My son, the war hero. I see you have the mark of a champion!"

The young prince's voice was light but it could still be heard clearly. "Father, I have missed thee." He handed him a golden war pike. "I was rewarded for defeating a goblin champion one on one."

He had a flashback in his mind of the giant goblin: taller than a troll, more muscular than an orc, covered in the blood of the humans he had killed in battle, and surrounded by normal-sized goblins.

The prince regained his composer. "Our allies on the continent of Crast awarded me with this tattoo of the highest honor." He held his father's arm. "I ended the war as fast as I could after I heard what had happened to Uncle."

He stood tall and was handed a glass of wine by a servant. "I toast that I shall avenge my uncle's death and make sure this kingdom prospers for all time."

The people raised their glasses for his toast and drank. King Loux slowly moved back to his throne and sat down. He waved his arm to signal his son to join him.

He nodded his head. "Sorry, Father, for I am tired from my travels. I shall call it early to bed." The young girls blushed at the sight of him. Every detail of him was dignified.

"Excuse me, I am lost and cannot find my room," He waved down one of the maids. When he entered his room, he slowly removed his armor and sat on his bed. His mind flashed back to his time in the other kingdom that he'd helped. He was offered a princess to marry who had dark brown eyes, long black hair, and dark skin.

"I have to be sad and show sadness. I am to be heartbroken. I am to be weary of battle and wishing for peace." He remembered a moment during the reception. A monster made of shadows—a wraith—had come in and devoured her in front of everyone. Though it was a tragic experience, he was not bothered by it. He sat there calmly as if there was nothing to it.

He fell asleep for a short while before waking in the middle of the night. He could hear a voice in the back of his head say, "You have great power. You will be much more important to me than your father. I have chosen you." The voice would terrify everyone who would normally hear it but the prince was unfazed. He treated it as if it was a regular voice.

King Loux entered the room to wake up his son. He was already awake and sitting in a chair with a cute little doll in his arms. The king's face turned white as he screamed, "Son, put that down at once!"

He looked at him calmly. "Oh, hello Father. I saw this thing when I woke up. Sitting here in this chair." The king tried to examine his son to see if there were any marks of devouring. To his surprise, there were none.

He kneeled by his son and gently took the doll. "Come on now. A man of your stature caught with a doll." They both chuckled a little as he walked off with it.

He turned to his son. "Oh, you have a delegate wanting to meet you. Remember, we are trying to form new human alliances." The prince stood up and stretched. The expression on his face was emotionless; even his eyes showed no emotion.

He stared out the window and sighed. "I shall do what is needed of me, Father."

The king ran to his room muttering and gently placed the doll into a chair. "We had a deal!"

She stared at him with her button eyes. Her face always seemed the same. She rubbed her chin as if to ponder. "I, Agrona, broke a deal?"

She moved her head from side to side. "I do not recall that my movements were in our agreement. I freely choose where I go." She hovered above the ground to look out the window. She could see the young prince riding his horse with the delegates. They seemed to be showing off their showmanship on horseback.

A blue glow emitted from her eyes. "I will grant you a new deal— your son. I shall grant him the gift of the gods when I get my true body."

A dark feeling filled Loux's deepest pits, as if he were hollowed out from the inside. He hunched over a little bit from the pain. Something about the deal felt off to him but he had no choice but to agree. After he nodded to accept, blood slowly ran down his nose.

He fell to the ground gasping for air and Agrona turned with a creepy giggle. "Remember who you just yelled at. I shall allow it to slide this one time. I still have need of you." Air rushed back into his lungs and he slowly stood up. He was trying not to lose composure as he left the room.

I've never heard her say her name before. That is not the name that was in the book. Who is she? He thought to himself. *Did I summon the wrong Fallen?*

A few weeks passed and the young prince was seen with the doll more often. "Son, why do you always carry that silly thing around? Are you still in mourning? I know you were to get married and she was killed in front of you by a wraith."

Tourmaline sighed. "Yes, she was killed, but I do not really care about the matter. Every night, I've been having the same dream. It is of a woman with long black hair, golden eyes with the whites of her eyes are black, and black wings. In the dream, she is holding me and rocking me like a baby. She sometimes hums a tune—a song that I've never heard of, and she rubs her fingers through my long hair. I dream of her every night. I feel that I need to find her."

He held up the doll. "It is weird but every time I dream of her, this doll is in my bed."

King Loux kept an eye on the doll every day, worried she would try to consume him. There were moments in which he refused to show up to important summons so that he was able to keep an eye on the doll. Rumors started to spread among the people that the king's mind was drifting over the loss of his brother, and they worried he had become mad.

One night, Agrona woke up the king. "The dwarf has left the grave. We must act quickly, now!"

King Loux, in an angry tone, grunted and stumbled up. He picked up the doll and rushed to his horse. Some of his guards tried to accompany him but he demanded that they stay put.

He headed towards the area and could see battle damage spread around the site. Standing in the middle was Aeron. Some of his wounds that had healed up had started to reopen. Blood was pouring into pools around his feet.

The king held his nose. "What is that dreadful smell?"

Aeron grunted at him. "Filthy human. Keeping this body alive required means that are unsavory to you mortals."

Agrona looked at him, and with a hint of concern in her voice, said, "Your cursed body is starting to die. I need you as an important guard while I recover my power. You must recover your scale."

She moved her hand around; the ground glowed a dark purple. Eerie sounds and voices echoed everywhere.

Even Aeron was a little unsettled by the sound. "I can feel it. Deep. Protected." She took a breath and souls popped out of the ground. The souls screamed as she consumed a handful of them and floated off.

"If I consume too many, they will know. We must start digging as fast as we can." She was unable to hide her excitement.

Loux cleared his throat. "The elves will be here to protect this place in his absence. Seeing the signs of the events that happened here, they will know something is up."

Aeron grabbed him by the neck. "Master, may I finally end this human now?"

She nodded. "No, he is right. You may hate the mortals, but their short life makes them capable of thinking things in remarkable ways. We are so close. I cannot lose my body now."

She made a magical map in the air. "Remember this location. There is an artifact there. It shall replenish your body for a time. My sister used it to save a mortal."

He walked off. "Yes, my master. I shall find it and recover my scale."

Agrona looked at Loux with anger and desperation. "We need to hurry with the offsite digging. Will you be able to hire workers that can dig faster than our slaves?"

Loux held his hand under his chin. "I can think of a few groups that would be willing to work with no questions asked. I shall get it done as soon as possible." The second he closed his mouth, his heart dropped into his feet. He knew that when they found it, he would be done for.

After they arrived back at the castle, he rushed into his study. He moved around some books and a hidden passage opened. He quickly closed it behind him and made his way down a spiral stairway. He entered a room with glowing amulets and runes. He passed through a barrier that was protecting a book in the center.

He opened the book and looked for the name Agrona among a list of titles of the Fallen. Nowhere could he find the name. He carefully combed through each page to find any mention of her, but he still came up empty. He looked for artifacts that could harm a Fallen god and his eyes lit up.

He rubbed his face, and his body shook with excitement. "The Sword of Etharia!"

"Was used to slay and imprison many of the Fallen. It had been used three times by mortals to defeat demons, greater wraiths, and mighty ancient dragons. It was last located in the great city of Burth-

Fell. If that bitch thinks she can stab me in the back. . ." He danced with excitement.

He rushed into his son's room. "I am going on a mission to the city of BurthFell. I am leaving you in charge while I am gone."

He handed his son some papers. "These are the things that need to get done no matter what." They were contracts for mining offsite near the mass grave.

The prince looked at it. "Father, I think the elves would have a problem with this."

Before he could finish, the king interrupted him. "Son! Do not take this contract lightly! It is of the upmost importance for the future of humans. Remember my goal?"

His son had a smile that even the king was bothered by. "Yes, Father. Make all the other races kneel to us."

Loux ran to his room and slammed the door behind him. The doll stood there emitting her anger. "You are leaving? If you are unable to stick to our agreement, I will have no use for you, lower mortal."

He shouted back in an attempt to make it sound important, "I gave the plans for the mine to my son. He is sure to complete the task. I have something I must attend to as king to our allies." Her aura vanished, and she sat in his chair with her hands perched on her chin.

He cleared his throat; it was hard though, because it was dry. "If I do not visit other kingdoms, I would be ignoring my duties. If I do that, people would get suspicious and start to watch our movements." He could tell his words were working as she looked towards the fireplace. "This is the most important part of the stage. If we are not careful, we can lose everything."

The doll smiled. "I trust you know what you are doing. Very well. I trust your son will get the job done."

The king left with a few hundred troops as his guard to visit other kingdoms. Agrona closely watched him as he left and sneaked into the prince's room and waited till night for him to return. The young man sat in his bed, tired from trying to act as king.

As he lay down, he could hear a voice say, "Your father is a weak man. I need a strong man by my side, and I have chosen you."

"That voice is a heavenly voice. Are you the woman from my dreams?" He turned his head, looking around to find her. In the corner of his room, the doll stood with a dark purple aura, which became black as it burned more.

"You are unaffected by my voice; most mortals would bleed from their eyes. There is something about you." She hovered in front of him.

He looked at her with tears of joy. "I have been dreaming of this. Of you. The one I am to be with."

Agrona's mouth opened wide with a grin as she thought to herself. *I have found a mortal born without a soul. The one my sister doubted existed, the one immune to our nature to devour. He shall be my king and I shall be his queen.*

Chapter Twenty-Eight

DRAGON GOD

*P*eople were running and screaming as the fire spread. Aeron randomly slashed at people with his clawed hands. Not a single movement was wasted. A true master of his skill, every swing killed a person. He slowly walked towards the castle where Aluxes and Azaroth were.

Azaroth was deeply troubled. "He got hold of something to restore his body. His power is even greater than it was before." Aluxes's eyes widened in shock. He managed to beat them with barely taking any damage himself, and he was in a weakened state. It was the first time she felt true terror from a creature not in her dreams.

Aeron opened his mouth and a ball of energy shot from it and caused an explosion. It was magical fire in its purest forum. Only some of the strongest of ancient dragons were able to create such fire and with difficulty. Yet, Aeron did it as if it were the only type of breath he had.

He walked towards them like he was on a mission, causing as much chaos as he could. He became drunk off his newly revived power. The evil grin on his face would scare even the king of the gods himself.

Azaroth grabbed a crossbow and aimed it. The amulet around his neck glowed brightly. He fired a bolt and Aeron grabbed it with an uncontrollable laugh. He lowered himself into a squat and leaped towards the castle. He moved so fast that Azaroth was caught off guard. He smashed through the wall as if it were made of paper. Before he could react, Aeron grabbed Azaroth's head and tossed him through a wall into the main gallery.

Aeron sniffed the air. "You have the scale on you, whelp. Give me that linen around your waist."

Aluxes screamed a little in fear, but quickly recovered. His voice was more intense than it had been before. She reached for her waist but remembered that she had did not brought her sword.

She looked at him in the eyes. "How do you know I have it on me?" She could feel it under her dress. It slowly started glowing red and felt like it was burning.

He grabbed at her, but she dodged him. "Whelp, I can feel it. I can smell it. I can hear it calling out to me." He tried to grab at her again but missed.

He growled in anger. "Master wants you alive, pup. If it was not for that, I would have killed you already."

Samantha managed to sneak up and stab him in the back. He laughed as he swung around at her. She leaped over just in time and slashed his face, but before she touched the ground, he snagged her with his other hand.

He slowly squeezed her neck. "I would expect this much from a vampire hunter but your little game ends here. However, before you die, I will let you know the cure for your curse. Only he can reverse it but he has to be alive to do it." Tears fell from eyes as she thought about her life ending. She had a flash of memories from when she was little with her family before she was kidnapped.

There was a loud explosion and pellets ripped Aeron's face apart. Onyx stood there reloading a blunderbuss. He shouted at Aluxes, "Hey lass! Stop wasting wee time and get that blasted sword of yours. It be too heavy for that kikimora!"

Aluxes looked over and saw that the bird-girl was barely able to lift it. Aluxes quickly snagged it and swung at Aeron. He blocked it with his arm, allowing it to cut into him. She tried to pull it out but he grabbed it with his other hand.

With a twisted smile, he snarled. "Whelp, that managed to cut deep." He kicked her, sending her flying into a wall. She gasped for air as blood popped out of her mouth. He was about to throw her sword at her when a spear pierced his back and was struck by lightning. It managed to knock his aim off and the sword missed Aluxes. Aeron turned around and Alisa stood there trying to ready another spell.

Light encircled her as she chanted the spell, "Mulungu, grant me the energy to smite the fools who defy your power." A bolt of lightning flew from her fingertips, hitting him, but he just stood there unfazed and smiling. He slowly walked towards her as the lightning scorched his body.

He pulled the spear from his back and stabbed her through the stomach and lifted her off the ground. He let go of the spear and she landed on the ground. He looked at his hands and licked the blood off them. Everyone stared at him and felt hopeless.

Azaroth jumped in, punching Aeron in the face so hard he fell to the ground. Azaroth's eyes and hair were a dark crimson color. His hair looked like flowing blood.

Aeron stood back up with a huge smile on his face. "So, I guess that part about being half-devil was true. Maybe we can—" Azaroth kicked him hard enough that he flew through a wall.

He looked down at his hand and summoned a fire blade. "It is forbidden for me to use my divine powers in the mortal realm, but the gods turned a blind eye to you."

Aeron slowly walked towards him and snickered. "I consider you a man. You have my respect. But you lack the experience in handling an ancient god like me."

He opened his mouth and shot another high intensity fireball. Azaroth was barely able to dodge it, but the explosion it caused still managed to hurt him and he dropped his blade. Without hesitation, Azaroth closed the distance before he could get another shot off. As the second attack was about to leave his mouth, Azaroth punched Aeron's jaw shut and caused it to explode inside him. The shock-wave was intense and Azaroth's arm broke when he shielded himself.

Aeron's body lay there like it was dead. Myka quickly started a healing spell on Alisa and Evalyn ran to Aluxes's aid. Aluxes was mostly healed. She just needed help popping her shoulder back into place.

They looked at the body. There were pools of blood around it and the head was missing. They had just started to relax when he slowly stood up and his head regenerated itself. Once the vocal cords and mouth formed, he laughed.

Azaroth walked up to Aluxes. "That amulet is giving him his new power. It restored his ability to retain his body. We must remove it."

She looked at his neck and could see the charm. It was two triangles with an eye in the center. She lunged at it but Aeron caught her sword with his hand. He tried to swing at her with his other hand but she ducked and rolled, pulling her sword out of his hands.

She ended up back next to Azaroth. "Where did he get that?"

He moved closer to her ear and whispered, "It belonged to your mother. She gave it to your father to save his life the day they met."

When Aeron's face fully healed, he stood there with a big grin. "My master found its location from reading one of the secret books of Dumas that the king kept hidden away. The dumb king has no idea. He is playing Master's game."

Samantha tried to sneak up on him again, but a dragon tail came out from behind him and hit her across the chest, breaking a few ribs as she hit the ground.

Azaroth and Aluxes both leaped in. They were in sync as if they'd been doing it their entire lives. Azaroth with his mighty blows and Aluxes with her fast swings overwhelmed the dragon god. The fight seemed to drag on for ten minutes.

All three of them took blows and damage but also healed as they fought. However, it was obvious to everyone watching that Aeron was the better fighter. If it were one on one neither of them could have taken him on and survived. Onyx slowly walked up, closely looking for an opening. He was armed with a goblin boom stick.

He chuckled a little. "Aye, I saw this be in the armory. I have been hit by one. I wonder if it will hurt this beasty enough to give us an edge."

Aeron did an uppercut to Aluxes and sent her up into the air. He then quickly turned the other hand into a dragon fist and clawed at Azaroth's chest. A loud echoing explosion ripped through the air as a metal ball went right into his heart. It stunned him enough to allow Aluxes to swing down with her sword as she fell, cutting him nearly in half.

Before she was able to pull her sword out, Aeron grabbed it and healed his body around it, keeping it stuck in place. He smiled and let out a loud beastly growl. Blood oozed out of his mouth all over her now torn up dress. Before he could speak, she grabbed the amulet and kicked him in the groin.

Onyx chuckled. "I told ya, lass. Hit them in the balls." He quickly reloaded another shot and took aim.

Aeron held up his hand. He was now was holding the linen that Aluxes had tied around her waist. He'd managed to rip it off from a small hole on the side of her dress when she was busy trying to escape. The smile on his face was larger than his head. The sky became the color of blood as the linen turned into a piece of flesh.

With glee in his voice as he talked, it combined with a hole on his thigh, "I am now complete. My curse is over. My master will rule all."

His body slowly grew, and he started to look more like a dragon. He kept getting taller and wider, all the while laughing. Horns sprouted from his head and his nose. Azaroth tried to take a few swings at him with his flaming sword, but it did nothing. Soon, the tallest of the group could only reach his ankle, yet he kept on growing.

Onyx tried to shoot him in the eye but his head was too high and out of range. He gasped. "I seen an ancient dragon once. He be so large he filled up a lake. I think he already surpassed that size."

Aeron stopped changing and growing. He was finished. They stood there, unable to handle what they were seeing. He was taller than a mountain and almost as wide. His red scales were larger than a boat.

The horns on his nose and head were longer and thicker than the tallest tree. He truly was the embodiment of a powerful god.

With a voice so deep and loud it caused quakes, he said "I, Demon God Aeron, have returned!" With just one flap from his large wings, the entire city was wiped off the face of the earth. People were flung all over, many to their deaths.

He opened his mouth, and a loud whistling could be heard as a ball of fire projected out, causing a large explosion that could be seen for hundreds of miles. The cloud dust was over a hundred miles high and was shaped like a mushroom.

Azaroth stood there with a look of helplessness. Aluxes had never seen him look weak, but she could not blame him. It made him look more normal. It made her love him more.

Alisa ran up to him and shook him. "You a god, right? Why cannot deal with him? Use some godly power?"

He stared at her and cried, "When the pact babies are born, we have our essences removed. Each time I use any of my powers, I use up some of my own life force. The stronger the spell, the more life I drain." He turned his head away. "He is a godly being, I would have to kill myself to destroy him."

Alisa stood there staring at him with regret that she'd asked him. "I sorry, did not. What we do?"

He looked around. "Nothing."

When Aeron flew into the sky, it was like he was in slow motion, but there was no mistaking the force that was generated with each flap. Trees were uprooted, boulders were flung everywhere, and water became unbound to the ground.

He boasted as he left, "I shall go and help my master get her body back on my own," and ignored the group of people as if they were nothing. A massive lightning bolt struck him in the head, causing him to crash into the ground.

As they approached to see what caused it, they saw a figure floating in the sky. Samantha's skin was enveloped in goosebumps, her eyes start to turn red with rage.

Without blinking, she grunted out, "Turiacus!"

Chapter Twenty-Nine

THE DERANGED GOD

*A*eron rolled around a little and growled in pain. The blood that flew out of his wounds was as hot as magma. He looked towards the sky and could see the vampire god Turiacus smiling at him.

Aeron, with puzzlement in his voice, asked, "Why do you fight me? Have you been cursed and tossed aside? You are more Fallen than I."

With a smile on his face and in pure ignorance of the situation, Turiacus gleefully said, as if his mind were gone, "Oh, my, Lady Etharia, my love. I love you so much I will take care of him for you. He planned to destroy this world you loved so much. Will you return my love for you if I defeat him again?"

Like he was intoxicated, he was unable to fly straight and unleashed another bolt of lightning, which caused Aeron much pain. Aeron managed to strike him with his tail, smashing him into the ground. As his tail slowly lifted up, he could see Turiacus's body in a pool of his own blood.

He smiled as he healed. "Oh, you have forgotten, my poor beastly god. I remember how you used to look before you trapped your soul in your favorite beast. I did it for you, my love Etharia."

Giant spikes of ice flew out of his hands and pierced the dragon's thick scales. Aeron tried to bite at him but his larger size made it hard to keep up. It became obvious who was the stronger of the two. If Turiacus decided to stop toying around, he could finish the fight easily.

"Ahh yes, devour. I must feed on the life force. I need the energy now. Oh, my dear sweet Etharia, is that why you left me? Because I took your curse?" He started to cry and stopped moving.

Aeron managed to bat him with his hand. "My sweet, I took your curse into my own body. You left me because I reminded you of it."

The dragon readied a fire breath but Turiacus became angered. "That filthy human—he took you from me! That is why I must kill him." He lunged at the dragon with his fist. The impact caused the attack to miss and fire up into the sky.

"I am sorry, my love, to hurt you so, but I was the one that reported to them. They had to know. Where did you go after that, my love?" He stopped moving and looked around. "My love, Etharia. Are you here to see me save the world for you again? Will this make you run into my arms and forgive me?"

Aeron used the moment to swallow him. He gloated, "When you imprisoned me in that form, your mind was still stable. Now you're nothing but a shadow of someone who was a rival."

He had started to fly off again when lightning surrounded his body. He rolled on the ground, smashing everything in his way. Dead people and animals could be seen in his path. The bolts kept striking him over and over. The pain forced him to gag and vomit.

Turiacus stood up from the excrement and smiled wickedly, which made Aeron quiver in fear. He raised his hand and let out a howl, and thousands of vampires came charging, covering the dragon. They bit and clawed at him, each causing some damage.

Turiacus spoke a little more soundly, "I am no fool to allow your master to destroy what is mine to devour. I have created the life that they both wish they could, and I have the same power that they do."

Aeron began to panic and tried to shake them off. As they consumed his blood, their bodies turned red; they were devouring his godly essences and becoming evolved.

Aeron chuckled a little after he calmed down. A large circle surrounded him that had a yellow glow. The vampires and even Turiacus were thrown to the ground. He had increased the weight of the air. He kept increasing it until the force crushed their bodies into dust. Some of the vampires that had drank his blood managed to escape.

Aeron looked at Turiacus and smiled. "I see. You are trying to find a new way to make your kind survive better. I think you should know that even though you made me human, I still hold you in the highest regard with respect." Turiacus smiled as Aeron charged another breath attack.

The words, "Samantha, my love. I am sorry," escaped his lips. There was another loud explosion, with a bigger dust cloud than the one before.

As the dust cleared, there was an aura. A god-like image. Turiacus was now almost a hundred feet tall. His eyes had a bright glow to them, and when he moved, there was an eerie afterimage, much like what they had seen from every divine being.

As they battled, the ground broke apart. It was clear why gods never fought their own battles and why they were forbidden to be in the mortal realm. Their devastating power could destroy all that was nearby.

Each strike, every kick, and all the magical attacks brought chaos in their aftermath. The plane of existence was ripping apart. Even their blood had a dire effect when it touched the ground. It was like lava, burning everything that it came in contact with.

They clashed for what seemed like forever until Turiacus's mind started to get lost in rambling again. "My love, I did this for you. Why can you not love me?" He looked around. "I became a monster because of you."

Aeron grabbed the chance and bit his arm off. It was an easy feat considering he was much larger than Turiacus. If it were not for his unstable mind, he would have won. But now his limbs were being bitten off one by one as he still rambled on, unaware of what was going on.

Before Aeron could bite off his head, Turiacus regained his mind a little and quickly made eye contact with the dragon. A large explosion surrounded Aeron's head. Molten blood flew all over, burning everything in its path.

It gave Turiacus time to regrow his limbs. He summoned another lightning bolt and used the moment to stand. Beams of light came from the ground and bound Aeron, preventing him from moving. The fight was almost over. When Turiacus was aware of the battle, it was obvious who was the more powerful of the gods.

Turiacus smiled. "In the old days, I would have just returned you to your cursed form but now my hunger is stronger than ever." He opened his mouth, exposing razor-sharp teeth. A monstrous roar came from him as he opened his mouth wider.

As he was about to bite Aeron, a spear-like tail impaled him. It ripped him in half and he fell to the ground in shock. He coughed out blood.

He begged, "Etharia, save me please. I need you to save me from myself. I know you felt guilty for what had happened to me. I forgive you for getting married to that human."

Aeron lowered his head with a grin. "You have one flaw. You are too powerful. You left yourself wide open." And without giving him time to gain his mind back, Aeron ate his top half in a single bite.

The other bits of Turiacus slowly turned into dust. Aeron bellowed and rolled around in joy. He had been able to defeat the one that had cursed him many thousands of years ago. He flew off towards his master. In his mind, nothing could stop him now.

Chapter Thirty

CURSED SON

A deep monotonous voice, as if it was from a lifeless person, said, "But, Father. The plan seems too reckless. And she will be there, so it will be hard for me to contain myself if I see her."

He stood there alone in the woods. He was naked with pitch black skin, red eyes, and long white hair. His fangs were long and his closed mouth was unable hide them.

He moved some bushes over. In front of him, a mile away, he saw her. He stared at them as they watched the fight between Turiacus and Aeron. He fixated on Samantha. She had a tingling feeling that someone was watching her and looked in his direction. Though she was too far away to see him, he ducked behind the bush, afraid that she saw him.

He rocked back and forth. His mind was at war like Turiacus's but more stable. "Mother, my mother. I wonder if you can forgive me mother. Can you love me?"

He looked up and watched the fight. "It is almost time." He stood there, mind wavering between his mission and Samantha. He twitched at moments, a sign of being at conflict with himself.

In the depth of his mind, he could hear Turiacus speaking to him. "Malikai, it is time to save your kind."

He looked at Turiacus. "Yes, my father."

As soon as Aeron fell on the ground and his guard was down, he let out a loud howl, and thousands of vampires ran out and latched on to the dragon and drank his blood. The newly turned vampires and the weak burst into flames from the divine energy in his blood. As he rolled around, thousands of them died. The goal was to gamble on a few who would survive.

After a few moments, some let go and took off running. Out of the thousands, a few hundred managed to escape his spell. One by one, they started to glow red and turned to ashes, looking like embers from a flame.

Unbeknownst to him as he ran in a random direction, Malikai ended up in front of Samantha. He stopped only a few feet away from her.

As she reached for her crossbow, he quietly whispered, "Mother."

Samantha stopped and stared at him. She did not know why but she felt as if she knew him. She stood there with her hand on her crossbow looking at him. His eyes slowly turned red, and then his veins as well as his body. He let out screams of pain and tried to run off, but she managed to get a bolt out into his leg.

He stared at her with tears of blood that ran down his face. "I forgive you. Please remember me. She never met me; she does not know who I am. No, he erased it. Part of his plan." Then, quietly under his breath, he said, "Mother."

Samantha stood there looking at him. She lowered her crossbow and tears started to run down her face.

"Who are you? Why can I not bring myself to kill you? Why do I feel sad after I just wounded you?" she cried out, unable to control her tears.

Evalyn came running up with her whip in hand and managed to whip it around one of his arms. The metal glowed white and burned his skin. Samantha cried out as he screamed in pain and knocked the whip out of her hand.

He took off running into the woods. Evalyn tried chase him. After a few moments went by, she walked back out, holding her whip.

She scoffed at Samantha with a look of fury. "What the hell is your problem?" The entire party was able to hear her shouting.

Samantha placed her hand over her heart and tried to find her words. "I do not understand. But I felt that he was connected to me somehow. I had an instinct to save him."

Malikai rushed to an area where five other vampires stood. He looked around. "Is this all that made it?"

One of the others who was strong enough to speak grunted under pain. "No, Master. Some are slowly recovering. Only twelve survived. The rest were not strong enough to survive the power in the blood."

In his mind, he could hear Turiacus's voice in the back of his mind, asking, "My son, did it go as planned?"

He looked straight, as if he were standing in front of him, and said, "Yes, Father. It went better than we had planned. Twelve have survived." Their bodies slowly changed. Their skin became a dark blue color and eyes turned red. They stared up at the battle between the two gods and witnessed Aeron defeating Turiacus.

Malikai looked around and nodded. The group darted off into the woods towards Turiacus's castle. Deep in his mind, he was thinking. *Father, your plan will be carried out.*

They made a quick stop—an abandoned building covered in moss. Inside were remnants of a happy family that had once lived there. Malikai picked up a book that oddly looked new, though the dates on it were of over a thousand years old. Inside it there was a vial of blood and charcoal drawings of a happy mother, a little child, and a man that resembled Turiacus.

Malikai looked at the pictures. "Elder brother, I will not make the same mistakes as you." Being unaware it was still in hands he ran off with it.

The trip was far, but with their new power, the sun no longer had its sway over them and they were able to keep moving. They also noticed that they no longer needed to feed. After a month of non-stop running, they made it back. Some lower vampires greeted them and all of them kneeled.

Malikai looked around. What used to be a broken town in ruins was now being rebuilt to its former glory. He had heard his father tell stories about its grandeur and had seen a few paintings.

A familiar voice echoed off the walls, "Did you remember to bring the vial, my son?" There, sitting on the throne, was Turiacus, slowly regenerating. He looked like a grotesque mangled body without flesh.

Malikai handed him the vial. Turiacus held it and ranted, "My dear, my love, my Etharia. I am sorry. I did not mean to cheat on you. But I loved her. This is all I have left of her. All that is left of my original mind, so I must take her again. I am sorry."

He slowly drank it, and though his face was mostly bone, his demeanor changed and his mind was different. He was no longer ranting under his breath, but he still twitched every now and then.

With a smile, he spoke in glee, "They have fallen for my trap. Now we must begin with my master plan." Malikai bowed and turned around. "What is that you have there? Tucked away behind your back?"

Malikai moved his hand in front of him and saw the book. "I am sorry, Father. I did—"

Before he could finish, Turiacus interrupted him, "No, my son. It is not of your doing; it is why I avoided it for so long. The curse of fate to remind me when I was more of what I am today." He snatched the book from his son and opened it to the family sketches.

He looked at Malikai and twitched a little. "This was my wife—a human. Our son became the first vampire. He was known as the vampire king. Her blood had a rare trait. It cured me of my affliction for some moments and she died as a mortal." He gently rubbed his finger across it, trying not to taint it with blood.

He stood up. "The vial will only last me about a year. I need to be fully mentally stable to complete this task. After I set it in motion, it will not matter if I am still of a sound mind." He slowly walked into the courtyard, which was full of people under a sleeping spell.

Chapter Thirty-One

THE KING'S EMBERS

King Loux eagerly rode off on his horse with his knights as his personal guard, glaring at the castle as it disappeared. He looked around and recounted his men— a little over a hundred. He was still unable to keep his mind at ease. He kept having flashbacks of what the doll had said to him and the smile she had given. He knew deep down that she was going to dispose of him and replace him with the prince.

If only I did not love my son, it would have been easier. He thought to himself

His mind kept filling up with his task as he rode off to find the relic —the Sword of Etharia. Though he was unable to bring the book with him, he did have a few pages copied. During every break they took, he would comb through it. Just like Agrona, Etharia was not in any of the lists except for a small mention that read, *"Etharia, the first created immortal to walk the earth, was punished most dreadfully by the god king."*

He wished he'd copied the whole book but it was too late. They only stopped to rest the horses. Eating was done while riding and they got little sleep. Three months passed before they took a real rest.

Some of the knights started to waver in their duties to the king, thinking that he had become mad. Around thirty deserted him and the rest stayed out of pity as he seemed to go deeper into madness. He constantly went through each page to make sure that he had not missed a single word.

He would constantly pull out a map to go over the plotted course, once again to a forgotten ancient library—the place where he had found the book.

They finally reached the destination and everyone was impressed by what they saw. Giant runes covered in overgrowth could be seen for miles. The knights sat there in amazement. One of them mentioned that it had to be bigger than the largest city in the world. Broken stones of unknown material littered the ground. They were bright, polished, and had a shine to them even in the shade. The king took a dagger and hit one of the stones; the blade broke and the stone received no damage.

He looked at them. "Stay near me. Do not wander off. There are ancient beasts, that time has forgotten, hiding here."

Some parts had been flooded by the nearby sea as the walls that held the water back gave away to time. The sounds of something huge could be heard swimming underneath. In the dark areas, heavy breathing echoed off the walls, deep enough that one could tell it must be a large monster.

One of the guards saw a little flower in the middle of the path. He looked at it and said, "This is a very lovely flower. My wife would love to have a seed from this." He bent down to touch it, and spikes popped out of it and pierced his hands. He screamed for a moment, but then his body stiffened as he became paralyzed. As the other guards tried to grab him, he was lifted high into the air. A giant plant-like beast with an odd, almost human-looking face came out of the over growth and ate the man.

The king yelled at them, "Do not touch it or you will all die!"

The monster must have been over eighty feet tall. It slowly placed its hand on the ground and the flower sprouted back.

Some stared at Loux in fear. He cleared his throat. "That is the tamest of what lurks here. We must move quickly before nightfall."

They ran along the main road to a tall building. It was round in shape and was the only building that looked like it was somewhat maintained. Even though there were fifty guards, they were dwarfed by the main hall. The king closed the door and told all but four to stay behind.

They moved towards a large pillar that had stairs inside. They walked up for what seemed like hours till they reached the top. In the center of the room was a round obsidian orb hovering above a hole.

One of the guards with a dry throat asked, "Sir, what this room be?"

He smiled as he walked towards the orb. "This, my friends, is the doorbell to the forgotten library." As he touched it softly, chimes were heard all over. It was as if someone was ringing church bells across the city.

An old but wise-sounding voice came from the shadows, "My my, the young prince has come back. Oh, but I see he is a king now." An old man walked out. He looked like an elf but was short like a dwarf. His back was hunched, had ears twice as long as that of an elf's, and a nose shaped like a bird's beak. Most of his hair were gone, and instead of the normal green eyes that male elves have, his eyes were an amber color.

One of the guards shouted, "Who is you be? You not a gnome or a elf. State what creature you be." He stepped between the old elf and the king.

Loux tried to stop the guard, but the man waved his hand. "It is all right my old friend. It is a fair question; you're only doing your duty."

He tried to stand straight to look tall and proud. "I am one of the last of the original elves. I am an Eternal, or I was." His voice still had an amazing sound despite his age.

He looked at his hands. "There are only maybe fifteen of us left." He held up his hands, showing twelve fingers on each. "We do not die of age. When the gods made us, we were to live forever. Boredom is what normally kills us."

He slowly walked up to the guard. "As for my name, well, I am a cursed Eternal. Even just hearing my name would cause death. The gods wanted to make sure no one would learn the true history." He moved his finger to tell the guard to lower his head. The old elf whispered in his ear.

The guard stood up with a confused look on his face and slowly started bleeding out of his pores. After a few seconds, he screamed in pain. Blood flew from his eyes, nose, and mouth. As time went on blood came from his armor as if he were bleeding from other regions of his body.

He ran towards one of the other guards, but one of his legs snapped off as he melted away into a red puddle.

The old elf smiled. "That was from hearing my name." He laughed in a sinister manner.

He walked towards the king, and with a pleased sound in his voice, said, "Well, my friend. I gather you need information about something." He waved his hand at the orb and the floor became glass. Underneath them were millions of books going down in a spiral.

King Loux looked at him and tried to hide his anger. "You told me that if I performed the contract spell, the one whom I summoned would do my bidding as per the contract. But she refuses to do anything I say and is starting to conspire behind my back."

The elf smiled in a way that made the king's hair stand on end. "My friend, you are just overthinking it. But if there is a problem, I am sure one of these books can help. But there is a price, and you know what it is."

The king crossed his arms and placed a finger on his temple, tapping long and hard. He understood that everything he had worked for would be destroyed if he refused to make the agreement. He had flashbacks of his son, remembering when he was young.

With sadness in his voice, he said, "Yes, you may have him."

The elf waved at the orb again and it began to glow, and with a different type of smile, he tapped the floor with his toes. "Now, what is it you seek?"

Loux looked at him, and with a stoic voice said, "I wish to know the location of BurthFell so I can find the Sword of Etharia." The elf's smiled vanished and the orb stopped glowing.

He walked back and forth. "This city was once a mighty city. The greatest in the world. Etharia is why it fell to shambles. If she stayed out of it, I would have been the king of that place." He looked at Loux with anger in his eyes. "My friend, I have seen the gods. I have met the devils and I allied myself with the Fallen." He pointed out the window.

In the distance, there was part of a castle that barely stuck out. Most of it was underwater. "That is where the king of the Fallen reigned—King Apophis sat. He was a god among gods. This sword was almost able to almost slay him. She was a one-of-a-kind weapon created by them. Hearing her name makes me want to vomit."

Loux tapped his feet and clenched his fists. "I gave you what you asked for. By the laws of your people, you must obey your end. Is there anything else I may add to make the deal?"

The old elf smiled right away. It was as if he had been waiting for this moment. "I need about half. It has been a while and I am starving."

The king clenched his gut. He understood that he had been tricked. He stumbled a little with his words but then nodded.

In the lobby, the men were setting up for dinner. Drinks and merry-making were bringing their spirits up. One of the men noticed something shining in one of the shadows. Before he could say a word, a giant spider leg shot out and impaled him. A dozen spiders with bodies bigger than horses and legs three times the size of their abdomens came rushing out. A man managed to hit one with a spear but it made the sound of metal hitting metal and bounced off. The screams were so loud even Loux was able to hear.

Lights of energy started to flow through the air and the elf began to feed off them, restoring some of his youth. It barely did anything for his skin but it repaired his hunched back. He reached in his robe and pulled out a book, as if he already had the book this entire time.

He handed the book to the king and in a serious tone said, "The name Etharia may not bring death like my name, but it is more forbidden to say it in the mortal realm. Do not say her name in any unprotected areas."

He looked at him, a little confused. "Who is—"

Before he could finish, the elf put his finger on his lips. "Even though we were enemies, I have to say that she was the greatest warrior that ever lived in all the realms. My Fallen comrades also think it would have been better to not have erased her from mortal memory. But she is one of the many names that I wish people remembered."

Loux looked at him, a little puzzled. "I thought she was your enemy? Why give such praise to your foe? Is it not standard to erase them from history?"

The elf chuckled. "Etharia was a real hero and deserved the respect that she earned, despite being created. If you have a real foe, it is your duty to make sure they are remembered forever." He slowly walked into the shadows and disappeared.

The king and the guards returned to where the group was. There was blood and webs all over. Half of the men were still alive but were cocooned. They quickly cut them free except for one man. As the king tried to cut the webbing, one of the large spiders came up and snatched him away. They could hear his screams bounce off the walls.

One of them opened the door and was grabbed by a large beast. It was too dark out. They were unable to see what it was but they could hear their comrade scream in pain. They quickly moved into one of the stairwells in the pillars—an area too small for the spiders to fit. None of them managed to sleep. Even the king was too scared.

As soon as they could see some light shining from under the door, they knew it was day. They ran out without any problems. The king looked back and could see a figure standing on top of the library. He knew deep down that it was the elf with his evil smile.

The elf stood there giggling with a slight sparkle in his eyes. He was excited about something.

He pulled out a communication crystal from his robe and cheerfully said, "Master, the deal has been made. He is going to get it as we speak."

"Good, I can now move forward with my plans. Did he suspect anything? I do not want any complications. If there is even a little setback, I will devour everything you hold dear. Starting with your books." The other voice had a terrifying sound.

He stopped and sounded a little bothered as he said, "No, Master. He took the deal with no complications. I followed your instructions and left him with enough to get the item." The crystal broke and turned to dust.

He stared at the sun and sighed. "If I never became a Fallen, would this empire still be around? How foolish I was to trust her."

He looked over the edge of his balcony and hesitated with his words. "I will see it till the end, I suppose." With a wave of his hand, he disappeared.

Chapter Thirty-Two

EMBERS OF HELL

"*B*urthFell was a city founded by the first alliance among mortals. The high elves, dwarves, giants, gnomes, and pixies. It was an advanced city with many towers reaching the clouds.

It was the time of the great war between the gods and devils. Their creations went to war to show which gods were the best at creating life. When the groups joined, they noticed that their chance of winning was more likely, and because their end goals were almost the same, they did not mind forming a monument of their peace.

The sounds of smiths could be heard from all parts, making weapons and armor for their great army. Over ten million residents and armed forces lived here. But not all had it easy, outside the walls were their slaves, the humans.

They were undesired by all, viewed mostly as filthy beasts. Races that lived off magic were able to harvest their life force, which was stronger than most. Being created by the earth, they were self-contained beings of their own destiny. This was viewed as filth by the gods, and in consequence of the creations the gods had created.

The alliance decided that their ability to reproduce faster than most other mortals made them an ideal work force. They were also able to live in harsh conditions. They were taller than most, and had above *average strength. Reproduction was a new concept among the older races. The gods saw it as a way to increase their numbers without using energy.*

But soon, this would all change for the humans. It started as their entire race was in the process of being wiped out, which became their greatest answer. It was when the great city was attacked.

First, waves of lesser monsters such as hobgoblins, gnolls, and imps attacked. Since the humans were considered lesser beings, they were not saved. Being killed off by the thousands, they struggled to survive. But much to the surprise of the other races, they managed to drive off the beasts.

They managed to arm themselves with the weapons of their kills and learned basic combat in a short time. For days, they fended off the bests but they were slowly wearing out. Eventually, all of them that were outside the gates were killed off.

Impressed with how the humans were able to learn the art of war, the ones in the city as house slaves were thought to be guards. But their value was so little that it did nothing to improve their fate. Orcs and trolls, by the millions, showed up demanding that the humans be turned over to them to be sacrificed to their gods. Their abilities had made their gods worried, and they wanted them wiped off the mortal realm.

Not wanting to die for slaves, they were willing to hand them over if they agreed to leave. What was left of the humans were rounded up and brought outside the gates.

This was to end their kind in a total genocide, until a bright light fell from the sky. It hit the ground, causing a great cloud of dust, like an explosion. Everyone stopped what they were doing to see what was going on. This was the day everything changed. It was the day Etharia arrived.

Her high output of godly energy made it look like she had an after-image following her. It was bright, hard to look at, and could be felt among everyone as the energy flowed through her every movement.

Swiftly, she moved through the crowd of monsters, cutting them in half. In just a few blinks she was already where the humans were, killing thousands of orcs and trolls. Without speaking a word, she killed the elves that were escorting the slaves to their deaths. She had made it evident that she did not care for any of them.

She stood there with a proud and powerful stance. Holding her sword towards the sky, she declared, 'I am Etharia, and I am here to claim the humans as their guardian.'

The largest orc to ever walk the earth showed up, oozing with power. He was one of the original orcs—an Eternal. He boasted to her with grand speeches of killing angels, the messengers of the gods. With a happy grin and an evil glare, he looked at her in the eyes and insulted her with his words.

'If you are truly a god, then you must be a weak one, to be cast down to the mortal realm.'

He stood about thirty feet tall. He was a beast among beasts. He picked up his glave and took a swing. A flash of light was all that was seen as his sword and body were cut in half. She then turned towards the gate and made a large fireball. The gate was no more.

She took the humans away with her towards the mountains, leaving the other two sides to fight. It was the end of the alliance, the end of BurthFell.

I am the only survivor, an old gnome who writes this before his time is up. I remember the days of the city burning. It went on for weeks. My family was killed by the flames. I do not blame her for what had happened. It was because we forgot that they were living creatures like anyone else.

The victor was no one but the humans. Both armies lost so many that their numbers were never again that high. It was not the orcs that set the city on fire; it was overuse of magic. The smith forges and no one was skilled enough to replace the human slaves at these jobs.

She was not the only god I would see in the realm, but she was the first to do so that I know of. We must blame ourselves for this; each one brought more death to our realm. Many races are now gone for good. I have not seen a single gnome after the fall. I fear I may be the last. I will never forget her golden eyes and blue hair. She was the most perfect looking woman I had ever seen, even compared to my new master, Melania.

Take what I say as a warning. All living things should be treated dearly; it matters not who created them. Or you will evoke someone's wrath."

The Old Gnome

Bwindle Bird

Loux had a surprised look on his face as he read more. He never knew that gods had stepped on the mortal realm, except for the Unnamed Goddess. He thought about the months of the year. Melania was the month after harvest. He wondered if the months were named after the gods that lived among the mortals.

He tried to think hard but was unable to recall anything named after Etharia. For such an important person to the salvation of all humans, one would think there would be something of her.

He turned to the next page and his face changed as he saw a map in great detail in the book, outlaying an area. He looked to the sun to get his bearings.

He asked one of the guards where the nearest port town was that had ships sailing east. None of them really knew where they are, but one had been drawing a map in his journal.

He looked at the king and hesitated. "Sir, I... I think I may know where to go."

He pulled out one of his maps and tried to pinpoint their location. "Sir, it is about a week's travel from here. But the town of Salvest would be the best bet."

The king shouted, "Men break camp! We make for Salvest. We are heading to the Immortal Sea." The men stood there looking at each other.

"Sir, we be no cowards, but what happened earlier and where we are going? We all know of the stories about legendary beasts that live there. We also know you gave permission for us to be killed for that book." Some of the soldiers teared up.

Loux looked at his men and could see it in their faces. He knew he had to inspire them and tell them some of the truth.

With a heroic tone but still sounding as if he was as hopeless as them, he said, "Men, I know your fears. Many have died, and for what? A king to find some idol to expand his riches?"

He looked around to see them surround him. "I must tell you something. I did not want to say it before to prevent starting a panic." With a deep breath, he paused for dramatic effect. "The truth is that the darkness that destroyed the Holy City is now in the new capitol, and it will not stop until every human is wiped off the face of the earth. The object that I am looking for is the only way to defeat it."

The men whispered as he continued to talk. "I am risking my life and all of your lives to protect our families and our very race as humans. If we few shall die but end up saving every single person in this world, is that not worth it to give your children a future?" He could see it; the men were inspired. Some even clapped as they praised him.

He removed his armor to show his scars; a few looked as if they were horrific. "I got these from learning about the truth of the events. My life, like all of yours, is on the table."

They bought it. He knew that they were all willing to die for what needed to be done. He still had power over his subjects, and they would follow his every order.

They set off and managed to arrive at the port with no problems. They found a boat with little effort. The people at the dock said that it had already been paid for and was set up. When the king stared at the sun, he swore that he could see the man of the library hovering above the water, following them.

The trip was long and harsh. Time was hard to judge while sailing. Only the gods knew what the date was when they landed at another dock to gather more supplies. To them, it seemed to be almost a year before they reached the Immortal Sea, but it had only been three months. The ocean was black. They could barely see a few inches below the surface. The air had the foul smell of stagnated water, which they could even taste in the air. There was a tiny island where a smaller boat was waiting. The sailors got off and went to it. The soldiers and the king were on their own.

The boat that they were on was a large galley but it was the smallest object around. There had been moments in which they could see eyes in the water. At night, it would have a greenish glow and stare at them. The smell of evil was thick and the sea was motionless.

In the book, it said that the Immortal Sea was where the first god to die in the mortal realm was killed. His death created a great hole to trap all the evil monsters. Then, a mighty rain flooded the area, making a sea. Anything that drank from the water would die a horrid death, and fishes turned to bones as soon as they touched it. It was a place that no mortal had been to since the war ended. It was a lower god that had served Melania and tried to overthrow her, and this was his fate.

One of the men gagged as he rushed towards the edge. Before he could vomit, a long, gray, slimy arm reached up and grabbed him. He barely let out a scream. They all swore they could hear the water laugh at their misfortune.

For three days, they paddled towards the shore that they could see, but it seemed like it was never getting any closer. It was as if it went on and on. When they had lost all hope, they hit a giant root. It punctured the bottom of the boat and slowly filled it with water. They looked over to the edge and noticed that they were thirty feet from the shore.

They hesitated a little about jumping into the water, not knowing what was in there. The sea was as black as tar; only the surface was visible.

One of the men shouted, "Strip your armor and place it in these barrels!" He pulled out a few empty barrels, and they put their equipment inside so they could get across without sinking. They tied a rope around themselves and the man. The king patted the soldier on the shoulder with a hopeful smile for him. The man jumped as far as he could.

He landed in the water with a large splash. Even the droplets were black. Not knowing if he was all right or not, they all looked over as time stood still for them. He leaped out onto the shore as they feared the worst.

He waved. "It is really deep. Did not even touch the bottom. I used the root to pull myself towards the shore." He tugged on the rope. They tossed the barrels into the water, and he pulled them to shore.

The men, excited to get off the ship, all jumped into the water. As the men reached the shore, they noticed that the first man was gone, and all that remained was a puddle of blood. The king quickly looked in the barrels and found his book.

With determination in his voice, he said to them, "Men, if we turn around now, then their deaths were for nothing. We are here, and we will find the item that will save us all."

One of the men tripped over a small hole. He noticed that it was a window opening, and that the boulders were in fact, parts of buildings sticking out of the ground. They were in BurthFell.

Chapter Thirty-Three

DOES DARKNESS DREAM?

*I*n a realm of complete darkness, nothing could be seen except a small shining light off in the distance. Every now and then, a body would float by only to be devoured into the nothingness. People who adventured into the unknown died from not being prepared. It was not their fault—not knowing what to expect in the Darkness. But the more they ventured out and settled, the brighter and bigger the light became.

The Darkness felt nothing until the moment it could see what was living in the light. They were tall beings. They could speak, write, and travel. Darkness was only able to consume. However, the light was growing faster than it could consume. It felt fear and anger. Not able to make life, it took matters into its own hands. Bodies that would float off into the land of nothing would be tested on. It would try to put its own force into the dead. Each time, it ended with failure.

With no living bodies to experiment on, it had no idea how any of it functioned. One day, as luck would have it, a group of explorers drifted off too far from the light. They ended up trapped within the Darkness. Eons went by as it became better at creating dark life. Soon, it was able to infect twin sisters perfectly. When they came into the light, they were welcomed openly but they had their own plan.

"Sister, we must corrupt them. Their life force is tasty," one of them said emotionlessly.

Everything became hazy as they feasted in secret; it was the first time they felt any emotions. One sister felt happiness and joy while the other experienced shame.

"Sister, we will rule over all of nothingness in no time," she said with the normal lack of emotions.

Everything slowly turned to smoke as it changed to another time. She was now staring at the back of a girl's head. Her body was enveloped in a bright light. "Sister, do not leave me!" She tried to attack her but before her hand could reach the girl, she spun around and grabbed her.

All she could see were her lips. "Sis, I am sorry, but life is worth protecting." Her voice was more defined, with greater confidence.

She smiled at her and said softly, "Sister, I decided on a name. To remind me of where I came from and who I am now. I am Etharia. Maybe you should pick a name too. It is fun."

The other yelled at her in bitter hatred, "We are the same sister! You betrayed Father." Before the shadows disappeared, she screamed out, "I will make you pay!"

Pain filled her body as she lay bleeding on the ground. Blood black as tar oozed out of her. "Sister, I have picked a name—Agrona," She smiled. "I hope it haunts you for all of history."

Before her eyes closed, she could see a sword and words being spoken. "I love you, sister. I hope your name will not define you. I want you to experience love like I have. I will do everything in my power to save you. For now, you must rest until we are ready to heal." There was a loud explosion as a stone appeared in her vision.

The doll woke up and screamed. The noise could be heard throughout the city, causing all who heard it to panic.

The prince burst through the door. "Is everything all right?" He saw her sitting by a fire, dark liquid slowly dripping from her eyes.

She quickly calmed down, and with a hint of confusion in her voice, asked, "Did it not make you afraid to hear my screams?" She pointed out the window. A guard ran around shouting; he held his head tightly as he jumped off the tower.

The prince rocked her softly in his arms. "No, I was worried about you. I feared something was going to destroy you." As he looked into her stone eyes, he felt a connection that he'd never felt before.

She slowly snuggled her soft head on his chest and wiped her tears on his shirt. "It was just a bad dream about my sister. She is why I am stuck in this body."

He walked her to his room and whispered, "It is all right. You can stay with me for as long as you like." Without him seeing her face, she smiled the evilest of smiles that a cute doll could give.

She placed her soft hand on his bare chest and rubbed circles on it. "I shall have my true body back soon. My sister died in vain." She pointed at the fireplace in his room.

He had installed a doll-sized chair by it and gently put her on it. "Why do you like sitting by the fire?"

She looked into the flames. "I feed off its destruction. When I rest, I can slowly feed from it to control my hunger. Your father may be a fool, but he does know how to not get caught." She turned her head to stare into his eyes. "I am still too weak like this and can be defeated by the weakness of this body."

The prince looked deep into her black stone eyes. "What will you do with me once you get your body?" He had his usual monotonous tone, as if he had no emotions and no feelings.

She smiled. "You will be my chosen. I too shall change like my sister." She reached out for his hand and they touched. He blacked out into a vision.

Wind blew dust around and lava spewed out of volcanoes. Standing in front of him was a woman much taller than him. She was naked with long black hair, large black wings, golden eyes, and dark ooze flowing from her eyes. Her hair covered the nipples on her hand-sized breasts.

She smiled at him. "This is my true body that I am after. This is the world I dream of making. How does it make you feel?"

He looked around. For most of his life, he had never showed any real emotion, but this time, he showed true joy in his eyes. "A world of nothingness is all I wanted. How can this be achieved?" He grinned oddly, as if he had never smiled before in his life.

She looked at him and held his hands. "My name is Agrona. I am the embodiment of nothingness. I wish to make you my king. Will you help me achieve this reality?"

His smile became more depraved and a sinister look took over his eyes. "I have never felt true love for anyone till today. I shall do everything you desire."

They embraced each other. Since she was much taller than him, she shrank herself to his height and they leaned in for a passionate kiss. As the dream world disappeared, he was left kissing the little doll.

They backed off from each other and the prince sighed with disappointed seeing the real world again. His emotions faded and his eyes became lifeless. Agrona looked at him. Her head tilted to the side with her hand under her chin.

She lifted up her other arm and patted him on the shoulder. "Now, now. I need you to stay focused. Your father is bringing all the parts we need to restore my body." Some life got restored in his eyes again.

She grinned a little. "The tool that can revive me is also the only tool that can kill me. I will need your help in making sure the latter does not happen."

As if he was hit with new life, focus, and determination, he put his hand on his heart as a salute of devotion. "I, Tourmaline, will do everything it takes to see your true body again." They started to plot by the fire.

Chapter Thirty-Four

IS THERE HOPE?

The large dragon, joyful from his victory over the vampire god, flew off. With the big match that he had in killing his rival, he forgot about Aluxes and Azaroth.

Bits of earth lifted off the ground each time he flapped his wings. Even over a mile away, the gusts of wind hit them with enough force to knock them off their feet.

They eventually found a way to gain some footing so they could watch him and figure out what they could do to stop such a large monster.

Azaroth said softly, "I was once allowed to visit the devil realm. My mother showed me a story of someone they feared." He closed his eyes. "He was so power-hungry that he almost destroyed their realm. He was finally pushed out into the mortal realm, taking many lives with him."

Samantha stood there trying to find a hint in his story. "How was he defeated?"

He looked at her. "Turiacus—when he was still sound of mind. He singlehandedly defeated Aeron during the war with the Fallen."

Evalyn grabbed her bladed whip and spun it around. She tossed up a few runes into the air. They glowed red as a bright light came from the whip. *"Banish the Unholy Monster with your grace, oh Goddess Siristeen,"* she chanted right before she hit the stones with her weapon.

Aluxes tried to stop her but it is too late. A quick crack from the whip sent the stones flying. They made flaming trails in the air towards Aeron.

All five hits caused enough damage to make him bleed a little. He let out a loud grunt of pain as the lights burned his wound.

Myka slowly walked backwards. "You cast a spell that hurt him. What was it?"

Evalyn, with a big smile on her face, said, "It was the spell Daddy used to slay the vampire king." She turned around and noticed that everyone but Aluxes was gone.

"Hey, I know how to defeat him." She cheerfully smiled. "The vampire told us during his battle."

Aluxes grabbed her and ran with her on her shoulders. "You fuckin' idiot. Dragons have a breath attack that follows pain."

Evalyn kept trying to shout, "Aluxes, listen. It is his body. His soul is a god but his body—"

Aluxes pinched her leg. "Shut your mouth! I need to run faster. It is hard to concentrate when your trap is yapping."

As Aeron recovered, he growled, "You little rodents. I forgot all about you." He took in a deep breath. Dirt, trees, rocks, and other loose objects were lifted off the ground. The area was extremely hot. The debris that flew into his mouth became lava as it slowly oozed out like drool.

With a whipping motion of his head, he let out a fire blast large enough that it made the ground split apart before it hit. Trees vaporized instantly, sand became glass, and the spot it hit turned into a huge cloud. As the dust slowly dissipated, the group was barely on the edge of the affected area. Covered in bruises, cuts, and scrapes, they walked around in a daze.

Onyx laid on the ground, screaming for help. The runestones in his artificial parts broke; he was now helpless. Some of the others noticed that they had a few broken bones.

Aluxes placed Evalyn on a patch of grass. "What did you do to my back? It is all wet." Her hand was covered in blood, but she had no wounds.

She became paralyzed when she noticed that it was Evalyn's blood. "Oh my, Aluxes, why do you look so glum? I am perfectly fine, my dear."

Part of her face was missing, almost down to the bone. Blood poured out from where her nose used to be. Samantha ran over and applied some bandages with medicine on them to stop the bleeding and pain that would catch up.

Evalyn sat there full of smiles, talking in a dazed state, "My dear Aluxes, I know I was always prettier than you. Remember that boy you liked? I purposely asked him out to make you angry."

Aluxes looked at her and tried to hold the tears in her eyes. "You are the prettiest girl I've ever met." She slowly patted her back.

"I do feel tired. I must tell you that the vampire told us how to kill him. His soul is a god but his body is a dragon. He said that you placed your soul into your favorite beast. Well, I am extremely tired now. Wake me up when we have won." She drifted off and was asleep.

Samantha patted her to make sure that was the only injury. "The medicines are very strong. She will be asleep for a while."

Myka came up behind Aluxes. "Fix her in Elvish Forest we can. But she be never the same."

Alisa helped Onyx and glared at Azaroth. "God devil, yes? You save all us?"

He looked around as he slowly healed his wounds. "I can kill him. I know what I must do. His body is not a god. It is his weakness."

He stared at Aeron as he flew away. "I might be able to stop him, but I would not be able to survive the backlash."

Aluxes lifted up her sword, and with confidence, shouted, "I will cut him up if I must!" She bolted towards the dragon.

Myka picked up Evalyn. "To my home I take her." Alisa nodded as she helped move Onyx. Azaroth and Samantha took off after Aluxes.

The beast flew faster than they could run. They eventually tired out, but he was still going. Not knowing whether or not he would need to rest in his flight, they knew it was impossible to catch up.

Azaroth looked at Samantha, "Do you know how to do a teleportation spell?"

She nodded a little. "Yeah, but only a short distance. I lack the power to do more."

He found a stick on the ground. "Write the spell down on the dirt with this. Aluxes has to only look at it and she can cast it."

She was confused but wrote the incantations in the dirt. As Aluxes stared at it, her eyes glowed a little as if she was absorbing it.

Samantha finished writing it and stood by and watched. Hesitantly, she said, "The backlash. Does she have a—"

He cleared his throat. "She will be fine. The effect will be minor for her."

She walked closer to Azaroth. "How is she able to do this?"

He chuckled a little. "It is a gift and a curse from her mother."

Aluxes smiled as she talked. "I think I got it. Are you sure this will work?"

He winked at her. "Yes, I am sure it will work. The three of us, let's go." She grabbed their hands and looked at an area ahead of Aeron. The ground rumbled a little and time stood still. In a blink, they disappeared and reappeared on the top of a mountain. The dragon was only a few miles behind them but was quickly getting closer.

Aluxes readied herself. "So, what is the battle plan?"

Azaroth looked at Samantha and she nodded. She knew what his plan was. Samantha started to chant a teleportation spell.

Azaroth grabbed Aluxes by the shoulder and kissed her deeply. The softness of his lips on hers made her mind go blank. An eternity went by and her body relaxed. Maybe too much, because she dropped her sword.

He slowly pushed her back a little and looked into her eyes. "I love you." She stood there blushing; it was as if she had forgotten how to speak. All she could do was stand there in a daze as he hit her in the back of the head with his hand and knocked her out.

He grabbed her before she hit the ground and gently handed her off to Samantha. Both of them nodded since they knew what they needed to do.

Samantha finished the spell and before they were pulled away, she said with concern, "If you survive, we will be in the Elvish Forest," and then they vanished.

He looked at the beast flying towards him, and took in a deep breath and closed his eyes. His green hair started to glow red. His body had a white shine like a beacon and the area slowly lit with energy.

Aeron was slightly blinded by the light. He still pushed on. "Little whelp, if this is how you wish to play it, then I shall accept your sacrifice. So that everyone will know that nothing can stop me."

He slowed down his flight to give Azaroth time to finish his spell. He opened his eyes; one was red and the other was a bold gold, and half of his hair slowly turned white. He did not use the teleportation spell so he would have as much energy as possible to summon this one spell.

Aeron chuckled. "Boy, I admire you willing to kill yourself to stop me. Now, hurry up for I must see my master. You will be lucky to even damage me." He started to speed up a little, heading straight towards Azaroth with no intention of dodging him.

Onyx was able to see the glow and he told everyone to stop. "Aye, the *god smite*. Lasses, if this spell does not work, we be done for. Even if it works, whoever the caster be will be gone." Everyone stood there watching Aeron fly straight into it.

Aluxes woke up and screamed, "Azaroth no!" Samantha grabbed her to prevent her from moving.

A few seconds later, the entire area exploded. Bits of the dragon could be seen flying off in every direction. Dirt and blood mixed, making red muddy rain pour from the sky. The ground that the light touched vanished, and in its place was a big scar on the land.

After the dust cleared, Aeron was seen lying there, most of his body destroyed by the blast. He shrank to the size of a normal dragon as his power leaked. It gave off an amber glow as it flew out in a mist.

Soon, he had become the size of a person. The once mightiest of all dragons reduced to a speck. He smiled in his own disbelief. He could see Aluxes as she slowly walked up to him. His body was regenerating but not fast enough to be a threat.

He added more insult to the heartbroken girl. "He killed himself to destroy me, and yet he was still weak and pitiful. His whore has to finish the job."

Tears poured out of her like an endless river. Unlike her usual angry eyes, she had real hatred as he laughed at Azaroth's failure. She stabbed Aeron in his exposed heart.

Being unable to recover from his wounds, he slowly faded into ashes. But before he fully died, Aluxes tried to smile at him and said, "Your master will be joining you next."

He chuckled as if her threat was empty. After the rest of his body turned to ashes his laughter could still be heard as they were carried off into the wind.

Samantha walked up behind Aluxes. "All I could find was his sword. It survived because it is a divine weapon. I think he would have wanted you to have it."

Aluxes pounded the ground and looked up at the stars as she cried out, "If they did not take away his divine essences, he would have survived! I hate the gods for being so cruel to their own children."

As Samantha tried to help her up, she noticed a small boil that was growing rapidly on her arm. "Shit, I was worried about this. We need to—"

Aluxes interrupted her. "There is no point of this world for me. I am not even allowed to have love." She screamed in pain as the boil burst. Blood spewed like a savage volcano.

Samantha tried to stop the bleeding. "I knew it. Unless you have a soul stone, the spell has a high tax. It normally kills the caster. Four Hells, I can see bone."

"Just let me be. It is what I deserve. This pain is all that is left and it is starting to get dull. Everyone I care about dies." Aluxes said as she gave in to her depression.

In the distance, Samantha could see the kikimora slowly dragging their stuff in a sack. "Her feathers are falling off. What happened to her?"

The kikimora stood in front of them out of breath. Her eyes made it look like she had a smile as she let go of the sack. She plucked off one of the few feathers that had not yet fallen off and placed it on Aluxes's wound, and the bleeding stopped.

"What is wrong with her? She looks sick," Aluxes mumbled.

Samantha held the creature's hand. "She is at the end of her life. She is dying." As the last feather dropped, her body shattered like glass and was no more.

Aluxes scoffed. "This realm is cursed. Nothing happy ever happens. I hate this world. It would be better if everyone just died. A world of nothingness." She said it quietly. No one heard her words.

Samantha held on to one of the feathers as it turned to glass and remembered what had been said on the boat. "A clay doll or befriend a dream beast. The kikimora is a dream beast. Aluxes, hey." She turned her head and noticed that Aluxes had fallen asleep.

As she bandaged up the wound, she noticed something different. "Huh, her circlet is a dark gray." She combed her fingers through her hair. "And some of her hair is turning black."

Their victory was not unnoticed. Thousands of miles away, the little doll was able to feel the loss of Aeron and was unsettled by it. She let out a horrendous scream that echoed across the entire castle.

The prince ran to her room and shouted, "My queen!"

She was sitting by the window. It vibrated violently and shattered. "Aeron has been defeated and died. This is a major blow and has weakened my forces by a large portion."

The prince was confused. He had no idea who Aeron was and ignorantly spoke ill of him. "Well, if he was defeated, he must not have been that good of a fighter."

The doll looked at him and pierced his shoulder with one of her tar-like vines and lifted him. "He was an Elder god. The fact that he decided to join me without me tainting his energy made him more important than you. You can be replaced but he was not replaceable, remember that." She let him go. Though the prince was stabbed, he showed no emotion of pain nor fear. He smiled and bowed to her.

Chapter Thirty-Five

THE KING'S JOURNEY

It had been over a month that the king and his men had become stranded in a forest of hellish nightmares. He had ten men left in his party. Some of the horrors they'd witnessed had never been seen by mortal eyes in over ten thousand years. They managed to make camp in what looked like the remains of a barrack. What race lived there they; did not know.

The weapons and armor that they found were still usable and much stronger than what they had brought. It gave them the ability to blend into the surroundings. The monsters were unable to see them while they searched.

They found a pond with a temple and agreed that what they were looking for was in there. But they did not dare go near it for the monsters that had taken residents there were far too numerous. The king cursed his trip and threw his book. Would they never be able to find this relic? Was it a fool's journey?

One of the men came back after doing some recon. He noticed a rabbit, of all things, wandering on a small trail. He noticed that the monsters were unable to touch it on this narrow path. He said that he tested it by walking on it and was able to see that the beasts that they were unable to see were there. They reached for him, but they could not touch him.

The man ran out and rushed to the trail. "Stay in the light, men. The things I saw could not touch anything in the light."

King Loux held the book tightly and cleared his throat. "Men, as the leader of this fool's quests, I shall head in first. If anything bad is to happen, it will be my payment for the lives we lost." He walked into the area, followed by the scout.

The light was bright enough that they could see what had killed their fellow comrades. They were not invisible, just so hideous that the mind was unable to make them out. They were like spiders but not spiders. The had eight arms, eight legs, and a human skull for a head, and were covered in webs.

The king looked around and noticed that the light went to the temple. He shouted to his men, "Stay strong!" There were some men who were scared but were able to keep a clear head. One of the men stopped and stared at one of the beasts.

The king walked up to him. "What do you see, Malvrick?"

Malvrick looked at him and calmly said, "It's strange. They are three times the size of us but their heads are of normal size. I get a strange feeling that there is more to this." The beast stared into his eyes with its eyeless skull.

Malvrick slowly said with a dry throat, "When I look at this beast, I think of John. He was killed by one of these things last week."

No one was looking when Malvrick took a small step off the lighted path, but they all stared when he started to scream. The monster quickly grabbed him. None of them turned away when they saw a small stinger protrude from the monster's arm and poke him, rendering him motionless. He was still alive as they could see tears falling from his eyes. The beast then shoved what looked to be an egg into his mouth. It was at this point that they understood that the skulls that the monsters possessed were indeed human skulls.

They pushed forward towards the building at the end of the light. When they made their way inside, they noticed that the air was refreshing and they felt more alive. No longer did they feel hunger or thirst. They felt relaxed and fell asleep.

The king woke up to a voice calling out to him. It was a male voice; it did not seem threatening, but was nowhere near friendly.

He walked down a small hallway till he reached a large worship area. In the middle was a statue of the Unnamed Goddess holding a sword. Next to it was a man who looked to be human.

He was a little intimidating. He had no eyelids or lips, and he had a large scar across his chest. They stared at each other without breaking eye contact.

Loux was the first one to break the silence. "Wh–"

The man interrupted, "I am Dumas. I am the protector of this blade." His voice was deep and powerful.

He pulled out a double-bladed staff and stood there in a pose, not knowing what Loux would do next. "What is it you want, mortal?"

The king cleared his throat. "Mortal?"

Dumas had no lips but Loux could tell that he was smiling. "I was a human like you, but I was chosen to be the history that was erased by the Goddess. You may have seen a book or two written by me."

He pointed towards a wall. "The area you came onto by boat is where she landed. It used to be the center of the largest city that the world had ever known."

Dumas then pointed to the king. "I know why it is that you are here, and I know what is going on in the world. But before I hand you what is most sacred, we must talk. I have been here for a long time and desire to speak to a fellow human while I still have some humanity left."

The king sat down on what used to be a bench. "Tell me what it is you wish to say."

Dumas looked at him. It was obvious that he had a lot to say. "What I am about to tell you is a history that the gods wish none would know. It is why all that has happened to this day has come to be. We humans were not wanted, but one took pity on us."

He waved his hand and a mural on the wall cleaned itself and moved. It showed his story as he spoke. "I was just a young boy, put into the slave camp by the elves and dwarfs. They were killing us off every day by working us to death. It was here that the mighty forces of the dark races marched their mighty army onto the city. To slow them down, our masters tossed us out, expecting us to be killed off, the last of the humans."

He looked at the king right in the eyes and raised his fist. "We won the battle. They provided us with no weapons but we still managed to drive off an orc army on the first night. This made even our masters fear us."

The mural showed an open gate. The Light races were armed to kill off the humans with the Dark races on the other side ready to wipe out what was left.

Dumas watched the slaughter, and he remembered it like it was yesterday. "We put up as much of a fight as we could but it was point-less. Then, from the heavens, she landed, destroying most of the city. She was our salvation, an immortal that took pity on us and decided to defend us personally." In the mural, all that was visible of her was a bright light aura and white hair. She slaughtered both armies as if they were nothing.

Dumas chuckled a little. "She killed off over eighty percent of everything, expect for the humans. She stood in the middle between us and declared that we are now protected, and she will destroy anything that dared to defy her."

He looked back at the king. "On both sides, some did not think that she was really a goddess and tried to attack her but they were quickly cut down. She was not alone, however, another being that looked just like her came but was darker and had much evil surrounding her."

He pointed to a corner, and over there was a sight that the king knew; black tar-like substance sitting there, devouring anything that touched it. "The monsters that you saw were influenced by this evil and changed." He moved his fist to his face. "I have also been altered by this. But thanks to the Goddess, I maintained my human mind."

He slowly walked around the king. "This led to a war that lasted almost a thousand years before this evil was stopped and placed inside a stone by Etharia."

He nudged Loux towards the sword. "I have been placed to watch this sword, only allowing those that are deserving to take it. You are not one of them, but my time is near, and it will get to its proper owner if you remove it."

King Loux picked up the sword and turned around. "What—" Before he could say another word, Dumas interrupted him again. "You will not live long enough to use it. Nor will you live long enough to tell anyone about the story that I just told you."

Dumas pointed at him and touched his nose. "Mark my words, king. You have one chance to redeem your soul. I know it is your hands that helped awaken this evil. It is the only way to save your son."

Loux shouted at him, "It was your fuckin book!"

Dumas chuckled as he tried to speak. "My dear king, you only read volume four out of thirty-eight. It was you who refused to do proper research. Did you not stop to think that a forbidden history was written in code? It was stated on the first page. There is one mortal in this entire world that has read eight of them, but she would rather kill you."

He looked down the hall. "I have been hungry for a long time, having only stray rabbits. To make sure that you tell none of your men, I shall partake of something with more meat." His body turned into an unkindness of ravens and flew towards the sleeping men. Screaming quickly followed and ended shortly.

Loux slowly made his way down the hall and feared what he would see next. All but one man had been pecked to death. Ravens ate the eyes, tongues, and other loose bits of flesh.

Deep inside of his very being he felt like he had a lead weight on his soul. He was afraid of the warning he had gotten. He was worried for his son even more, and he started to feel bad for killing his own brother. He'd done all of this because he wanted to be remembered forever as a great king. Now, he would be known as the king that destroyed the world. His only thought was that the way to save his legacy was to make sure that his son would become a great ruler.

The ravens all flew into a spot and formed back to Dumas. He stood there and grabbed the only soldier left alive by the neck. He talked, not to the troop he had by the neck, but to Loux.

In a dark tone, he said, "Great King Loux, your actions will cause the great suffering that will fall onto everyone. Since it is the gods' fault for pretending it never happened, the world would not be ready for it." He placed his hand on the eyes of the soldier, and he fell asleep.

Dumas looked at Loux. "He will replace me once I am gone. You will take this sword to its rightful owner, and in return, I will save your legacy in exchange for what is left of me."

He had no lips, but Loux could tell that he was smiling. "How does it feel knowing your end is near, Great King? You are a foolish king, but you still can be remembered as a hero."

The king held the sword tightly to his body and ran off as Duma's haunting laughter could be heard for miles. Dumas looked into a corner with glee in his eyes; the king had forgotten his book.

Dumas looked up towards the sky in a sigh of relief. "Etharia, I have accomplished the mission I promised you. I hope I am able to finally rest after all these years. May the Unnamed Goddess take my soul to the promised place, after I set forth my plan."

CPSIA information can be obtained
at www.ICGtesting.com
Printed in the USA
BVHW031525050821
613731BV00006B/27